HEROES

Valerio Massimo Manfredi is an archaeologist and scholar of the ancient Greek and Roman world. He is the author of sixteen novels, which have won him literary awards and have sold 12 million copies. His 'Alexander' trilogy has been translated into 38 languages and published in 62 countries and the film rights have been acquired by Universal Pictures. His novel *The Last Legion* was made into a film starring Colin Firth and Ben Kingsley and directed by Doug Lefler. Valerio Massimo Manfredi has taught at a number of prestigious universities in Italy and abroad and has published numerous articles and essays in academic journals. He has also written screenplays for film and television, contributed to journalistic articles and conducted cultural programmes and television documentaries.

Also by Valerio Massimo Manfredi

VALERIO MASSIMO MANFREDI

HEROES

Translated from the Italian by Christine Feddersen-Manfredi

PAN BOOKS

FOR MARZIA, FLAVIA, VALERIA AND MARCELLO

First published 2004 as *The Talisman of Troy* by Macmillan

First published in paperback 2004 by Pan Books

This edition published 2014 by Pan Books
an imprint of Pan Macmillan, a division of Macmillan Publishers Limited
Pan Macmillan, 20 New Wharf Road, London N1 9RR
Basingstoke and Oxford
Associated companies throughout the world
www.panmacmillan.com

ISBN 978-1-4472-7138-3

Copyright © Valerio Massimo Manfredi 1994
Translation copyright © Macmillan 2004

Originally published in Italian 1994 as *Le Paludi di Hesperia* by
Arnoldo Mondadori Editore S.p.A., Milano

The right of Valerio Massimo Manfredi to be identified as the
author of this work has been asserted by him in accordance
with the Copyright, Designs and Patents Act 1988.

1 3 5 7 9 8 6 4 2

A CIP catalogue record for this book is available from the British Library.

Typeset by SetSystems Ltd, Saffron Walden, Essex
Printed and bound by CPI Group (UK) Ltd, Croydon, CR0 4YY

Visit **www.panmacmillan.com** to read more about all our books
and to buy them. You will also find features, author interviews and
news of any author events, and you can sign up for e-newsletters
so that you're always first to hear about our new releases.

KEY TO MAP

ITALY

Mountains of Ice – The Alps
Lake of the Ancestors – Lake Garda
Eridanus River – River Po
Mountains of Stone – The Ligurian Alps and Carrara Mountains
The Blue Mountains – The Appennines
Mountains of Fire – Vesuvius to Etna
Island of the Three Promontories – Sicily

BALKANS

Hyster River – Danube
Epirus – Albania
Land of the Achaeans – Greece
Palus Maeotis – Sea of Azov
Pylum – Capital of Messenia
Pontus Euxinus – Black Sea

AEGEAN

Ilium – Troy
Tyre – Tyre
Assuwa – Asia
Keftiu – Crete

Ah, could we but survive this war
to live forever deathless, without age,
I would not ever go again to battle
nor would I send you there for honor's sake!
But now a thousand shapes of death surround us,
and no man can escape them, or be safe.
let us go . . .

Homer, Iliad XII, 322–8

1

SILENCE FELL OVER THE room. Everyone was watching the guest, the castaway tossed up by the sea between the rocks and the sand. His hands were still bruised and scratched, his eyes red and his hair as dry as the grass at the end of the summer. But his voice was beautiful, deep and resonant and, as he told his story, his face was transfigured. His eyes shone with a mysterious fever, reflecting the hidden fire within him, burning brighter than the flames licking the hearth.

We understood his language because we lived near the land of the Achaeans and we had once had commercial dealings with them. I myself am a singer of tales among my people and I know wonderful stories, stories so long they take up a whole winter's night, when men lend an ear and linger over their wine, but I had never heard such a beautiful and terrible tale in all my life. It was the story of the end of an era, the story of the decline of the heroes . . .

Sad, it was, especially for a singer like me, because when the heroes disappear, the poets die as well, without a world to sing of.

I am an old man now and I have no desire to live any longer. I have seen flourishing cities devoured by flames and reduced to ashes, I have seen ferocious pirates roam the seas and sack the coasts, I have seen unspoiled maidens raped by bloody barbarians. I have seen all those that I love die, one by one. Yet, from those far away days of my youth, no memory is more vivid in me than the story of that stranger.

He had witnessed the most famous enterprise ever attempted.

The taking of the mightiest city of all Asia! He had fought alongside one of the most powerful men of the earth, an indomitable and generous warrior who had dared to challenge the gods themselves, wounding the hand of Aphrodite and slashing open the belly of Ares, god of war, dark and unforgiving fury who never forsook revenge.

Now you will listen to my story, sitting here on the hay and drinking goat's milk, and perhaps you will not believe my words. I know, you'll think that these are just tales that I've spun to entertain my audience, to gain me food and lodging. You are wrong. Before this uncultured, miserable era, a time existed when men lived in cities of stone, dressed in fine linens, drank inebriating wine in goblets of gold and silver, navigated on agile ships to the ends of the earth, battled on chariots of bronze with shining weapons in their grasp. In those times, poets were welcomed into the palaces of kings and princes. They were honoured as gods.

Everything I am about to tell you is true.

*

Our foreign guest stayed at the palace for several months until one day, at the end of the winter, he disappeared without a word and we never heard of him again. But I hadn't missed a word of the tales he would tell in the evening, after dinner, in the assembly room. The echo of the great war fought on the shores of Asia had reached us, but that was the first time we had ever had the opportunity to listen to the words of a man who had taken part in it.

The chief of our people and the nobles would ask him time and again to tell the story of the war, but he always refused. Too bitter a memory, he said. When he finally did begin to tell his story, he began with the night of the fall of Ilium, the city of Priam, which we know as Troy.

And so, I will now tell you the story of what befell the city as I heard it from his lips. You shall learn how such a long and oppressive war was fought for nothing.

Yes, before he disappeared the stranger revealed a secret to me: the true reason why Ilium was razed to the ground and her people destroyed. No . . . it wasn't about a woman. It wasn't over Helen. I should say, instead, that she was one of the combatants, perhaps the most fearsome of them all. Why else would Menelaus have taken her back without making her pay for her betrayal? Some say that the sight of her naked breasts made the sword fall from his hand. No, the reason was another: a reason powerful enough to compel a king to put his queen into the bed of another man . . . for years. Unless what I was told is yet another imperfect truth, concealing an enigma within an enigma.

Anyway, that stranger, cast up by the sea on to our shores, had wanted to reveal it to me, a mere boy. In part he told me what he had seen in person, in part what he had heard and in part, I believe, what the gods themselves had inspired in him.

Perhaps he thought that no one would have believed me, or perhaps he needed to free his heart from a weight he could no longer bear.

Here is what he told me. Muse, inspire my story and sustain my memory. You are about to hear such a story as you have never heard, and you will pass it on to your children and to your children's children.

*

For seven days and seven nights burned the city of Ilium. The proud citadel burned and the fifty rooms of the royal palace burned, while her inhabitants, those who had survived the massacre, were massed together in the fields like sheep in a pen. There they waited to be assigned to the victors as spoils of the war. The women lay on the ground with their gowns torn and their hair loosed, their eyes cried dry. Almost all of them were the brides or daughters of Trojan warriors who had fallen during the night of the betrayal. They were destined to serve the wives of the victors or to be called as concubines to their beds, to be possessed and profaned, deprived of everything but the bitterness of their memories.

The children cried, dirty and hungry. They lay on the ground until sleep overcame them and when they awoke they cried again.

The Achaean chiefs assembled in the tent of Agamemnon, their high commander, king of Mycenae. They were discussing whether they should leave immediately or whether the army should remain to offer sacrifice in expiation for all the innocent blood spilled. The victory they had awaited for so many years had not brought them the joy they would have expected. Spoils were scarce because the exhausted city had long consumed all of its riches. The atrocities committed the night the city was taken had left in the heart of each one of them the dark expectation of inevitable punishment. They felt like drunks who had reawakened after a night of revelry, with their clothes soiled and the taste of vomit still in their mouths.

They sat in a circle on seats covered with skins. First came Ulysses, the victor: the inventor of the horse, the machine which had tricked the defenders of Troy. But as the army had poured into the city, he had disappeared, and Eurilocus, his cousin, had taken command of his men, Ithacaeans and Cephallenians from the western islands. He had reappeared at dawn, pale and silent. He, the destroyer of the city, had taken just a small part of the spoils. Strange, really, since he was one of the poorest kings of the coalition, the sovereign of dry and rocky islands. And, what counted the most, the victory had been entirely his doing. No one had argued or sought to know what he had hidden in that meagre booty, so small that it aroused neither the jealousy of the other chiefs nor the envy of his men. And after all, he would be returning to Ithaca with the weapons of Achilles, which alone were worth the price of one hundred bulls.

Ulysses, versatile and cunning! He sat, and listened, keeping his left hand on the hilt of his sword and the right on his sceptre, but he heard nothing of what was said because his labyrinthine mind was following paths hidden to all.

Next to him was the seat, empty, of Ajax Telamon. Great Ajax with his sevenfold shield, his immense size a bulwark on both battlefield and ship. The only one of them who had never received help from one of the gods in battle. He had died in shame and grief, throwing himself upon his own sword because Ulysses had denied him the inheritance most sought after: the weapons of Achilles. His father, who day after day trained his gaze out over the waves pounding the rocks of his island, would wait for him in vain.

Then came Nestor, king of Pylus, a wise counsellor whose true age no one knew, and after him Idomeneus, king of Crete, the successor of Minos, the lord of the labyrinth. Agamemnon was next, and then his brother Menelaus, exhausted by the night of blood, of death and delirium. It was said that Menelaus had possessed Helen, his wayward queen, that night in the bed of Deiphobus, her last husband, that he had taken her in a pool of blood, alongside the mangled corpse of the Trojan prince. But no truth may come of such a night of trickery and of deceit!

Ajax Oileus, Little Ajax, sat with his brow contracted and his hands tight between his thighs. The night before, he had raped princess Cassandra in the temple of Athena. The goddess herself was struck with such horror that she had closed her eyes so as not to witness the abomination. He had pinned Cassandra to the ground and ripped off her clothes, he had penetrated her like a ram, like a raging bull. For a moment, just a moment, he had met her eye and in that moment he understood that the princess had condemned him to death. To a horrible, certain death.

Agamemnon then took Cassandra for himself. Only she knew the secret hidden in the king's heart. But he, the great Atreid, eyed Ajax with great suspicion, knowing that he had been alone with her first.

Last came Diomedes, son of Tydeus, king of Argos, he who had conquered Thebes of the Seven Gates. No one after the death of Achilles could rival his valour and courage. He had been inside the horse along with Ulysses and had fought the whole night through, searching for the only remaining Trojan adversary worthy of him, Aeneas. He found no trace of the Dardan prince. But he had slipped into the citadel as morning was breaking and had disappeared into one of its secret passages. Diomedes's armour was now covered with dust and the crest of his helmet was full of cobwebs. And he watched Ulysses of the many deceptions warily, because they two alone, among all the Achaeans, had managed to steal into the city before the night of the wooden horse. They had got in one night long before the city's fall, disguised as dirty, blood-stained Trojan prisoners. Only they had been familiar with the hidden conduits of the citadel.

The chiefs went on with their discussion at great length, but could not reach an agreement. Nestor, Diomedes, Ulysses and Menelaus decided to depart regardless with their fleets; Agamemnon and the others would stay behind to offer a sacrifice of expiation to appease the gods and win their safe return. Or so they claimed, but perhaps there was yet another reason behind their staying. Agamemnon had been seen roaming with Cassandra through the still smoking ruins of Ilium, searching for the only treasure that really interested him; the one for which the war had truly been fought.

The fleets of those who had set sail stopped for the night at the isle of Tenedos. But the very next day, Ulysses changed his mind about leaving. Agamemnon had been right, he said, a hecatomb must be offered to the gods. He turned back, although the others were all against it, and his comrades begged him not to take them back to those cursed shores where so many of them had fallen. Their pleas were useless. The Ithacaean ships turned sail with the wind against them, forcing their oars through high black waves that the northerly wind churned up and topped with livid froth. Ulysses, standing tall at the stern amidst a shower of sea-spray, had taken the helm of his ship himself. He was never seen again.

It was rumoured that he had returned, in the deep of the night, to the shore where the Achaeans had raised a cairn over the bones of Ajax. Driven by remorse, while the heavens were rent by lightning and the mountains shaken by thunder, he had laid the weapons of Achilles on the votive altar. Too late, even if this were true, because the actions of the living are of no help to the dead. They mourn endlessly their life lost, and wander in the dark chambers of Hades longing for the light of the sun which they will never see again.

What I think is that Ulysses realized that he had been deceived, and this realization was intolerable. No possible doubt could cloud the mind of the astutest man of the earth. And thus he defied the wind and the waves of the oncoming storm.

I know for certain that the other companions, those who had remained behind with the great Atreid on the shore of Ilium, never saw them arrive, neither Ulysses nor his Cephallenian warriors. When he landed Agamemnon had already set sail, and Ulysses never succeeded in reaching him later. Perhaps he waited too long to return out to sea and was forced to fight the hostile winds of winter. Perhaps a god envious of his glory pushed his ship towards the Ocean without wind and without waves, or was holding him prisoner somewhere.

The first of the Achaean leaders to pay for the excesses committed on that cursed night of the fall of Troy was Ajax Oileus. His ship was taken by a storm, run aground on the Ghirèan cliffs and rent in two. His comrades were immediately engulfed by the waves of the storming sea, but Ajax himself was a formidable swimmer. Clinging to a wooden crate, he fought off the billows and managed to save himself, hoisting himself on to a rock. Sitting on that crate, he berated the gods, claiming that he was invincible and that not even Poseidon could defeat him. The god of the sea heard his words and rose from the depths of the abyss, clutching his trident. With a single blow he shattered the hard rock: Ajax fell between the crumbling splinters and was crushed like wheat under a millstone. For a moment, his screams of pain could be heard over the din of the storm, before they were scattered by the wind.

The others had managed somehow to brave the storm. Having reached Lesbos, they held council to decide whether to sail north of Chios towards the isle of Psirìa, on their left, or south of Chios, rounding the Mimantes promontory. In the end they decided to cut through the sea in the direction of Euboea, by the shortest route. But although the sea had calmed and the temperature was mild, Menelaus disappeared during the voyage, on a moonless night with all of his ships. I will tell you more about him, and what happened to him, later.

Nestor reached sandy Pylus with his men, his ships and his booty after having rounded Cape Malea. He reigned for many more years over his people, honoured by his sons and their wives.

Quite a different fortune befell Diomedes, son of Tydeus.

He berthed his ships on the beach of Temenium while the night was still dark. He had sent no herald to announce the fleet, and no one knew of his homecoming. He had Ulysses's warning in mind: 'Don't trust anyone,' his friend had told him, 'upon your return. Too much time has passed, many things will have changed. Someone may have taken your place and be plotting against you. Above all, no matter how grievous this may seem, do not trust your queen.'

Diomedes set off with Sthenelus, his inseparable friend, and reached his palace in Tiryns under the cover of night. He hadn't seen it for ten years. It seemed changed, although he couldn't say how. He was deeply moved as he contemplated the walls of the citadel, walls which were said to have been built by the cyclops. The gates of his palace were posted with armed guards. He recognized them: mere children when he had left, they were now in the prime of their youth and strength.

He left Sthenelus out of sight with the horses to wait for him, and entered from a passage known only to him. He found the postern on the southern side of the walls, obstructed by the mud brought by the rains and by the roots of the trees which had invaded the passageway over the many years in which no one had used it. It joined the outer fortification to the palace walls and had been used, in times of war, for surprise attacks on the enemy. As Diomedes advanced he felt choked by emotion and by the sense of oppression created by the narrow conduit. He had envisioned his return much differently: his people in celebration, running to greet him along the road, the priestesses of Hera scattering flowers to welcome his chariot. And above all, Aigialeia, his bride, meeting him open-armed and taking him by the hand to their fragrant bed to make love with him after so many years of longing and of separation.

Aigialeia ... how many nights he had dreamed of her, lying under his tent on the Ilium plain. No woman, not even the most beautiful of his prisoners, had ever satisfied his passion. The women captured in battle are only full of hate and of despair.

Aigialeia ... her breasts were white and hard as cut ivory, her womb always burned with desire, her mouth, flushed with fever, could cloud his mind and drive him out of his senses.

Perhaps this was why he was approaching his own home so furtively, stealing into the palace from a hidden subterranean passage. A thousand times in war he had faced death by the light of day. But now an unknown and much greater fear made him crawl through the darkness. The fear of having been forgotten. Nothing is more terrible for a man.

He had reached the point where a narrow tunnel branched off from the postern passage; it ended up directly behind the niche in the throne room which housed an effigy of the goddess Hera, wife of Zeus. This most ancient simulacrum had always adorned the wall opposite the throne. The jewel which embellished the statue's breast was a translucent stone of clearest quartz; it looked black when seen from inside the room but, when looked through from behind the statue, if the throne room was lit, it was as transparent as air. His father Tydeus had had it cut by the artificer Iphicles, who had set it with great expertise. No one could have guessed the trick unless they knew about it. And sounds flowed perfectly through the well-modelled ears of the statue as well.

The throne room was empty but still illuminated although the hour was late, and the hero remained concealed behind the statue, wary that something was about to happen. He was not wrong. An armed man soon appeared and sat down; from another door entered the slim figure of a veiled woman. She uncovered her face only after she had closed the door behind her: Aigialeia!

She was in the full prime of her beauty, more seductive than when he had left her, more desirable. Her shoulders, soft and round, had lost the cold purity of adolescence, her eyes were deeper, darker and bigger, and her mouth was like a ripe fruit, moist with dew. Two lines creased her forehead between her eyebrows, making her gaze both harsh and sorrowful. Aigialeia . . .

The man said: 'They've pulled aground at Temenium in the dark near a pine forest. They evidently don't want to be seen. They're hiding, as if they were afraid.'

'And you're sure that it's them?' asked the queen.

'As sure as I'm alive. I recognized the emblems on their ships and on their weapons.'

'And . . . him?'

'He's surely on his ship, the one with the royal emblem and the polished shield at the stern. His best warriors are on armed guard all around the ship. They're on their feet, in the dark, in two rows: the first facing the ship and the second, back-to-back with the others, facing the sea and the countryside.'

Aigialeia's face lit up with joy and Diomedes, from his hiding place, felt his spirit fill with immense happiness. He was on the verge of revealing himself to the woman who seemed so joyous over his return. He hadn't even felt such elation the night Troy had fallen after years of siege.

Aigialeia said: 'No. They're not for him, the guards and the double row of warriors. He never protects himself. No one could ever surprise him in his sleep, not even by stealing up in bare feet on the sand. And no one could hope to save his skin after having roused him and challenged him to combat. If what you say is true, on that ship are the spoils of war. All the treasures that he took from the city of Troy. And, perhaps, something more important still. We must eliminate him before the people find out. We'll say that the ships were full of pirates who had landed to sack the fields and to steal slaves and livestock.'

The man answered: 'The army is ready. Nearly all of his men are sleeping, exhausted from the voyage. We'll wipe them out in their sleep and then it will be easy to crush the guards around the king's ship. And when I have seized the treasure I will bring it to you.'

'You fool,' said Aigialeia, 'you can't defeat him with weapons!

The din of the battle will infuriate him; he'll leap out of bed with all his armour and mow you down like heads of wheat. Only I can sway him. I shall go to the ship wearing the dress of the ancient queens that bares my breasts. I will paint the tips of my breasts red, and when he has taken me, again and again, only then will he sleep in a slumber so profound that he won't feel the air parting for my dagger as it plunges into his back. You will attack then, and you will not spare a single one of the comrades who fought with him under the walls of Ilium.'

The man trembled and sweat poured down his face. He said: 'And will you wear the dress of the ancient queens for me as well, the dress that bares your breasts? And will you paint the tips of your breasts red for me?'

Aigialeia stared at him with her harsh, haughty gaze. 'Perhaps. But now do as I've commanded.'

Diomedes felt his heart splitting in his chest. For an instant he wanted to break into the room and slay them both, but fear stopped him. He did not know if he could plant his sword between the breasts of the woman he had dreamed of for years as he slept under his tent on the plains of Ilium. He realized that he would never be able to sit on the throne of Argos without her, nor sleep in his empty bed without going mad.

He thought, in those moments of acute pain, that he had to reach his comrades and save them from the attack.

His men were all that were left of his kingdom and of his family. There was no one in Argos who desired his return if his own queen were prepared to kill him. And if his own army was prepared to spill the blood of those who had fought for so long far away from their homeland and who had finally returned to embrace their wives and their children.

He made his way back through the secret passageway at a run, and found Sthenelus silently waiting for him in the shade next to their horses.

'We must return to the ships,' he said. 'The queen is plotting to kill me and to kill all our men by sending the army out against us.'

Sthenelus did not move. He grasped Diomedes by the shoulders and said: 'They'll never win. We will wake our comrades and march against the city. You have conquered Thebes and Troy: no one can challenge you and get away with it. And when we have won you will choose a just punishment for the queen.'

But Diomedes was no longer listening. 'I wounded Aphrodite,' he said. 'I thrust my spear through her delicate hand as she stretched it out to protect Aeneas her son, and now the goddess of love has twisted Aigialeia's feelings; she has filled her with hate for me. The gods never forget. They have their revenge, sooner or later.'

'It's better to die fighting, even against the gods, than to flee,' said Sthenelus. 'Tell me what you saw in the palace.'

Diomedes told him everything, without holding back. 'Do you understand now why I have to go? This is no longer our homeland! I left my queen in the royal palace when I departed for the war. I held her in my arms that morning, and kissed her. And she swore that she would make a statue in my likeness and lay it in our wedding bed and sleep alongside it until I came back. Now I find a monster who only looks like Aigialeia . . .' He bowed his head. 'Yet even more beautiful, if such a thing is possible. Even more desirable.'

They mounted the chariot; Sthenelus grasped the reins and urged on the horses. They galloped swiftly over the dark plain towards the sea, towards Temenium where the ships had been berthed and the comrades slept waiting for dawn.

Diomedes woke them and called them to assembly. They were expecting him to announce their triumphal return to Argos, the city that they had left ten years before. Instead their ears heard bitter words, words they would never have wanted to hear.

When the king finished, he asked them to forsake Argos and to follow him: he would bring them to a new homeland, to a distant land in the west where the memories of a futile, bloody war could not follow them. To a place where they would meet other women and father other children, where they would build a city destined to become invincible.

'The world,' he told them, 'is very big, much bigger than we can imagine. We will find a place ruled by other gods, where our gods cannot persecute us. I am Diomedes, son of Tydeus, conqueror of Thebes of the Seven Gates and conqueror of Ilium. Together we shall conquer a new kingdom, a hundred times bigger than this one, and we will have plenty of everything we desire. We will drink wine and feast every night to drive away our memories.'

Some of them, the youngest, the strongest and most faithful, went right to his side, swearing to follow him anywhere. Some pleaded to be allowed to join their wives and bring them along. Others, most of them, stood in silence, their heads bowed. And when the king asked them what they intended to do, they answered: 'Oh lord, we have fought at your side for years without ever sparing our courage. Our chests and our arms bear the scars of many wounds but now, we beseech you, give us our part of the booty and let us go. It is only right that you leave the wife who would betray you, but we are not kings. We want to return to our houses, to reunite with our wives and with the children we left in swaddling when we departed with the other Achaeans to follow the Atreides under the walls of Troy. We want to grow old in peace, to sit in front of our homes in the evenings and watch the sun go down.'

Diomedes entreated them: 'You mustn't stay behind! I supplicate you, leave with us. Either all of us should remain or all of us should go. If we stay, I will have to kill the queen and then live the rest of my days persecuted by her Furies, and all together we will have to combat against the Argives, against our own blood. And there will be more bitter mourning and more, infinite pain. If only some of you remain, you will certainly be overwhelmed and slain as soon as they realize that I am not there to defend you and guide you in battle. An evil spirit has taken possession of the palace and of the city. If this were not true, my wife, who adored me, would never have dishonoured my bed and my home. She would never have plotted my death.'

This is what Diomedes said, but his words did not convince

them. They had been waiting too long to return to their homeland and their families and now that they had arrived they couldn't bear the thought of leaving once again.

A slender crescent moon was rising at that moment from the waves of the sea and the stars began to pale. The time had come. The men embraced one another, weeping, as the booty was lowered from the ship, the plunders of war to be divided.

There were bronze tripods and urns, jewels of gold and of silver. Pelts of bears, lions and leopards, finely engraved shells from the sea, helmets, shields and spears. And there were women with high, rounded hips, with black eyes still moist with regret for all they had lost.

The king took very little for himself. He kept the golden armour which had been gifted him by the chief of the Lycians, Glaucus, after they met in battle, and he kept the divine horses he had taken from Aeneas. Only he and Sthenelus knew what was hidden in the hold of the royal ship; the reason why Diomedes could promise his men that the city they would found would be invincible, a kingdom destined to reign over the world.

Diomedes bid his comrades farewell and turned to Sthenelus to give him the orders of departure for the fleet. But Sthenelus turned towards those who had decided to stay, and said: 'I shall remain here with them. I want to see the sun rising over the sky of Argos. I want to enter through the southern gate, to see the people and the market where we played as children, chasing after one another with little wooden swords. I've fought long enough. Not even for you, my friend, could I return to sea and face the weariness, the cold, the solitude.'

Diomedes understood. And although he felt oppressed by immense sorrow, he knew that his friend was not speaking out of fear. He simply could not abandon their remaining comrades to their destiny. He would enter Argos with them and he would die with them. He was the other half of Diomedes, as Patroclus had been the other half of Achilles: and so he had to remain with his men, those who would not take to the sea again.

'Farewell, my friend,' said the king to him. 'When the sun

rises high in the sky of Argos and over the palace of Tiryns, look up at it, touch the door jamb for me as well. And if you see Aigialeia . . . tell her that . . .'

He could not go on. Emotion overcame him and his words died in his throat.

'I'll tell her, if I can,' said Sthenelus. 'Farewell. Perhaps we'll meet again one day, but if we don't, remember that although I've decided to remain, I am your friend. Forever.'

And thus the son of Tydeus, Diomedes, left the shores of the land which he had desired so fervently, to face the sea once again.

It was still dark when they weighed anchor but the sky was turning lighter at the horizon. He ordered his comrades to row as fast as they could and to hoist the sail. He wanted to be far off on the water when the sun rose: he couldn't bear the sight of his beloved land as he was being forced to abandon it and he didn't want his comrades to suffer for the same reason or to regret having followed him. He donned the golden armour of Glaucus and stood straight at the stern under the royal standard so that all of them could see him and take courage.

When the aurora rose from the east to illuminate the world he was far away: on his right loomed the high rocks of Cape Malea.

He would never know what fate befell the comrades who remained behind. In his heart he hoped that they had been spared and that, with Diomedes gone, the city would no longer have any reason to destroy valiant men, formidable warriors.

But I imagine that a wretched destiny awaited them, no different from the fate of Agamemnon and his comrades when they returned to their homeland. The only word that was ever heard about those men was that Sthenelus had become Aigialeia's lover. I believe that it was the queen herself who spread this story. Since she could no longer reach Diomedes and kill him herself, she hoped that Rumour – a winged monster with one hundred mouths – could overtake him more rapidly than her ships, shattering his mind and making him die of desperation.

Sthenelus died with his sword in hand, honourably, as he had always lived, toppled from his chariot by the cast of a spear or perhaps pierced through his neck by an arrow. The horses harnessed to his chariot were no longer the divine steeds that Diomedes had taken from Aeneas and he could no longer fly like he had over the plains of Ilium, swifter than the Trojans' arrows, faster than the wind. A man of no worth, perhaps, tore the armour from his shoulders as he fell, crashing into the dust. And watched as his soul fled, groaning, to the Kingdom of the Dead.

2

THE SUN HAD SET and all the paths of land and sea had darkened when Agamemnon's fleet cast anchor at Nauplia. Victory weighed more heavily upon his shoulders than defeat would have and the gods had chosen for him to behold his homeland under the veil of night as well.

He descended from the ship and breathed in the unforgettable odour of his own land. For a moment that scent rushed to his head like the aroma of a strong wine. But then it swiftly called to mind his daughter Iphigenia, sacrificed on the altar to propitiate their departure for war ten years before, and he realized that all the glory he had won, that the priceless treasure that he was bringing back – the one and only reason that he and his brother Menelaus had set off this war – were not worth the breath of his lost daughter.

How bewildered were her eyes as they took her to the altar! He remembered how she had drunk the potion that would numb her, believing that it would induce the sacred sleep of prophecy. 'The goddess will appear to you in a dream,' they had told her, 'because you are pure. To you she will reveal the reason for her ire. She will tell you why she will not send favourable winds and allow the fleet to depart. When you awaken you will reveal her words to us.'

He, the Atreid, remembered how he had turned away from the altar when the priest grasped the flint knife he would use to open the vein of her neck. He had to be present so that the sacrifice would be accepted, so the gods would be satisfied with his pain and with the life of a still-innocent child.

He thought of how the demon of power invades the soul like a disease. A king is branded by the gods, cursed by a destiny impossible to avoid. Kings are made to do things that no other man could do, in good and in evil. They give death like the gods and suffer like mortal men, and they cannot count on one or on the other.

I have long pondered on what Agamemnon did to achieve his ends and I have asked myself if it is possible for a man to go so far solely to lay claim to power. Still today I cannot answer that question. But in the light of what happened later, perhaps an explanation does exist; perhaps his intentions were good, perhaps he thought he could save his people from total disaster and ward off the end awaiting them all.

As king, he knew that the war would bring death to thousands of his people's sons. As king he showed them that he was prepared to offer the life of his most beloved daughter.

If this is true, then his death was a terrible injustice. After suffering all that a man could suffer in his life, he was made to suffer the most shameful death, the same that would have befallen Diomedes had he not been so prudent.

Agamemnon had the Trojan prisoners disembark, and among them Cassandra, daughter of Priam, but left the spoils of war on board the ships; he would send men and carts the next day from Mycenae to load it all up and bring it to his palace. His charioteer accompanied him, as did all his most trusted comrades, the noblemen who had fought by his side during the whole war. The others remained on the beach to sleep and wait for the booty to be divided up the next day so they could return to their families. They could not go home empty-handed after having been away for so long.

Silence shrouded the countryside, but as the armed column passed, the dogs sleeping in front of the sheep pens and the farms awoke and started barking, and a horn sounded from on high. But its long, wavering blow was full of anguish, as if it signalled the passage of an invading enemy.

When Agamemnon came within sight of Mycenae, he realized that the city was expecting him: armed guards on the bastions held flaming torches, and more torches were burning at the sides of the great gate. The coat of arms of the Mycenaean kings, two gold-headed lions facing each other on either side of a red column over a field of blue, stood out on the huge architrave, on the gigantic jambs, over the wide black opening. The king was moved to see his emblem, the symbol of the mightiest dynasty of the Achaeans, but the dark gateway below loomed before him like the door to the House of Hades. The soldiers on the bastions clanged the spears against their shields to greet him, as his horses plodded up the ramp that led to the palace.

Beyond the gate, to his right, more torches illuminated the tombs of the Perseid kings, the first to have reigned over the city. They had descended from Perseus, the city's founder, he who had defeated Medusa. The sacred enclosure had been restored when the new Pelopid dynasty had come to power, signifying continuity and respect for tradition. On the other side of the valley, the enormous stone dome of Agamemnon's own tomb rose on the mountainside, the tomb he had prepared for himself before he had left for the war. One day he too would rest under that immense vault, wrapped in white linen, his face covered by a golden mask that would perpetuate his features through eternity . . . if it was the will of the gods to grant him a dignified death and the honour of solemn funeral rights, at the end of his existence.

But no one stood along the street, the sounds of the horses' hoofs and the chariot's wheels rang against dark walls and closed doors. The hinges of the gate groaned behind him and it swung shut suddenly with a loud clang. Many of his comrades put their hands to the hilts of their swords. The eyes of Cassandra, who stood beside him on the chariot, were as empty as the circle of the new moon. But as he was about to descend in front of his home, she touched his arm. He turned towards her and she whispered something into his ear. Agamemnon's face turned white with the pallor of death: only then did he realize that he had been tricked. He realized that the Achaeans had fought for ten long years in vain and he understood that the princess was giving him the chance to save his life. But his was a life worth nothing now.

He entered the palace and the maidservants knelt and kissed his hands as though he had been away just a few days, off hunting boars. Then they led him to the bath chamber to ready him for meeting the queen. Cassandra and his comrades were taken to the throne room.

Agamemnon allowed them to remove his armour, to undress him and bathe him. The girls' hands lingered on his hard body, furrowed with scars, they squeezed hot water on his shoulders from big sea sponges, they poured scented oil on his head.

He died that night.

They say that the queen's lover, Aegisthus, smote him down during the banquet, as he ate. He lowered the axe on his neck and Agamemnon fell to the ground like a bull slaughtered at the manger. But he did not die then. He dragged himself across the floor, bellowing and spurting blood from the wound. He tried to defend Cassandra as the queen murdered her with a dagger. He died at her feet as the palace rang with the cries of his comrades who were falling one after another under the blows of their assailants. They fought to the very end, bare-handed, even with arms maimed and legs crippled, because they were the best of the Achaeans, chosen by Agamemnon to depart with him for Troy.

The floor was slick with their blood and the commander of the guards could barely stand upright as he passed from one to the other to cut the throats of those who were still alive. Their bodies were all buried together in a large empty cistern, before the sun rose and the people of the city could discover what had happened. Then the maidservants washed the throne room floor and purified it with fire and sulphur.

On that same night, other armed men left on war chariots, directed towards Nauplia, where the fleet was anchored. Queen Clytemnestra had ordered them to seize the king's ship but her designs were not to be fulfilled. Before entering the city, Agamemnon had ordered his shield-bearer Antimachus to climb up on to the hill that overlooked the city. He had told him: 'I fear that some sort of misfortune may befall me. I do not know if the queen's heart is still true to me. Go all the way up to the top of the hill; you'll be able to see the palace perfectly. When the banquet is finished and the lights are extinguished in the rooms, I shall go up to the tower that stands over the chasm with a lit torch in hand. When you see me, you may enter the palace yourself, you may eat and drink and take your rest. But if you do not see me, this will mean I have been betrayed. Light a fire on the top of the hill. The wind will lick up the flames and make them visible from the sea. The men will know what to do.'

Thus had said the king, and Antimachus had obeyed him. When he heard the cries of the wounded, when he saw his comrades' corpses being carried out of the palace, he understood what had happened. He lit a fire and the flames rose high, driven by the wind that blows all night on the hilltop, and his signal was seen from afar by the sentries standing watch on the deck of the king's ship. They knew what Agamemnon wanted and they set fire to the ship, burning it with all its treasures. The other ships weighed anchor and sailed off into the night.

No one was ever to know what became of his men. Perhaps some of them sought a new land to settle, perhaps others became pirates and brought ruin to the coast dwellers. Perhaps others still found a hidden landing place and secretly reached their homes and re-embraced their wives and children.

One day later, a messenger from Queen Aigialeia arrived at Mycenae bearing news of what had happened at Argos.

Clytemnestra received him alone, towards evening, in a throne room dimmed to hide the signs of her sleepless night, the circles under her eyes and her ashen cheeks. She learned that Diomedes had barely managed to escape death but that his fate would certainly catch up with him on the sea where he had sought refuge; the hostile wind and waves would take care of him. Clytemnestra had the messenger report back to Aigialeia that Agamemnon had died in expiation for his crimes and that Menelaus had not yet made return. And in Crete they had had no further news of

Idomeneus. She had even sent a ship to Ithaca, to her cousin Penelope, and was awaiting her answer. As soon as Helen returned, the queens would once again reign over the Achaeans.

The messenger departed as dusk fell and Clytemnestra remained alone next to Agamemnon's throne. The silent, empty room still echoed with cries and curses, as though the slaughter would never end.

*

In the meanwhile, Diomedes's ships were far off at sea and had rounded Cape Taenarum, passing within sight of Abia, the city that Agamemnon had promised to Achilles had he agreed to set aside his ill will and return to combat. A pale sun lit the houses facing the sea, the fishing boats and the ships pulled aground on the beach. The season for navigation was over.

They were entering the kingdom of Nestor and Diomedes pondered whether to stop and ask for hospitality or to continue north, where it was said that the passage to the Land of Evening could be found. Those who had been there spoke of vast plains on which thousands of horses grazed and of tall mountains always covered with snow that only Hercules had ever crossed, when he had set off to reach the Garden of the Hesperides and the house of Atlas, who bears the sky upon his shoulders. It was an incredibly rich land, crossed by the Eridanus river, which was said to be so wide that the sea itself changed colour for a huge expanse at the river's mouth and became fresh-watered. There lay the Electrides islands, where drops of pure amber fell from the sky at night and were harvested by their inhabitants, who sold them to the merchants that ventured so far.

Diomedes knew that Nestor would ask him the reason for this voyage; why he had abandoned his homeland after years of yearning and endless war. Nestor would offer him his fleet and his army to help him win back his city and his kingdom. But Diomedes would have to refuse, and explain that there was no life left for him in Argos or in his palace.

And so Diomedes preferred to continue on. From the railing

of his ship he saw Nestor's palace brushed by the last glow of the sunset as it stood against the sky already dark. The lamps and torches were just being lit in the palace halls, fires were being kindled in the hearths, maids were taking out the cauldrons and putting meat in them to boil. The king was just coming down from his rooms to share a banquet with his strong sons and their blooming wives. Diomedes thought of how good it would have been to sit down together and hark back to all the misadventures of the war, to drink wine and take pleasure in the songs of the poets until late at night. Lamps were being lit in the houses of the fishermen and craftsmen and he envied them as well; he would have much preferred to be a poor man, a man of no means, but to have a house and a table to sit around with his children and wife, to talk about the changing weather and the labours of the day. Instead he travelled towards an unknown destination on the back of the cold, sterile sea.

The lights of Pylus reflected in the water and accompanied him for a while before they were extinguished by the night which swallowed sky and sea. Not a sound was left in the air, only the swash of water against the ship and the whisper of wind in the sail.

The pilot governed the helm, keeping his eye trained on the star of the Little Bear. The king had ordered him to follow it until he told them to stop. For days and days they would ride the waves towards night and darkness, leaving behind daylight and sun until the water of the sea changed colour and its taste became sweet to the palate. The mouth of the Eridanus.

Exhausted by fatigue and by the emotions that racked his soul, Diomedes finally fell asleep on a bed of pelts, laying his head on a coil of rope, and he dreamed he was in his palace, lying next to Aigialeia, nude and white-skinned. Her hair gave off an intense scent, her lips were half open, her skin made golden by the reflection of the lamp. He drew closer to caress her but his fingers touched cold, slimy scales, as if a serpent or a dragon had slithered into his bed. He suddenly felt its fangs sink into his hand, and his flesh became livid and swollen with poison.

He slept fitfully as his comrades took their turns at the helm and stirred up the flames in the braziers so the ships would not lose sight of one another.

At dawn they sighted the islands of Ulysses: Zacynthus first, then Dulichium and Same, and then Ithaca itself. The first were illuminated by the sun, but the last was still shrouded by the night, cloaked by the shadow of the Thesprotian mountains.

Diomedes planned to berth at Ithaca after hiding the other ships behind the little isle of Asteris. He wanted to know what had become of Ulysses, whether he had reached his homeland or was still afar, but he dared not reveal himself to queen Penelope without knowing what she had in her mind. If he found Ulysses, he would ask his advice for the journey he was embarking upon, because no one knew the perils of the sea as he did, no one could counsel him as Ulysses could.

He went ashore without weapons, dressed as a simple merchant, and he walked to the palace.

There was a boy of about ten playing in the courtyard with a dog. The boy asked him: 'Who are you, foreign guest? From where do you come?'

'I am a sailor,' he answered. 'I left Pylus last night and I wish to see the king. Take me to him, if you can.'

The boy lowered his head. 'The king's not here,' he said. 'They told me that he was coming back, that he would be here any day. But the days go by and he has not returned.'

Diomedes looked at the boy and he recognized him. He clearly saw Ulysses's features: his dark eyes which flashed with ever-changing light, his wide cheekbones, his thin lips. He felt moved; he remembered when he was a little boy himself, sitting on the palace steps waiting for his father who was fighting far away. And he remembered when glorious Tydeus finally returned. He was stretched out on a ox-drawn cart, suited in his armour, covered by a blood-red cloak. His ashen face was wrapped in a bandage that held his jaw shut. His body jolted whenever the wheels hit a hole or a stone, and his head banged against the wooden cart. Women dressed in black raised piercing screams . . .

He laid a hand on the boy's head. 'Telemachus,' he said. 'You are Telemachus.'

The boy looked up in surprise: 'How do you know my name? I've never seen you.'

Diomedes answered: 'I knew your father, king Ulysses. I was a friend of his. I recognized you because anyone could see that you are his son.'

'Do you think my father will come back?' asked the boy again.

'I do,' replied Diomedes. 'He will return with the swallows and bring you beautiful gifts.'

'Do you want to see my mother?'

'No, my son, I do not want to disturb the queen and distract her from her pursuits. She must have much to do in the palace.'

The young prince insisted: 'Please come, it will make my mother happy to speak with a friend of my father's.' He took him by the hand and led him into the house.

Diomedes followed. Penelope had never seen him, after all, and he thought he could keep his identity a secret.

The queen received him in the grand hall. Her nurse set out a stool for him and put bread and wine before him. Penelope was small, but very beautiful. Her hair was dark and her eyes light, her hands were tiny but strong, her hips were round and her breasts were high and firm like all the women of Sparta.

'Did you fight the war?' she asked him.

'Yes. I was with Diomedes.'

'Why did you abandon your king? Is he dead?'

'It is as if he were. But why, queen, do you ask me of Diomedes? Why don't you ask about Ulysses, your husband?'

'Ulysses . . .' The queen dropped her head and the two curls adorning her temples shadowed her cheeks. 'We're waiting for him. He should be back soon . . . don't you think?'

'Ulysses did not come with us. He returned to Troy, where Agamemnon had lingered to sacrifice one hundred oxen to the gods in expiation for the war. We knew nothing more of him . . . but I am sure that you will see him again. Perhaps he tarries in order to plunder the coasts and augment his spoils. Or perhaps the bad weather has delayed him, and he waits in a sheltered place for better conditions. Ulysses is prudent; he always calculates the risks he must face.'

'He didn't want this war. He did not want to leave, to leave me, our son . . .'

'But he is the one who won the war. The city fell thanks to his stratagem.'

'My cousin, Queen Helen . . . has she returned?'

'No. She was with Menelaus but they disappeared one night before we rounded Cape Sunion. Perhaps the wind carried them astray, to Cyprus or to Egypt. Who knows?'

'Why, when I asked you about Diomedes, did you say to me: 'It's as if he were dead?' Tell me the truth. Has he been killed? Imprisoned upon his return?'

Her voice betrayed a touch of trepidation, as if she feared the worst. It seemed that somehow, she knew something.

'Queen Aigialeia laid a trap for us. I barely managed to save myself, with some of my comrades. We know nothing of our king. That is why I said: 'It's as if he were dead.' He loved his wife. It was easy to take him by surprise. The bitch betrayed him after he had escaped so many perils on the fields of Ilium.'

Penelope shivered. 'Do not say that. War is much harder on women than on men. What do you men know of what passes through the mind of a woman living alone for years, for thousands of days and nights, in expectation? In continuous illusion and continuous delusion? Love can be transformed into hate . . . or into madness. And madness can strike indiscriminately, like an illness. Queen Clytemnestra . . . she too . . .'

'Has betrayed her husband?' asked Diomedes.

'No. She too . . . pursues an ancient destiny. Long ago the queens reigned over this land, and a great goddess, the mother of all living things, reigned in the heavens. The race of the queens lives on. While men destroy themselves through war, the queens are preparing for a return to the time when the ancient order had not been disrupted, when the wolf grazed alongside the lamb, when Persephone had not yet been carried off into Hades, when eternal spring reigned always.'

'The conspiracy of the queens . . .' whispered Diomedes. 'They say it has gone on for centuries. Medea against Jason, Deianeira against Hercules, Phaedra against Theseus, the fifty daughters of Danaus who slaughtered their husbands. Are you among them? Are you preparing to murder Ulysses? You will never succeed. No one can surprise him through deceit. I know him.'

A ray of light lit Penelope's forehead: 'You know him? Give me proof, if you want me to believe you.'

'He has a scar on his left leg and a birthmark over his knee. He has a wide face and thin lips. Broad shoulders and chest, long legs for his stature. And a strange smile . . . he always smiles as he is about to deal the death blow . . . Why do you want to kill him, *wanaxa*? Why?'

'No,' said Penelope. 'I will not kill him, though I have been asked to do so. And do you know why? Because it is not he who chose me, but I who chose him. My father Icarius was against it, but I covered my face as soon as I saw him because I knew he would be the only man of my life. I covered my face with a veil so he would understand I wanted to be his bride. He or no other. I chose him: he was the poorest of the kings, sovereign of dry, rocky islands, but his voice was resonant and persuasive. When he spoke everyone listened, enchanted.

'He did not want this war. The blood of the ancient race lives in him as well. He opposed force with astuteness . . . in vain. When Agamemnon's messenger came to ask him to depart for the war, he found Ulysses ploughing the beach with an ass and a bull at the yoke. They took Telemachus from his cradle and laid him down before the beasts. Ulysses rushed to gather the little one to his chest, proving that he could not be mad. They gave him no choice but to leave . . . He made a wedding bed for me amidst the boughs of a tree, the arms of an olive tree, like a bird's nest. What other man would have done the same? The kings of the Achaeans built nests of stone for their brides, gelid walls that ooze blood.'

'How do you know about Clytemnestra? And about ...
Aigialeia ... you knew about her too, didn't you?'

'Yes. All of the kings will be driven away: Idomeneus from
Crete, Diomedes from Argos, Menelaus from Sparta ... or killed.
Clytemnestra will kill. If she hasn't already.'

Diomedes hid his face in his cloak. 'Oh great Atreid!' he
murmured to himself. 'Watch your back! We are no longer beside
you, we are no longer ... we are no longer.' He wept. The tears
fell copiously from his eyes, they dripped from the golden curls of
his beard.

'Who are you?' asked Penelope.

'My name is Leodes.'

'Who are you?' demanded Penelope again.

'A man on the run ... I would have liked to ask counsel from
your husband, wise Ulysses, before facing the unknown but the
gods have denied me even this.' He rose to leave but Penelope
stopped him. She had a sly look in her eyes, as if seeking his
complicity.

'Tell me: he sent you, didn't he? He is hiding nearby and he
sent you to discover the truth and report it all back to him. I
know, that's the way he is, and I'm not offended. I understand
him. Tell him that I understand but that he must return immediately, I beg of you. I'm sure that I'm right, aren't I? Am I not
right?'

Diomedes turned away: 'No, *wanaxa*. I'm sorry but you are
not right. I've told you the truth. Ulysses left us at Tenedos and
he turned back towards Ilium.'

Penelope began to tremble. Her lips trembled and her hands
trembled and tears trembled under her black lashes. 'I beg of you,
do not torment me,' she said. 'Do not continue lying to me. You
have put me to the test. If it is he who sends you, run to tell him
that our bridal chamber is intact, I have conserved it like a sacred
enclosure. Tell him to come back. I beg of you.'

Diomedes rose to take his leave. In his heart of hearts he
envied the son of Laertes, for his bride loved him still.

'I'm sorry, *wanaxa*. I'm not who you think I am. I seek Ulysses as well and I do not know where he may be. But if one day he does return, tell him that a friend came looking for him, a friend who was at his side on the fields of Ilium the night he donned the helmet of Merion. He'll understand. He will tell you all about me. Now please allow me to go, to straighten my bow towards the northern sea. Farewell.'

He walked away, and Telemachus scampered after him. 'Tell me,' the boy said, 'have you seen him of late? What does he look like? What does my father look like?'

Diomedes stopped for a moment. 'He looks like you imagine him. When you see him, you'll recognize him.'

'I don't want to stay here to wait for him,' said the little prince. 'Take me with you to search for him at sea. I'll work for you, I'll earn my bread as a servant. Please take me with you so I can find him.'

The hero ruffled the boy's hair. 'I can't,' he said. 'I can't, although I wish I could.'

The boy stopped following him and sat on a stone to watch as he walked off in the direction of the port. A dog ran up to his young master and curled up at his feet. He stroked and hugged him tightly, calling him by name: 'Argus, Argus.'

Diomedes turned at the sound of that word. He looked at the boy and the dog and he said: 'When your father comes back, never let him leave again.'

He continued down the road and reached the port as night was falling. Some fishermen had approached the comrades he had left behind on the ship and were talking to them, trying to sell them the fish they had caught in exchange for resin and pitch, if they had any. Diomedes went aboard and had them cast off. His comrades began rowing and he steered towards Asteris, where the rest of the fleet was waiting. The men slept on their rowing benches and set off again at dawn. A southern wind had picked up and the ships hoisted their sails. The current carried them north as well, towards darkness and night.

His pilot, Myrsilus, asked him: 'Was there news of Ulysses? Did you see him?'

'No,' answered Diomedes. 'He has not returned. I begged him not to go back to Ilium, remember? The weather was worsening. Perhaps the storm caught them as they were leaving and the wind cast them up on some unfamiliar beach. Ulysses is the best of us all on the sea. If he has not returned, who could have been saved? What have you learned of the route which awaits us?'

'There is land before us, towards the west,' replied the helmsman. 'Some say it is an island, others a peninsula. Land lies to the east as well. Not one of these Ithacaeans has ever gone far enough north to find other lands in this direction. But they have heard tell that the winds are perilous and unpredictable, the reefs treacherous. The land which stretches out to the north is different from ours; it is low to the sea, often enveloped in mist and clouds. The sun's rays don't touch it for long periods of time, neither when it rises in the morn nor sets in the evening. The people who inhabit these lands are strangers to all and their language is incomprehensible.'

'That is where we shall go,' said the king. Then he went to the bow and stood there, motionless, his head in the wind and the sun on the blond hair that fell to his shoulders. He threw off the humble cloak that he had worn to Ithaca with a mind to surprise Ulysses. But Ulysses was not to be found. His voyage would lead him into the unknown, and only the memory of his friends could follow him there.

They sailed for many days, and stopped every night on dry land, where a promontory stretched out from the continent into the sea or where an island offered shelter. A few of the men would go inland to look for food and water. They cast out their nets sometimes and caught fish or gathered up crabs, shellfish and other sea foods along the beaches.

The coast did not change much; inlets and promontories, islands small and large. At the horizon, towards the east, a chain of mountains always followed them, some low and others tall, towering over the sea. They often saw men fishing near the coast, tossing their nets from small boats carved from a single tree trunk. Sometimes, at night, they would see lights twinkling in the dark, fires burning on the mountain tops. They would hear shrieks echoing amidst the craggy cliffs, sounding like the cries of eagles.

The further north they travelled, the more the sky became grey and dark, mirrored by the sea.

One day his comrades asked Diomedes to go ashore. They had seen the mouth of a river, with a small village. They wanted to take what food and women they could, before continuing their journey. Diomedes consented, although he was against the plan. Fierce people often inhabited such poor lands, and he was afraid they might be lying in wait behind the mountains looming nearby. They beached at a small cove and dropped their anchors. Myrsilus led a group of men to the top of a hill to observe the village. It was a cluster of huts standing along the banks of the river; each hut had a pen for animals. They heard bleating, the braying of donkeys and barking of dogs. But not a human voice.

Evening fell, but the menfolk had not returned to their huts; they could sense the presence of the enemy. They sat all together out in the open, armed. They sniffed the air like sheepdogs guarding their flocks, lifting their snouts to pick out the scent of a wolf.

3

WHEN DARKNESS FELL MYRSILUS led the attack. Diomedes was against it and did not take part. He had agreed to them taking women and food, but he ordered the population to be spared, as much as possible. He remained on his ship with a few comrades as Myrsilus and his men charged forward shouting.

Other shouts answered from the bottom of the valley and from the houses of the little village, and the skirmish began. These were poor men, bearing rough, primitive arms, but they fought furiously to save their wives and children.

Their resistance did not last long. Their weapons broke as soon as the conflict started and they withdrew, continuing to throw stones, but they could not make a dent in their assailants' large bronze shields and crested helmets. They would have been all slain then and there, had not something that terrified even their assailants occurred.

A horn sounded shrill and long from the mountains, followed by shouting so loud it seemed to come from thousands of men yelling at once. A great multitude of warriors appeared at the pass that descended between the valley and the sea. The blazing torches they carried formed a river of light that ran down the wooded slopes of the mountain.

The village men and the Achaean warriors fighting in the little field near the town took no heed at first, absorbed as they were in the brawl, but the women turned towards the mountain and then towards the sea, raising their arms in a gesture of despair. In just a few moments, their tranquil existence had been completely overturned; they were being attacked both by land and by sea, by strangers who knew nothing of each other.

Diomedes saw what was happening from his ship and immediately realized the danger his comrades were in. He called his slave, a Hittite named Telephus whom he had taken prisoner in Ilium, and ordered him to sound the signal for retreat with his bugle, but the valley was already thick with battle cries, with clanging weapons and neighing horses. Myrsilus and his men did not hear and continued to strike out at the villagers.

Diomedes saw the invaders' advance guard racing down from the mountains behind the village. They were wild and relentless, flying like shades from one hut to another, riding their horses barebacked. They carried off everything they could find, accumulating it in great heaps, and then set fire to the huts. The wind licked the flames high, lifting columns of smoke and sparks towards the sky. The native warriors, crushed between the two enemy formations, would be soon overcome, and once they had fallen, Myrsilus and his men would find themselves surrounded, with no hope of escape.

Diomedes donned his armour and ordered the rowers to direct the ships to the coast.

His ship was the first to enter into the circle of light which the flames cast towards the sea, and he stood tall at the bow, clad in blinding bronze, under the standard of the kings of Argos. He threw out his arms, gripping his spear in his right hand and his shield in his left, and he let out the war cry. The cry that had terrified the Trojans, throwing their ranks into disorder and panicking their horses. Diomedes's war cry echoed again and again, and the din on the beach ceased. The invaders turned and were struck dumb by the sudden apparition. Behind them the long column continued to descend the mountain, massing inland with great commotion. Myrsilus and his men took advantage of the moment to retreat with their backs to the sea. They pressed close, side by side, shoulder to shoulder and shield to shield.

One of the invaders strode towards the beach and let out a cry of his own, waving his weapons in the air and gesturing for his men to fall back. It was evident that he wanted to take up Diomedes's challenge to single combat. The royal ship advanced until it was nearly at the beach and Diomedes leapt into the water fully armed and advanced towards his adversary. Myrsilus's men opened their ranks to let him pass, closing tight once again behind him. The waves lapped calmly at the pebbles along the shore but on the western horizon a long rip in the clouds revealed a strip of crimson as if the sky, wounded, were bleeding into the sea.

The warrior who had come from the mountains was a shaggy giant. His head was protected by a leather helmet, his chest by a bronze plate held in place by chains crossed at his back. A loincloth covered his hairy groin.

He flung his spear first. It struck the centre of Diomedes's shield but the metal boss deflected it. Tydeus's son planted his left foot firmly forward, weighed the long, well-balanced spear in his hand, and then hurled it with enormous strength. The ashwood shot through the air like lightning, ran through the enemy's shield and struck the bronze that protected his heart. It grazed the plate but did not pierce it. A shout arose from the men gathered behind him. The warrior tossed the shield that would no longer serve him and unsheathed his sword.

Diomedes drew his sword as well and he advanced, glaring at his enemy from the rim of his shield; his eyes behind the visor were burning with ire as the mighty crest of his helmet fluttered in the evening breeze.

The hero then delivered a violent downward blow on his enemy's head, but the other succeeded in fending it off with his own sword. Diomedes struck another even stronger blow, but the blade which had once torn through the belly of the god of war fell to the ground shorn in two as if it had been made of wood! A chill seeped into the hero's bones. His adversary yelled out a wild threat, and the words sounded strangely familiar even though he did not understand them.

His outburst reminded the Achaeans lined up on the shore of a language once common but long forgotten. Myrsilus tried to toss his sword to the disarmed king, but Diomedes did not see him; he could not tear his eyes from the enemy, who advanced jeering and brandishing his sword. It was made of a shiny metal which glittered with blue and scarlet sparks; its surface was not smooth and perfect like their blades of bronze but rough rather, as though it had suffered innumerable blows. The vault of the heavens must be made of that metal; perhaps this man had received the sword from a god and nothing could defeat it! The warrior suddenly leapt forward and dealt a daunting blow. Diomedes raised his shield, but the blows came faster and stronger. Sparks sprayed out at each strike; the polished rim was breaking up, the fast-joined studs falling off. He would soon find himself with no means of defence. But then his Hittite slave, Telephus, shouted behind him:

'Wanax! His spear is stuck in the sand just three paces behind you!'

Diomedes understood. He backed up slowly at first, then, in a flash, hurled his shield at his adversary and spun around like lightning. He pulled the spear out of the ground and as his foe flung out his arm to deflect the shield that had been thrown at him, Diomedes threw the spear straight at his chest. The point pierced the plate, cleaved his heart and came out of his back. The warrior swayed for a moment like an oak whose roots have been chopped off by woodsmen, black blood pouring from his mouth. Then he crashed face first into the sand.

A long groan sounded from the ranks of the invaders, a wail of lament that swiftly became a howl of fury as they all lunged forward at once.

They were hundreds of times more numerous than the Achaeans, even now that all the comrades on board the ships had come to their aid. Diomedes saw that opposing them was futile, and ordered his men to toss their shields on their backs and run towards the ships. They obeyed, but many of them were struck and killed as they ran towards the sea and scrambled up the sides of the ships. Others were wounded and fell into the hands of their enemies; they were cut to pieces, their heads stuck on pikes and hurled back at the ships. The men all rushed to the thwarts and began to row as fast as they could to escape, as a band of enemies seized the anchor cable of the royal vessel and attempted to hold it back. Others rushed upon the ship and clusters of them hung on to the sides so that the rowers, no matter how mightily they arched their backs, could not overcome the increasing weight and resistance of the enemy. The sea boiled all around but the ship could not haul off.

The glow of the fires lit up the ever-growing host of men tugging on the cable. Diomedes realized that they were pulling the ship back to shore; his comrades at the oars were failing to get the better of the hundreds of enemies dragging them towards land. The other ships were already far off at sea; their pilots had not realized in the pitch dark that the king's ship was not among them.

Diomedes ordered all the men not at the oars to take their bows and let fly at the mob pulling on the anchor cable. He himself seized a two-edged axe and leaned out over the prow to chop off the cable. The enemies were quick to realize what was happening and their archers advanced as well, shooting swarms of arrows at the ship. Myrsilus ran to protect the king with his shield. In mere moments, the shield became so heavy with the great number of arrows stuck in it that Myrsilus could no longer hold it alone. He gasped: 'Wanax! Hurry, or we'll all die!' Diomedes once again raised the axe over the rope at the point in which it sat on the railing and swung down with all his strength. The axe sliced through the cable and stuck deep in the wood. Suddenly free, the ship shoved off, urged on by the oars. The hull groaned as the stern sunk into the waves but Myrsilus tenaciously shouted out the tempo for the oarsmen, and the ship finally wheeled around and set its bow to sea.

As they moved off, the king saw a man desperately swimming towards the ship in an attempt to reach it. Believing it was one of his comrades trying to escape the enemies, he had a rope lowered so the man could catch hold of it. As the ship finally drew away from the shore, the cries of the mob fading and the blaze of the fire dimming in the distance, the man was hoisted aboard. He was not one of their comrades; he must have been one of the inhabitants of the wasted village. Deprived of home and family, horrified by cruel enemies, he had chosen those who seemed less ferocious. He looked around bewildered and then, picking out the king, threw himself at his feet and embraced his knees. Diomedes had the men give him dry clothes and food and he returned to the bow. He would turn back now and again to watch the tremulous flames, and then scanned the open sea in search of the other ships. Myrsilus had the brazier lit at the fore so they could be seen, and other fires were soon lit on the waves. He counted them. '*Wanax*,' he said, 'they're all there.' The king had the ship stopped and looked back towards the shore. The column of enemies was on the march again and a long line of torches snaked along towards the south as the burning village offered up its last faint flashes of life.

'They're going south,' said the king. 'Towards our land.'

'It is no longer our land,' said Myrsilus.

'You are wrong,' said the king again. 'It will be ours for ever, as a man's father and mother will always be his father and mother, even if the son abandons them.' He turned towards the foreigner and pointed at the torch lights heading south through the night. Who are they?' he asked.

The foreigner shook his head and Diomedes repeated: 'Who are they, who are those men?'

The man seemed to understand what he was being asked; he widened fear-filled eyes in the dark and in a whisper, as if fearful of his own voice, said: '*Dor*.'

'I've never heard tell of these people, but I say that nothing will stop them if they have swords like the one I saw . . .'

His Hittite slave approached. 'It was made of iron,' he said.

'Iron?' said Diomedes. 'What's that?'

'It's a metal, like copper and bronze, but infinitely stronger. Fire cannot melt it, but only serves to make it softer. It is laid on burning coals and then shaped with a hammer on an anvil. All of our noblemen in the city of Hatti, the king and all the dignitaries, are armed with swords and axes made of that metal. They have conquered all Asia with them. No one believed me when I spoke of the existence of this metal. Now you know I was telling the truth.'

As they were speaking, one of the ships drew up and the pilot called out: '*Wanax*, are you safe?'

'I am,' replied Diomedes. 'But we all risked death. Is that you, Anchialus?'

'Yes, *wanax*. And I am happy to see you.'

'Not for long. You must depart.'

'Depart? I have departed, to stay with you. And I do not intend ever to leave you.'

'You must go back, Anchialus. Have you seen that multitude of wild men? They are called . . . *Dor* . . . They are armed with a metal that can cut the best bronze, they ride the bare backs of their horses as if they were a single being, like centaurs. They are as numerous as ants and they are headed towards the land of the Achaeans. You must turn back, you must warn Nestor and Agamemnon; tell Menelaus, if he has returned, and Sthenelus at Argos, if he still lives. Tell them what you have seen. Tell them to ready their defences, to build a wall on the Isthmus, to send the black ships out to sea . . .'

'What does it matter, *wanax*?' replied Anchialus. 'We have chosen to sail towards the night, towards the land of the Mountains of Ice and the Mountains of Fire. What happens beyond the horizon we leave at our backs no longer concerns us.'

'I am your king. I want you to go. Now.'

Anchialus lowered his head, gripping the railing of his ship with his hands.

'I will do as you say,' he replied. 'But then I shall return. They say that this sea is really a gulf. I will catch up with you, when I have done as you have ordered me. I will sail up the coast until I find you. Leave a sign on the beach that I can recognize.'

'I will. Seeing you again will fill me with joy.'

The other three ships had joined them. The fires burning in the fore braziers cast a crimson halo on the waves, like a blood-stain.

'But before you go, let us render our lost comrades their last honours, ship by ship.'

They all stood, gripping an oar in hand and, one ship after another, looking towards land, they shouted out the names of their lost comrades, massacred by the enemy, hacked to pieces, abandoned without burial on a wild and hostile shore. Then Anchialus raised his hand in salute and pushed his ship back, his oarsmen at their places. The night swallowed them up and the wind carried afar the names of their comrades.

Diomedes walked back to the stern and covered his head in mourning for the loss of such gallant men. Strange quivers of blood-coloured light shot through the clouds crossing the sky. Perhaps it was their souls, seeking the light of the stars one last time before plunging into Hades.

The foreigner that they had hoisted aboard followed Diomedes and went to sit at his feet. He had chosen him as his master and awaited his command. Myrsilus, at his side, had taken the helm, keeping his eye on the Little Bear whenever it appeared between one cloud and another. It was too dark to seek a safe landing place, for they risked being smashed to pieces against the rocks, nor could they remain still and allow the wind and the waves to set them adrift. They had to navigate, confiding in the help of the gods and in good fortune. Telephus, the Hittite, sat on a basket near Diomedes, sharpening his knife on a whetstone.

'What land are you from?' asked Myrsilus, to break the silence and fear.

'You call us Chetaeans but we are Hittites. My native name is *Telepinu* and I come from a city of the interior called *Kussara*. I fought at length as the captain of a squadron of chariots in the army of our king Tudkhaliyas IV, may the gods preserve him, against the league of *Assuwa*, which we defeated. But when you arrived from the west, the league was reconstituted in support of Priam and his city *Vilusya*, which you *Ahhijawa* call Ilium. We were willing to help Priam at that point, setting aside our past conflicts with the league in order to repel our common enemy, but only a small contingent could be sent. Other peoples had come from the east, from the *Urartu* mountains, and invaded our land. Our king sent a legation to the king of the Egyptians but Egypt was being invaded as well, by multitudes from the desert and from the sea. If we had been able to draw up our whole army and all of our war chariots against you we would have chased you back into the sea! Nothing can withstand the charge of a battalion of Hittite chariots.'

Myrsilus smiled in the dark: 'That's what they all say. *Ahhijawa* . . . so that's what you call us . . . it's strange, a people do not exist because of who they are, but because of what others consider them to be. Have you seen Egypt as well?'

'Oh, yes. I was sent to escort one of our princes who had gone to visit their king, who is called Pharaoh. Their kings know the secret of immortality, but reveal it to no one. Two thousand years ago, they were already building stone tombs as tall as mountains. Their priests know how to obscure the sun and make it reappear at will. And they have a gigantic river whose waters beget monsters with mouths full of teeth and backs covered by armour that no weapon can penetrate.'

Myrsilus smiled again. 'What lovely stories you tell, Chetaean. By chance, do you know something of this land we are seeking?'

'No. I've never heard speak of it. But all those people marching south worry me.'

The shrieks of a flock of cranes broke the silence of the night. The Hittite pulled his cloak close around his shoulders. 'We're heading where they're escaping from. We're going the opposite direction from the cranes, who are wise enough to abandon inhospitable places where the winters are too harsh . . . Have you noticed those strange lights behind the clouds? I've never seen anything like it in all my life. And never, as far back as man can remember, have so many peoples left their own lands and set off to cover such immense distances. Something has terrified them, or perhaps something urges them on without their knowing why . . . like when the locusts suddenly, for no reason, gather and begin to migrate, destroying everything along their path . . .' He turned to look at the king, who stood still and silent by the railing, his cloak pulled up over his head. 'You are all running as well . . . without knowing where. And I with you.'

He found a blanket and curled up between the baskets and ropes, seeking shelter from the damp night. Diomedes turned to the pilot then: 'Are you well awake?' he asked.

'I'm awake, *wanax*, I'm holding the route and keeping windward. Sleep if you can.'

The king laid out a bear pelt and lay down upon it, covering himself with his cloak. He sighed, grieving for the comrades lost.

The Hittite slave waited until the king was asleep, then walked over to the pilot and pointed at a box tied to the mast. 'Do you know what's in there?' he asked.

Myrsilus did not even turn towards him; his gaze was riveted to the sky. 'In what?' he asked.

'You know. Inside that chest tied to the main mast.'

'Ask me once more and I'll chop off your head.'

'Who do you think you're talking to?' insisted the slave. 'Do you think you can treat me like a mouse just because I've fallen into servitude? I am a Hittite warrior. I was the commander of a squadron of chariots. And I wasn't born yesterday. There's something strange in that box.'

'One more word and I'll cut off your head,' repeated Myrsilus. The Hittite slave said nothing. The other men were laid out on the bottom of the ship and were sleeping under their cloaks.

The foreigner who had been taken aboard was sitting against the ship's railing with his legs close against his chest and his head leaning on his knees. The Hittite slave watched him for a while, then approached him. The glow of the brazier at the stern lit up his dark face. 'What kind of a man are you?' he asked him in his own language.

The foreigner raised his head and in the same language answered: 'I am a *Chnan*.'

'A *Chnan* . . . what are you doing here? And you speak Hittite . . . where did you learn it?'

'The *Chnan* speak many languages because we take our wares to all the peoples of this earth.'

'Then you're not one of those wretches whose village they destroyed?'

'No. We were pushed up here by a storm two months ago, at the end of the summer. My ship sank and I barely saved myself. They welcomed me, gave me food. They did not deserve to die.'

'We do not deserve to die either. Do you know anyone who deserves to die? To sink into darkness, leaving behind forever the scent of the air and the sea, the colours of the sky, of the mountains and the meadows, the taste of bread and the love of women ... is there someone who deserves such horror, just because he was born? Who were those ... *Dor* ... you were talking about?'

'That's what the people who took me in called them. They are a powerful, ferocious race. They live on a great inland river called the Ister, but for some time now they have been restless, and they make continuous raids towards the sea. Those whom you saw were but a small group of them; if some day all of them decide to move, no one will be able to stop them. They have weapons of iron, they ride the bare backs of their horses ... did you see them?'

'I did. Do you speak the language of the Achaeans as well?'

'I can understand much more than I speak. But it is better they don't learn that ... until I know them well. But tell me, what men are these that sail in this sea, in this season and in this direction? They must be mad, or desperate.'

The Hittite looked into the sky again. The strange lights had been extinguished and the vault of the heavens was as grey and smooth as a leaden bowl.

'They are both,' he said.

*

At that same hour, Clytemnestra lay on her wedding bed alongside Aegisthus. She was not sleeping; she lay with her eyes open and the lamp lit. She had killed her husband without hesitation, as he

42

returned after years of war, but she could not bear the visions that crowded round her head if she closed her eyes. She could not bear the hate of Electra, the daughter who remained to her. Since that murdering night, she had often gone up to the tower of the chasm at night, in the wind, and there she had remembered the days of her wedding, the night in which a choir of maidens with flaming torches had accompanied her to the wedding bed of the king of Mycenae, the king of the Achaean kings.

They had undressed her and perfumed her. They had combed her hair and loosened her belt, laying her on the bed. She remembered how the king had appeared, the copper reflections on the thick locks that shaded his forehead and cheeks, mixing in with his full beard. She remembered his chest and his arms shining with scented oil, and she remembered how she had done her duty. How she had pretended to cry out with pleasure when his scourge lacerated her womb.

She had used her allure wilfully but without abandon, without ever letting herself be moved.

Men have to submit or die. As when the great queen, the *Potinja*, once reigned. Once a year she chose her bedmate, the male who would render her fertile, the strongest and most fearless, the most vital. He who after having fought duel after duel with the others had earned himself the privilege of being king for one day and one night before dying.

Clytemnestra got up and went to the throne room. She sat on the seat that had belonged to the Atreides and waited there for the sun to rise.

Even before the maidservants had left their beds and lit the fire in the hearth, the man whom she had been expecting for days arrived. He entered and, seeing that the room was still dark, he sat on the floor near the wall to wait for someone in the household to awaken. The queen saw him and called to him.

'Come forward,' she said, 'I've been waiting for you. Did you see my cousin, the queen of Ithaca?'

'Yes, *wanaxa*, I have met with her.'

'And what did she tell you? Has she agreed to our requests?'

'Yes. All will be done when Ulysses returns.'

'But . . . how? Did she tell you how? The king of Ithaca is the most cunning man on earth.'

'She is no less able than he. Ulysses will never suspect anything.'

'What of him, did you see him? Why didn't you wait for his destiny to be fulfilled?'

'I waited, but king Ulysses did not return. He should have reached Ithaca no longer than three days after Agamemnon and Diomedes returned. But when I left, a month had passed and there was no word of him.'

'A month is too long. It couldn't have taken him so long.'

'Perhaps his ship foundered. Perhaps he is already dead. While I was in Ithaca, a ship arrived at port and a man came ashore and spoke with the queen. I learned that they were Achaeans and that they had come from Argos, but I could find out no more.'

'Argos?' repeated the queen, getting to her feet. 'Did you see that man in the face?'

'For just a moment, at the port, as he was boarding the ship.'

'What did he look like?'

'He had long blond curls that fell to his shoulders. His eyes were dark, bright and watchful. His hands were strong and his gait was forceful, as if he were accustomed to carrying a weight on his shoulders.'

'The weight of armour,' said the queen. 'Perhaps you saw a king escaping . . . or preparing to return.' The man shook his head without understanding. 'My cousin is with us. I am sure of it. And when we have extinguished the mind of Ulysses, the last obstacle will have been brought down.'

The man left and the queen walked out on to the gallery of the tower of the chasm. The clouds were low on the mountains and swollen with rain. Suddenly, Clytemnestra saw a woman wrapped in a black cape leaving from one of the side gates below; she walked swiftly towards the bottom of the valley, and stopped at the old abandoned cistern. There she fell to her knees. She rocked back and forth, gripping her shoulders, and then she

lay flat and placed her forehead against the bare stone that covered the opening. Electra. She mourned her father, contemptibly
murdered and contemptibly buried, and the gusts of wind raised
the soft echoes of her laments all the way up to the bastions of the
tower.

*

Meanwhile, on the distant northern sea, Diomedes's ships
advanced in the light of dawn. Their beaked prows ploughed
through the grey waves, passing between deserted islands and
rugged promontories reaching out like hooked fingers into the
sea. Little villages perched high above, surrounded by dry walls
like nests of stone. They could see the inhabitants venturing out
with their herds of goats, wild men these too, covered in fur like
the animals they tended.

That night they found shelter near the mouth of a river, and
the night after that as well. At dawn, Diomedes decided to walk
upstream with Myrsilus and other companions in search of game.
But they were soon to be confronted with the strangest of
prodigies. Having gone round a hill and descending on the other
side, they saw that the river had vanished. They searched and
searched for it, but could find it nowhere. After a long stretch on
foot they reached a place where the river reappeared but was
immediately swallowed up into the ground, sucked into a sink-
hole. Diomedes realized that the hole must lead to Hades and he
sacrificed a black goat to Persephone so that she might propitiate
his journey. The victim's blood stained the river water red and
disappeared into the ground.

They dared not draw water from the cursed river that fled the
light of day like a creature of the night, and so they continued
inland in search of game and water. The land opening up all
around them was quite different from any Diomedes had ever
seen; it was covered by stunted, twisted trees and furrowed by
deep gorges and wild, overgrown ravines.

A little group of deer appeared and the hunters closed in. The
Hittite and the foreigner were armed with bows and hid behind

some brambles; Diomedes and Myrsilus took position opposite them with their javelins. A flock of birds took to the air with shrill cries, startling the deer. As they bolted, Myrsilus hurled his javelin but missed the mark, while the Hittite had had the time to take aim and he hit a large male which collapsed to the ground, dead. The others tied him by his legs to a branch and began to make their way back to the ship. Although the territory they crossed seemed deserted and uninhabited, the eyes of the foreigner kept darting here and there, as though he sensed some presence.

He was not mistaken. One of the men suddenly yelled out in pain and dropped to his knees; an arrow had pierced his thigh. They all turned; behind them, just topping a hill, were a mob of wild-haired savages with long beards, wearing goatskins. They were armed with bows and wielded heavy clubs with stone heads. They ran forward, shouting loudly and waving their bludgeons. Diomedes ordered his men to retreat to a gorge where they would have some hope of resisting, although they were so thoroughly outnumbered. Some of the attackers were letting out shrill, high-toned cries, like those of sea birds. Their cries echoed in the distance, bouncing off the rock walls, the precipices and the caverns; they must have been calls for reinforcement, because the enemy strength soon swelled to an enormous number of men.

The Achaeans continued to fall back but shortly found themselves in a deep, narrowing gully. Their enemies were soon upon them, looming from above at the rim of the steep crevasse and pushing huge stones down below. The stones roared down the rock walls, picking up speed and dislodging others on their way to the bottom of the gully. Diomedes ordered his men to flatten themselves against the walls and then to run as fast as they could in the direction of the sea, but some were struck nonetheless by the stones and crushed to the ground, while others met an even worse fate. That cursed gully was rife with pits and swallow holes, covered with thick bushes and brambles. As they ran, many plunged below to their deaths, while others lay helplessly on the bottoms of the pits howling with pain, their bones shattered.

Diomedes took stock of the tremendous danger and, as the

enemies rushed to close off every path of escape, he ordered his men to stop and to seek cover among the bushes and the rocky crags of the gully walls. He glanced around and saw that the ground was all scattered with white animal bones. That was how this fierce people hunted game! By herding them towards that gorge and raining down stones on them from above, just as they were now trying to destroy him and his companions. He, King of Argos and son of Tydeus, was forced to scramble like a wild animal being hunted down by savages, was forced to listen to his wounded warriors' cries for help without being able to raise a hand for them. They hid among the bushes and waited, perfectly still, although the stones never ceased to fall from above, just barely missing them at times. Thus they waited until nightfall. Then the stones stopped falling and fires were lit on the rim of the gully. Their enemies were not going anywhere. They were waiting for the sun to rise and then they would slaughter them all.

One of his men crept towards Diomedes; it was Cleitus, son of Leitus of Las, who had fought at his side at Ilium. He said: 'This is the fate that has befallen us for following you! To be massacred by ferocious savages without any chance of defending ourselves, to be stoned to death like beasts without ever drawing our swords. If we had remained at Argos we would have at least been able to fight on an open field in the light of the sun, and we would have died in our own land.'

Myrsilus interrupted him: 'Hold your tongue. No one forced you to follow the king. You did so of your own will. If you don't stop whining I'll break your jaw and make you spit blood. What we must do is find a way to escape while it is dark and they cannot see us.'

Telephus, the Hittite slave, approached him as well, and said: 'The wind is blowing from the sea, and the ground above us is covered with dry grass and branches. Where I come from, when the peasants want to burn the stubble on their fields, they wait until a strong wind picks up from the east; the whole plain soon becomes a sea of flames.'

'What do you mean to say?' asked the king.

'Listen, *wanax*. While we were running like madmen down this abyss, I noticed that on the left side there was a way of getting back up to the rim. It won't be easy, but I come from the mountains and I'm a good climber. If any of your men can climb as well, allow them to come with me. When we get up there, we'll set fire to the grass all around the enemies. The wind will do the rest. There's no other way, king. If we don't try it, we will all die and our bodies will lie unburied, like the bones of these animals.'

'I will come with you myself,' said the king. 'As a boy, I often stayed with my grandfather Oineus and my uncle Meleager in Aetolia; I climbed the steep slopes there with no fear. I will take Diocles and Agelaus, Eupitus and Evenus with me; they are Arcadians and lived as boys on the mountains.'

Myrsilus wanted to come as well, but Diomedes ordered him to stay with the others.

They set out and followed the Hittite slave in silence. When they got to the foot of the escarpment, they began their ascent, stopping every time a stone was knocked out of place for fear they would be heard and discovered. As they made their way up, they could hear rowdy laughter and shouting, and the crackling of the fires. When they pulled themselves up over the rim of the gorge, they could see the savages all sitting around the fires, eating roasted meat. They were yelling and belching, throwing bones and pieces of meat at each other.

Diomedes and the others encircled the bivouac and headed for the most isolated fire, slipping behind the men sitting there and killing them before they had even suspected their presence. They seized firebrands then, and spread out. The Hittite slave guided them, just as he had as a boy, helping the peasants set fire to the stubble fields in the immense high plains of Asia. He tested the direction of the wind and touched his brand to the grass and dry branches covering the ground. The flames rose up vigorously and spread, carried by the wind. The other men, lurking in a half circle around the camp, did the same all around their enemies. In mere moments the high plain was a sea of flames and the wind was getting stronger.

The enemies were terror-stricken and yelled out in alarm, as some of them fell, run through by the arrows of invisible assailants. They could see nothing beyond the circle of flames that enveloped them on all sides. Forced back by the unbearable heat, they were soon caught between the yawning chasm and the wall of flames. Some tried to lower themselves down but panic overwhelmed them as they tumbled over and ended up smashed against the rocks, while others tried to run blindly through the fire.

Agelaus caught one of them alive and tied him to a tree, to deliver him over to Diomedes once it was all over.

By dawn the fire had burnt itself out and the ground was covered with scorched bodies. The king leaned over the side of the gorge and shouted to his men: 'You can come up now! There is no more danger.'

The survivors clambered over the side, but Myrsilus hesitated as he heard groaning coming from the concealed pits. He could barely make out one of the men lying at the bottom of the hole; a fractured leg bone had broken through the skin and gleamed sharp white. His low, constant moaning was laden with pain. Myrsilus cautiously made his way along the narrow-sided gully as far as he could go, bending over the pit as a ray of light illuminated the face of the wounded warrior.

He recognized him: it was Alcatous, son of Dolius. He had long ago left Mases, a town on the coast where he had made his living as a fisherman, dreaming of glory and a rich booty. He had followed Diomedes on this last adventure hoping one day to be among the first in a grand new kingdom, with a place of his own in the assembly. He could never have imagined that destiny would bury his life on the bottom of a dark, miserable pit.

Myrsilus leaned over the edge of the pit and took aim with his arrow, while his dying comrade, who had understood, tried to drag himself to clear ground where he could offer an unhindered target.

The arrow pierced the pit of his throat and he collapsed against the wall. As his soul, groaning, fled his wound, his eyes rolled backwards and he could see within himself, for an instant. He found his native town, the glittering water of the sea and his own boyish steps along the shore, he felt the splashes and the foam, the sand beneath his feet and the heat of the sun on his bare shoulders. He wished he had never left as he descended forever, weeping, into the cold and the dark.

Myrsilus approached another hole but he could not get close enough because the walls were too steep, nor could he see inside because the opening was covered with thick bushes. All he could do was to toss down his knife, a sharp blade of bronze that he had never parted from, in the hopes that another one of the men could retrieve it and put an end to his suffering. He shouted: 'There's nothing more I can do for you, my friend!' Only an echo answered: 'Friend!' And he climbed out of the gully and up to the rim with a heavy heart, the last of all of them.

Diomedes came close: 'How many?' he asked. 'How many comrades have we lost?'

'Alcatous . . .' began Myrsilus, 'shattered on the bottom of one of those holes.'

'Schedius and Alcandrus,' added another, 'crushed by their stones.'

Each of the men looked around, naming the companions he found missing. Agelaus drew close to the king, and pointed at the prisoner he had taken: 'I got one of them alive, and tied him to that tree. Avenge their slaughter on him.'

But Diomedes said: 'I've already killed so many of them . . . what would one more change? Let's go now, back to the ships. Our comrades will be worried about us.' He started off, but Telephus and the *Chnan* turned back first to retrieve the deer they had left down in the gorge, so that its meat would not go to waste.

Myrsilus, who had not taken part in the battle but had listened to the cries of his dying friends, lagged behind; he desired nothing but revenge. He waited until the others had gone on and he approached the prisoner. He was a vigorous man, and in trying to get away was shaking the whole tree to which he was tied. Myrsilus came close and tied him even tighter, and then he unsheathed his sword. The man stared at him without trembling, his head held high. Myrsilus cut the straps that held up the goatskin that covered his body, leaving him naked. Then with the tip of his sword he cut his skin just above his groin, making his blood drip copiously between his legs. The man understood the end he was meant for and widened his eyes in terror, trying desperately to twist free with all his remaining strength. He shouted and pleaded in an incomprehensible language but Myrsilus had already gone off to catch up with the others.

When he had walked for a good stretch, he turned back and saw that a wolf or a wild dog was approaching the prisoner, attracted by the smell of blood. It would stop, doubtfully looking around, before approaching again. The man was trying to scare it off, shouting and kicking, and the animal would draw back, only to reapproach a little more courageously each time, until it started to lick at the blood seeping into the earth. Myrsilus saw it go close to the man and lift its snout towards his groin, and he knew that his aim had been achieved. He turned and started to run down the slope, to join up with his comrades. Just then, an excruciating scream sounded through the valley and they all stopped short with a shudder. The scream echoed again, even louder and more frenzied, following them at length as it bounced again and again off the rocky cliffs, until it died away into a dreadful whimpering.

They started on their way again with heavy souls, eager to leave a land that could swallow up a live, glittering river and regurgitate it back into the sea, cold and black.

4

WHEN THEY REACHED THE beach and saw that the ships were all there, they felt relief but dared not abandon themselves to joy, for they had lost many companions.

Diomedes wanted a trophy erected nonetheless to commemorate victory over their enemies, and since they had neither spoils nor booty, he dedicated a suit of armour he had won in Ilium. He hung it on two crossed poles and had his name carved on to a stone, so that a memory would remain of his passage through that land.

They raised a lofty cairn on the shores of the sea and celebrated the funeral rites of their fallen comrades, so that they might find peace in Hades.

Telephus and the *Chnan* lit a fire and roasted the deer; when it was cooked, they carved it into portions and distributed them to everyone. Diomedes had wine brought from his ship and thus, as long as their cups were full and there was food to eat, their sadness was dispelled, although they all knew in their hearts that it would return, grim and oppressive, with the shadows of night.

They took to sea again and the ships sailed the whole day without ever losing sight of one another; towards evening, the *Chnan* approached Myrsilus who was at the helm and said: 'The wind is shifting; soon it will be athwart of us and will push us towards the open sea.'

'I feel nothing. How can you say that?'

'I tell you the wind is changing. Strike the sails and dismast, and order the men to row to shore. And signal to the others to do the same, while there is time. Have you ever heard of the *Borrha*? It is a freezing wind born in the Hyperborean Mountains in the land of night: when it blows on the sea, no one can withstand its force. It raises waves as high as hills and even the most well-built boat will sink in no time.'

The hint of a chilly breeze brushed the shrouds and Myrsilus started, looking around uneasily.

'Do as I say,' insisted the *Chnan*. 'If you don't, we will all die. There's no time left.'

Myrsilus went to the king: '*Wanax*, we must go aground. The wind is changing. I ask for your permission to signal to the other ships.'

Diomedes turned towards him: 'The light of day is still with us, why should we do so?'

A sharp gust of wind bent the mast and tensed the sails. The hull listed to its side with a groan.

'The next will break the mast and sink us!' shouted the *Chnan*. 'By all the gods, do as I say!'

The defiant wind roused Myrsilus and transformed him. He shouted for the men to sink the right oars and to row with all their might on the left ones. He posted another at the helm in his stead and rushed with all the crew to strike the sail. The wind had become very strong and snapped the free end of the great sheet of linen like a whip. They flung themselves upon it and held it down with their weight. When they had restrained it, they began to extract the mast from its step.

'Too late!' shouted the *Chnan* over the roar of the wind. 'If you dismast now, it will fall on you and kill you.'

Myrsilus returned to the helm. 'Row hard on both sides now. Set the bow to the wind! Bow to the wind or we'll go under!'

Diomedes had climbed up to the curved stern and had hoisted the signal to strike sail; some of the ships responded immediately. But one of them appeared to be in great difficulty as it was tossed to and fro in the enormous foaming waves by the powerful gusts of the *Borrha*. Through a cloud of sea spray, he could see the men struggling with the rigging, but the force of the wind had become overpowering. He saw one of them flung into the sea by a wave and disappear under the billows; another, thrown overboard, grasped on to the railing, floundering and calling for help, before going under himself.

A sudden strong gust cracked the mast and tossed it into the sea along with the sail. The hull seemed to disappear for a moment but then resurfaced and the king saw the men chopping with axes at the shrouds still entangled in the broken shaft of the mast.

Once free of the water-filled sail which had been dragging the ship down like an anchor, the hull dipped at the stern and, as the oars struck the surface of the sea, straightened up again. The king was watching all this with such anxiety that he had not even noticed what was happening on his own ship. He turned and saw the thwarts being washed by the waves; the men were drenched, yet they arched their backs and dug in their feet with every stroke of their oars. Myrsilus shouted out the rowing tempo, his voice overcoming the noise of the squall and the ominous creaking of the hull. He knew that their lives were in the hands of the men at the oars; the moment they were sapped by fatigue, the ship would sink.

The *Chnan* was at the bow, grasping on to the ship's railing, scanning the sea desperately for a safe haven. He turned all at once towards the stern and yelled out with all the breath he had in him to Myrsilus: 'Put about! Veer to starboard!' Myrsilus shouted the order to the rowers and leaned into the helm, trying to push it left.

Diomedes ran to his side and the king's strength got the upper hand over the sea. The hull twisted, forced by the might of the hero who guided the toil of over one hundred arms racked by spasms, and the bow veered to the left, taking the brunt of the wind on its right side. The ship picked up speed and listed sharply and Myrsilus feared for a moment that the vessel would smash to pieces. But the *Chnan* knew what he was doing; he was directing them towards a strait wedged between two tongues of land. Before long, something miraculous happened: from one moment to the next, they found themselves in a vast mirror of calm waters barely rippled by short, close waves.

'Oh gods!' gasped Myrsilus, not believing what he saw. 'Oh gods, what is this?'

The *Chnan* traversed the ship from bow to stern, looking down at the still waters and up at the open sea, whipped by the squall.

'To shore!' shouted the king. 'Hurry, we must guide our comrades to this place or all of them will die!' The men rowed first to a little island on their left and then to another on their right; on each Diomedes set fire to a jar of resin and pitch, lighting them from the embers which were always kept burning in a covered urn under the curved stern. The comrades at sea saw the two lights and steered their ships towards the narrow strait, as the king's vessel had done. Four ships made it but the fifth, the last one, could not overcome the force of the sea and the wind. From the island, all the men shouted loudly to encourage their comrades still at the mercy of the sea, but the crew was exhausted by the long struggle. Diomedes saw the oars stop moving, one by one, and slip into the sea, he saw the hull, no longer animated by the strength of its crew, turn in a spin. It offered its side to the sea, and sank.

The king clenched his fists and lowered his head.

The men began to gather the branches and tree trunks that the tides had abandoned on the beach, and lit fires to dry themselves, their clothing and cloaks. They then hauled the ships aground and took refuge inside. They stretched the sails over the thwarts and lay down beneath them, holding each other close to keep warm. The wind continued to blow all night without cease, not subsiding until dawn. The next morning the sea gave up the bodies of some of their comrades who had drowned in the storm. They were green with algae and their eyes were open in a watery stare, like those of fish that a fisherman tosses on the beach to die.

They were buried in that low, grey land, among the cane thickets and brushwood on a clear, cold morning, and when the king had finished their funeral rites, the four pilots of the ships, including Myrsilus, approached him.

'Let us stop here, *wanax*,' Myrsilus said, speaking first. 'We have already lost many men. The days are getting shorter and the weather is worsening. If we go on, we will all die. How will you be able to found your kingdom then? Who will you share your destiny with?'

The king turned to face the sea and seemed to be absent-mindedly watching the swell of the waves which stretched out over the sand until they licked at his feet. The *Chnan* spoke then: 'I heard tell of this place from a sailor of Ashkelon who had learned about it from an Achaean of Rhodes who imported amber. I think we have reached the coast of the Seven Seas: seven lagoons which pour into one another until they reach the mouth of the Eridanus. There lie the Electrides islands, where amber falls from the sky, they say ... or where amber arrives on mule-back from the lands of the long nights, I say. From this point on, the paths of the sea are calm and sheltered. We need only steer clear of the shallows, but a man with a sounding line at the bow will suffice to avoid them.'

Diomedes turned to him: 'You know many things, and you saved my ships yesterday. When I found my kingdom I will build you a house and give you weapons and a cloak. I will give you a beautiful woman, tall with rounded hips. But tell me, why is it that yesterday you spoke in the language of the Achaeans? You've been with us for some time and you've never spoken a word in our language.'

'Because there had been no need,' replied the *Chnan*, 'but I thank you for your promise. I would ask you to do the same with your Hittite slave as well. He saved you and all of us by setting the grasslands on fire.'

The king shook his head: 'I owe my life to a slave and to a foreign merchant! I wonder whether our gods still have power over these lands ... What you propose is only right; when I found my kingdom, the Chetean slave will have the same things I've promised you.' Then he turned to his men and said: 'Let us go forward and explore these lands. We will seek a landing place where we can find water and food. There's nothing here; not even the possibility of shelter.'

The men obeyed and put the ships to sea, first the king's and then all the others. The *Chnan* stood at the bow, dropping a line every so often to gauge the depth of the water. Not much time had passed before they saw a group of low islands on the surface of the waves. They followed a wide channel that wound like a serpent through the small archipelago and soon sighted the mainland and went ashore. The place was deserted. The silence was broken only by the shrieks of sea birds flying low over the cane thickets. Diomedes sent some of the men hunting with bows and harpoons and then called Myrsilus. He ordered him to advance inland with a group of men, to see who lived in that land and whether they could settle there. He sent the *Chnan* with him as well.

As soon as they had left the coast and were out of sight, the *Chnan* said to Myrsilus: 'Hide your arms here under the sand and keep only a dagger or sword under your cloak. We'll move forward in small groups, at a distance from each other. In this area there should be a market where the goods that come from the north are exchanged with those that come from the sea. Merchants won't attract attention, but armed men would.'

Myrsilus was reluctant to abandon his arms, but remembering how the *Chnan* had saved the fleet the day before, he thought it was best to heed his advice. He ordered his men to do as he had said. He took the lead in the first group, scanning the territory continuously as they advanced. He felt exposed, alone and naked in that flat solitude. In all his life, he had never crossed a land from which neither the mountains nor the sea could be seen, in which the countryside was not bright with myriad colours. Here, as never before, the land was a uniform, endless expanse, all the same pale green. They saw, towards midday, a herd of horses, hundreds of magnificent animals grazing peacefully, twitching their long tails; their long wavy manes nearly touched the ground. A pure white stallion galloped around a group of mares and ponies, his tail erect. He would stop and rear up, whinnying and pawing at the air, and then start to gallop again. No one guarded over them; that immense wealth seemed to belong to no one.

Here and there, marshes glimmered on the ground, and the land would suddenly become soft and spongy under their feet. Thick oak groves sheltered groups of boars rooting about in search of acorns and tubers. Deer with majestic horns would stop suddenly at the edge of a wood and stare at the intruders, blowing little clouds of steam from moist nostrils.

They walked and walked until they could see a wisp of smoke rising in the distance, as the western sky began to redden in a muted sunset. There was a little town of grass-roofed wooden huts covered with mud. There also seemed to be a camp at a short distance from the settlement.

'If we had brought our arms we could have had food and women!' said Myrsilus.

'Instead, we'll go to them and ask for their hospitality; that way we'll find out where we are. You don't say a word. I know better how to deal with them.'

They got closer and saw that around the little town were droves of small, black swine and flocks of sheep. Ducks and geese dipped their bills into the mud on the shores of a little marsh. A group of children swarmed towards them and a dog started barking, soon joined by others. Several men came forward then as well; the *Chnan* raised his hand and told Myrsilus to do the same. The men got closer and were staring at them. Their legs were covered with tanned skins and they wore long-sleeved tunics of thick wool, belted at the waist with a strip of leather decorated with carved pieces of bone. They carried no arms, at least, none that could be seen. They spoke among themselves for awhile and then one approached and said something.

'What did he say?' asked Myrsilus.

'I don't know. I've never been around these parts before.' The *Chnan* loosened his belt, raised his tunic and slipped out something he wore against his skin: a long string wound several times around his waist, strung with brightly coloured glass beads and bronze clasps adorned with amber or glass.

Myrsilus looked at him in surprise: 'Where did you find all that?' he asked.

'This is my personal treasure; I always carry it with me. I was wearing it when you pulled me from the sea.'

The men instantly drew closer and behind them, Myrsilus noticed some women as well. They raised up on tiptoe to admire the wares that sparkled in the hands of the *Chnan*. Soon they were all chattering away, each in his own language, and it seemed that they could all understand each other well enough. The *Chnan* moved his hands with the skill of a juggler as his face assumed a great variety of expressions; he soon was directing all his attention towards the women and ignoring the men. He would place the shining clasps on their rough-hewn woollen clothing, and those little trinkets seemed to light up the beauty of those coarse, wild women, much as a bare stone is brightened by the colours of a little springtime flower.

The *Chnan* gave up a couple of the clasps and a few beads in exchange for hospitality for the two of them and for the comrades who were waiting just outside the village, in addition to a sack of barley bread and five whole cheeses for their return journey.

He and Myrsilus ate in the house of the man who seemed their chief, the only one who had bought ornaments for himself, his wife and his eldest daughter. His arms hung on the walls of the only room that made up the house: a long bronze sword, a studded shield and a dagger. The floor was made of flame-hardened dirt.

The *Chnan* spoke during the whole dinner and it was evident that as time passed, he was rapidly learning to understand them and make himself understood. At times he accompanied his words by drawing signs with his knife in the barley loaf in front of him or on the curdled milk in a bowl in the centre of the table. The dogs lay near the entrance, waiting to lick the bowls once the meal was finished.

After a while, they heard low noises outside the door, the sound of hushed words; the reflection of flames flashed under the door. The door then opened and a man entered, to speak with his chieftain.

'Could you understand what they were saying?' Myrsilus asked the *Chnan*.

'Not much of it. But I think I've convinced him that I understand much more than I really do; that's what's important. No one would talk to a man who understood nothing.'

Myrsilus shook his head: 'So what's happening now?'

'Someone has just arrived. Perhaps from the camp we saw as we were approaching.'

The *Chnan* followed the chieftain out of the house and saw a group of men gathered in a nearby field. They were carrying lit torches and were dressed in a style he did not recognize. He turned to ask Myrsilus whether he had ever seen similar people, but his companion had drawn back, into the shadows behind the door. The *Chnan* turned back. 'What are you doing here?' he asked. 'Aren't you coming to see the new arrivals?'

'Trojans,' said Myrsilus in a low voice, his head down. 'They're Trojans and we are unarmed.'

5

THE NIGHT THAT MENELAUS disappeared, many wondered how such a thing could have happened. Some said that a sudden wind had pushed him south, sweeping him away for days and days, until he was cast ashore in Egypt, or at the mouths of the Nile. But on the other hand, at that very same time, at the end of the summer, Nestor had reached Pylus safely and without difficulty, Diomedes had landed on the beaches of Argos and even Agamemnon had seen Mycenae again, although it would have been better for him to have died in Ilium.

It is hard to believe that only Menelaus met with hostile winds. And it is difficult to believe that none of the sixty ships that accompanied him found their way home. An entire fleet does not disappear like that unless preordained by the gods. Things went quite differently, I believe.

*

Those years were cursed. Something unknown and relentless, perhaps the will of the gods, perhaps some other obscure force, drove many peoples from their homes. In some places, the land grew dry and the sprouts were scorched by drought before they could ripen, while oxen collapsed all at once under their yokes, dying of hunger and strain. Other animals became sterile or stopped reproducing; if they did bear young, the monstrous creatures they engendered were hurriedly buried at night by terror-stricken farmers and peasants.

Elsewhere, the earth was scourged by storms of wind and rain, flooded by torrents and rivers that overflowed their banks, inundating the countryside with mud that rotted when the sun rose over the horizon. That decay generated an endless number of repugnant creatures: toads, salamanders and serpents that spread everywhere, infesting the fields, the pathways and the dwellings of men. Animal carcasses were abandoned by the rivers to rot along the shore as the waters subsided, attracting crows and vultures which filled the sky with their shrieking by day and jackals which let out their mournful howls by night.

Only the sea seem to be spared these disasters: her clear waters continued to nurture every kind of fish, as well as the gigantic creatures of the abyss. And trade continued as well on the paths of the sea, albeit greatly diminished. Thus, many peoples entrusted their destinies to the sea, preferring to face the unknown rather than wait in their own lands to die of starvation, hardship and disease. Others, who already inhabited the seas, gave themselves over to raiding and piracy.

A sort of coalition was formed, joining the *Peleset* and the *Shekelesh*, the *Lukka* and the *Teresh*, the *Sherdan* and the *Derden*, and many other peoples as well. They were warmongers, desperate, ready for anything, and they decided to try their luck against the richest, most prosperous and powerful nation of the earth: Egypt. They did not know that the land of the Nile had been stricken by the same scourges, although there the wisdom of the priests and the architects, the patience of the people, and the strength of their sovereign had managed to attenuate the frightful effects.

They say that a group of Achaeans joined forces with this coalition as well; these were the Spartan warriors of Menelaus that a strange destiny had dragged to those distant regions.

The night in which they had disappeared from sight, Menelaus's ships sailed in the direction of Delos. His men were told that the queen had convinced him to consult the oracle of Apollo, the god who had protected the Trojans during the war. The king sought to know what sacrifices of expiation he must perform for having taken part in the destruction of the city, in order to escape the ire of the god who would otherwise have annihilated them.

Apollo had answered that they would have to offer a sacrifice in the land of Danaus, and then consult the oracle of the Old Man of the Sea on the deserted shores of Libya. The land of Danaus was Egypt; Menelaus decided to set sail at midday along with his entire fleet, and thus he left the land of the Achaeans behind him, as his brother Agamemnon went to his death.

The gods who know all and see all perhaps allowed Menelaus, lost in the arms of Helen, to hear the last gasp of his dying brother; perhaps they passed on, in a cold shiver, the stab of the sword that cut the throat of the great Atreid. And when the king abandoned himself to the act of love, he was invaded by the same chill of death, by the same terror of infinite emptiness.

The fleet crossed the sea, sailing with favourable winds for eight days and eight nights until they came within sight of the coast, near the western mouth of the Nile. But as fortune or chance had it, in those very days a multitude of other ships were present there. The Peoples of the Sea; the *Peleset* and the *Lukka*, the *Derden* and the *Teresh*, the *Shekelesh* and the *Sherden*, were attacking Egypt as allies of the Libyan king Mauroy.

Pharaoh Ramses, the third of this name, decided boldly to counter-attack rather than to wait for the clash with the enemy; he sent out his fleet from the western branch of the Nile and from the eastern branch of the Nile and moved them out to sea on both sides, exploiting the land wind of the early morning. Menelaus's army, finding themselves in that place by mere chance, were attacked from the west before they could establish any contact, and they were forced to defend themselves. His warriors, accustomed to years and years of fierce fighting, drove back the attackers several times, but a steady stream of Egyptian ships continued to descend from the mouth of the Nile. To their left, a group of *Sherden* vessels full of warriors with round shields and conical helmets adorned with ox horns were battling tenaciously against a number of Egyptian ships which manoeuvred with great expertise in the shallow waters along the coast. In the skirmish that ensued, the *Sherden* ventured too close to the shore and ran aground on the shoals. They were shortly surrounded on all sides and massacred.

Menelaus could not understand what was happening: wherever his gaze fell, the sea teemed with ships and warriors from every nation. But although their number was enormous, they were thrown into confusion because they could not communicate; there was no one giving precise orders that could be heard by all. The Pharaoh's fleet, on the contrary, moved with supreme skill in those treacherous waters. They separated into squads, only to join back together again like a phalanx on a battlefield. Most of the heavy Egyptian warships continued to fan out towards the open sea; their crews exchanged signals by hoisting cloths of various colours on their ladder masts and by sending flashing light signals using their gleaming copper shields.

His men tried to convince Menelaus to engage in battle with all he had; they thought that if the coalition were victorious they would be able to divide up the booty and return to Sparta with immense riches, but Menelaus feared the loss of his fleet in those dangerous waters and signalled for his crews to get out as soon as it became possible.

Those who could did so, but some of the ships had penetrated too far into the enemy formation, and were forced to fight so as not to succumb. Some ships were set aflame by incendiary arrows and had to be abandoned. Their crews perished or ended their days in slavery, labouring over the construction of colossal monuments in the land of Egypt. Menelaus attempted to break through the encirclement with the surviving ships, but his was a hopeless endeavour. A vigorous sea wind had picked up and it drove his ships, together with the vessels of the coalition, towards the shore and against the sandy shoals. The Egyptian fleet, which had taken advantage of the morning land wind to move out to sea, now had the sea wind aft and closed in on the invaders like a pair of pincers, forcing them into the shallow waters of the delta.

Menelaus managed to save his ship thanks to the strength of his rowers, who struggled against the wind and propelled the ship against the Egyptian fleet. They rammed the side of a great vessel and sank it, then led the surviving ships of their fleet out to sea through the breach. The helmsman, an old sailor from Asine, realized that the sea wind was shifting west, and he had the sail hoisted immediately, as the other crews followed his example. The ships picked up a certain speed and, although they risked capsizing aport, they held their course until they reached an island where they could take shelter.

Meanwhile, the *Peleset* had succeeded in breaking through the encirclement on the east side of the formation, and escaping to the open sea. Some ships put out to sea, while others, most of them, retreated to the *Chnan* coast and settled between Gaza and Joppa. They gave this land the name of Palestena.

But the rest of the coalition fleet found no way out; driven on to the sand and the mud of the delta, the hulled ships ran aground while the light Egyptian craft, nearly all made of papyrus, easily drew up alongside them. The bundled stems used to build the pharaoh's ships were soaked with water and would not catch fire. Their high prows and high sterns allowed them to navigate the waters of the sea, while their flat bottoms and pliable structure let them slip over the shallowest of shoals with the agile movements of a water snake.

The weather did not change until sunset, when a strong wind picked up from the desert and blasted out over the sea, dragging with it the remaining coalition ships and casting them into the high waves; the *Teresh* and *Shekelesh* were scattered in every direction.

That very evening the pharaoh was already celebrating his triumph over the invaders. He had the great royal parade vessel put out to sea, and he himself, standing at the prow, drew his bow and ran through the shipwrecked sailors still floundering in the waves. His concubines, stretched out on soft cushions, watched with admiration and called out with glee each time his arrows hit their mark. The wretches who sought to escape along the banks of the river were sucked up into the mud or ended up devoured by scaly monsters with webbed paws and huge mouths full of sharp teeth.

The Libyan chieftain, Mauroy, managed to save himself, but his end was no less terrible. They say that once he returned home, his own people impaled him and left him to rot, preyed upon by crows and vultures.

At nightfall, Menelaus walked to the beach on the little island where they had taken refuge and looked out towards the coast. The glow of the fires still quivered on the horizon; from the darkness descending over the water came the cries and laments of shipwrecked sailors whom the wind was dragging into the open sea to sure death. He suddenly perceived, along with the smell of burning wood and scorched bodies, the scent of his queen and he turned. Helen was at his side, staring steadily at the horizon without blinking. The wind pressed the light fabric of her Carian gown to her high breasts and slender legs. She observed the corpses crowding the expanse of sea with the same firm, proud gaze he had once seen on her face as she watched her suitors competing to win her favour.

The moon was rising between the lotuses and papyruses of the delta. The king thought he heard a low groaning; he turned, and saw that it was coming from a man dragging himself on to the shore, bleeding copiously from many wounds. He saw him raise both his arms towards the disc of the moon, he heard him pray, weeping, in one of the hundred languages of the great defeated coalition. And he saw him fall face down with a loud thud. He was no longer the man who had departed from his city or village one day, leaving his wife and his children. He was a dark, shapeless thing that the sea rolled in the mud with its incessant swell.

*

Menelaus's fleet was hauled aground by the men for the winter, and for months they all laboured on the ships to repair and restore them, so they would be ready to put out to sea as soon as the conditions were favourable for navigation. They were mistaken about that. They were forced to remain in that forgotten place for nearly three years. First, an epidemic broke out; many died and many ships were deprived of their crews. Then, impetuous northern winds beat down on the sea all the next spring and summer, bringing with them storms and squalls, gales and torrential rain. When the weather gave them a little respite, they attacked passing ships, or fished or hunted in the interior, but they never ventured on to the open sea. When the third springtime arrived, Menelaus departed with his ship and several of his men to sail to a place on the coast where he had heard he could consult the oracle of the Old Man of the Sea. He sought to know his destiny, which seemed more dismal and incomprehensible with each passing day.

The oracle struck dread into the hearts of men. Few had ever seen his face. Sometimes his voice was said to issue from the mouths of animals who lurked in his cave; jackals or foxes or even marine animals that lived in his lair. At other times, the cave was deserted, and his voice came from the flames of the sacred fire that burned in the brazier. For this reason he was known as the 'ever-changing' one.

When Menelaus disembarked, he found a deserted beach scattered with the bones of men and animals, and with the remains of shipwrecked vessels.

He left his men at the ship, laid down his sword on the sand and entered the cave alone. The walls were painted with scenes of fishing and hunting; men in long pirogues chasing huge sea cetaceans, others in groups, armed with bows and arrows, hunting fabulous beasts with long spotted necks, and short-maned asses or mules with black and white stripes. A sudden barking startled him and an animal that was half dog and half fish ran off towards the sea, rolling on fins that took the place of his legs. The king had heard say that the Old Man used similar beasts as his guard dogs.

He went forward and found himself before a great basin lit by a ray of sun that entered from a crack in the cave ceiling. At the sound of his steps the water suddenly boiled up and a scaly back emerged from its depths, then a bristling tail and a mouth full of teeth. A monster the likes of which he had never seen in all his life. Along with a stink of rot and putrescence that turned his stomach.

'Where are you, Old Man of the Sea?' shouted Menelaus.

'I am he,' answered a deep, gurgling voice. 'I am the dragon who swims in these waters. In this land they call me *Sobek* and they worship me as a god in a great sanctuary at *Nbyt*. But beware, do not approach me! Or your human existence may finish up between my jaws.' Menelaus backed off in dismay and his hand fell to his side, defenceless.

'I am he!' screeched another voice. 'Son of the night!' and Menelaus saw an enormous bat lazily swinging from a crevice in the vault. 'I am blind but I can fly through the darkness and see things that no human being can see.'

'I am he,' said another voice, soft and hissing. And Menelaus saw a serpent raise his head and swell his neck, darting his forked tongue at just a span from his knee. 'I am the child of the sun, and the guardian of the night.'

The king of Sparta did not move as the serpent swayed back and forth on his rolls of coils before slipping silently away between the pebbles and the sand. He walked forward then, towards a tunnel at the back of the cavern that seemed to penetrate into the bowels of the earth. He entered and continued at length in the dark, in absolute silence, until he saw a light reverberating at the top of the passage. The light became more intense as he advanced, and he soon found himself in a large grotto invaded by a bright ray of sun which poured in from above, illuminating an old man with his head veiled. He sat on a wide stone seat on the banks of a dark, clear spring. His skin was black and wrinkled, while his beard and the hairs on his arms and legs were pure white.

'Are you Charon, perhaps, who ferries souls to the undergloom?' asked Menelaus. 'Must I die here? Here, so far from my homeland, forgotten by all?'

The old man raised his head and showed two deep, glittering eyes.

'I have come to learn my destiny,' said Menelaus. 'I have

suffered greatly, I have sacrificed my life and my honour. I want to know if this has any meaning.'

The old man did not move. His gaze was locked into a fixed stare. Menelaus drew so close he could touch him.

'I am a king,' he said. 'I was a powerful sovereign, father of a daughter as lovely as a golden flower, husband of the most beautiful woman on earth. Now my life holds naught but poison and despair. My warriors die without glory and I am going mad in this torrid, flat land. Oh Old Man of the Sea, they say that you have the wisdom of the gods. Help me, and when I have returned I shall send you a ship laden with gifts, with all those things that can gladden your heart. Help me, I beseech you, tell me if I will return, if I will escape an obscure death in a foreign land after enduring such pain for so many long years. Shall I ever return to live with the queen in my palace? Will I ever forget the shame and dishonour that keep me awake at night?'

He sat down in the dust and lowered his head like a suppliant.

The old man neither moved nor opened his mouth.

'I will not go from here,' said Menelaus, 'until I've had an answer. I will starve to death if you do not answer me.' And he too fell into silence.

Nothing happened, for some time. But then all at once, the ray of sun spilling down from the ceiling of the cavern touched the surface of the water, and the spring shone with myriad reflections, lightening even the walls of the cave with a pale glow. The old man shook out of his torpor and pointed his finger to a point at the centre of the pool. Menelaus stood and stared at that point, as his soul was invaded by a strange, untried trepidation. He heard the voice that had already greeted him in the guise of the dragon, the bat and the serpent; it was different now, with a deep harmonious sound like that of a song whose words he could not understand. But that melody roused images from the surface of the water, as if it were a mirror. Menelaus saw and heard as if he were present in the events that flowed beneath his eyes, but unable to speak or react.

He saw an impostor seated on the throne of Mycenae alongside queen Clytemnestra, grasping the sceptre of the Atreides. He saw the funeral mask of his brother Agamemnon rising like a golden moon from behind the palace and weeping tears of blood. He saw a maiden escaping from a hidden doorway, dragging behind her a blond boy with terror-stricken eyes. They ran through the windy night, stopping often behind a tree or a rock in the fear they were being followed. And then they ran again, until they found a man awaiting them with a chariot to which two fiery black steeds had been harnessed.

The maiden clasped the boy to her breast in a long embrace, kissing his face and forehead. Her lips moved as if she were imparting warnings, advice, encouragement. And the light which flickered in her eyes blazed with passionate love and with fierce hate. She hugged her brother again and spoke more hurried words, turning often to check behind her. Then the young prince got into the chariot next to the driver who held the reins still; the wind filled his great dark cloak like a sail in a storm. The maiden turned over her charge to him and she cried as they left. The man whipped the horses and the chariot departed swiftly in a white cloud. They were Agamemnon's children and his own niece and nephew: princess Electra and prince Orestes, forced to hide and to flee, orphaned and persecuted.

He shouted and wept with rage, shame and grief, as he never had before, so loudly that the surface of the water trembled and darkened. His cry shook the walls of the cavern, stirring up hosts of squeaking bats who flitted away and halting the strange melody that had accompanied his visions.

The black-skinned man sitting on his stone throne in the shadows now was roused: 'Why did you set off the war?' said his voice. But his lips were sealed and his face was still, like that of a statue carved in wood or sculpted in stone.

'To divert a river of blood. To ward off the destruction and the end of my people.'

'What destruction?'

'It was written that the sons of Hercules driven away by Euristheus would return . . . that they would return to annihilate

Mycenae and Argos and all of the cities of the Achaeans. There was only one single thing on the entire earth that could save us: the talisman of the Trojans. But how to win it? It was hidden away in Ilium, protected by layer upon layer of inviolable secrets. Our only hope was for someone, one of us, to gain entry to the innermost parts of the city and the citadel by living there for years and years. Only thus could we hope to learn their secrets and penetrate their defences . . . we needed someone who could win over the minds and the souls of the princes and the trust of the king.

'Only Helen could succeed! All women and all goddesses live within her; love and perfidy, purity and deceit. Only she dares wield the infinite weapons that make her more fearsome than a phalanx drawn up on an open battlefield.

'The responsibility for saving our people fell to the Atreides and solely to us: we bore more grief than any of the other Achaeans, more than Achilles and Ajax, who died under the walls of Ilium. Agamemnon sacrificed his beloved daughter . . . and I was asked to sacrifice my bride, the only love of my life, and my honour. We made war to hide our true intent, and we knew that the final attack would not be launched until the last secret had fallen. Until Ulysses and Diomedes had entered the city by stealth and discovered where the talisman of the Trojans was hidden.

'Useless, all of it useless. My brother is dead. I have seen an impostor sitting on the throne that belonged to Perseus and Atreus, I have seen the young prince and princess, terrified, fleeing in the night . . . All useless . . .'

He fell to his knees on the banks of the spring and wept, hiding his face in his cloak.

'You did not do your part! You did not pay the price that was asked of you!' thundered the voice of the Old Man. Menelaus started. 'Isn't that so? Isn't that so?' he shouted, even more loudly.

Menelaus stood and walked towards him, his eyes filled with stupor: 'How is it possible that you know this? Your oracle is truthful, then . . .'

'Admit your blame!' said the voice. 'Or leave now and never come back.' The Old Man's eyes were closed but his forehead and face dripped with sweat. The drops that slid over his dry skin were the only signs of life on that ashen face.

Menelaus lowered his head: 'All of the kings of the Achaeans would have wanted her as their bride. She was given to me. Can't you understand? Can't you understand me?'

'As you journeyed to Delos your brother was butchered like a bull in the manger,' said the voice. 'If you had stayed with the others, this would not have happened. You are to blame. The blood of your brother is on your hands.'

It seemed completely, both in timbre and tone, the voice of his dead brother accusing him; he thought of the persecuted prince and princess escaping in the night, swarms of pursuers at their heels. His heart cramped in his chest, as though pierced through by a spear.

He cried out, weeping: 'Oh Old Man of the Sea, if you speak in truth, tell me whether I will be granted an honourable death. Because I have nothing else left to hope for.'

'What do you want?' demanded the voice.

'To return, to avenge my brother, if he has been murdered. I will ask for help from the other kings, Ulysses, Diomedes. They will not abandon me.'

But as soon as he pronounced those words, he realized that he was in a different place.

He was walking on the deserted beach of a sunny island. The warm air was fragrant with pine and myrtle and he felt a powerful, invisible presence hovering about him. The water of the sea lapped at his ankles, the sand slipped between his toes like a rough caress. A rock jutting out into the sea blocked his way, and he clambered on to it, so as to descend on the other side and continue his walk. But when he was at the top, he looked down and saw a man sitting on a stone, a white cloak wrapped around his bare limbs. He recognized him: it was glorious Ulysses, son of Laertes. He looked out over the horizon, eyes glazed with deep sadness. And a female voice called out: 'He is mine, for seven years!'

'Oh lady hidden in the air,' shouted Menelaus, 'allow my friend to depart! Allow him to take to the humid paths of the sea. He is needed in the land of the Achaeans; we need his wits, his invincible mind!'

'He is mine, mine for seven years,' sang the voice again. And her words hit him like a gust of wind, making him spin like a dead leaf. He fell into the sea, sinking into the cold embrace of the abyss for the longest of times, until he emerged once again from the centre of a dark lagoon, under a sky laden with low clouds. Before him was a miserable camp, with shelters made of reeds and swamp grasses. The men were emaciated, livid with cold and hunger. Among them was Diomedes, son of Tydeus. His beard was long and unkempt, his hands were dirty and his cloak was soiled with mud. Menelaus turned away from that pitiful sight and then found himself immersed in the waters of the spring, under the vault of the immense cavern, standing before the black-skinned man, the Old Man of the Sea.

A noisy laugh exploded under the great vault: 'Have you seen your companions? Do you still think they can help you?' asked the voice. Menelaus covered his head with his cloak.

'Old Man of the Sea,' he said, 'I cover my head and deliver myself to the infernal gods. I recognize my guilt and I am ready to suffer my punishment. But one thing you must tell me, and I will do the rest: where is the talisman of the Trojans now? Did Queen Clytemnestra take it from Agamemnon after killing him? Is she hiding it somewhere ... or has she destroyed it? Tell me only this, I beg of you. I alone remain; I alone can stave off the misfortune that weighs upon the Achaeans.'

'Who else, besides you, knows your secret?' asked the Old Man.

'No one ever suspected anything ... except for Ulysses.'

'All was born in deceit and in deceit it is destined to end. But you can turn the evil you have done into good. Ulysses can help you, far away as he is. Use his mind. Carry out what he has imagined,' said the voice. 'No more than this can I tell you.'

The ray of light dimmed until it nearly disappeared and the hiss of the wind issued ever stronger from the top of the cavern.

The Old Man of the Sea seemed to have dozed off on his stone throne. His limbs hung limply, his mouth fell half open. The king of Sparta turned back, traversing the tunnel and the great chamber until he found himself once again in the open. The wind had become very strong and his men struggled to secure the ship's lines to the ground so that the sea would not steal it away.

Menelaus watched them through the swirling sands that obscured the light of day, and he hardly recognized them, as if they were foreigners pushed there from distant lands by the force of the sea and the wind.

Only the next day were they able to return to their island in the delta. The queen saw the ship coming to shore, and yet he tarried. After a long wait, she walked to the beach and found her king sitting in silence, watching the waves. She asked him what the response of the Old Man of the Sea had been and Menelaus, without turning, said: 'His response was quite auspicious, for me and for you, my queen. The old man said:

Menelaus, it is not your destiny to die in the bluegrass land
    of Argos,
but in the Elysian fields where the gods will send you,
there where life is lovely for mortal men.
No snow, nor chill, nor rain there,
but always the gentle breeze of Zephyr blowing
sonorous from the Ocean, soothing and refreshing.
For the gods hold you, as Helen's lord, a son of Zeus.

'One day sorrow and wounds and death will end, my queen. We shall live in a happy place, far from all others, for ever.'

He fell still again, watching the foam of the waves that died at his feet, and then said: 'We must return.'

6

MYRSILUS THOUGHT THAT HIS last day had come when he saw armed Trojans in such a far-off land. But the *Chnan* had no fear and he approached the new arrivals, mingling among them, watching and listening to try to understand why they were there.

It was evident that the village chieftain and the man who seemed to be the chief of the Trojans did not understand each other, but that they had become accustomed to communicating using gestures, and even the *Chnan* could understand these gestures well.

'I think,' he told Myrsilus later, 'that the foreigners want to remain here. They are prepared to exchange bronze for wheat, milk and meat for the winter, and seeds for the spring. They want to settle down in this land.'

'When Diomedes finds out he will march here with his men and wipe them all out! I am certain he wants no Trojans in the land in which he will found his new kingdom.'

'Then don't tell him,' answered the *Chnan*. 'We cannot wage war in these swamps, in this bitter cold, and those wretches mean no harm. They're just trying to survive the winter. When the seasons change they will sow wheat and, if they manage to harvest it, a new people will be born, in a new land, under a new sky. Let the seeds take root, warrior. This land is big enough to nourish many peoples.'

'Perhaps you are right, *Chnan*. There's only one thing I do not understand; why it is deserted. If we were in the land of the Achaeans, there would be at least six or seven villages in the land that stretches from here to the sea. Here we've found nothing but these four huts in an entire day's journey. And no more, as far as the eye can see.'

'You're right. Perhaps the land is inhospitable, perhaps it is infested with wild beasts. Perhaps the people who lived here were driven away by famine or killed off by a plague. Man persists in living everywhere, even if the earth doesn't want him. Do you know that there are men who inhabit the great sands, where not a blade of grass grows? And men that live in lands covered with ice? But the earth, sooner or later, frees itself of men like a dog scratches off fleas. Perhaps it is best that we rest now. Tomorrow morning we will have to start off for the ships before dawn, or your king will set off looking for us and get all of us into a fine mess.'

'What about our comrades out there on the plain? They have no shelter; they'll die of cold when the frost sets in.'

'I'll go tell them to come here with us. There's plenty of room.'

'No,' said Myrsilus. 'Someone must remain outside the village in case something happens.'

'I understand,' said the *Chnan*. 'I'll go . . .' He took a pile of pelts from one of the corners and stole away, disappearing into the darkness. He returned not long after. The Trojan camp was lit up by a few scattered fires. The village was just barely illuminated by the ash-covered embers that still burned in the centre of the main clearing.

As he groped around for the entrance to the hut, he felt a heavy hand fall on his shoulder. He spun around and saw that it was one of the women who had looked with longing at the goods he had set out. No one had offered to exchange pelts or food for an amber-beaded clasp for her. But she knew she had something even more precious that perhaps the foreign merchant would appreciate: herself. Tall and buxom, her blonde hair fell loose on her shoulders and a leather cord decorated with bits of bone adorned her white neck.

She smiled at him and the *Chnan* smiled back. Small and dark he was, and with his short, curly hair he seemed like little more than a boy next to her. She slipped a hand under his tunic to feel for a trinket that she liked, taking his right hand at the same time and placing it on her breast. The *Chnan* was flooded by a heat he had not felt since he had left his land; he felt like a boy reaching out to gather ripe clusters of grapes from the vine. He put his other hand under her gown and he realized she wore nothing underneath; it was like caressing the soft down of a newborn lamb. He kissed her avidly, and it felt like sucking a honeycomb at high noon in the fragrant mountains of Lebanon.

She left him leaning against the wall of the hut, exhausted, walking away with the supple, solemn roll of a mare and the *Chnan* realized that he had made the best deal of his entire life. Even if she had carried away all the wealth he had laced under his tunic, what he had had in exchange was worth as much as a herd of horses, as a load of cedar wood, as a caravan of mules laden with all the copper in Sinai.

He entered the hut and by the dim light of a wick stuck in tallow took stock of what was left to him. Oh virtuous woman! The girl had taken nothing but a clasp with three beads of coloured glass, one yellow, one red and one white, streaked blue. In the dark her fingers had recognized what her eyes had desired by the light of sunset.

'Did you see them?' asked Myrsilus's voice in the dark.

'I did not see much but I felt the earth shake . . .' answered the *Chnan* as if talking in his sleep.

Two hard, woody hands threw him against the wall. 'I asked you if you'd seen our comrades,' repeated Myrsilus, and his voice was a low growl.

The *Chnan* regained his wits: 'I did see them and they were dying of cold. Now they're fine. Better than before, without a doubt. Calm down, warrior, let us get some sleep as well.'

Myrsilus was placated and lay down once again on his mat, pulling up a cover made of sheepskins sewn together. The warmth was soothing, and sleep descended rapidly on his eyelids, but he was soon saddened by anguished dreams. He realized that he had left his homeland for a cold, muddy place where the sky and the ground were always sodden, as if it had just rained or were about to rain. Even his king was changing; he was shedding his splendour with each passing day. The days of Ilium were distant, as if centuries had passed since they had left the shores of the Hellespont.

It was the *Chnan* who woke him, shortly before dawn. They took their things and left without making a sound. At their backs, a pale sun illuminated a group of hills that rose from the plains like islands in the sea. Myrsilus had not noticed them before, and he had the sensation that they had emerged overnight. And perhaps that is what happened.

They reached their comrades outside the village and they took the road of return towards the sea.

'The Trojans are not alone,' said the *Chnan* abruptly. 'There are others with them, who followed them across the sea.'

'How do you know?' asked Myrsilus.

'I had awoken before you. I wanted to say farewell to a girl; I owed her a gift. She's the one who told me.'

'Who are these people?'

'*Enet*, I think. They're called *Enet*.'

Myrsilus continued on his way for a while without speaking, as if he were trying to recall something.

'Enetians,' he said.

'What?' asked the *Chnan*.

'Perhaps they are Enetians. A nation allied with the Trojans. Fine combatants, both with spears and with bows. They were almost always drawn up on the left wing; they faced the Cretans of King Idomeneus and Ulysses's Cephallenians. I never met them myself. I wonder what they're doing here. And I also wonder why they're with the Trojans. The gods are truly persecuting us; they have cursed us.'

'Don't you know how many peoples have abandoned their settlements in these past years? Didn't you ever notice those strange lights in the sky when we were out to sea? No man alive has ever heard of or seen such a thing, I'm certain of it. And I'm sure that all this means something, although I don't know what.'

'If only the seer Calchas were with us!' said Myrsilus. 'He would know how to interpret these signs, and he would know what they meant.'

They journeyed that whole day without seeing a soul, and towards evening came within sight of their camp. Myrsilus reported to the king, telling him everything they had seen without making mention of the Trojans. He did not want to march back inland and start up a war again that he hoped finished for ever. He could not know that it was only a sign, and that a man can not escape the destiny that the gods have placed on his scale.

His comrades offered the food given to them by the villagers and someone lit a fire for their evening meal. There were fish from the sea as well, and partridges and teals that some of the men had downed with their bows.

The sun was setting over the plain and a mist was rising from the ground, looking something like a cloud, a milky foam crossed by whitish streaks. It veiled the sun, and everything that was near the ground was swallowed up within it. The men looked around in dismay. Not even the king, Diomedes the hero, knew what to do or what to tell them.

After a while, only the tips of the tallest poplars emerged from that shapeless expanse that fluttered like a veil. Sounds were muffled and even the birds called to each other with weak laments. A heron, passing over their heads in slow, solemn flight, vanished all at once into the void.

'What is this?' the king asked the *Chnan*. 'You who have seen so many lands, can you tell me what this is?'

'I've never seen anything like this, *wanax*,' said the *Chnan*, 'but I think it may be a cloud. I have met men who come from the land of the *Urartu* where the mountains pierce the clouds, and they have told me that it is like this inside a cloud. But I cannot explain why the clouds weigh on the ground in this land instead of sailing in the sky. It is a strange land indeed.'

When darkness fell nothing could be seen at all, and the men stayed very close together for fear of losing their bearings, and kept the fire burning that whole night. Diomedes thought that

that land must be similar to Hades, and perhaps he believed that he had truly reached the limits of the other world, but he neither trembled nor sought to flee. He knew that only heroes and Zeus's favoured sons can face that which is impossible for all others.

He lay down on his bearskin and covered himself with a fleece. Myrsilus slept nearby.

At dawn the next day, Diomedes gave orders to set sail and the fleet began to navigate slowly through the mist that steamed on the surface of the water, amidst the cane thickets on the shore and the little woody islands that cropped up on the sea.

They advanced in this way for most of the day, when suddenly, they all thought they had heard calls of some sort.

'What was that?' asked the men at the oars.

'I don't know, but it's best to stop,' replied Myrsilus.

The king agreed and went to the bow to scan the foggy expanse in front of them. The other ships stopped as well and the splashing of the oars ceased. In that complete silence, the calls sounded more clearly and then long rostrated ships emerged from the mist slowly, like ghosts. A standard with the head of a lion stood tall at one of the bows, and a red cloth hung loose on the mast.

Telephus, the Hittite slave, approached the king. 'Peleset pirates,' he said. 'They must have got lost in this accursed cloud. Let's hope they don't attack us.'

'Why?' said the king. 'I do not fear them.'

'It's best to avoid clashing with them,' said Myrsilus, who had handed the helm over to one of the men. 'We have nothing to gain, and much to lose. Since they've seen us, we must speak with them. The Chnan surely knows their language. Have him come.'

The king nodded and the Chnan succeeded in arranging an encounter. The Peleset flagship and Diomedes's ship both left their formations and met half-way. They manoeuvred slowly with oars and helm until they were nearly touching, side to side. The Peleset chief and King Diomedes, both armed and carrying a spear in their right hands, faced one another.

'Tell him to let us pass,' said Diomedes, 'and we will do them no harm.'

'The heavens have sent you, powerful lord,' said the *Chnan* instead, 'to free me from indescribable suffering.'

'I am glad you speak my language,' said the *Peleset*. 'We'll have no difficulty understanding one another. Tell him to turn over everything he has and we will spare your lives.'

'The chief pays you his respects,' translated the *Chnan*, turning to Diomedes, 'and he asks if you have wheat or barley to sell him. They are short on food.' Then, without waiting for an answer, he turned again to the *Peleset* chief: 'If you want my personal advice, you'd best attack these people immediately, because the rest of the fleet will be here at any moment; thirty battle ships loaded with warriors are close behind us. This is just the advance guard. In exchange for this information, I beg of you, take me as your slave! These people are savage and cruel. They have sown death and destruction wherever they have passed, burning down villages and setting whole cities aflame! They subject me to the worst of torments for the mere pleasure of ill-treating a poor wretch. With my own eyes I have seen my master, this man here, at my side,' he continued, indicating Diomedes, 'rip the beating heart out of his enemy's chest and devour it avidly. Free me, I beseech you, and you will not regret it.'

The *Peleset* chief was dumbfounded, and in Diomedes's stern gaze he thought he saw all of the terrible things that the slave had warned him of. 'You can die for all I care,' he said to the *Chnan*. 'We're going our own way.'

'We have no food to sell him,' said Diomedes.

'Of course, *wanax*, I took the liberty of giving him this answer, already knowing what you would say. They'll be off on their own way now.'

The *Peleset* ships paraded past them, one after another, about twenty in all. They turned to the right, heading south. The fog was thickening again and the damp chilled them all to the bone. The last *Peleset* vessel passed at just a short distance from them, but before it was swallowed up into the mist they heard someone shout from the deck: 'Achaeans! I am Lamus, son of Onchestus, Spartan. I was made a slave in Egypt! Remember me!' His words were followed by the sound of blows, moaning and then silence.

Diomedes started: 'Gods!' he said, 'an Achaean like us in such a distant land . . . and *Peleset* . . .'

'And Trojans, and Enetians . . .' said Myrsilus.

Diomedes spun around to face him: 'What did you say?'

'There were Trojans and Enetians in the village we visited last night.'

'Why didn't you tell me? I could make you pay dearly for lying to me.'

'Not a lie, *wanax*, silence. I waited until now to tell you. If I had told you then you would have launched an attack.'

'Certainly. They are our enemies.'

'Not any more, *wanax*. The war is over.'

'Only when I say so. Did you recognize anyone? Aeneas? Had he been there, would you have recognized him?'

'Of course, *wanax*. But he was not among them. Their chief was an older man with grey hair, but his beard was still dark and his black eyebrows thick. Tall, with slightly bent shoulders . . .'

'Antenor,' murmured Diomedes. 'Perhaps you saw Antenor. It was Ulysses who asked Agamemnon to spare him the night of the fall of Troy because Antenor had treated him with respect and had given him hospitality when he had gone that first time to ask Priam to give Helen back. But why here? What does he seek in this land?'

The *Chnan* drew closer: 'Something terrible must have happened. Perhaps a war greater than the one you fought, perhaps a gigantic battle, or some cataclysm. The *Peleset* would never have ventured so far! Those Trojans must have known, and have chosen to seek out a place far away from everything, a tranquil and solitary place.'

'Do you have orders to give me, *wanax*?' asked Myrsilus.

'We'll go forward, but stop as soon as you find a suitable

place. If we can, we'll try to free that wretch. Those ships can't be too far.'

They proceeded until darkness fell, without ever sighting the *Peleset* fleet. They moored their ships on the beach of a sandy island, low on the surface of the sea, and lit a fire. The coast of the continent was very close. The king called Myrsilus: 'They must be anchored somewhere near here, on the mainland. Go aground with a group of selected men and see if you can liberate that Spartan. Take the *Chnan* with you; he understands their language and he'll be useful to you. I don't want you to suffer any losses; if the endeavour proves too difficult, turn back.'

As the others went ashore on the island, Myrsilus and the men he had chosen walked to the mainland; since the water was so shallow at that point, they were no more than knee-deep. A breath of wind was picking up from the sea, dispelling the fog and letting a little moonlight through. Myrsilus had never seen such a land in all his days; the coast was a vast expanse of fine white sand that sparkled in the pale glow of the moon. The waves swept across the wide beach and then withdrew with a gurgling sound. Here and there were gigantic trunks, abandoned on the waterline, stretching their enormous skeletal arms towards the sky.

'There must be a great river near here,' said the *Chnan*.

'Why?' asked Myrsilus.

'Those trunks. Only a great river can uproot such colossal trees and drag them to the sea, where the waves wash them back to the shore.'

Myrsilus was once again astonished at the wisdom of this foreigner that they had rescued from the sea; all he knew must come from having journeyed so far and having met diverse peoples with different languages. They walked and walked, so far that the moon had risen by nearly a cubit at the horizon; finally, at the end of a small bay, they saw the *Peleset* fleet at anchor. The place was completely deserted and there were only a couple of sentinels standing guard near a small campfire. Every so often one of them would break some dry branches from a trunk lying on the sand to add to the fire. Myrsilus and the *Chnan* crept close, so close that they could hear the crackling of the fire and the voices of the two sentinels.

'How can we find the man we're looking for?' asked the *Chnan*. 'We can't search the ships one by one.'

'You're right,' said Myrsilus. 'The only way is to make ourselves heard.'

'But then they'll all be upon us!'

'No, not if something is keeping them busy.'

'Like what?'

'Like their fleet catching fire.' The *Chnan* widened his eyes and shook his head incredulously. Myrsilus turned to his comrades: 'You go that way, to the edge of the forest, and lure the sentinels away from the fire, then kill them. We'll take firebrands in the meantime and go set fire to the ships. When the confusion is at its peak, I'll call him out and we'll all meet up at the big dry trunk. If you are careful and do as I say, none of us will die, and we will have liberated a long-suffering comrade.'

A small group of men went off towards the woods; soon after there was a sound of branches being broken, followed by the close beating of wings and a loud rustling.

The sentinels turned and stopped talking, straining to hear. More noise, and the two *Peleset* each took a brand and headed to where the sounds were coming from; presumably a wild animal was roaming about their camp, since the place seemed completely deserted and uninhabited.

As soon as they had left the halo of light of the fire, Myrsilus and his comrades seized blazing firebrands and rushed off towards the ships. They ran barefooted on the sand like shadows, without making any noise at all. Each chose his ship and set fire to it. The pitch and caulking pressed into the seams of the planks ignited immediately. Flames licked at the hulls and dense spirals of smoke curled upward. The two sentinels turned back to raise the alarm but they were stricken down at once by the men hiding in the wood.

In just a few moments, four of the ships were completely

enveloped by the blaze. The men sleeping on board flung themselves out through a barrier of flames, yelling for help. Their comrades rushed from the other ships, carrying jugs and buckets of water to douse the flames.

In that confusion of blood-red light and crazed shadows, Myrsilus raised a cry in the language of the Achaeans, knowing that only one man aboard would be able to understand him. He shouted: 'Spartan! Join us at the dry tree trunk at the seashore!' In that chaos of cries and laments, Myrsilus's words floated like the peak of a mountain above the clouds of a storm and Lamus, son of Onchestus, heard them.

He jumped ship and began to run towards the burning vessels where, amidst all the uproar, he slipped away from the area illuminated by the raging fire and took shelter in the darkness, by the great dry trunk. He looked around, seeking the voice that had called him; he saw no one and feared he had imagined the whole thing. As he was about to return to his destiny, a voice rang out behind him: 'We are Argives and we heard your voice. We have come to free you.'

Lamus embraced them one by one, sobbing like a baby. He could not believe that he had escaped the grievous destiny already marked out for him. Myrsilus urged them all to leave that place at once and to rejoin their comrades, but before they started their march, he was seized by doubt. He felt he had to make the freed Spartan understand that the fate awaiting him might be worse than any he had faced up until then.

'Before you join us, consider what you are doing; you are still in time, surely no one will have noticed your escape. You must understand,' said he, 'that we shall never again return to Argos and the land of the Achaeans. We fled our homeland where betrayal awaited us, and here we seek a new land where we can settle and found a new kingdom for our king, Diomedes, son of Tydeus, victor of Thebes of the Seven Gates and of Troy.'

'Diomedes?' said the Spartan and his voice trembled. 'Oh gods . . . oh gods of the heavens! I fought with you in the fields of Ilium. I was with Menelaus.'

'Then think about it, I tell you. If you remain with those pirates perhaps you will return home some day, perhaps someone will pay your ransom. It was a storm that drove them here; they have not come of their own free will. We instead have come here to stay. Forever.'

The man was struck by those words. He turned towards the *Peleset* ships and his face lit up with their scarlet glow. Then he turned towards Myrsilus and his face was sundered by the darkness, as were his thoughts.

'I'll come with you,' he said. 'For you, I am a man, a comrade. Anything is possible for a free man. I thank you for having faced all this danger for me.'

They set off in haste and did not notice that behind them a wounded man was dragging himself through the sand; it was one of the two sentinels whom the men had attacked after luring him away from the campfire. He was bloodied, but alive, and he had seen everything.

Myrsilus and his comrades began to sprint along the beach, and when they were out of danger, past the little promontory that closed off the bay, they looked back. The burning ships were destroyed; all that was left of them were their fiery masts which sank sizzling into the dark water. Around them, many tiny black shapes scurried in every direction, like ants whose nest has been devastated by the farmer's hoe.

The king awaited them, standing vigil at the fire, alone. All of the other comrades, done in by their hard labour at the oars, had succumbed to sleep in the ships, or stretched out on the sandy beach. When he heard the men splashing through the shallow water that separated the beach from the island, he went out to meet them.

'We've brought back a Spartan,' said Myrsilus. 'The one who made his voice heard in the midst of the fog. We told him that perhaps he would be better off staying with the *Peleset*, but he decided to join us nonetheless.'

The man advanced towards the fire, then threw himself at

Diomedes's feet and kissed his hand: 'I thank you, *wanax*, for having liberated me,' he said. 'I fought at Ilium as you did, and I never would have thought I would see other Achaeans in this desolate place, in this land at the ends of the earth.'

They remained near the fire at length, and Lamus told of how he had ended up in Egypt. During a great battle, he had fallen into the sea grasping on to a piece of flotsam. He was fished up by the *Peleset*, who intended to sell him in the first city they landed at. But the wind had pushed them north for days and days until they had ended up in that sad, dreary place.

'What do the *Peleset* plan to do?' asked Diomedes.

'They want to return to their home territory, but they fear facing the winter sea. Perhaps they will seek a place where they can pull their ships aground, where they can find food and water to drink until the season changes.'

'Your king . . .' Diomedes asked again, 'King Menelaus . . . did he survive?'

'He was alive when I last saw him, but I have heard nothing more since then. Oh *wanax*, the gods blew us out to the sea, and our small vessels were tossed to and fro, on to the shores . . . the gods toy with our lives like a boy playing in a pond who pushes his boat back out whenever the waves bring it close to shore . . .'

'The shore . . .' said Myrsilus. 'Perhaps there are no longer shores where we can land. In this place the water, the earth and the sky are all mixed together. We are returning to Chaos.'

'Perhaps,' said Diomedes. 'Are you afraid, helmsman?'

'No,' replied Myrsilus. 'I feel no fear. Grief, sorrow . . . melancholy, perhaps. Not fear. It's as if we were fleeing from life, descending into Hades before our time and without a reason.'

The king turned again towards the Spartan: 'What do you know of this land?' he asked. 'And of its inhabitants, if there are any?'

'Very little, *wanax*. In the many days we've navigated here we've never seen another human being. Those who were sent inland reported that there is, first, a thick, nearly impenetrable forest of pine and oak to cross, populated by boars and huge wild bulls, but then an open plain as vast as the sea beyond. I know no more than this.'

The *Chnan* approached their Spartan guest and asked: 'Did you see the strange signs in the sky as well? What did the *Peleset* have to say about them?' A shiver of fear was visible in the man's eyes. 'Did you see them?' insisted the *Chnan*.

'We saw them. The *Peleset* tell a story that they learned from an old man who lives in a hut in the forest.'

Silence fell, and they could hear the heavy breathing of the men sleeping inside the ships and the light murmur of the tide lapping at the sand.

'What story?' asked the king.

'The old man stayed with them nearly three months, but I do not know how well he managed to learn their language. He too had seen the strange lights in the sky, and he spoke of a terrible thing that wiped out the inhabitants who lived on the plain, one village after another. He claimed that the chariot of the Sun had fallen to earth not far from here, near the great river.'

'The chariot of the Sun? What kind of a story is that?' protested the *Chnan*. 'The chariot of the Sun is still in its place and every day crosses the vault of the sky from east to west.'

'Maybe they saw something similar to the sun falling on to the earth. The old man spoke of a specific place, not far from the mouth of the great river, but no one has dared to go near there. The waters of the swamp boil up, incomprehensible sounds are heard. Laments, like the weeping of women, fill the night . . .'

Another long silence followed, broken by the solitary screech of a scops owl in the distance. The *Chnan* started: 'Someone may have mistaken the cry of a night animal for the shrieking of mysterious creatures. This land breeds ghosts.'

'We will soon learn what land we've reached,' said the king sharply, 'and we'll know whether the chariot of the Sun has truly fallen into these swamps.' He raised his eyes to the ship which transported his weapons and his horses. 'I can harness the divine horses to that chariot, the only ones who could draw it . . .' There was blind, stubborn conviction in his voice. 'But we must sleep now,' he added. 'The nights are long, but the dawn is no longer far off.'

They lay down near the fire, leaving a sentinel to stand guard, but the king was pensive. The cry of the owl seemed even sadder now, in that immense silent night, and reminded him of when as a boy that screeching would keep him alert in the palace of Tiryns as he stared out open-eyed into the endless darkness. That boy believed that there were creatures whose eyes were made to see in the gloom, creatures with eyes of darkness who saw the other half of the world, the half that the sun never visited. But those were times in which he thought he saw centaurs descend from the mountains in the golden twilight, and chimeras flying among the rocky gorges with shrill screams. Now he felt those empty eyes staring at his men and at his ships from the wooded shore on the mainland, and he was afraid, as he had been then, long ago.

The next day they resumed their journey. Myrsilus made a wide turn towards the open sea to avoid engaging the remaining ships of the *Peleset* fleet in battle. Towards midday, they met with a rather strong eastern wind and so he hoisted sail and hauled back towards land. The sky was covered with clouds and the air was biting cold but the sea was calm and made for clear sailing. All at once the look-out at the prow shouted that he could see something which looked like the mouth of a river. Myrsilus had a jug dipped into the water; when it was full, he hoisted it aboard and tasted the water with his finger: 'It's fresh water, *wanax*,' he said, handing the jug to Diomedes. 'We've reached the mouth of the Eridanus!'

'I told you that I would bring you to a new land,' said the king. 'It is here that we shall stop and build a new city.' He asked the helmsman if the wind was strong enough to allow the ship to sail upstream.

'Yes, *wanax*,' replied Myrsilus. 'I think so.'

'Then let us go,' said the king.

He took a cup and filled it with strong red wine, the same that he would drink before battle in the fields of Ilium. He poured it into the river current, saying: 'I offer you this libation, oh god of the waters of Eridanus. We have fled our homeland, after suffering all that men can suffer in a long war. We seek a new land and a new era and a new life. Show us your favour, I beseech you.' He threw the precious silver cup into the water as well; Anassilaus had melted it and engraved it with supreme art one day long ago at Lemnos, never imagining how far away it would end up.

He went to Lamus, son of Onchestus, the Spartan that Myrsilus had freed from slavery: 'Could you recognize the place where the old man said he had seen the Sun fall?'

'I think so. But why do you want to know?'

'If we want to remain here, I must know every secret of this land. You show me the place, as soon as you see it, and do not fear.'

The ship began to sail up the river; it was immense, so wide that the banks could barely be seen from the centre of the current, and the tallest oaks seemed mere shrubs.

'A river like this receives many rivers, and descends from mountains as high as the sky, always covered with ice, in the winter and in the summer, higher than the mountains of *Elam* and *Urartu*,' said the Hittite slave, Telephus.

'You are right,' said the king. 'And perhaps one day we shall see them.' The wind picked up from the west and north, and the ships had to counter its thrust with their helms, so as not to run aground on the river's southern shore. They crossed a dense forest from which immense flocks of birds would suddenly rise, blocking out the pale autumn sun like a cloud, and then finally entered the open plain. Every so often they would meet with big wooded islands whose gigantic trees stretched out their branches to touch the surface of the water. Every puff of wind snatched a host of brightly coloured leaves from those branches; yellow, red and ochre, they whirled through the air before alighting on the current.

To their left and right, instead, the land was bare, with scattered groups of trees here and there. The Spartan pointed to a place in which a branch of the river broke off from the main current, crossed a large pool and then headed south towards the sea. 'Here,' he said, 'this is the place the old man told us about; where the pond water is sparkling.'

Diomedes ordered them to stop the ships. One after another they furled the sails and cast anchor. The king armed himself with only a sword and set off on foot, taking a small group of warriors inland with him: Licus, Eumelus, Driop and Evenus, all from Argos, as well as Crissus and Dius of Tiryns.

The sun was already low, and transformed the still water of the marshes into mirrors of gold. They would stop every so often and listen: silence, everywhere, wringing their hearts and chilling their souls. They had never felt anything similar, not even in the midst of the fiercest fray on the field of battle. Even the birds were still and all they could hear were the small sudden thuds of the frogs jumping into the water.

They advanced as far as the shore of the pond and Diomedes signalled for his men to wait under an oak that stretched its bare branches towards the water. He went on alone, as the dusky light dimmed and the sun sank into the mist that veiled the horizon.

He stopped all at once, vaguely sensing that the place was infested by a powerful, dark presence; he glanced back at his men, who had so often faced death on the open field. They were glancing about helplessly, seized with dismay.

Just then he thought he heard something: a sound, or a moan, perhaps, was that the voice that Lamus, son of Onchestus, had spoken of? The cry of wailing women? He looked at the surface of the waves and heard the sound even more distinctly. It was a wail, yes, a chorus of weeping as if many women were grieving over the slain bodies of their sons or brothers or husbands. Diomedes the hero sought the voice of his own mother in that chorus, the voice of Aigialeia, his lost bride, but he could not hear them. He drew even closer to the pond which had swallowed up the chariot of the Sun and he saw a shiver run over the water although the wind had calmed and the air was still and stagnant. And as the sky darkened the surface of the pool stretched and curved as if pushed upward by the back of a monster. To his left the sun disappeared with a last tremor of light and the sky suddenly blackened above the pale layer of fog. A gurgling rose from the pool and beneath the surface, deprived of its golden reflection, Diomedes could see a shape, like a wheel . . . the wheel of the chariot of the Sun? The water gurgled again and the wheel dissolved in the rippling waves. Diomedes turned towards his companions: 'I don't need you any longer,' he said. 'But I'm going to stay here, I want more time.'

'Come back to camp with us, *wanax*,' pleaded the men. 'These are unknown lands.'

'Go,' repeated Diomedes. 'This place is deserted, can't you feel that? Nothing can harm me, and the goddess Athena will watch over me.'

The men departed and the rustling of their passage through the swamp reeds could be heard for a while, until silence descended once again over the pond. The hero leaned against the trunk of a colossal willow that wet its branches in the water. The ground had become as dark as the sky.

Time passed and the cold become pungent but he continued to stare at the surface of the water, black as a burnished mirror. He had nearly decided to return to the ships when he saw a pale flash of light animate the bottom of the swamp. He turned his eyes to the sky, thinking that the moon had emerged from behind a bank of clouds, but he saw nothing. The light was emanating from the bottom of the pool. The surface of the water arched again, becoming a dark globe which covered something that continued to remain invisible. The hero could not believe his eyes. The water did not fall; it adhered to the bulging beneath like a fluttering cloak. The light flashed again, stronger and brighter, and struck the clouds of the sky which quivered as if pervaded by lightning in a storm. These were the lights that had accompanied them since they had left the land of the Achaeans, sailing over the sea, these were the unexplainable flashes that had frightened the men at the oars and filled the helmsmen with wonder. He was afraid to stare at the light, which now seemed directed towards him. How could his body resist a bolt that could penetrate the clouds of the sky? The light darted now from the hub of the wheel like a sunburst, and when the ray struck him, the veils that prevent us from seeing that which has existed before us and that which will exist after us, fell suddenly from his eyelids. The hero saw, as if in a dream, the origin of his life and of his human adventure.

He saw the war of the Seven against Thebes; he could distinctly hear the neighing of the horses and the cries of the warriors. It was there, in that blind massacre, that everything began. War of brother against brother, blood of the same father and of the same mother. He saw his own father, Tydeus, scaling the walls and hurling the defenders down from the bastions, one after another. Shouting, shouting louder and louder for his comrades to join him and follow him. It was at that moment that the spear of Melanippus, flung with great force, stuck into his belly. And his father, Tydeus the hero, ripped the spear from his flesh, holding the bowels that burst from the wide wound with his left hand, while with the other he whirled the mighty two-edged axe. Melanippus took no care – how could a dying man find the strength to harm him? – and the great axe was whirled and then flew through the air. It fell on his neck, cleanly chopping his head off.

His mutilated body collapsed to the ground shaking and kicking but his head rolled away, far from the bastions, and ended up between the feet of the warriors facing off in frenzied battle. Diomedes's father, Tydeus, dragged himself over the stone, leaving a long wake of blood; he reached the severed head of Melanippus, seized it and bashed it on the stone with both his hands, forcefully, until he split open the robust skull. He neared his mouth and devoured the still warm brain. And the goddess Athena who had rushed to aid him, to heal his wound, turned away in horror, closing her eyes so she would not see. Tydeus died alone, breathing the last breath of life on that stone, far from his bride and his son. The goddess shouted out with her eyes closed and full of tears: 'This is your stock, Diomedes! This is your race and your blood!'

Diomedes turned and shouted out himself: 'Did you see that? Did you hear?' But he had forgotten that his companions had all gone. He himself had ordered them to go.

The mysterious power that loomed in those waters forced him to look again into the rays of light. And he saw Amphiaraus, the father of his friend Sthenelus, fleeing on his chariot, fleeing over the plains in a cloud of dust, whipping his horses cruelly, fleeing Thebes to flee the Fate of death.

But the earth suddenly opened beneath the hooves of the horses and the infernal Furies emerged, spouting flames from their mouths; their hair was woven with poisonous serpents, their eyes veined with blood, their skin red and scaly. They grabbed the reins of his fiery horses – who tried desperately to get free, rearing up and neighing wildly – but the Furies dragged them under the ground, and Amphiaraus with them. The voice said: 'And this is the race of Sthenelus, the blood of your faithful friend!'

'Sthenelus!' shouted Diomedes. 'Where is he? Where is he?'

But there was no answer. He knew in the bottom of his heart that Sthenelus was dead, long dead; he had felt his vital force vanish from the world like smoke, like the vapour of the morning mist is dispersed by the sun.

He collapsed against the tree and said: 'Oh god, you who inhabit these waters and make the clouds throb with your gaze, I have seen what was. I have seen that the blood of my race is like poison. Now let me see what will be. If there is still a way to bend a bitter destiny.'

He mustered up his courage and advanced to the edge of the pond. He stood still in its blinding light. The globe trembled and the water which covered it began slowly to drip and then to pour downward, raising splashes from the surface of the pool. The light quivered, the wheel turned and he could once again hear the chorus of laments.

Diomedes sensed that there was someone at his back and he turned: he saw a warrior wrapped in a cloak advancing towards him from the depths of the darkness. A white crest swayed on his helmet, a Trojan sword gleamed in his hand. The warrior came closer, surrounded by silence and by a halo of fog, and he was enormous to see, much larger than a real man. Only when he came into the ray of light was his face recognizable. His eyes blazed with hate and revenge: it was Aeneas!

Diomedes drew his sword. 'This is destiny, then! This is the future, the same as the past!' he shouted and he hurled himself at his adversary, but the sword pierced an immaterial shape, an empty image. He spun around, still shouting: 'Where are you? Fight and let's finish this forever! It's either me or you, son of Anchises! How many times did I force you to flee on the fields of Ilium? Show yourself! I'm not afraid of you!'

He dealt blow after blow, until he collapsed, exhausted, on to his knees in the damp grass.

The lights in the sky had gone out and the surface of the pond was once again still. A hand touched his shoulder: 'Let's go, *wanax*. This land breeds nightmares. Let's go back to the ships.'

'Myrsilus! Why are you here? You shouldn't have left the ship. The ship must always be guarded. With all it contains.' He got to his feet and walked towards the river bank.

'Our comrades are guarding the ship, *wanax*. You can trust them.'

They walked in silence, guided by the light of the camp fire that blazed far off in the night, and by the torch that Myrsilus held in his hand.

'What did you see in that place, *wanax*? The others returned in a great fright. They said they saw you shout and wave your sword, chopping down swamp reeds, willow bushes and poplar saplings. They heard sounds and cries and moans but they did not know how to help you.'

'I saw only what I carry within me,' said the king.

'What about the chariot of the Sun? Is it true that it fell into those waters?'

Diomedes did not answer. He was thinking of the arched surface of the water, of that thing that launched rays of light towards the sky and then sank back into the mud and silence.

'I don't know. But it is from there that the signs that cross the night sky come. The signs that have frightened so many peoples and scattered them in every direction like crazed ants. The sky should never touch the earth. The storm of the elements will not subside yet for a long, long time. Our suffering will continue.'

'I know, *wanax*,' said Myrsilus. 'I saw it in your eyes. But let us rest now, for every day has its sorrow.'

7

MYRSILUS WENT TO REST under the ship's stern, but he stayed awake for some time listening to the voice of the river. He thought of the lofty mountains of ice which must have generated such an enormous current. Perhaps the Hyperborean Mountains or the Rhipaean Mountains he'd heard tale of as a boy. It was there, in a deep grotto sustained by a thousand columns of ice, that the cold wind of the north was born, to upset the waves of the sea and bring snow to the earth during the winter.

He was thinking of what the king had seen in the swamp; something that had troubled his mind, moving him to rage against the swamp reeds and bushes. The same thing had happened to Ajax Telamon! He had slashed the throats of sheep and bulls, sure he was killing his enemies. But Myrsilus did not fear that the king had lost his mind. In his eyes he had seen suffering and terror, but not madness. Diomedes was still the strongest.

But Lamus the Spartan, son of Onchestus, crept close to the king: 'Was the chariot of the Sun really there, *wanax*?'

The king was not sleeping. He was leaning against his shield. 'I don't know,' he said. 'If it truly fell from the sky, it is trying to get free now, to return whence it came. Those flashes of light flung towards the sky are like a cry for help, cries that no one can understand, only fear. The earth no longer bears fruit, peoples are abandoning their homelands . . .'

'And you still want to proceed inland? Isn't that cry – that lament – a sign from the gods to make us understand that we must stop challenging fortune? I beg of you, let us turn back. King Menelaus is alive, I'm sure of it, and so are nearly all my comrades.

They are bound once again towards our homeland. I've heard that you lost your city, but if we return he can help you; he'll ask Agamemnon, the great Atreid, to join forces with him to retake Argos and restore your command. This land is cold and deserted, not gracious and warm like our land on the banks of the Eurotas. Like your land, with abundant harvests and grazing flocks. Let us return, *wanax*, the kings will fight for you, and so will we . . .'

Diomedes turned towards him, but his eyes seemed to stare beyond, into the dark night. 'Perhaps you should have stayed with the *Peleset*,' he said. 'We'll go forward, as far as the Mountains of Ice if need be, or the Mountains of Fire, until we have found a place to establish a new city and a new kingdom. For years we suffered all the pain and fear of a cruel war. We have already gone beyond the bounds of fear. This land is worthy of us because it is unlike any other. It is barren, like our hearts, cold, like our solitude. It is austere and immense; we will conquer it and settle here, a new people.'

Lamus walked away, his soul heavy with sadness, fearing that he would never again see his city and his father, already so advanced in years. Diomedes called him back: 'Spartan!'

'Here I am, *wanax*.'

'One day we will return to the sea, and you can decide then whether to leave us or stay with us. But for now you must do your part; we must be able to count on your help.'

'You can be sure of it,' said the Spartan. 'My king loved you as a friend and honoured you as a god. What is right for him is right for me.'

'Listen,' said Diomedes again, 'while we were navigating towards this land we met up with a savage people who were marching along the coast towards the south. I sent a ship to warn the kings of the threat to the Achaeans; the comrade piloting it was Anchialus, one of my best men, whom I would have wanted with me. It's not I who have forgotten my homeland. It's my land that has refused me. Understand?' Tears quivered on his eyelids, but the ardour of his gaze dried them before they could descend to his cheeks.

'I understand,' said Lamus, and walked away.

King Diomedes thought of Anchialus and his ship; he imagined that it had already reached the land of the Achaeans and had cast its anchor in the sandy bay of Pylus. Anchialus would have made his way to the palace of Nestor and would be enjoying his hospitality. Diomedes would have liked to be in his place, warming himself before the blaze of a big fire, eating roasted meat sliced into big pieces by the carvers, drinking wine late into the night and then lying beside a white-necked, soft-eyed maiden. He imagined this to be the privilege that his companion Anchialus was enjoying in that moment, and he stretched out with a sigh.

But the immortal gods were otherwise inclined.

*

After Anchialus had brought the ship about as he had been ordered by his king, he did not go far forward, because the wind was against him and the night dark. Having reached the closest island, he had dropped anchor in the shelter of a small promontory. He thought he would wait in that place until the wind had changed direction and could push him south towards the land of the Achaeans. He had stretched out on the bottom of the ship to look at the sky and the stars that would guide him. His heart was assailed by conflicting feelings. He was sorry to leave his king, whom he had fought with for years, who had saved his life in battle time after time. But he was also filled with joy at the thought of seeing his land again, and his old mother and father, if they were still alive. He thought that Nestor and the other kings would thank him, and give him rich gifts in exchange; weapons, garments and perhaps a beautiful, high-flanked woman to take to his wedding chamber.

He waited ten days. On the eleventh the wind changed and began to blow from the north, violently, raising wild waves. Anchialus waited until it had expended its energy, then hoisted the sail and began his voyage. The wind had shifted direction and was blowing aport so that the pilot had to frequently compensate with oars and helm to keep from being dragged westward into the open sea.

They proceeded the whole day and stopped for the night near a promontory on the coast. The place was deserted; the only dim lights to be seen were a few isolated huts up on the mountains at quite a distance. He chose Frissus, a man from Abia, to stand guard, and told him to wake a companion, whoever he preferred, to relieve him when the stars had covered a quarter of their course across the sky. He himself went to rest.

But Frissus was deceived by the peace that reigned in that place and by his own weariness, and he fell fast asleep. He saw no danger gathering, he heard no sound, because the murmur of the wind and the splashing of the tide were like a soft, reassuring voice, like the lullaby that invites a child to sleep. He started awake shortly before dawn when the cold stung his limbs and the shrieks of the seagulls brought sudden anguish to his heart.

He got to his feet, but Anchialus was already standing opposite him, his sword in hand and a look of stupor in his eyes. He was not looking at him, but at something behind him. Frissus turned and saw a host of white wings in the sky and a host of black sails on the sea, barely distinguishable from the black of night by the pale glimmer of dawn.

The others awoke as well and ran to the ship's side, looking at each other in silent dismay.

'We must flee,' said Anchialus. 'If they reach us, it's all over. No one journeys by sea in this season and at this time of day, with so many men and so many ships, unless he is forced to. They can only bring us harm.'

'Hoist the sail!' he shouted. 'Man the oars!' The crew swiftly obeyed, the ship left its mooring and thrust forward. Anchialus flanked the pilot aft, to aid him in governing the ship. But the bulk of the island had hidden part of the fleet from view, and no sooner had their ship left shore that they found four vessels bearing down on them at full tilt. One tried to bar their way, but Anchialus managed to dodge him by veering towards shore. The two ships were briefly side to side, so close that the Achaean warriors could see their adversaries in the face. They were dark-skinned, with black, tightly curled hair like the Ethiopians, armed with bronze swords and leather shields, and they wore leather helmets as well. Their commander spoke a rough Achaean. He yelled out: 'Stop or we will sink you!' But Anchialus only urged his men to row harder.

'Who are they?' asked the pilot.

The enemy commander leaned overboard, hanging from the stays by one hand and grasping a sabre in the other. '*Shekelesh!*' he shouted. 'And I'll chop off your nose and your ears when I catch you!'

'Siculians!' said Anchialus to the pilot without losing sight of the enemy. 'Oh gods . . . what are Siculians doing here? Put about!' he ordered the pilot. 'Put about, get the ship to the other side of that rock.' The pilot obeyed and they pulled away from the *Shekelesh* ship, which disappeared from sight briefly behind a little rocky island.

'I've been to their island, when I was once a ship-boy on a merchant vessel carrying wine. They were said to have come from nearby Libya, populating the island even before Minos ruled Crete. They are poor people, renowned for their fierceness; they will fight for anyone and against anyone. Their name itself sounds like the hissing of a snake! We must out-distance them. If they take us, they'll sell us all as slaves in the nearest market.'

They rounded the island, but soon found two more ships on their left.

'It's a trap!' shouted Anchialus. 'If they wedge us between them, be ready to draw your arms.' One of the light *Shekelesh* vessels had already caught up with them and was cutting them.

'Ram it!' shouted Anchialus. The crew struck the sail. 'Now!' he shouted again. The oarsmen increased their pace and the pilot veered left, colliding full force with the enemy vessel. The little ship was rent and foundered instantly, but the others had the time to draw up alongside and board the Achaean ship. The *Shekelesh* clambered over the sides of their ships, shouting and wielding swords and daggers. The Achaeans abandoned the oars and launched an armed assault on their enemies. Anchialus shouted 'Argos!' with all the breath he had, as they would once shout on the plain of Ilium at the moment of unleashing their attack. 'Argos!' he shouted. And the mêlée spread like wildfire, filling the ship with screams and blood. The Achaeans fought with desperate energy, killing many and throwing many overboard, but they were outnumbered when a third ship drew up to join the battle.

The pilot spotted Anchialus in the midst of a group of enemies; he swung his double-edged axe, chopping the head clean off one of the *Shekelesh* and shearing another's arm, but it was evident that he would soon be overwhelmed. He burst into the circle, pushing them aside with great force, and hurled himself at Anchialus, shouting: 'Save yourself! The king gave you an order!' The pilot threw him into the sea, before he was surrounded and massacred by a swarm of assailants.

The other comrades were done in as well, one after another. The *Shekelesh* took only two of them alive, and tortured them all that day to avenge the heavy losses they had suffered without any advantage, for there was nothing on the vanquished ship worth plundering.

Anchialus gripped a piece of planking; he could hear the cries of his comrades and he bit his lips bloody in rage, but he could do nothing to help. His pilot had given his own life to save him and allow him to carry out the task that Diomedes had given him. He had no choice but to try to survive and go on his way.

His limbs numb from the cold, Anchialus swam to the island and from there, before nightfall, to the mainland. He was drenched and starving, and the chill of the night would surely have killed him had not fortune finally come to his aid. He found a little shack made of sticks and dried branches, a shelter for animals.

There were no animals, nor even a bit of hay, but there was plenty of manure. Anchialus took off his clothing and buried himself naked in the pile of dung, whose warmth kept him alive that night.

The next morning, he bathed in the sea and put on the clothing which had dried overnight. The *Shekelesh* ships could just barely be seen at the horizon; the wind was carrying them west, towards the land of Hesperia, where king Diomedes was directed or perhaps had already arrived.

He was cold, for he had lost his cloak, so he ran southward all that day, to keep warm and to dismiss thoughts of hunger and fatigue. He ran, his heart heavy with pain, thinking of his lost comrades lying on the sea bottom, food for fish. He feared that he would never succeed in reaching the land of the Achaeans, to launch the alarm so that the kings could prepare their defences.

He would stop every so often when the path touched the seashore and collect molluscs and little fish, eating them raw to assuage his hunger pangs, soon resuming his journey. When he crossed a forest, he would gather snails and larva attached to the shrubs in their winter slumber. When night fell, he sought shelter in a little cave, lining the floor with dry leaves which he also used to wall up the mouth. He fell asleep disparaging such a pitiful existence, more similar to an animal's than to a man's. In just one day, he who was the commander of a ship with fifty Achaean warriors had lost everything, and was reduced to a brute who slept in animal dung and ate raw meat. He clenched his jaw, closing his wounded soul between his teeth; he knew that if he gave in to despair, his world would be engulfed and annihilated by that horde of barbarians that scoured land and sea with no end in mind. More desperate, perhaps, than he was, more lost, even, than his king Diomedes, who sought a kingdom in the mists of night. Perhaps an entire world would continue to exist, with its labours and hopes, if he, Anchialus, found the strength to go on.

The next day, as he left his shelter with his limbs aching and his eyes puffy, he saw a woman, standing before him. She was covered with hides from head to foot and was bringing a flock of sheep to pasture. He looked at her without saying a word and she did not draw back; she was not frightened by his wretched appearance. She had him stretch out next to one of her goats and squeezed the animal's teats into his mouth, satiating him with the milk.

She took him that night into her hut near a stream, a shelter made of stakes and branches and covered with mud, where she lived alone. She milked the sheep and goats, making a curd which she shaped into cheese and placed on grates hanging over the hearth. She fed him smoked cheese and flat millet bread roasted on the embers and gave him milk to drink. When they had finished eating, she took off her coarse garment and stood before him nude, in silence. Her hands were large and cracked and her nails were black, her hair was dirty and tangled, but her body seemed lovely and desirable in the glow of the fire. Strain and exertion had marked her face, but had not erased an austere, simple grace; her nose was small and straight, her deep, dark-eyed gaze modest, nearly frowning.

Anchialus drew close and took her into his arms. He lay with her on the sheepskins which covered the floor near the fire. She caressed his hair and shoulders with her dry, rough hands as he entered her moist, warm belly and her ardour blazed within him like the heat of the embers.

He spent the whole winter with her. He helped her to tend to the animals and milk the goats and sheep. They hardly ever spoke and, when the snow fell to whiten the mountains and the valleys, they would sit in silence watching the big flakes whirling in the cold, grey sky. And so Anchialus survived and waited for the season to change, so he could begin his journey once again. He was certain that not even the *Dor* or *Shekelesh* could proceed when the snow covered the ground and the storms raged at sea.

One evening at the end of winter, she crouched near the fire and took some bones out of a little sack, shook them in her fist and then threw them on to the floor, three times. She suddenly stopped, looked at the knuckle bones scattered over the ashes, and raised her tear-filled eyes to his. She knew that the moment had come to let him go. The next morning she filled a sack with food and gave him a skin with fresh water drawn from the stream, pelts to protect him from the chill of night, and a walking stick. Anchialus took his smoke-blackened sword from the wall and departed. When he reached the mountain ridge that had closed off his horizon towards the south for so many days, he turned back. She was small and very far away, a dark figure standing in front of a solitary hut. He waved his hand but she did not move, as though her grief and the cold wind which blew from the mountainside had changed her into a statue of ice.

*

Diomedes left the mouth of the Eridanus and sailed yet another day up the river, taking advantage of the wind blowing from the east which swelled his sails, without finding any signs of human presence. The men heaved the ships aground on the southern side of a bend in the huge river. They had cast their nets before going ashore and caught a great deal of fish, which they roasted on the fire. Some of them were so big that they had had to run them through with their spears to stop them from destroying the nets.

The next day the king decided to venture inland. He had a trench dug and a palisade built for the men who would remain to guard the camp and the vessels. He had them unload the ships' cargo so that maintenance work could be done on the hulls. He had the crew put ashore the chest that he always kept tied to his ship's mast and disembark his horses, the ones he had taken from Aeneas after he had fought and wounded him on the fields of Ilium. He appointed Myrsilus to take command in his absence. He instructed his escort to wear battle gear and to take enough food rations for three days. They departed, following what seemed to be a torrent that strangely took water from the river instead of feeding into it. They marched the entire first day along the little stream, and towards evening they sighted a village. It was surrounded by a wide moat fed by the canal that they had been following all day. Within the moat was an embankment topped by a palisade, beyond which the roofs of a great number of large dwellings could be seen, apparently all quite the same, arranged in orderly, parallel rows. A wooden footbridge had been lowered over the moat at the entrance to the village: a door of tree trunks flanked by two towers, made of tree trunks as well and covered by roofs made of branches. The fields all around revealed the signs of man's labour, yet seemed to be abandoned; they were scattered with patches of stubble and with piles of hay, now soaked through and covered with whitish mould. Rotten or dried fruits hung from trees planted in lines along the borders of the cultivated lands; the ground at the base of the trunks was thick with fallen fruits. Not a wisp of smoke rose from the rooftops of the village houses, nor could a single sound be heard: not a voice, not the bleating of a sheep nor the lowing of a calf.

To the west, the sun was emerging from a dense bank of clouds just before setting, and it cast its last light on to the village and the fields, scoring the earth with the long shadows of the Achaean warriors on the march.

Diomedes signalled for them to stop and he advanced with two or three men, those closest to him, towards the bridge. He called out but there was no answer, only the barking of a dog that sounded after a while from behind the palisade. He advanced cautiously over the bridge and entered the village. The dog they had heard, which was gnawing on the fleshless bones of a carcass, growled, then slunk away whining, and the whole place fell into the most profound silence. Diomedes called out again, and still receiving no response, began to advance along the road that crossed the village from one side to the other. As they moved forward, his warriors patrolled the side roads that divided the town into regular districts.

He sought the residence of the chief, but could not find it; all the dwellings were equal in size, made of gratings of intertwined branches coated with fire-hardened clay, and topped by straw and hay roofs.

'All men seem equal in this city,' said Evenus. 'All of the houses have the same dimensions and are made in the same way. How can the people understand who is to command and who is to obey?'

'There are no people here,' said Diomedes. 'Not any more.

Something happened. Something that killed them or forced them to flee.'

'What could it have been?' asked Evenus. 'In all my life I've never seen a similar thing. Could it have been . . . the chariot of the Sun?'

'We shall see,' said the king. 'Look inside the houses and tell me what you find.' He himself entered one of the houses. There was only one room inside. Along the wall were a series of dusty mats topped with gleaming white skeletons. Their mouths were stretched wide in a spasm of agony, their arms curled on their bellies, backs bent as if cramping over a point of piercing pain. At the centre was a hearth with a thick layer of ash; dark jars of varying dimensions, carved with simple decorations, stood all around. Half-burnt animal bones were mixed with the ashes, fish bones, walnut shells and fruit pits. There were no lamps, nor were there tables or other furnishings. The only other thing Diomedes saw was a bronze horse's bit hanging on the wall, still fitted with its reins.

One of his men was waiting for him when he walked out. He could read the fear in his eyes: '*Wanax*, the houses are all empty . . . we've found only corpses, what's left of them. But in one of the houses, down there, we've found something strange.'

Diomedes followed him and entered a house located at the crossing of the two main roads. The door was open and the light of the setting sun poured in, striking an object lying on a sort of raised platform at the centre of the house, a bright disc that glittered like a little sun. The king approached it and saw that it was made of embossed gold with spiral decorations which looked as if they were moving; it sat on four little wheels. On the ground was a clay basin full of rainwater, adorned with bulls' heads, with a little fragment of gold taken from the edge of the disc, at its bottom.

'What is it, *wanax*?' asked the warrior. 'It seems like magic, like sorcery . . . I don't like this place . . .'

The king stretched his hand towards the disc and suddenly the shimmer vanished. The sun had just descended below the horizon.

He looked at the little wheels and at the fragment at the bottom of the basin.

'A piece of the chariot of the Sun has fallen into the swamp . . . that's what it means.' He said nothing else, so as not to frighten his men, but he realized that those people had wanted to leave a sign for those who would come, perhaps to warn them, or perhaps to leave a token in memory of their end.

'Let us go now,' he said. 'Do not touch anything, because this place is like a sanctuary.'

They walked out through the southern door, opposite to where they had entered. They passed the bare bones of a calf; nothing was left but a few strips of dried skin around the horns and the ribs. The empty eye sockets seemed to stare with surprise at the line of crested warriors who advanced through the dead city.

There was a broken bridge at the southern door as well, which crossed the rushing waters of the canal, but what they found on the other side was much more sinister than what they'd seen within.

Two rows of scorched stakes crossed a recently ploughed field; at the top of each stake was the burned head of a ram with great twisted horns, with scraps of skin and scorched flesh still clinging to the skulls. At the end of these eerie rows was an even more disturbing scene: the skeletons of two oxen lay on the ground under the yoke of a plough still stuck in the ground. The remains of a man lay nearby. Dogs had ripped him apart, fighting over the pieces: the gnawed, fleshless arms and parts of the legs lay at some distance from the torso, which was still protected by a sort of large leather tunic. The satchel he wore around his neck was of leather as well.

The king neared the man, took the satchel and opened it: teeth, the large pointed fangs of unknown animals. Diomedes looked around and saw that more teeth had been tossed into the furrows that the plough had made.

Evenus approached: '*Wanax*, what does all this mean? That man was sowing teeth . . .'

'Dragon's teeth . . . like Jason, in Colchis. Dragon's teeth, to call a new race of warriors from the ground.'

'And those rams' heads!' murmured Evenus, looking around as darkness descended over the valley behind him. A thin lick of fog was rising from the moat, creeping across the earth, lapping at the bases of the stakes, enveloping the bones of man and animal.

'Perhaps this man was performing a ritual to propitiate the sowing; an ancient, sacred rite of his ancestors, called upon out of the deepest despair.'

'Let us leave this place, *wanax*! It is inhabited by the shadows of the unburied, shades without peace. They'll drag us down to Hades with them if we stay here. All of our comrades are afraid as well; we have faced many dangers, fought without sparing our strength, we fear no enemy! But this land populated only by shadows has filled us with dread. It is not in this land that you shall found your kingdom!'

The king paused to look at the blackened skulls driven into the stakes, and the fog which crept over the earth and submerged everything, the skeletons, the abandoned plough.

'This is a land shrouded in the chill of winter. Springtime comes here as well, and the meadows are covered with flowers; the tall grass will hide the signs of death. You mustn't be afraid. But now let us return to the village and prepare for the night. Tomorrow we will return to our camp.'

'*Wanax*,' said Evenus, 'no one will follow you over that moat and behind that palisade. If you order us to do so, no one will shut an eye. Allow us to turn back now! We can follow the banks of the canal. We have brought our fire with us; we can light torches. Heed my words, *wanax*, I beg of you.'

Diomedes saw the terror in his eyes, even though his gaze was steady and his hand firm on his sword's hilt. If they were attacked during the night, anything might happen. He agreed to take them back to the camp they had left on the shores of the Eridanus.

They ate something so as not to march with hunger in their bellies, then gathered branches which they fashioned into torches, lighting them from the ash-covered embers that they had brought with them in a jar. They began their journey: Diomedes walked at the head of the line and Evenus was last. They marched on in silence, accompanied only by the screeching of the night birds. Weariness began to weigh upon them, and the men slowed their pace, but Diomedes urged them on as if suddenly he had a reason to hurry to the camp.

The sun had not yet risen when a bloody flash appeared at the horizon, a throbbing reddish light.

Evenus ran from the rear guard to the king's side: 'Do you see that, *wanax*? It looks like a fire.'

'I see it. Fast, we must make haste. It could be our camp.' The men took off at a run and covered the last stretch of road stumbling and falling, since they could not see the ground they were treading on. As they drew nearer, a confused uproar could be heard; swirling flames and sparks rose towards the sky. When they were finally close enough, they realized what had happened: the ships pulled aground had been spotted by the *Peleset* fleet during the night, and set ablaze. Myrsilus and his men were engaging the enemy on the beach, while others tried to put out the fire.

Diomedes beheld that terrible spectacle and the flames consuming his ships set off another fire in his mind: that terrible day that Hector had overwhelmed the Achaean defences and put Protesilaus's ship to the torch on the beach of Ilium. Fury raged through his veins and the strain of their endless march vanished all at once. He seized his sword and raised a great yell: 'ARGOS!' Just as he had when he ordered his men to attack on the battlefield in Ilium. He lunged forward, all the others close behind. He broke through the ranks of Myrsilus's warriors, who were being overpowered by the crushing force of the enemy and he burst into the front line, throwing himself into the fray.

The king was out of his mind. The brawl raged around him like a dream of the past: the battle under the wall of Thebes, the duels fought to the death before the Scaean gates, the Trojan warriors mowed down as their women watched. The king was like the wind that bends the oaks on the mountainside, like the hail that destroys the harvest, like the bolt of lightning that first blinds, then kills.

His cleaving blow ripped open the belly of the *Peleset* warrior in front of him, making his bowels spill down to his knees. He decapitated the comrade who had come to his aid and he horribly disfigured the face of a third who had dared to creep up on his left.

The blood drove him wild with anger and yet filled his soul with deep sorrow, like the sea tousled on the surface by a storm remains dark and still down beneath. And thus the force of his blows was invincible.

Myrsilus and his men, eager to prove themselves worthy in the eyes of their king, counter-attacked vigorously, repulsing the enemies towards the shore of the river. The *Peleset* chief realized that the situation had been completely reversed and that if the battle were to continue his men would be annihilated. Satisfied with the damage he had inflicted on his enemies, he shouted out that upon his signal, all his men should run to the ships and set sail.

Only Lamus, son of Onchestus, understood what he had said, but he was near the palisade and had no way of letting Diomedes know, as the king was in the thick of the battle and his ears were full of its din. He shouted: 'Stop them, they want to escape! We must not let them get away, or we will have no ships for ourselves!' But his cries went unheard. At their chief's signal, the *Peleset* turned and fled rapidly to their ships, setting off towards the centre of the river, where the current swiftly carried them out of sight, towards the sea.

The Achaeans remained on the gravelly shore of the river and not a one had the heart to raise the cry of victory although they had defeated a numerous, war-seasoned enemy. Almost all of their ships had been destroyed. Those which had not burned down were in such a sorry state that they could not imagine repairing them.

The king assembled them all near the palisade; he took off his helmet and, dishevelled and blood-spattered as he was, said: 'We have won the battle but we have lost our ships. We have no choice now. Although the comrades who came with me last night asked me to leave this land which shows so many signs of unexplainable destruction, today it is no longer possible to do so. We will push on and find a place suitable for founding our new kingdom. Perhaps the destruction of the ships is a sign from the gods who want to make us understand that this is the place they have destined for us. Let us go forward; there is always a new land on the horizon. If we must, we shall go towards the Mountains of Ice or the Mountains of Fire, or even beyond. No one is stronger than a man who has nothing left to hope for from fate.'

The men listened to him in silence. Many of them, especially those who had accompanied him the day before and marched with him all night, were distressed thinking of the hardships and privations they would suffer in that deserted, cursed land. But among them the most afflicted was Lamus, the Spartan; he was certain then that he would never be able to see his home and his city again. If he had been free to go as he pleased, he would not have known where to turn. He kept at a distance, head low, choking back his tears.

'Do not despair!' said Diomedes to his men. 'The enemy has deprived us of our ships, but they did not succeed in attacking the camp. What is most precious remains. Follow me,' he said, heading towards the camp. 'Since we have nothing left but our arms and our courage, it is time that you know the truth.'

He reached the centre of the camp, where alongside the pole with his standard was the chest that he had always kept tied to the main mast of his ship. He grabbed an axe and with a single stroke broke open the hinges. The lid fell to the ground and revealed what was within. A great silence fell over the camp and the men bowed their heads.

Myrsilus came forward and raised his spear towards the sun which was rising from the bare branches of the poplars and oaks to illuminate the waters of the Eridanus. 'We will follow you, *wanax*, even to the Mountains of Ice, even to the Mountains of Fire!'

All the men raised their spears to the sun and shouted: '*Wanax!*'

They were no longer afraid and they watched their ships sink under the river current, without tears. The ships that had brought war to Ilium, the ships that for years had been the hope for their return, the symbol of their homeland.

'Now we can only go forward,' said the king.

They loaded all they had on the backs of the horses. The chest was closed again and loaded on to the king's chariot, to which the divine horses of Aeneas were harnessed. When they were all ready, he gave the signal to depart and the column began its westward march.

The *Chnan* was one of the last, and he was distraught over seeing the ships destroyed. 'Madmen and fools!' he said. 'They've lost their ships and it's as if nothing had happened at all, just because they saw that thing in the box. Were you able to get a look at it, at least?' he asked Telephus, the Hittite slave.

'No,' he answered. 'They were all in front of me with those crested helmets. But I don't think it makes much of a difference for us.'

'Of course it does,' said the *Chnan*. 'With a ship, I could have brought you anywhere: to the ends of the earth, to the shores of the Ocean, to the swamps of the icy Borysthenes, to the mouth of the Nile, or . . . home. Even home . . .'

For the first time, his eyes were full of dismay and of terror.

8

THEY ADVANCED FOR SEVERAL days until they found another
of those strange square-shaped cities, surrounded by a canal, filled
with huts of the same size. There were still some people left here,
just a few families who survived by rearing a cow or two, or a
small flock of sheep. They took fright at the Achaean warriors,
but Diomedes ordered his men not to harm them and to take
only the women they could convince with gifts or words. A
pointless order; nearly all the remaining inhabitants were well on
in years.

They decided to stop there nonetheless because the weather
had changed again for the worst: first rain, then snow and intense
cold. They found food there as well: wheat, barley, milk and
cheese. And the forests were full of wood for lighting fires.

When the weather was fine, the king took his horses down to
the plain, far away from the square city. He brought them there
to graze, and the horses pawed the snow to find grass and scrub
to feed on.

He would return in the evening with a look of melancholic
peace in his eyes, and would go to his hut without speaking to
anyone. If snow fell during the night he would come out wrapped
in his cloak and linger there, watching the big flakes swirl through
the air in silence, his eyes bright and feverish. Sometimes he
wouldn't go to rest until it was nearly dawn, falling then into a
heavy, agitated sleep.

The men who stood guard outside his door said that they had
heard him calling out the name of Queen Aigialeia, in his sleep,
and that they had heard him weeping, but Myrsilus threatened

to cut off their tongues if they ever dared speak of such a thing again. He said they had to stand guard and nothing else, putting the rest out of their minds.

One day the king took only one of his horses with him and when he was far from the camp, he tried to mount him bare-backed, as he had seen the *Dor* do. The steed bucked and shook him off more than once, but in the end the king had the better of him and managed to stay on his back as he galloped through the snow-covered plain. It felt incredible, like flying, like squeezing an impetuous sea wave between his legs, and Diomedes felt as if he could feel the hot blood of that great animal flowing in his own veins.

The steed flew, flogging his flanks with his tail, blowing clouds of steam from his frost-whitened nostrils and letting out shrill whinnies. Diomedes let him run until he was exhausted, then dismounted, covered him with a blanket, and let him graze. Every now and then the horse would raise his proud head and shake his mane, seeming to stare at him with a troubled, intense gaze.

'You're thinking of your master, aren't you? Are you thinking of Aeneas?'

The animal shook his head as if nodding. 'He's no longer with us. Aeneas is dead. I'm all you have left, and it's me you must love. If we should ever meet up with him one day, I will challenge him, and if he wins you can return to him, if you wish, and carry him once again into battle. But until that day you must serve me, for I have won you in fair, honourable combat.'

He started back towards the village but a false trail brought him far from his path, very far, to the southernmost edge of the forest. Before exiting the thick of the woods, he saw a caravan advancing from the north through the deep snow. There was a small group of warriors armed with long swords and spears, clad in animal hides and wearing helmets of leather and bronze; behind them a pair of oxen were pulling a covered carriage.

When they were very close, a sudden wind blew at the mats covering the sides of the carriage. For a moment, a mere moment, the king saw a maiden of divine beauty, her blue eyes veiled by shadow, her forehead white and pure as ice, her hair like ripe wheat. She looked like Aigialeia, when he had seen her the first time! Her features were different, the slant of her eyes and the lines of her face, but her spirit and form were the same, as were the enticing ambiguity and directness of her gaze and, he imagined, the fire that blazed beneath her gown. Happy the man who would carry her to his wedding chamber.

He mounted his horse and followed the little cortège at a distance, at length, remaining within the forest so he would not be seen. He felt an invincible force pulling him towards that carriage that advanced, swaying, and leaving a deep trail in the snow. He realized some time later that the carriage was approaching one of those square cities surrounded by a moat and an embankment, but this one was much bigger, and could contain many people. Spirals of smoke rose slowly from the rooftops, towards the cloudy sky.

He came out into the open just as the carriage was stopping and a door was opened in the palisade to admit the new arrivals.

A man crossed the bridge at its centre, walking towards the carriage from which the girl was descending. The warriors also unloaded several wicker baskets, her dowry perhaps, and carried them towards the city.

Diomedes sank his heels into his horse's belly and got so close that the girl could see him; she looked into his eyes and he returned her gaze and made a sweeping gesture with his hand as if inviting her to follow him. The men who had been accompanying her turned towards him in alarm, then took their bows and began shooting arrows at him. He was beyond their range and he shouted to her: 'Come with me! No one is more beautiful than you on this earth! Come with me!' He spoke from his heart; he felt that that woman could become the queen of the city that he would found. Only she, perhaps, could wipe the image of Aigialeia from his soul. He wanted to attack then, and carry her off, but as he was about to charge forward, a great number of men appeared from behind the palisade and drew up before the carriage.

The maiden entered the city behind the man who had come

out to welcome her. Before the door closed behind her she turned towards the plain and looked back at that rash warrior who continued to call to her, prancing about on his bay horse and raising sparkling sprays of snow.

Diomedes understood what was happening. The chief of those people had had a bride brought to him from afar! A bride of another stock, who would ward off the fate of his dying race, inject new blood into a breed cursed by an obscure affliction.

And this made him want that woman even more, at any cost.

He returned to his village, following the prints left by his horse in the snow, and he called his warriors to assembly that very evening. He told them that he had discovered another one of those strange cities, large and prosperous, full of herds, of abundant food, of weapons and metal to be forged. This would mark the moment of the conquest of his new kingdom. By spring they would have land, women and riches enough to found a new city. The warriors pledged to assist him.

'I thank you,' said the king, 'and if we win I will take a queen for myself from this city and I will take her into my bed as soon as the good weather returns.' The warriors cheered and applauded and then they all sat on the ground for their meal. Telephus had roasted a goat and it was served to the king and his friends, but the wine had run out.

'We will plant vines as well!' said Diomedes. 'I have seen wild shoots in the forest. We'll cultivate them to produce fruit. We will drink wine together and make merry, just as we once did,' he said. 'Like in the old times,' he promised, but having no wine saddened them nonetheless.

Two months passed, and in that time the *Chnan* managed to make good progress in learning the language of the inhabitants of that land. They did not fear him because he had no weapons and because he spoke as though they could understand him. When the weather started to improve and the days to lengthen, the *Chnan* knew more about those places and those people than all the Achaean warriors put together. One day, towards sunset, he asked to see the king. Diomedes was sitting on a stool in front of his hut watching the sun descend over the boughs of the trees which edged the horizon. The *Chnan* told him: 'King, I come from a land of journeyers; we are always encountering different peoples, and thus is it easier for us to learn their languages. But this does not mean that we are not fond of our own land; when I saw the ships burning I felt like dying at the thought that I would never again see my land and my city. But if you promise me that one day you will find me a ship and you will let me depart, I will serve you faithfully and tell you everything I manage to learn.'

'I give you my word as a king,' replied Diomedes. 'When we conquer a territory that faces the sea, I will find you a ship and you shall depart on it.'

'And will you allow Telephus, the Chetaean, to depart with me?'

'I had hoped that you would remain with us . . . I would have given you a wife, and a house. But if this is what you want, I will let you go. And you can take the Spartan with you as well. His only dream is to return.'

'I thank you and take you at your word,' said the *Chnan*. 'Do not be offended that we desire to go. We do not even know what we will find, whether our homes and families will still be there, whether our parents are still alive. The Chetaean commanded a squadron of war chariots and I a merchant fleet; all that unites us is our condition as foreigners and our desire to return, something that you no longer feel.'

'You are wrong. I shall never forget Argos and my nest of stone on the rock of Tiryns, but I would have to slaughter my own people in battle to return. This is why I have chosen to seek a new land . . .'

The *Chnan* fell silent for a while, sitting on the ground with his back against the wall of the hut, then began to speak: 'The chief of the city you want to conquer is called Nemro. He is a valiant man, beloved by his people. He has lost two brothers and his first wife.'

'Why are these people dying?' asked the king. 'Why are their cities empty?'

'No one knows. But they say it began when the strange lights appeared in the sky . . . and after the chariot of the Sun plunged into the swamp. If we remain here, I fear the same fate could befall us.'

The king held his tongue, thinking of what he had seen and imagined in the swamp, of the ghosts thronging his mind since that moment. He thought of the corpse of the man who had died sowing dragon's teeth, of the skeletons of the oxen who collapsed at their yoke, of the rams' heads impaled on stakes and burned. It was a sight he would never be able to forget.

'When we explored the first city, the one we found completely deserted, we beheld a horrible scene,' he said to the *Chnan.*

'I know. Your men have spoken of it often sitting around the fire in the evenings. It frightened them greatly . . .'

'What do you think? Have you talked to these people about it? What does it mean?'

The *Chnan* seemed startled by a sudden thought: 'Did you walk among those stakes?' he asked. 'The stakes with the rams' heads?'

Diomedes did not take his eyes off the sun that was settling into the mist on the horizon. 'Yes,' he replied without batting an eye.

'You shouldn't have! They say that—'

But the king interrupted him, as if the answer to his questions no longer interested him: 'The woman brought from far away . . . do you know who she is? Did she come as his bride?'

'She comes from the land beyond the Mountains of Ice and has journeyed through clouds and forests to come here. Nemro wants a son from her.'

The king lowered his head. He thought of the light, inviting glance of the girl who had come from the ends of the earth, and of the empty eye sockets and mocking grins of the rams' heads perched on the blackened stakes. What did destiny have in store for him? In his heart he envied the comrades who had fallen under the walls of Ilium. But perhaps that woman could restore his desire to live.

'I will attack that city and take that woman,' he said.

The sun had set and a diaphanous fog rose from the forest, covering all the earth. From the thick of the forest came the defiant bellows of the wild bulls readying for their springtime battles, but there were other voices as well, cries not human and perhaps not even animal, whimpers of creatures no longer alive, not yet dead. Shades, they must be.

The *Chnan* strained his ears as if trying to decipher those remote, bewildered cries. His features were drawn, his mouth twisted, his forehead moist.

'You will attack a dying people? You will snatch the woman, and the last hope, of a man who has done nothing to you? On what pretext?'

'No pretext,' said the king. 'A lion needs no pretext for killing a bull, and a wolf feels no remorse at slaughtering a ram. If I find a good reason for living, my people will find one as well. If I lose it there will be no hope for anyone.'

*

Myrsilus prepared the men and gave instructions for departure. He loaded the carts with whatever could be used to build shelters suitable for sustaining a siege, and all the food he could find. Very little remained to the inhabitants who still lived in the village, although their livestock would probably ensure their survival. The warriors offered no farewells, even though they had lived with that folk for many days, and when they walked off into the plain the people of the village crossed the moat and watched them in silence. Diomedes took a last look at them before mounting his horse; all old people, they were, with white hair and dead eyes. It was no life, what they were living.

The army proceeded in a column, the carts at the centre pulled by the oxen. They arrived within sight of Nemro's city just before dusk, and the king ordered his men to take position on the access paths and around the two wells where the inhabitants were accustomed to draw water. Others unloaded the carts and made makeshift shelters for the night by covering them with hides and cloths. Myrsilus planned to make fixed shelters using the wood from the forest if their siege was prolonged. If it could be called a siege: two hundred warriors around a wooden palisade, a muddy moat, an assembly of straw-and-mud huts. Where were the proud walls of Troy built by Poseidon? Where was Thebes of the Seven Gates? Where were the shining phalanxes, the tens of thousands of fully armoured warriors? Diomedes felt a stab of pain in his heart, and he turned his gaze towards the deserted plains to hide his confusion and the tremor in his eyelids. But it was just a moment; the force of his spirit was still intact. Before his men could stop him, he mounted his horse and galloped on alone straight to the access bridge. His horse's hooves pounded the wooden trunks and the sound filled the city walls. No one showed up to bar his way, no one stopped him from entering.

He advanced through the half-open door and looked around: the place seemed deserted. The doors of the houses were closed, the animals' pens were empty; there was total peace and silence in the wavering twilight. He abruptly heard an odd sound; a crackling, like something catching fire.

He pressed his horse on to the centre of the city, where the two main roads crossed. He turned to his right and then to his left, and his eyes filled with horror: twenty rams' heads stuck on sharp stakes were enveloped by flames. A sharp, repugnant odour, a dense, pungent smoke, filled the air. For a moment, he saw a figure wrapped in a cloak of black wool, who set fire with a torch to the last stake and vanished down a side road. Myrsilus's voice rang out behind him: 'Stop, *wanax*! It could be a trap! Wait until the other comrades arrive!' But the king, after a moment's hesitation, lunged forward on his horse and wove his way through the rams' heads. He caught up with the man before he could slip into one of the houses; he blocked him off and thrust his spear at his throat. It was a bony old man with deep, dark rings under his eyes; he backed up against the wall and waited without blinking for the bronze blade to pierce through his flesh. The king lowered his spear and got off his horse and when Myrsilus reached him, panting, he said: 'Call the *Chnan*. I want this man to answer my questions.'

Myrsilus obeyed, and ordered his men to search the city house by house to flush out whoever was hiding there.

'Who are you?' asked the *Chnan* when he arrived.

'Your chief is dead,' answered the old man. 'His head will burn like these!'

'Our chief has already passed between the severed heads and he is still alive, as you can see.'

The man glanced furtively at Diomedes, and then glared at his questioner: 'You lie. It is impossible.'

'He is a great hero who has destroyed two immense cities enclosed in stone walls. He saw the place where the chariot of the Sun fell and he spent the night there.' The old man's eyes widened until they showed white all around, and his chin began to quiver. The words of the *Chnan* had filled him with dread.

'Tell him I'll drag him to the swamp where the chariot of the Sun fell,' said Diomedes, when he realized the cause of the man's terror. 'I'll tie him to a tree and leave him there to go mad.'

The old man shook his head, then flung himself to the ground with his face in the dirt. His body trembled uncontrollably. The *Chnan* helped him to his feet and tried to calm him. He promised that he would be allowed to go free if he told them where the others had gone.

'They are safe by now,' said the old man. 'You will never catch up with them. Tomorrow they will cross the river and march towards the Great Lake of the Ancestors at the foot of the Mountains of Ice. There they will immerse themselves in the clear, pure waters to free themselves of the curse which brings death. They will build houses on the water that can not be touched by any sorcery. Our people will be reborn.'

Diomedes realized that Nemro was directed north, towards the shores of Eridanus. If they managed to cross the river, he would never see that woman again.

He called Myrsilus and ordered him to harness the horses to

his war chariot. He told his comrades to hold the old man until he returned, then leapt into the chariot and passed the reins to Myrsilus. They rode to the north side of the city where they found evident traces of the migration. The king then urged on his horses like he had long ago on the plains of Ilium. He let out a long, high, warbling cry; the steeds pawed the ground and reared up, shaking the yoke, then hurled forward on the dirt trail, raising a cloud of dust. Myrsilus let out the reins at their necks and the divine animals picked up their pace, neck to neck, head to head, in a riot of shining muscles, manes billowing in the wind. The king was silent now. His right hand gripped the rail and his left the spear. The low sun cast a blazing reflection on his face and hair.

The chariot flew over the deserted trail in the last dim light of the sun and Myrsilus managed to keep up a steady gait until it was almost completely dark, accustoming his eyes to distinguish between the pale dust and the green fields. He was forced to slow down when the last reflection of light vanished, but just then the king pointed to a distant point: 'Look,' he said. 'It must be them. Don't stop, we'll be upon them when they least suspect it.'

They saw lights in the middle of the plain, reflected like a mirror: the waters of the Eridanus! Dark figures were moving all around the fires. Myrsilus slowed the horses to a walk and continued to approach until, under the cover of darkness, they could see what was happening in the camp before them. The people were on their feet in a circle around several large fires. At their centre stood Nemro, wearing his armour and a cloak of dark wool. Facing him was the blonde maiden who had come from afar, her head covered in white bands that fell softly around her neck. They were about to celebrate their wedding.

A long-bearded old man held their hands, and an attendant poured white flour on their heads and milk at their feet.

Diomedes saw in an instant where his chariot would be able to slip in and how it could curve away in escape; he explained the manoeuvre to Myrsilus who nodded, clenching his jaw and twisting the reins around his wrists.

'Now!' shouted the king.

Myrsilus incited the horses and cracked the reins across their backs repeatedly. The steeds raced forward, directed at the only point of light in all that darkness. Their neighing and furious galloping, the thunder of the wheels and the shouts of the two warriors, threw the onlookers into a total panic, but Nemro turned and understood. He grabbed a spear and hurled it at the chariot that was advancing straight at him like a meteor. The point ripped through the shoulder of Myrsilus's tunic; he had done nothing to dodge the blow. Nemro was forced to throw himself sideways, losing his grip on the hand of his bride, who stood petrified staring at the warrior on the chariot which was flying directly at her. The hand of Diomedes passed under her arm and lifted her as if she were a twig, over the red-hot rim of the chariot wheel; he delivered her gently inside like a dove in its nest. He stretched his left arm around her waist, clasping the parapet with his other hand. Myrsilus in the meantime was racing through the camp without so much as a backwards look; he curved near the bank of the river before hitting the sand that would have hindered his flight and urged on the divine horses once again with shrill cries until they reached the open plain.

He wheeled full around the camp and hurled back towards the point from which he had launched his attack.

Nemro had got to his feet in a fury and assembled all his men but Diomedes caught him off guard again by bursting through at the same point, where the men were now grouped around their chief. One was hit straight on and trampled under the horses' hooves, while two more were maimed under the chariot wheels. Nemro himself was struck at his side by the left horse and thrown to the ground in a daze.

Then the chariot of bronze and fire disappeared into the night.

*

For three days, the woman refused to eat or sleep. She lay curled up on her mat with her knees drawn up and her hair completely covering her face. Sometimes towards evening she would let out a melancholy, quavering song like a lullaby crooned to rock a child to sleep. It seemed to be her way of soothing herself, of relieving her pain. She was rapidly wasting away; her face thinned and seemed even tinier than it was in reality. When she lifted her eyes they were puffy and red with tears.

'Perhaps she loved him,' said the *Chnan* to Diomedes. 'Nemro was to be her husband, after all.'

'She had never seen him before, I'm sure of it. Her family had sent her from a distant land, how could she have loved him?'

'Maybe you left her too long with him: just a few days can be enough to win a woman's heart, especially if she knows that the man she has been given to will be her husband for the rest of her life.'

'Do you think she knows the language of the people of this land? There must be some ties between her people and these people if she was sent as a bride to a chief of this land. Perhaps she knows a few words . . . You could try to talk with her.'

The *Chnan* shook his head. 'One deaf person speaking to another: how could we understand each other? My knowledge of this language is so scarce; hers must be even less. She probably doesn't know more than a few words, if any at all. Perhaps a caress would count more than any word. She's only a frightened girl. She doesn't know who you are, what you want from her. She is almost certainly a virgin, never touched by man.'

'No one has harmed her! We have offered her food, a bed, we share with her what little we have.'

'She's afraid. She won't eat because she fears you.'

'I don't understand,' said the king.

'It's her only defence. By not eating, she'll become ugly and thin, and you will no longer desire her. Perhaps, if you made her understand that you don't want to hurt her . . .'

'You know many things, man of *Chnan*, things that I do not know . . . or have never wanted to learn. I've been taught that all that matters in life is the honour and the glory that a man conquers in battle. Perhaps this is why I lost Aigialeia, my queen. Or perhaps it was Aphrodite's revenge.'

'We call her Isthar,' said the *Chnan*. 'And she can be a terrible goddess indeed. What did you do to anger her?'

'I wounded her in battle, as she stretched out her delicate hand to shield her son who had fallen to the ground under my blows. Since then I have feared her revenge. The gods never forget. They can strike us whenever they want, in the most atrocious of ways. If the worst thing in the world for a man is to fall into the hands of another man, can you imagine what it means to fall into the hands of a god who hates you?'

'But perhaps there is also a god who loves you. Or a goddess; you are a king and you are handsome and strong.'

'The goddess who loved me has abandoned me. I haven't seen her for a very long time, I haven't felt her presence . . . We are a cursed race: my father Tydeus devoured the brain of a man while it was still warm. But I admire him all the same. The greatest courage in life is embracing it all until the bitter end, until the last horror, if necessary . . .'

The *Chnan* lowered his head and held his tongue. The king's gaze was fixed on the sky, covered with black clouds frayed with white towards the bottom, towards the earth. A cold, damp wind penetrated their bones and shook the fragile walls of the reed and clay houses in the little dying city. The *Chnan* bounded across the road and entered the hut he had chosen as his dwelling.

The wind had begun to blow stronger and thunder exploded in the sky directly above the village, making the ground tremble. The rain pelted down, streaming over the road. The king had never felt time flowing away from him like this: fast, unstoppable, like the muddy water spilling into the moat from a thousand streams. He went out into the tempest that swept the village with its biting gusts of wind. The rain poured over his face and his chest and dripped down his back; his feet sank into the mud up to his ankles. He stood, head bent, in the downpour as if to purify himself, and then he went to the hut where Nemro's woman was being held.

Two of his warriors stood guard, motionless, one in front and one in the back of the house, sheltering as they could under the overhanging roof. They were faithful, patient men, capable of enduring anything. Seeing them like that, immobile in the wind and water, in that wretched place, he felt compassion for them; he felt stronger and sharper than ever the desire to give them a life and a land, to give them women and herds of oxen and fat sheep. He ordered them to go and find a warm fire and some food. They obeyed with a nod, pulling their cloaks over their heads and running off. The king entered.

It was dark inside: a single earthenware lamp was smoking, burning sheep's fat. In the corner was the food that had been brought to her and that she had refused to touch, left to be gnawed at by the mice. This was his wedding chamber? The perfumes and the scents? The wedding torches? He couldn't even see the girl until his eyes had become accustomed to the gloom. And when he did see her his soul filled with despair: she was scrawny and pale and he could barely see her face behind a tangle of dirty hair. She startled at his entry, and began to whimper softly. Then she backed away, creeping, into a corner and hid her face.

Diomedes took off his cloak and began to approach her, but when he saw her shaking in fear, he stopped in the middle of the bare room. He brought his lamp close to his face: 'Look at me,' he said, 'I need you too.'

At the sound of his voice, the girl turned slowly and the king could see her bewildered eyes, the pale flicker of her gaze. But he also perceived, greatly wounded and broken, that remarkable, ambiguous force of spirit that had struck him the first time he saw her.

The fire in the hearth had gone out; Diomedes put a little wood on top and lit it with his lamp. The flames licked up while outside the rain pelted down even harder.

'I don't want to hurt you,' he said, adding more wood to the fire. 'I won't hurt you,' and he held his head low as if he, too, suffered from the same desolation as she.

The girl seemed to revive and moved slightly away from the wall.

'Come closer,' said the king. 'Come warm yourself by the fire. Come; don't be afraid.'

The girl raised her head and looked at him. Then she got to her feet and walked slowly towards the fire. She was trembling, and her step was uncertain after fasting for so long. She stumbled, but Diomedes, who had not taken his eyes off her, caught her in his arms before she could fall. He set her gently next to the fire, then removed his own wet clothing and took her delicately into his arms. She stirred and the king opened his arms so she could go. If she wanted to.

She didn't go, and the king held her without speaking, listening together with her to the sound of the rain on the straw roof.

Time passed, so long that it stopped raining and the sun began to shine through the cracks in the door. The *Chnan*'s voice could be heard, saying: 'The men have made bread, *wanax*.' And the little hut was invaded by a ray of light and an intense aroma. The king got up, went to the door and took the bread, then went back to the girl and offered her a little piece. She opened her lips and ate it while the king lightly stroked her hair. He took some bread himself and ate it while looking into her eyes, without moving his other hand from her head. And in that moment, the beam of sun that entered through the door lit up his hair from behind, bathing it in blond light, like a god's. He gave her more bread and she ate from his hand and accepted his caresses.

*

It didn't take long for Nemro to learn where his enemy was hiding. The weather was bad and the incessant rain had wiped away the traces of Diomedes's chariot and horses, but as soon as he could, Nemro had sent his men to search the land far and wide.

A group of them encountered the old priest who they had left behind when they had set off for the Lake of the Ancestors, to officiate the rite of the severed heads in the deserted city. He was wandering through the countryside with a satchel at his neck; he did not even seem to recognize them.

'It is us, Oh Man of the Sun and of the Rain,' they said. 'Stop! We seek the blond foreigner who flies on a chariot. He has abducted the bride of Nemro and has kept her for himself. Without her, Nemro cannot guide his people to the Lake of the Ancestors and build a city on the water. She is our only hope; her blood is not contaminated by the Sun of the Swamp.'

The old man blinked repeatedly as if a violent light were wounding his eyes: 'He has passed twice among the burnt heads and he is still alive,' he said. 'His flesh is harder than your bones. And he has spoken with the Sun of the Swamp: I saw it in his eyes. How can Nemro hope to combat him and win?'

'You leave us no hope, then. But at least tell us where he is; we will do anything we can to have Nemro's bride back. We fear nothing any more in this world.'

The old man pointed south towards the horizon and then set off again with his slow, shuffling step in the other direction. They would never see him again.

That evening they reached the city occupied by the invaders, and they slipped in during the night. They watched them from their hiding places for days and days. They watched the men train with their weapons, hurling their spears and shooting their bows, wielding sword and axe. They watched them fight each other, and stand guard at night with fine weather or with rain. They realized that their own forces could never defeat such warriors.

When they returned to report to Nemro, he listened to them in silence without a blink of his eye, then withdrew to his tent where he remained at length. He finally came out and assembled his men. He said: 'We cannot go to the Lake of the Ancestors without my bride and we cannot fight our enemies alone; they are too strong and too fierce. We need help, and we will find it in all the surviving villages and among the other peoples. We shall ask the *Kmun* of the Mountains of Ice and the *Ambron* of the Mountains of Stone. We will tell them what has happened, and they will tell the other peoples who live near them: the *Pica* and the *Ombro*. We will say that the foreigners of the flaming hair have come to kill us and carry off our women . . . that they have come to steal everything from us, even our hope. They will help us, and our enemies will find ambushes in every forest, traps in every valley. The water they drink will turn to poison, every birdsong or animal call will hide a signal for attack. They will die, one after another . . . as we have been dying until now.'

Nemro lowered his head with a sigh and said: 'Whoever survives, of the two of us, will have the bride for himself and will generate a new people with her. If I am the one who remains alive, I will take you to the Lake of the Ancestors, at the foot of the Mountains of Ice whence our forebears came. If it is he, the man who flies on the fire chariot . . . if it is he who remains alive on the battlefield, then his seed will generate a new race of exterminators and there will no longer be any room for anyone else in this land . . . for no one, between the mountains and the sea. We must destroy him, because he, perhaps, has come from the Sun of the Swamp himself! Perhaps he is the last and most terrible calamity.'

Nemro's men took his message to the *Kmun* on the Mountains of Ice and the *Ambron* on the Mountains of Stone, and these warned their neighbours, the *Pica* and the *Ombro*, and these in turn told the *Lat* who had settled at that time in the plains of the western sea. Whatever path the invaders chose, they would find it fraught with mortal danger.

*

Meanwhile, the Man of the Sun and the Rain, the old priest, continued his solitary journey towards the place where none of his people had ever dared to venture. He knew that his energy would not suffice to follow Nemro in his quest for survival, but he thought that perhaps enough remained to discover where the poisonous seed of death had come from, when it fell from the sky like a globe of fire and sank its roots in to the swamp.

Although it was already late in the spring, it continued to rain hard and long every day. But he never stopped; he walked all the same through the tall grass and reeds that had overrun the fields once flourishing with crops and rich pastures for numerous flocks.

He would rest now and then in a deserted village or an abandoned house when the inclemency of the elements prevented him from going on. And then he would take up his journey once again.

After seven days he reached the swamp where the seed of destruction had fallen. He was exhausted with fatigue, hunger and pain; his hands and feet were full of sores, his legs attacked by leeches. And yet he thought he heard the gentlest dirge, like the soft wailing of women grieving for their lost husbands. He followed that song, dragging himself to the shores of a large pool with a surface as smooth as a bronze mirror.

He leaned over to peer inside and saw his own image reflected in the shiny black water, nothing else. Only his own thin, dazed face. He moved all around the liquid mirror, forcing a passage between the thick reeds, the willows and millet stalks.

The wind rustled in the boughs of colossal poplars, filling the air with their white down, but not a bird took wing, not a chirp could be heard, nothing but the ancient lament that still echoed very faintly in the misty undergrowth.

Utterly disheartened and defeated, the old priest let himself slip to the ground and sat propped up against a big trunk, uprooted like a little twig by some immense force. He had hoped not to abandon life before learning the truth, but now he felt his energies forsaking him on the shores of that dead water, although nothing had happened. No vague idea had formed in his mind, no sign had appeared before his eyes. His weariness weighed so heavily upon his eyelids that sleep finally overcame him and he sank back, head lolling and arms outspread. In his uneasy sleep he saw the deserted cities of his people crumbling into ruins, one after another; the canals filling with reeds, the palisades rotting away, swarms of rats invading the roads. A turbid grey sky covered all, swollen with disease. His closed eyes filled with tears and his heart brimmed with anguish.

But then he saw the black lagoon fill slowly up with mud and sand, becoming a swamp, first, and then a marsh, until it became solid ground and was covered by a forest of aged oaks. And over that land he saw that the sky was blue again, and the sun shone, and a new people descended from the wooded mountains to occupy the deserted plain. Many, many years . . . but one day life would flourish again in the great valley of the Eridanus; the newcomers would mix with the last descendants of his unlucky people.

He saw men tilling the earth, digging canals and building cabins. Ripe wheat rippled in the summer sun and exuberant grapevines stretched their cluster-heavy shoots towards the sun.

He did not see the warrior of the flaming hair who had passed twice between the severed heads without harm, but he felt his shadow vanishing beyond the wooded mountains, beyond the blue summits.

The old man never stirred again, and the wind covered his wasted body with white down, like a larva in its cocoon. But his spirit was soaring with great butterfly wings over the sea of swaying reeds, over the waters of the Eridanus, high above the swollen grey clouds, through the pure, transparent air, towards the infinite light.

9

Diomedes advanced westward with his warriors, journeying up a muddy little river in the hopes of finding more welcoming lands and less hostile skies, but as soon as he had left his refuge and ventured on to open land, he immediately felt the presence of a hidden enemy who seemed to be everywhere.

By day the men would hear distant sounds, like animal cries, in the midst of the plain or the deep of the forests. By night, fleet, faint shadows passed in the glimmer of the moon; shapes, similar to beasts or fantastic birds, appeared out of nowhere before the sentinels who stood watch in the darkness, only to vanish like the creatures of a dream.

Telephus, the Hittite slave, warned everyone to stay alert; to take care not to be lured away from the camp or guard post. He said that he wouldn't be provoked by a shadow; crossing swords was the only way to challenge him. No flimsy shade could frighten him; he had never heard of anyone being killed by an apparition or a ghost. Only a good span of bronze or iron would do that job.

'You don't believe in invisible creatures and gods, then?' the *Chnan* asked him one evening as they were roasting a wild pig they had snared in a trap.

'I believe in the gods of my land when I am there, but here . . . who could ever desire to live in a place like this? There can be nothing but the spirits of animals or of trees here; nothing that can worry us. Stay within call and within reach, always, and no harm can come to you. I commanded a chariot squadron in the Hittite army, but I've had to patrol the mountains and forest of Toros and Katpatuka on foot, as well. Those places are crawling with fierce, treacherous savages. We simply watched each others' backs; no one ever went out alone to look for water or forage for the pack animals.'

As he was saying this a shrill sound whistled through the air and one of the sentinels on guard at a short distance collapsed with a sigh, run through by an arrow. The king was notified immediately, and he rode out on horseback with fifty armed men to encircle the area the arrow had come from, but the darkness and the rough terrain protected the aggressors. They never found a trace of them, as if they had never existed.

The king returned to the camp in the middle of the night, full of impotent rage, and stopped beside the dying warrior: his name was Hippotous, from Lerna. He had been only sixteen when they left for the war. His father Phaillus had been among Tydeus's most faithful friends and Diomedes had always loved him like a younger brother. His comrades had brought him close to the fire, and the *Chnan* was wetting his lips with a linen cloth. He was delirious.

'They're attacking!' he would shout out, trembling and trying to lift up on his elbows. 'Deiphobus and Aeneas, on the right! Beware, *wanax*! Watch your left side! The Maeonian chariots are upon us, those cursed bastard dogs . . .'

The king knelt beside him and placed a hand on his burning forehead. The *Chnan* had managed to cut the arrow shaft with a knife blade, but he had not been able to extract the tip.

'Rest now, my friend. The enemy has been routed. They've taken to their heels.'

'Really, *wanax*? And what will I have? What spoils will be mine?'

'A pair of horses: two superb sorrels, still be to broken in,' said the king, stroking him tenderly. 'A helmet; it's beautiful, decorated in silver and . . . two spears . . .'

But the god of eternal sleep opened the youth's eyes for an instant and he saw the truth in his king's mournful gaze. 'I'm dying . . . *wanax*. To no purpose.'

His head dropped back and his still eyes were filled with death.

The fire was going out, and its bluish reflection made the pallor of his forehead look like marble. The king bit his lip and wept.

*

After that night, Diomedes tried to be even more prudent; he would send Myrsilus forward with a small group of his fastest men: Evenus, Agelaus, Krissus and even Lamus the Spartan, son of Onchestus. After long days of bewilderment, Lamus had finally recovered his spirit and determination. He seemed to feel that any moment in which the column was not moving was a waste. He was never ready to stop in the evening, and in the morning he was the first to awaken and to stir up the fire.

At their sides, the king posted two small squads of Argive warriors from his personal guard. He himself marched in front of the main body of the column and posted a small rear guard behind, at a good distance. His wooden chest was at the centre of the column on a little cart pulled by a couple of mules. Alongside the chest, sitting on a bench and protected by a shelter of intertwined wicker, was the bride come from beyond the Mountains of Ice. She was as yet untouched by man.

But even in this way, Diomedes continued to suffer losses: clusters of arrows would suddenly fall from the sky like hail, although the men could not understand where they were coming from. Or the earth would open beneath their feet, plunging the warriors into pits studded with sharp spikes which pierced them through like fish that a sharp-eyed fisherman runs through with his harpoon. Sometimes, as they slept, their entire camp was inundated with water, so that they had to abandon their sleeping mats, gather up the supplies and run to repel the danger that loomed in the shadows, spending nights awake, eyes stinging with fatigue, bowels gripped by cramps.

The king always showed his men the same dauntless expression, the same imperious gaze, but those who were closest to him, Myrsilus and even the *Chnan*, often saw the muscles of his face quivering uncontrollably under his skin, his eyes blinking rapidly and a light sweat beading his forehead, whether it was hot or cold. The king was suffering and his pain worsened with every passing day.

The bride would raise her head, sometimes, and the king exchanged glances with her, but that contact gave him no comfort or warmth. Her eyes were like a cold springtime sky, continually crossed by light and shadow, cloudy and clear practically at the same moment. The king could not speak to her. He tried, sometimes, in the intimacy that at night his men left to him in respect of his rank and because of their fondness for him, but he obtained no response. But the *Chnan* noticed that when Diomedes seemed most alone and despairing, when it seemed that fate and events did naught but torment him, then, it seemed to the *Chnan*, then her eyes would flicker a look like a furtive caress.

And the *Chnan* would notice that the king would suddenly turn his head then, as if someone had touched him.

'All they want is the girl,' said Telephus, the Hittite, one night. 'If we let her go, this persecution will stop. We can no longer bear up under this strain. If we go on like this, we will all die. Someone has to tell him,' he said, nodding towards the king, who was standing alone near his horses. 'We've been marching for days and days and we've never seen their faces, but they are murdering us. How many men have we lost? Ten, maybe fifteen, I've lost count. And how many of them have we killed? Not one. They're different; they will never agree to face us on the open field, phalanx against phalanx. They don't think there is anything shameful or wrong about attacking us in secret, at night.'

'You don't think he already knows?' replied the *Chnan*, indicating the king as he advanced through the mud, leading the horses by their reins. 'They say that he once wounded a god in battle, but here there is no one to cross swords with, not even a savage or a shepherd . . .'

'Why is he doing it then? I know he is a generous man. How could he sacrifice his people this way?'

The *Chnan* walked at length without answering. In the distance was a low line of bluish mountains.

'See those mountains? Perhaps that is where this accursed land ends. The king believes that if we manage to leave this place, we'll finally be able to build a city and raise a temple. He thinks we will be invincible then, and that this girl will give him sons, and a dynasty. And that he'll get other women for his warriors; that's what he's thinking. He knows there is no alternative. We can't turn back, and facing the enemy is impossible. We have no choice but to go onwards . . . hoping that some of us remain, in the end.'

'But why won't he give back the woman? He'll find other women, more beautiful ones.'

'He wants this one. If she was sent to regenerate the tribe of Nemro, she must bear a great life force within her. This is what he thinks. And perhaps he loves her. Have you seen how he looks at her?'

'I have. But we will all die, this I know. Those mountains are still too far away; how many of us will fall before we get there?'

The column had stopped because Myrsilus had found a dry clearing, a large grassy knoll protected on one side by a group of ash and oak trees, just turning green with new leaves, and on the other by a torrent that edged it on three sides like the ocean around a peninsula. Gigantic clouds were gathering over the mountain peaks, shot through by blazing bolts of lightning.

'We must inflict heavy losses on them,' said the *Chnan*, 'and convince them to withdraw.'

'Or resolve it by fighting a duel,' said Telephus.

The *Chnan* watched the big storm clouds clustering over the mountains: 'The west wind is pushing them this way,' he said. 'They'll be here right after dark.'

'Yes. And the rain as well.'

'There will be lightning; these tall trees may very well attract the bolts.'

'Do you mean to say we should camp elsewhere?'

'On the contrary. Perhaps they'll attack tonight, and we may manage to wipe them out, or at least to strike out hard. If the storms in this land move like the sea . . . and if the king will listen to me . . .'

As he moved off the surrounding forests began to echo with calls, like animal cries.

The *Chnan* went to the king: 'Your men say you have armour of gold.'

'They have told you the truth,' said Diomedes without turning.

'Is the shield made of gold too?'

'Yes, the shield as well.'

'Give it to me. If these cries from the forest are not night birds, as I don't imagine they are, they will attack again tonight.'

'Invisible and unfindable, as always.'

'Not any more, *wanax*. Give me a man who can help me light a fire on the highest part of the hill. Telephus, the Chetaean, will do. And give me your shield, enclosed in its case. The storm will be here soon, just as darkness falls. Sit down and eat now. Rest and gather your forces because I will soon make your enemies visible. Order the archers to draw up and to be ready with their bows, for they will have to aim and shoot as swiftly as the blink of an eye. Order your warriors to remain in their armour and to keep their hands on the shafts of their spears.'

The king gave him the shield and the *Chnan* went off with Telephus towards the top of the hill. Telephus held a burning firebrand, which he used to set a fire as soon as they had arrived. The men below lit fires as well and began to eat. The king ate, and offered some of his food to the girl. The storm was drawing nearer and the clouds galloped through the sky above the camp.

The Hittite appeared just then. 'Oh king,' he said. 'Rally your men. The storm is rushing towards us, and if the enemies attack, the *Chnan* will show you where they are, but only for a brief moment.'

'That will be enough,' said the king. He put on his helmet and fastened his cuirass.

The wind had picked up and was stoking the fires in camp and on the hilltop. Diomedes called his men and had them take position behind a group of trees facing the forest. He told them to stay ready, although he knew not what to expect. Suddenly, a blinding light flashed, immediately followed by the roar of thunder, and in that instant the king saw the enemy advancing in open order across the plain, towards the hill. The *Chnan* saw them as well, and he turned the golden shield so that it would project the light of the large fire that Telephus had built upon them, as he continued to feed it with all the wood he could lay his hands on.

'Now, *wanax*!' shouted the *Chnan*, and Diomedes rushed forth, followed by his men. The enemies had stopped for a moment, stunned by the thunder and blinded by the lightning, but the light of the fire reflected off the golden shield of the king made them visible; shadowy, but distinguishable. It was enough. The Achaeans fanned out as they ran down the hill at great speed. Diomedes burst into the midst of his enemies, and his shout was more terrible that the roar of the thunder. He ran one man through with his spear and brought down the next ones with his dagger and sword. The javelins of Myrsilus, to the far left, hit their marks one after another. Taken by surprise for the first time, the assailants were bewildered, uncertain whether to continue fighting or to flee, and in that uncertainty the hard blows of the Achaeans rained down, enraged as they were and eager for revenge.

It began just then to pour, and the bursts of heavy rain dampened the fires and extinguished them almost completely in just a few moments. The light of the golden shield went out as well and the battle ceased. Myrsilus took a burning brand and examined the dead, trying to recognize Nemro, but found no trace of him.

They took shelter under their tents and waited for the rain to stop so they could continue their search. Quite some time passed before the sky cleared, revealing the stars and the full moon that was just rising over the crests of the Blue Mountains.

The king scanned the fields to see if the dead were still there, and as the pale light of the moon freed itself of the mists of the storm, he saw a still, erect shadow among the lifeless bodies of the fallen. He was tall and powerful, and gripped a long narrow sword. It was Nemro!

At a certain distance behind him, his men were lined up at the edge of the forest, their hands on the hilts of their swords. The *Chnan* approached the king and said: 'It has happened sooner than I could have hoped: he is challenging you to single combat. Kill him, and we'll no longer have these sneaking demons hounding us.'

Myrsilus stepped forward: 'Oh *wanax*, that savage who has hidden in the shadows until now is not worthy to cross swords with the king of Argos. You rest and watch: I'll go.'

The king looked back and he saw the blonde bride standing behind him, staring at the plains beyond him. She was looking at Nemro.

'No,' said the king. 'I must fight him. Have the armour of Ilium brought to me.'

Myrsilus obeyed and Diomedes was brought the armour that he had worn when he fought the sons of Priam between the Scamander and the Simois. He threw the leather cuirass he had donned for the night raid on to the ground, and covered himself with bronze. He slung on his shield and grasped the enormous ashwood spear. He tightened the baldric adorned with golden studs and stretched his right hand out towards his attendant to receive his sword.

'The *Pakana*,' said Myrsilus. And the attendant handed him the heavy sword, its silver hilt set with a piece of amber embossed with the figure of a lion chasing a roebuck, crafted by Traseus.

The king hung it from his baldric and adjusted it on his side. Before donning the helmet, he turned to the bride and said: 'I am facing death for you. Do not disdain me in your heart.' He descended the slope with slow heavy steps until he was facing his adversary. The Achaean warriors, who had received no orders, all drew up into three long rows on the hillside, holding their shields and grasping their swords. When the king grasped his own and began to brandish it, looking for a gap in his enemy's defences, they shouted: 'ARGOS!'

Nemro's warriors shouted out something as well, but no one understood except the *Chnan*, whose eyes welled with tears in the darkness.

They had yelled out: 'LIFE!'

Diomedes observed him carefully, exploring every detail of the gigantic figure. He wore a conical bronze helmet and a great shield which protected him from his chin to his knees. He gripped a javelin and a long sword hung at his side. He was readying for the battle as well, weighing the javelin to balance it before striking. The air had become much colder than the earth after the storm, and a light mist crept through the grass and covered the field until it lapped at the foot of the hill where the Achaean warriors were lined up. The combatants, under the glow of the moon, were waist deep in it now. Nemro swiftly hurled the javelin, aiming at his enemy's forehead, but Diomedes saw the blow coming and raised his shield. The weapon penetrated the rim and its point stopped just a palm from his face, although the hero's eyes never so much as blinked.

A roar arose from the edge of the clearing. Diomedes dislodged the javelin from his shield by knocking it against the trunk of a tree, and he resumed his impenetrable stance. Nemro made to unsheathe his sword but just as he was lowering his arm to his belt, his shoulder was bared. Diomedes threw his spear, which ripped into his enemy's shoulder-plate and lacerated his flesh. Blood gushed down the warrior's arm but the blow had not severed his tendon; the muscle was intact, and he lunged forward, brandishing his sword.

The utter silence of the little valley was rent by the din of hand-to-hand combat. The clang of bronze striking, suffocated cries, jagged breath. The two men faced off in fierce, incessant fighting, without a moment of respite.

Diomedes suddenly delivered an unexpected blow from above, surprising Nemro's arm in an awkward position; the warrior lost his sword. Diomedes reacted swiftly, forcing back his unarmed opponent. Nemro turned and began to run, then stopped all at once and grabbed a tree trunk which was lying on the ground. He wheeled around and thrust it out like a battering ram towards his enemy, still in swift pursuit. As his men raised a cry of fear and surprise, Nemro charged forth holding the trunk in both hands and hit the running Diomedes full in the chest, knocking him to the ground. Cheers of joy came from the edge of the forest, while the rows of Achaeans on high seemed to dissolve like shadows in the fog which rose towards the summit.

Nemro dropped the trunk and picked up a boulder emerging from the grass. He stood above his fallen enemy, raised the rock high above his head and crashed it down upon him with all his might. But Diomedes had come to his senses; he twisted his torso and dealt a deep upward thrust with his sword. The boulder fell at his side without harming him as Nemro dropped to his knees, holding both hands to his wound. Gritting his teeth, he wrenched the sword from his ribs and lunged forward to strike his enemy with the blade red with his own blood, but his strength abandoned him and he collapsed, dying.

Diomedes rose to his feet and took off his helmet. Nemro raised a hand towards him and said something that the king could not understand, but the tone of that hoarse, sorrowful voice penetrated deep into his soul. He knelt over him, and when he had breathed his last, Diomedes closed his eyes.

He did not strip him of his armour as was his right. He picked up the spear and returned to his own men, who awaited him in silence, drawn up, unmoving, on the hillside. As he advanced through the tall, damp grass he heard a song rise up behind him and he shuddered. It was the same lament he had heard in the swamp at the mouth of the Eridanus; an inconsolable weeping, an endless sighing. The voice of a dying people. He turned slowly towards the forest and in the moonlight he saw a group of men approaching the lifeless body of the fallen giant. They gathered him up gently and carried him in their arms to the torrent. They washed away his blood and sweat, recomposed his limbs and adjusted his weapons, before covering him with a cloak. They fashioned a stretcher out of supple hazelnut branches where they laid him and stood vigil over him all night.

At the break of dawn they began walking. Diomedes stood on the hill and watched as they made their way with a slow step carrying the rough litter of their fallen king.

They soon disappeared from sight, but for a long time the funeral dirge could still be heard over the whole breadth of the plain, drifting towards the horizon, still oppressed by large black clouds.

They walked, stopping neither by day nor by night, until they reached the shores of the Eridanus and then beyond, until they reached the place where the rest of their people were camped. From there they proceeded to the Lake of the Ancestors, guided by the elders who had always known the way. When they reached its shores they laid Nemro's body in a hollowed log and pushed him into the deep, in keeping with the ancient rite of their fathers. The Great Waters welcomed the son who had returned after so long a time and rocked him at length in the sun and wind before burying him in the liquid darkness of the abyss.

*

Diomedes resumed the march towards the Blue Mountains with a heavy heart. Victory had given him no joy, and the land they were passing offered no place suitable for founding a city. They saw more square villages surrounded by moats and cultivated fields, but they were naught but islands in a sea of wild nature that had taken possession of all the territory. Many of the villages appeared to be deserted, as if the inhabitants had left, taking their things with them.

Boundless cane groves marked the slow snaking of the water over the earth. It seemed that a number of frightful floods had devastated the work of men, and that immense, prolonged fatigue had finally crushed the will of the village communities to withstand the constant onslaught of the elements. Everywhere they found signs of work begun and abandoned half-way: embankments, dams, canals . . .

The weather had begun to change and the high sun warmed the air and the earth. At first this brought welcome relief, but then the heat became intolerable because the water that flowed on the ground mixed with the air and produced a sense of suffocation and oppression. Only towards evening was there any respite.

The land seemed to change; the sun setting behind the Blue Mountains enflamed the clouds in the sky and set alight the marshy expanses at their feet. The water glittered between the canes like molten gold and the wind rose to bend the grass on the plains and rustle the green foliage of the oak and ash trees. The poplars shivered silver at every breath of the wind and the new leaves of the beeches shone like polished copper. At the edges of the forests grazed great horned deer and does with their newly born young. Packs of boars snuffled under aged oaks, and the sows called to their striped-back little ones with soft, continuous grunts. Sometimes, in the thick of the wood, they would glimpse the shiny pelt of a huge bear.

When darkness fell, an incessant choir of frogs would rise from the waters, joined by the chirping of crickets in the meadows and the solitary warbling of the nightingale in the forest. At that hour, the king would go down towards a nearby river or stream to bathe; he would throw his chlamys over his shoulders and remain in silence to contemplate the evening. Memories would overwhelm him then, of the furious battles fought under the walls of the city of Priam. His companions: Achilles, Sthenelus, Ulysses, Ajax . . . all dead . . . or lost. How he would have liked to sit with them and speak of the toils of the day, drinking wine and eating roasted meat . . .

For many years he had desired to return to the peace of his home and the love of his bride and now, incredibly, he regretted that the war had ever finished. Not the blind clashes he'd had in this land, but the loyal combat of the past, where two phalanxes would draw up in broad daylight on the open field, front to front. And where the gods could clearly choose whose side they were on, where a man could show what he was worth. He remembered the blinding glare of bronze, the din of the combat chariots launched in unrestrained attack against the barrier of the enemy infantry. He recalled deep sleep under his tent, and endless torpor. And he remembered how continuous familiarity with death made him appreciate enormously every aspect of life, no matter how humble or poor.

Now, for the first time in all his life, he was afraid. He was afraid of seeing his men die one by one, snared like animals in traps, betrayed at night, surprised in the shadows. He was afraid that he was marching, at the cost of great sacrifice and exhausting strain, towards nothing. This uninhabited wasteland was no land at all; it was a limitless, boundless magma that had already annihilated the people who had tried to settle it.

The bride who had come from the Mountains of Ice began to understand the language of the Achaeans, because Telephus and the *Chnan* spoke to her often and dedicated great attention to her, but she never spoke, never asked for anything and never even smiled, for she knew in her heart that she would never again see her land or her family.

One evening they camped along the river, which had become much more lovely and clear. The water ran sparkling over smooth pebbles and gravel of myriad colours. Long tongues of fine sand stretched into the bends, edged by little tufts of wicker which bowed in the evening breeze until they touched the current.

The girl descended towards a grove of willow trees, took off her clothing and walked into the water. It was still cold with the melting snow of the Blue Mountains, but very pleasant because it reminded her of the rivers in her native land. She let herself be carried by the current, she rolled and dipped, diving in where it was deepest until she could touch the sands at the bottom. She would turn on to her back and then on to her stomach, letting the water caress her hair.

When she got to her feet to return to the shore where she had left her clothing she found King Diomedes before her, sitting alone on a boulder.

The low sun struck him in full, setting his hair ablaze around his bronzed cheeks, mixing it with the curls of his beard like the waves of the river amid the willow bushes. He was wearing only his chlamys over his nude body, and his leg was propped up on a stone. She realized that he had been watching her for some time, without her knowing. She did not run away, because there was nowhere she could go. She was drawn towards him by the melancholy look in his eyes; the same that she had seen in Nemro's black eyes, but without his gleam of hope. In those few steps that separated her from the king she realized that he was sadder, more alone, more desperate; she understood that Nemro's death for him had been nothing more, nothing less than an unavoidable turn of fate.

She looked at his awesome hands, the hands of an annihilator. The strong fingers, the turgid veins under his skin. Hands that gave death or a caress without much difference. She looked into his eyes and laid her hands on his shoulders; they felt hard, and strong. She ran her fingers through his soft, smooth hair. She pressed his head to her bosom and he put his hands around her waist and kissed her breasts and her smooth stomach still dripping with river water. Without standing, he pulled her against him, pulled her into his lap and penetrated within her holding her in his arms like a child, letting her rest her head on his shoulder, as though she were sleeping. One drop of her virgin's blood stained the white chlamys of the king and she pressed her lips together without a moan. She clasped the hard body of the king with her tender arms and with her long, slender legs. She thought of Nemro's black eyes, dead, forever, she thought of her distant land, beyond the immaculate peaks of the Mountains of Ice, and she wept. She wept while the king laid her on the sand and unleashed all the power of his loins within her, gripping her by the shoulders, by her hair ... She wept because she felt the whole world stifled by sadness, in the murmur of the river and the woods, in the slow, opaque dusk, in the remote screeching of the scops owl, in the whisper of the wind.

The king cried out in the moment of supreme delirium, a cry as hoarse as the growl of a beast, then collapsed, exhausted, his fists clutching the river sand. The girl slipped away from under his heavy body and immersed herself again in the river to purify herself in its gelid waters. When she emerged, Diomedes had disappeared; there was nothing left of him but the footprints in the damp sand and his feral odour in the air, but as she was gathering up her clothing she found a flower resting on her gown, a wild melilot. She picked it up and brought it to her face, inhaling its scent. The moon was just rising between the boughs of the poplars and the day past was nothing but a thin vermilion strip on the mountain crest. She felt that the king had left her a kiss and a caress.

10

WHEN QUEEN CLYTEMNESTRA LEARNED that Helen had returned to Sparta together with her husband Menelaus at the end of a sultry summer, the news filled her with joy and at the same time with great anxiety. She was impatient to embrace the sister she had last seen when she was only twenty, and to learn from her many things about the long war that she still did not know; above all, she was impatient to know whether she would serve the cause of the great conspiracy. But she feared Menelaus.

The younger Atreid would immediately seek news of Agamemnon and it was not improbable that he would soon know the truth. Many witnesses to the massacre had been eliminated; only the most faithful had been spared. But how to establish who was faithful in a palace where the queen shared her bed with the accomplice who had helped her kill her legitimate husband, where son and daughter no longer trusted their own mother?

Her informers had told her that Menelaus had been greeted by a city astonished and troubled, but not hostile.

The mothers and fathers of the warriors who were returning after so many years had thronged along the road that led into the city from the south. They anxiously watched the ranks of foot soldiers, scanned the rumbling battle chariots as they paraded by with their gleaming decorations of silver and copper.

Some of them suddenly lit up, shouting out a name, and began to run along the column so as not to lose sight of the beloved face, not for a single instant. The man who answered to that name did not turn his head, remaining in the ranks, closed in his polished armour, but his gaze rested on those well-loved heads, on those faces so harshly lined by their long wait.

Others, after having watched the very last man parade by, dragged themselves back to the head of the line to have another look, or crossed to the other side, not willing to resign themselves to the despair of a loss, telling themselves that time and the war can make a son unrecognizable to the father who sired him, to the mother who bore him.

Still others, after having futilely called out the names of one or more of their sons, again and again, after having run up and down the ranks with their hearts in a flurry, and after having frantically searched the rows of warriors arrayed in front of the king's palace waiting to be discharged, gave themselves up to despair. The women raised shrill cries and soiled their hair in the dust, the men, their cheeks streaked with tears, stared silently at the dull, lightless sky hanging over the city.

At nightfall several guards exited the palace with torches, accompanied by scribes who had inscribed the names of the fallen on fresh clay tablets. Then came the king in person, armed, flanked by his field adjutants. He had been responsible for the war and he was responsible for the fallen, for all the young men run through by merciless bronze, buried in a foreign land, in the fields of Asia or the swamps of Egypt. He had to answer to the grief-shattered parents.

The great courtyard of the palace was packed with a silent crowd, but soon someone began to shout: 'Bring us back our sons! What have you done with them? You took the best of our young men and brought them to war . . . over a woman!'

The king was pale, subdued. He wore his long red hair tied at the nape of his neck and was barefoot, like a beggar.

'Even I mourn my dead!' he shouted suddenly. 'Where is my brother Agamemnon? And where are his comrades? Where are my brother's children, Prince Orestes and Princess Electra? Why haven't they come to welcome me?' He advanced towards the edge of the steps. 'The responsibility for the war was mine,' he said, 'and I will pronounce the names of my comrades fallen in a strange land, buried far away from their homes, so that their parents can raise a mound to them, with a stone remembering their name, should they so wish.'

'It's your fault that they're dead!' shouted another voice. 'Just so you could have Helen back in your bed! And you are alive!'

The king opened his robe and bared the scars on his chest. 'It is only fate that has spared me,' he shouted. 'A thousand times I heard arrows whistling next to my temples, many times did the bronze cut my skin. I never hid myself. Strike this heart if you believe that I trembled with fear, that I used the lives of the comrades you entrusted me with as a shield.' He lowered his head. 'I wept over them. Bitterly. Each one. And I remember every one of them.'

The crowd's shouts lowered to a diffused murmur. The king held his hand out to the scribe sitting on the ground near him, who handed him a tablet. He began to read the names of the fallen, one by one, with a firm, sharp voice, and the silence in the courtyard became so deep that the sputtering of the torches could be heard in the still air. Until late that night, the king pronounced the names of the fallen before their mothers and their fathers, before their tearful brides.

Among them he pronounced the name of Lamus, son of Onchestus, but the youth's old father did not hear him. He lay dying in his bed, his heart full of grief because he would have to descend into the house of Hades without seeing his son, the only son that his wife had borne him. For years he had dreamed of seeing Lamus return one day, of seeing him enter the gate to the vineyard under the arbour, made a man by the war and its hardships, of seeing him toss his spear and his shield on the ground and run forward to embrace him. But now his hour had come; his wait had been futile.

When King Menelaus had pronounced the last name, the moon was disappearing behind Mount Taygetus and old Onchestus descended weeping into the shadows. The gods who see all and know all did not permit him to know that his beloved son was alive. Lamus was marching in that moment under an incessant rain on a path which climbed towards the woody heights of the Blue Mountains, in the remote Land of Evening. He was following the son of Tydeus, Diomedes, towards an obscure destiny.

*

Helen met with Queen Clytemnestra of Mycenae and Queen Aigialeia of Argos in the sanctuary of the *Potinja*, the ancient goddess and lady of the animals, near Nemea, at night, by the light of a lantern. She had requested this herself, so as not to be recognized or arouse suspicion in the men of her escort. And she had also requested that when they met in the temple, the priestess of the goddess be present as well to celebrate her rites.

'You've changed,' Queen Clytemnestra said to her.

'So have you,' replied Helen meekly.

'We reign over Argos, Knossos and Mycenae,' said Aigialeia. 'We each have a man in the palace and in our beds, but he has no power. You must do away with Menelaus.'

'Does he know how his brother died?' asked Clytemnestra.

'He knows that he is dead. That he has been for some time. And he is suffering.'

'We've suffered as well,' said Aigialeia. 'Don't let yourself be moved. Men are bearers of death and it is only right that they die. It is women who bear life, and our reign will bring happiness back to this world.'

'He will soon know learn how Agamemnon died,' said Helen, 'if he hasn't already found out. Yesterday friends from Mycenae announced a visit.'

'Do you know who they are?' asked Clytemnestra, and fear flashed through her eyes.

'I don't know,' said Helen.

'You must kill him before he has time to take any initiative . . . or find allies.'

'One of the kings might come to his aid . . .' said Helen.

'Only Nestor remains,' said Aigialeia. 'The others are all dead or gone.' She handed Helen a vial. 'This is a potent poison. You must mix it with your perfume and spread it on your body where you know he will kiss you. He will die slowly, little by little, every time he makes love to you. When he is weakened by the poison he will no longer approach you, and it is then that you must entice him, provoke him, force him. He made war to have you back in his bed. And that is how he must die.' Helen accepted the vial and hid it in the folds of her gown. 'With Menelaus dead no one will be able to thwart our plan. Old Nestor will be completely alone; at his age, he won't want to take up a war, and I doubt that his sons will either. Pisistratus, his firstborn, is a bull, but he has everything to lose and nothing to gain. Penelope already reigns in Ithaca, and Ulysses is surely dead. If he were alive he would have returned by now. In Crete, Idomeneus has been dethroned after he immolated his only male heir to the gods. There is no one left in the palace of Minos but the women. We have won!' exulted Aigialeia.

She was the first to leave the sanctuary, as night was falling. Her driver was waiting for her, holding by the reins a couple of horses as white as the dust on the road. Helen was to go last, after allowing some time to pass. Clytemnestra approached her before taking leave herself. The sanctuary was dark by then and nothing could be seen but the image of the goddess crowned in pale light, although the priestess continued her woeful chanting.

'Have you seen anything strange among the things that Menelaus brought back with him from Ilium?'

'What do you mean?'

Clytemnestra smiled and her lips twisted into a kind of grimace. 'You know. They say that this wretched war was not fought over you, but over something else . . .'

Helen did not turn. 'The talisman of Troy?'

'But then it's true,' gasped Clytemnestra. 'It was all done for the mad dream of endless power . . . that is why Iphigenia was sacrificed, her throat slit at the altar like a lamb's . . .' Her voice trembled and her eyes filled with darkness; her forehead was creased and drawn. She bowed her head and gathered her thoughts in silence, then said: 'Aigialeia had all of Diomedes's comrades killed and requisitioned all their booty. She searched everywhere. She was evidently looking for something.'

'Yes,' nodded Helen. 'The same thing.'

'But you must certainly know then . . . Who took it? Was it Diomedes? Menelaus? Ulysses perhaps? Or maybe . . . perhaps it was Agamemnon. He was the great king, after all.'

'If Agamemnon had had it, how could it have escaped you? No one got away, as far as I've been told . . .'

'Many of his ships managed to set sail that night; we do not know where they went. No one has seen them since. Could destiny mock us so? Could it have been on one of those very ships?'

'I do not know who has the talisman of Troy. I know that many that night were looking for it: Diomedes, Ulysses, Ajax, perhaps even Agamemnon or Menelaus . . . there's only one person who surely knows where it is to be found: princess Cassandra, who is your slave, I believe. She was the priestess of the temple.'

'She's dead,' Clytemnestra said.

'Dead? But why?'

'She was his lover. I killed her.'

'How could you have done that? What did it matter that Agamemnon had a lover? You have destroyed the only chance we had to learn the truth.'

'What is done is done. Maybe Menelaus knows something nonetheless. It won't be difficult to find out if you use your wiles . . . You must learn everything before making him die.'

'Why do you desire that thing so? By wanting it, you're making us like them. Seeking power for power's sake.'

Clytemnestra was pale, and her forehead was damp: 'I must know why this war was really fought; I must know, at any cost.'

'Tonight I will go naked to Menelaus's bed, and I will be wearing the perfume you have given me. You will soon know whether your design will be brought to completion. And you will know all the rest, if there is anything more to know. But how will you remain silent, until then? Menelaus will surely demand to see the burial place of his brother, and will immolate a sacrifice to his shade. How will you explain his death? Will you shirk your own part in it?'

'Perhaps it would be better to kill him at once.'

'Impossible,' replied Helen. 'He is always accompanied by his guard, all veterans from the Trojan war who never leave his side for a moment. I am the only person to have intimate contact with him. Should something happen to him, I will be immediately blamed, and put to death. There are many who hate me. Especially the elders, who believe that the war was fought for my sake, and reproach me for the deaths of their sons in the fields of Asia. I must convince Menelaus of your innocence. Or at least leave him doubting your guilt.'

'I know what I can do,' said Queen Clytemnestra. 'I will send a legation to render homage to Menelaus and to invite him to Mycenae so he can learn the truth about his brother's death and make a sacrifice on his tomb. He will certainly sense a trap and refuse. At this point I will no longer have to justify myself, and I can accuse him of being in bad faith. You will take care of the rest.'

'That seems like a good solution,' responded Helen. Clytemnestra drew close to embrace her, but Helen flicked her eyes at the men of the guard who stood observing them at the threshold of the sanctuary. 'Better not,' she said. 'Farewell, my sister, may the gods enable us to fulfil our aspirations.'

They left, taking each her own road.

*

That same evening Menelaus met in his palace with old Hippasus, who had once been the *lawagetas* at Mycenae, head of the army under the Atreid king. His sons had brought him there in secret, disguised as a farmer on a hay cart.

The king approached him and clasped the old man tightly to his chest. Hippasus ran his hands over the king's face. 'The war has left its mark on you, my king,' he said. 'Where have the days gone when I would take you and your brother on my chariot to hunt boar in Arcadia?'

'Those days are long gone, my old friend,' said the king with moist eyes, stroking the old man's thin white hair. 'Days that will never come again. But tell me the reason for your visit. You certainly haven't come all this way in disguise just to welcome me back.'

He ordered the servants to bring a seat and a stool, and told the maidservants to wash his guest's feet. The old man sat down, while his sons remained standing behind him. There were four of them, big men all, with wide shoulders and powerful arms. The old man let the women wash his feet in a large basin filled with hot water.

'I have come to bring you unhappy news. Your brother Agamemnon . . .'

'I know. He's been killed.'

'Murdered in his own palace by Queen Clytemnestra and her lover, Aegisthus; he is a monster, generated by incest. His father and his grandfather are the same person.'

The king bowed his head: 'Much horror has gathered around our family. The house of a king is always a house of blood, but we must nonetheless do what must be done.'

'How did you learn of Agamemnon's death?'

'It's difficult to explain. I visited an oracle in the land of Egypt, where I saw, like in a dream, his body butchered and his funeral mask rise like a bloody moon behind the tower of the chasm. When I landed here and did not see him come to greet me, I understood that my dream was the truth.'

'Diomedes is gone as well. They say that he was killed in a trap set for him by his wife Aigialeia, but no one knows where he is buried. Some say that he escaped with his fleet and took on the winter sea. Idomeneus was driven away from Crete and we know nothing of Ulysses.'

'I am alone,' said the king, and he spoke with a deep, low voice, laden with sadness.

'Not all is lost. Your brother's children, Prince Orestes and Princess Electra, are safe. Electra lives in the palace but never leaves her rooms except to pay homage to her father's tomb. Orestes is in Phocis with your sister Anaxibia: I had him brought there myself, by one of my sons. Now that you have returned, you must put him back on his father's throne. King Nestor of Pylus will surely give you his help.'

'I know,' replied Menelaus, 'but it will be another bloodbath. How can I ask my people to begin another war? Another endless siege? The walls of Mycenae are unassailable. Tiryns could only be taken by the Giants. Certainly Aigialeia and Clytemnestra have joined to see their plot brought to completion.'

'We will help you from the inside,' said Hippasus. 'Many are still faithful to the Atreid dynasty and hate the queen and her lover for the atrocities they have committed.'

Menelaus remained silent in thought as the maidservants brought more seats and prepared the tables before each one of them. Hippasus's four sons sat and, as soon as the meal was served, reached out and devoured the large pieces of meat on the trays.

'Only if it becomes inevitable,' said the king finally. 'Blood disgusts me.'

Several days later, a legation from Queen Clytemnestra arrived to pay her respects to King Menelaus and invite him to Mycenae, but the envoys were told that the king was ill. He lay in his bed, seized by fever; the queen was at his side, wetting his dry lips with cool water. Machaon, the healer who had so often cured him in the fields of Ilium, was dead, slain by the sword of Euripylus. His brother Podalirius, no less gifted in the medical arts, had been lost on their return voyage. All trusted that the gods would come to the king's aid. As soon as the king was better, he would certainly go to Mycenae to meet with his sister-in-law and immolate a sacrifice on Agamemnon's tomb.

The envoys waited several days to see if there was any improvement, to no avail. They only caught a glimpse of Queen Helen as she celebrated a sacrifice to speed Menelaus's recovery.

They were so close that they could see the small mole on her right shoulder and smell the heavenly scent of her skin as she passed.

When the head of the delegation reported this news to Clytemnestra, the queen seemed anxious: 'There was something strange about her when I met her at Nemea. She always spoke softly, and stayed in the shadows.'

'I don't know why you say that, my queen,' replied the man. 'I saw her very closely, in broad daylight. Years and years have passed, but she is as beautiful as ever. Her skin still has the fragrance of violets, her voice is as sweet and harmonious as when she was a young maiden, when the Achaean kings were contending her hand.'

Clytemnestra asked no more, and was satisfied with the news she had received. The king's illness was doubtless the result of her poison. Helen was loyal to their cause.

Another month passed, and the news from Sparta was still more comforting: she was told that an artist had been called to the palace to make a mould of the king's face in damp clay and prepare his funeral mask. The great moment was close.

But the artist who made the mould of Menelaus's face would have been in no hurry to complete his work had he seen how quickly the king had leapt from his bed afterwards, stealthily gone down to the stables and had his fastest chariot prepared for him. His head covered by a hood, he stepped aboard alongside the charioteer and nodded for him to lash the horses.

Three days later they passed the Peloponnesian isthmus at night, so as not to be seen, and continued for a week until they reached Boeotia and the shores of Lake Copais. On an island at its centre rose the impregnable fortress of Arne. The armed sentinels standing guard were astonished to see a tawny-haired warrior descend from the boat; the herald announced him as Menelaus the Atreid, king of Sparta, shepherd of peoples. Soon thereafter Queen Anaxibia was awakened in the deep of night and accompanied to the throne room. The king stood still as a statue in the centre of the room, his long red hair tied at the nape of his neck with a leather string; he spun around at the sound of her steps. They fell into each other's arms and wept without saying a word in the middle of that large deserted room. They shed bitter tears, thinking of the childhood they had spent together, of the adolescent dreams of love they had confided in each other, of the memories of happy times and of their long separation, of the never-ending years of the Trojan war.

When they had given vent to their feelings, Menelaus looked at her as if he could not believe his eyes. 'Beloved sister,' he said, running the tip of his finger over a tear on her cheek. 'Only you remain in this hostile land. I have come to ask for your help.' A sudden gust of wind swept the hall from the windows open on to the courtyard. Menelaus's black cloak swelled for a moment and fell again, swaying, to his ankles.

'No,' said Anaxibia. 'I'm not the only one left. Sit down. Wait,' and she motioned to a handmaiden who had risen from her bed to do her queen's bidding. The woman moved off.

'What is your plan? You surely know of the death of our brother . . .' The woman was back already, standing at the threshold of the door. With her was a youth of perhaps seventeen. He wore naught but a sheet around his bare shoulders. A golden down covered his cheeks and a cascade of blond hair lit up his face. His hair was so blond it seemed nearly white but his eyes were pitch black. Queen Anaxibia held out her hands to him, and kissed him on the forehead and eyes, then, indicating the guest, said: 'This is your uncle Menelaus. We thought he was dead, but he has returned. He has just arrived from Sparta.'

Menelaus opened his arms. 'Son,' he said, his voice still trembling. 'My boy.' The young prince, still half asleep, returned his embrace a little uncertainly, and kissed the king on the cheek. 'Orestes, I have come to put you on the throne of your father, at Mycenae, if you so wish.'

'I do, *wanax*,' said the young man. He was wide awake now, and his gaze was firm and certain.

'Don't call me that,' said the king. 'I'm your uncle and I love you as if I were your father . . .' They sat down and the maidservant brought them warm milk and some wine. 'There is something that perhaps you do not know . . .' And as he was speaking, Menelaus sought the eyes of his sister to have her approval for what he was about to say. The queen nodded. 'My boy, your mother was not forced against her will . . . your mother made you an orphan of her own hand.'

The prince did not flinch. 'I know,' he said. 'And I will kill her for it.' He took a cup of milk from the table and downed it. He stood and took his leave with a slight bow: 'Good night, uncle. I'm happy that you have returned.' He crossed the threshold as weightless as the night air. The light of the torches burning in the corridor made the sheet covering his body transparent: he was as beautiful as a god.

Menelaus followed him for a moment with his eyes, then bowed his head. 'It will be a bitter, fierce fight,' he said, 'more cruel than the Trojan war.'

'Yes,' said the queen. 'Only members of the same family can truly hate each other.'

'I'm afraid,' said the king, 'that my strength will not suffice. I must face a powerful coalition, alone.'

The queen's lips curled into a smile. 'You're not alone,' she said. 'You have the most powerful ally that exists in the world. Come, I want to show you something.' She got up and walked down the corridor. Menelaus followed her to the end, then down a stair that led under ground. They reached a small door closed with bronze bolts. Anaxibia drew them and thrust her torch into the interior. Menelaus was struck dumb, his eyes filled with stupor.

'The talisman of the Trojans!' he gasped. 'Oh gods, gods of the heavens . . . then it was not all futile . . . all of that blood was not spilled in vain . . . oh gods, I thank you.'

The queen closed the door and bolted it. 'This is why you've found me here at Arne. This fortress in the middle of the lake is impenetrable; no one can violate it.'

'But how could you have . . .'

'When our brother was murdered by that bitch, a ship

managed to reach me here before anyone had thought of chasing it. Everyone thought that the talisman of Troy was to be found on Agamemnon's flagship, which was burned at port and sunk by its crew. Clytemnestra was led to believe that the men had carried out an order of the king, who had somehow sensed her betrayal. She even sent divers down to explore the wreck, but the sea bottom was too deep; not even the most expert sponge divers could reach it. She could not know that the talisman was aboard a little thirty-oar which escaped towards the north and went ashore at Aulis.'

'An action that seems inspired by the mind of Ulysses!'

'Who says it wasn't?' said the queen.

'Yes . . .' murmured Menelaus. 'Ulysses turned back . . . I've always asked myself why.'

Anaxibia shut the door that closed off the underground stair from the corridor and motioned to her handmaidens, who were waiting in a group, chatting with each other, each holding a lit lamp in hand. They rushed to hear her orders, then took Menelaus up to his room. They undressed him and bathed him with abundant warm water, then dried him off and dressed him in a fine linen dressing-gown. They asked if he wanted one of them to remain with him in his bed, whichever of them he preferred, but the king let them go and stretched out exhausted on the big pine-scented bed. An able craftsman had carved it from a trunk uprooted by the winds of Mount Ossa. Above his head was a bronze plate embossed with a line of warriors flanking charioteers on their swift war-cars.

*

One autumn evening some time later, princess Electra left the great Gate of the Lions at Mycenae and walked down the narrow valley of the tombs. She was carrying a basket filled with offerings, honey and milk and white flour, offerings for the shadows of the dead. But she didn't stop in front of any of the great mounds along the path. She continued with hurried step until she found a large slab of stone covering a cistern hollowed out of the underlying rock and there she stopped. She poured the milk on to the stone and then the honey and then scattered the flour, invoking the shade of her father.

Big congealed lumps showed how many times her hand had generously poured those offerings and were proof that not even the animals, the stray dogs and the foxes, had dared to contend with the angry shade of the Great Atreid. She prostrated herself on the bare rock and wept with her cheek pressed against the huge slab, wetting it with her tears.

The sun had dropped behind the mountains and its light was suddenly swallowed up by a dark mass of clouds that advanced from the most remote horizon. The wind slipped into the valley and its voice, in the narrow gorge, joined her lament. The princess got up on to her knees, her right hand still caressing the stone. Her head was low. She could hear the twittering of the birds seeking a shelter for the night. The last swallows circled low on the arid grass, crossing in flight between the dried amaranth and the thorny brambles.

The valley was nearly completely invaded by the shadows when Electra got up. 'Farewell, father,' she murmured, bringing her hand to her mouth for a kiss. 'I'll come back as soon as I can.'

She had seen him, for the last time, all covered with blood with his throat cut, being dragged obscenely across the floor like a butchered animal. Awakened in the night by the screams coming from the great hall, she saw everything from the gallery on the second floor but she could not cry out the horror and desperation gnawing at her heart; her soul was lacerated with pain and then invaded by the most implacable hate. Yet every time that she came to that wretched, unworthy tomb, she tried to remember her father as he was when she saw him leave for the war. He had come into her room where she, sitting on the floor in a corner, was trying to swallow her tears. He had put his hand on her head and had said: 'Iphigeneia will leave tomorrow to become the wife of a prince, but you must keep watch over your brother who is still small, and respect your mother. I will think of you every evening, when the sun descends behind the mountains or among the waves of the sea, and I'll dream of holding you in my arms and of stroking your hair.'

She had got up and hugged him. She had felt the cold contact of the bronze covering his chest and had been seized by a stab of pain, the same that she felt now, every time she laid her face against that stone, always so cold, even on the hottest summer evenings.

'Farewell, father,' she had said, crying, and she had raised her eyes to meet his. In his face she had read the mark of dark desperation, in his eyes the uncertain sparkling of tears. He had given her a kiss and had left, and she had remained to listen to the pounding of his wide steps down the stairway and the clashing armour on his powerful shoulders. She would never see him again. Alive.

A pebble suddenly rolled near her feet, from the left; Electra turned in that direction and saw a cloaked figure advancing at a cautious pace from behind the boulders in the valley. She shrank back, frightened; anything could happen in such a solitary place. The man stopped and bared his head, revealing the face of a young blond god.

His voice rang out, close and warm, in the silence of the evening: 'Electra.'

'Oh, gods of the heavens . . .' stammered the princess, peering in the near darkness so that her eyes might confirm what her heart already knew. 'Brother,' she said, 'is that you?'

The young man embraced her, nestling her head against his shoulder, while she could not hold back her tears. He led her to the shelter of a jutting rock and had her sit beside him. He held her tightly, nearly cradling her in his arms.

She suddenly started: 'You are mad,' she cried, 'to have come here! If anyone sees you, you'll be killed at once. Aegisthus's men are everywhere.'

'I had to see you and let you know you're not alone. We are gathering an army and when we are ready we shall lay siege to the city.'

'You'll never succeed,' said Electra. 'The city is invincible. The

Phocian forces have no chance against the squadrons of war chariots that Aegisthus can send into the field.'

'Uncle Menelaus is back. Haven't you heard?'

'Yes, but I had heard that he was very ill, close to death.'

'He's fine. But don't let the word out; no one must know. Nestor will send his fleet to sea to stop the Cretans if they should attack us; he'll send us one thousand men, commanded by Pisistratus, and one hundred chariots. Many others will join us from Argos, Tiryns, Nemea and from Mycenae as well.' He took a fleeting look at the slab covering the cistern. 'Our father will be avenged and he will finally have peace in Hades.'

Electra couldn't take her eyes away from him, and he stroked him gently as he spoke. When he had finished she dropped her head for a while as if gathering her thoughts: 'Do you know what all this means?'

'I do,' said the youth. 'It means the death of our mother. By my hand. If we win. If we are defeated, it means my death, and yours, and the death of all of our dreams.'

'You've never killed anyone. How could you kill your mother? Have you thought of how you will feel afterwards? Of the nightmares that will torment you for your whole life? Her spirit will give you no peace, neither by day or night.' She kissed his eyes, his forehead, his hair. 'You're just a boy . . . you would have the right to different thoughts. Oh gods . . . why? Why us, we've done nothing!'

'Do not ask, sister. There is no answer to your questions. Destiny is blind and has cast all this misfortune upon us. In this very moment someone else, in some other place, far away, is enjoying every happiness . . . even ours, the happiness that would be ours. But one day, who knows, perhaps more serene days will dawn for us as well. Perhaps we'll be able to live, and to forget.' Orestes rose to his feet. 'But now we will do what must be done. Don't cry as I leave you.'

He covered his head and turned, soon disappearing into the darkness that had descended to cover the land.

The chirping of the birds had ceased; they were sleeping in

their nests under their mother's wing. The dark valley now sounded with the hoots of the birds of prey and the howls of the jackals which roamed the darkness to rob the dead of the offerings left by the pious living. Electra pulled her cloak tight around her shoulders and started her walk back. As she was leaving the valley, her gaze flew to the citadel and the high walls of the palace. She thought she saw, for just an instant, a solitary figure dressed in black on the tower of the chasm. Then the wind carried the echo of a wail coming from a house near the road. A babe crying for fear of the dark, consoled by his mother's singing.

Electra listened to that lullaby and it called up lost images, forgotten long ago. A knot tightened her throat and an aching nostalgia filled her soul.

Then the baby's crying stopped, and the mother's song as well. Electra began walking.

11

ANCHIALUS JOURNEYED AT LENGTH amid steep mountains and thick forests, living on what he could find. When he came upon a village, he would remain and work there for some time, in exchange for food and shelter. He pushed on this way until one day, having decided that it was time to move on, he realized that the choice was no longer his to make. The people whom he lived with had come to consider him their property and intended to keep him as a slave. His sword was taken from him, and an iron collar was put round his neck, with a ring they used to chain him up at night. He remained in that state for a long time, without understanding where he was or who the people who held him prisoner were, until one night the village was stormed and sacked by a people coming from the north. The *Dor*.

He was spared because he was a slave and that day he traded one master for another. He saw that the *Dor* community was divided very rigidly: there were the warriors, those who did manual labour, and the slaves, nearly all plunder of war, like himself. The slaves had to attend to the animals and take the flocks to pasture.

He had never managed to learn the language of the people who had first kept him slave, but he realized that it was much easier for him to understand the language of the *Dor*, which sounded strangely familiar to him, similar somehow to his own.

He could not fathom the reason for this, and he tried to remember the traditions and stories that the elders of his people would tell when he was just a boy in search of an explanation, but he found none. At night when he dropped on to his mat of dried grass, he could not sleep, exhausted as he was. He thought of the comrades whom he had let die at sea, he thought of the others who had stayed with Diomedes; he thought of his king, to whom he had made a promise it would be very difficult to keep.

He implored the gods to free him, to remove the yoke weighing on his shoulders, to restore his shield and his spear. But much time passed before anything happened.

The *Dor* settled for nearly three years on a plain near the shore of a lake encircled by tall mountains, and he with them.

One day they gave him a woman, a slave like he was, so they could generate more slaves, but when he lay with her he spilled his seed on the ground so that he would not be bound to that life, so that he would have no wife and no children. Every day, at the break of dawn and at the setting of the sun, he repeated to himself: 'You are Anchialus, son of Iasus, and you fought with the son of Tydeus, Diomedes, under the walls of Troy. No one can keep you in their thrall.'

He feigned docility and cowardice, he pretended to tremble in the sight of his master, he grovelled and whimpered when they threatened punishment and soon no one had any more regard for him than for the sheep and goats they raised in their pens.

And so one night he strangled his master in his sleep, took his weapons and his horse, and escaped. He descended the banks of a river, leaving no traces, and he continued on day and night without ever pausing, never eating and never sleeping. When he was certain that he had put enough distance between himself and his enemies, he stopped to look for a little food so he could gain the strength to go on. He set traps, as he had learned from his first masters, and caught some game. He dug in the ground for tubers and roots with his sword, and he gathered wild fruit from the trees as he had done after surviving the pirates' attack.

When he felt strong enough, he took up his journey once again, keeping well clear of villages this time. Nearly two months passed in this way, although he could not say how much ground he had covered. He knew only that he was walking southward, leaving the darkness and night behind him.

One morning, just as day was breaking, he finally reached a rocky peak from which he saw an expanse of waves that shone like polished bronze. A strong salty odour was carried on the breeze and his heart swelled in his chest. 'The sea,' he murmured aloud.

Along the coast he found a village of fishermen who spoke his language. He asked them what land he found himself in, and they told him it was Epirus, ruled over by Pyrrhus, a youth just seventeen years of age. The fishermen told him that their young king had come by ship after fighting at length in Asia. It was said that he was the son of a fearful warrior who had died far from his native land. 'The son of Achilles!' thought Anchialus. 'Achilles's son, here . . . how could that be?' He was more convinced than ever that the accursed war had ruined them all, overturning kingdoms and dynasties, procuring no less trouble for the victors than for the vanquished. So the son of Achilles did not reign in Phthia and over the plains of Thessaly as would have been his right, but over a poor, primitive place at the edge of the land of the Achaeans!

He asked the fishermen where he could find the king's house, and they answered that he must continue along the coast, never losing sight of the sea, proceeding south until he reached a place called Buthrotum. There lived the young king, surrounded by his warriors, with a foreign bride, older than he, beautiful but very sad. No one had ever seen her smile, but neither had anyone ever seen her weep. Those who had known her said she looked like a statue, with skin pale as marble and lovely, lightless eyes.

Anchialus thought and thought of who that woman might be, but he could not remember anyone who fitted that description. He was pleased nonetheless; he thought that he would finally meet one of the kings who had fought under the walls of Ilium, and that he could report to him as Diomedes had ordered. He would ask for a ship, and he would set sail west once again. Sooner or later he would find Diomedes and the comrades he had left, and he would join them in their new kingdom, in their new homeland.

He walked for two days before he found a fisherman who was going by boat to the city to sell his catch of fish; he asked if he could go there together with him. They talked at length while the boat slipped calmly over the clear waves, under a brilliant sun. He felt as though he had never left those lands. They could see islands rising from the sea on one side and, on the other, the steep, rocky coastline with its low sandy stretches bordered by lush trees and thick bushes of fragrant juniper and myrtle.

Buthrotum appeared towards evening, walls reddish in the twilight, standing out against the deep green of the surrounding woods. Dogs were barking; gulls screeching over the jutting cliffs. Epirus seemed an untamed land.

Anchialus reached the palace and entered the courtyard to announce himself to the guard at the gate.

'I am Anchialus, son of Iasus. I once fought at Troy with my king Diomedes, son of Tydeus, the lord of Argos. Tell your king that I am here and must speak with him as soon as possible. A grave danger threatens these lands, and he must know of it.'

The man studied him carefully and only then did Anchialus realize what he must look like: his hair was long and unkempt, his hands rough and calloused, his fingernails black. 'I know, I seem a beggar, but you must believe me. I was enslaved and forced to put sheep and swine to pasture for years. I finally succeeded in liberating myself and I resumed my journey so I could keep my promise. I want nothing, although I am tormented by hunger. Just allow me to speak with the king.'

'The king has departed,' said the guardian.

'Departed? Where has he gone?'

'King Menelaus has asked for his help.'

'King Menelaus? He is alive then?'

'Yes. He is asking for help from all his allies to put together a large army and attack Mycenae, which is in the hands of his sister-in-law, Queen Clytemnestra. The queen has killed King Agamemnon, with the aid of her lover.'

Anchialus lowered his head. The Great Atreid had fallen! After having endured such suffering in the war, he had fallen in his own home, between the very walls he had so dearly desired.

'How long ago did he depart?' he asked.

'Two days ago. He is marching south, along the coast.'

'Can you tell me where he is headed?'

'I do not know. But I could not tell you if I did. The king's destination is a secret. No one must know where he is coming from. He will descend like a hawk into a flock of crows.'

Anchialus fell silent for a moment, trying to work out what he should do. If only he had been able to meet the young king, he would have given him Diomedes's message and his mission would have been over. He would have looked for some ship in a port and sailed westward. He wanted to return to Diomedes. As he was contemplating his course of action, his gaze alighted upon the figure of a woman who was just exiting a side door and heading towards a path that led to the mountainside. For a moment, their eyes met and he was thunderstruck: Priam's daughter-in-law, Hector's bride: Andromache!

He followed her without making himself seen and saw her stop in front of an earthen mound topped by a stone. Weeds had completely covered the mound and at its base a few wild thistles had opened their purple flowers. She knelt next to it and bowed her head until it touched the ground; she was weeping, her back shaken by sobs.

Anchialus turned away because he understood that those solitary tears should bear no witness. He knew who that mound had been raised to. Andromache had wanted a place where she could grieve for her lost husband, buried far away in the fields of Asia after Achilles had slit his throat, pierced his heels and dragged him behind his chariot. She was the sad bride that the man who had directed him to Buthrotum was speaking of. Queen of a miserable kingdom of shepherds and fishermen, prey to a violent and irascible boy who had demanded her as his trophy; she, the rightful spoil of his father had the gods not sent the arrows of Paris to fell him at the Scaean Gates.

After some time, Andromache rose to her feet, drying her eyes with the edge of her veil, then walked back down the path that led to the city. Anchialus approached her, bowing like a suppliant.

'Queen,' he said, 'stop and heed my request. I am a man who has nothing left to me, neither home, nor homeland, nor friends, but I think I can offer you something if you will help me.'

Andromache appeared startled, as if she could never have expected to meet anyone in so solitary a place. She looked him over calmly; her skin was pale as marble and her eyes were black as the gates to Hades, but the glitter of tears gave her gaze a mournful intensity.

She did not answer and hurried her step, head bowed.

'I beseech you, queen,' said Anchialus, nearly barring her way. 'Do not deny a moment of your time to a poor suppliant.'

'I am not who you think I am,' she said in a soft voice. Anchialus could hear her light eastern accent, the same as the women prisoners whom he would take to Diomedes's tent when they were dividing the spoils after a victory in Asia. Tears swelled within him as well, as the violence and futility of her pain pierced into his very bones.

'I beg of you, I must reach your husband Pyrrhus, valiant son of Achilles. I have been told that he has departed.'

'He is not my husband,' replied Andromache. 'He is my master. They have given me to a boy who could be my son . . .'

'They say he marches to join forces with Menelaus. Tell me the road he is following, if you can, because I absolutely must find him. If you tell me, I will help you to escape. I will take you with me; I promise you, you will not lack sustenance nor a resting place for the night. I will respect you as befits your rank and your sorrow, and I will never raise my eyes to you unless you wish to speak with me. I will find a peaceful, secret place for you. My own nurse will care for you, if she is still alive; she is a good, old woman who lives alone on a little island. If she is dead, I will find another house for you, and another woman to serve you for as long as you desire. More than this I cannot do, but I swear before the gods that I am sincere and will keep faith to what I have promised.'

'Sincere . . .' said Andromache. 'Like the vow Ulysses made to Poseidon on the beach of Ilium: an enormous horse, of wood . . .'

Anchialus dropped his head, unable to bear the look in Andromache's eyes.

He drew a knife from his belt and he held it out to her, kneeling before her. 'I was inside that horse,' he said. 'With lord Diomedes, my king. Kill me if you want, because if I cannot fulfil my mission, I prefer to die by your hand, so that at least a little justice may be done in this world, and so that you may be convinced that I am sincere.'

Andromache hesitated a moment, looking at the glittering blade, eyeing the edge slowly all the way up to the hilt. She stretched out her hand until she was nearly touching it with her long white fingers. Anchialus raised his head and saw in her gaze the ferocious tranquillity that he had so often seen in the eyes of warriors in the heat of battle. All their strength gathered in a still gaze and even stiller hand. The quiet that comes the instant before dealing the blow that will take a life.

Anchialus realized that he was ready to accept death without regret, on that dusty trail at the edge of the land of the Achaeans, from that gentle hand that had once caressed the head of a boy and the body of a hero. But all at once, the hand drew back.

'Pyrrhus has taken the road for Phocis; his aim is to reach King Strophius and Queen Anaxibia, Menelaus's sister. From there, he will continue with the Phocians towards the Isthmus to close off Mycenae from the north.'

Anchialus sheathed the blade and rose to his feet: 'Accept my offer, queen. You will live in peace, sheltered from all violence.'

'In peace?' said Andromache. 'Do you know why I haven't killed myself yet? After having endured the hands that hurled my son from the wall of Troy on my skin, do you know why I haven't killed myself?'

She turned her head towards the stone stuck into the pitiful, weed-covered mound, and the tears suddenly began to pour from her eyes again, trembling first on the rim of her eyelids, then trickling to meet the corners of her wan lips. Anchialus felt his heart unsteady in his chest.

'Because the sweetness of my memories is still greater than the horror of that massacre. And my memories are so dear to me that they give me the strength to live. Death would take even them from me. My Hector, my one and only love, and my beloved child: they would die entirely, and for ever. My life, as miserable and shameful as it is, prolongs theirs. Without me, their memory would be lost for ever.'

They began to walk again towards the little city and Anchialus realized that she would not separate herself from that place for any reason. Might that mound actually cover the bones of Hector, the greatest warrior of all Asia? If that were true, what terms did she have to accept in exchange for keeping those relics there? Was her shame the price she'd paid to live with her memories?

An icy shudder gripped him, although the sun shone high; it seemed to him that the sky had lost its light and the sea its splendour.

When he set off for the mountain, he was burdened by an obscure weariness that he had never felt before.

*

He reached Pyrrhus's column five days later, in a valley at the heart of the steep mountains of Acarnania. The only people of Achaean stock who had not taken part in the war of Troy lived in that land. They were so isolated and primitive that they cared nothing about anything. Ten years earlier, Agamemnon had sent Ulysses in vain to convince them to fight at his side; not even the persuasive words of the king of Ithaca had moved them. But what could be expected of a people who had no king nor cities, only wretched villages? Ulysses had spoken to a few old heads of family, who had no authority. They listened impassively as if he were speaking nonsense, and did not even deign to answer him. They neither agreed, nor disagreed; they said nothing. As Ulysses was still speaking, one of them stood and left, then another followed, and yet another, until they were all gone.

Anchialus had heard this directly from Ulysses when King Diomedes had once invited him to share the evening meal in his tent. And so he had avoided any contact with those people as he journeyed, for fear of not knowing how to deal with them.

He announced himself to the camp sentinels. One of them ran to advise the king that Anchialus, son of Iasus, a comrade of King Diomedes, had come to speak with him. Pyrrhus had him brought to his tent at once.

A wispy beard barely covered his cheeks, his hair was cut above his ears, and he had an incredibly powerful build for a boy his age. Anchialus had seen him on rare occasions, always at a distance and always flanked by two huge Myrmidons, Periphantes and Automedon. When his eyes had adjusted to the gloom in the tent, with a mere lantern to light it, Anchialus saw that Pyrrhus wore the armour of his father. His first suit of armour, the one that Patroclus had worn to trick the Trojans into believing he was Achilles and drive them from the Achaean camp; the armour that Hector had stripped from Patroclus's body, and that Achilles had won back by slaying Hector. The other suit of armour, the one that Hephaestus had forged for Achilles's last battle, had gone to Ulysses.

'You wear the armour of your father,' said Anchialus, gazing at the shield adorned with silver stars. 'How often I saw it shine on the chariot drawn by Balius and Xanthus! We Argives were usually lined up alongside the Myrmidons.' The youth seemed not to hear his words.

'Why did you ask to speak with me?' asked Pyrrhus, eyeing the guest with diffidence.

'Oh *wanax*,' began Anchialus, 'my lord Diomedes, king of Argos . . .'

'King of nothing!' snapped the son of Achilles. Anchialus stiffened, wounded by his insult. 'King of nothing,' repeated Pyrrhus, his voice dropping, 'like me . . .'

Anchialus understood. 'Do not say this, *wanax*. You reign over the Epirotes and Diomedes will soon have a great kingdom in the land of Hesperia, and I will join him there.'

'Diomedes was forced to flee, as was I. Thessaly is my kingdom, the Myrmidons are my people, my palace stands in Phthia, and yet I must live in these mountains in the midst of savages in a pathetic dwelling that I conquered without glory.'

'But I have heard that your grandfather, old Peleus, is still alive. How is it possible that you no longer live in your palace, enjoying your privileges? Has an enemy killed Peleus, perhaps, and driven you out?'

'No enemy,' said Pyrrhus. 'There is no enemy capable of driving me out. Only my own grandfather could do so. Peleus would not have me. One cannot fight such an enemy, but only flee. I fled my grandfather.'

Anchialus fell into silence, but his desire to know what had happened prompted him to speak. He said, '*Wanax*, pardon my boldness. Why did Peleus not keep you with him?'

'He doesn't like me. He's an old man and he thinks like an old man. "Why did you kill the old defenceless king," he said, "who your father Achilles had spared thinking of my white hair? Why did you kill the little prince, smashing him on to the rocks below? Why did you force his mother to lie with you after obliging her to witness such horror?" They'd told him everything, understand? He already knew everything. I swear that if I knew who it was I'd strangle him with my bare hands. I would rip out his eyes and his tongue and feed them to my dog.'

Anchialus was quiet, not knowing what to say.

'But there was something you wanted to tell me,' said the youth then. 'Where do you come from? How did you arrive here among these mountains?'

'I was following my king, Diomedes, sailing north on the western sea, when we fought a people marching towards the land of the Achaeans. They were as numerous as locusts and they possessed weapons made of an invincible metal. The sword of Tydides, a formidable arm, was snapped in two as if it were made of wood. The king barely saved himself, and we with him. He ordered me to take my leave of the other ships and to sail back, to warn the Achaean kings of the danger. "They must assemble an army," Diomedes said to me, "they must send the black ships out to sea!" I have travelled at length, I have endured every sort of suffering, I have been imprisoned and enslaved, but I have kept faith to my promise. You are the first of the Achaean kings I have met. Tell the others to prepare their defences and allow me to depart, for I must join my king in the land of Hesperia.'

Pyrrhus looked at him without batting an eye.

'Who told you where you could find me?' he asked, looking intently at Anchialus in the darkness as if to see inside of him. He rose to his feet and approached him, towering over him by a full head. 'My route was a secret. How did you find me?'

'I suffered and fought at Ilium like your father, like all the other Achaean chiefs and warriors, like you did. What does it matter how I found you? The gods guided my steps so I could bring you this alarm.'

Pyrrhus burst out laughing. 'The gods! If there are any gods, they amuse themselves by setting us down the wrong paths, by bringing us to remote, desolate destinations. They set us off one against another and they enjoy watching as we add wound to wound, as we slaughter each other. Like when we goad our dogs into a fight, and bet on which will be the first to rip out the throat of another. Don't talk to me about the gods. I'm young but I'm not stupid, don't make game of me. Tell me who told you where I was or you will die. I could care less if you fought at Ilium.'

Anchialus shuddered: in that boy was the awesome power of the son of Peleus, but not a crumb of his father's piety, nor his hospitable manners. He had not offered him a seat, had not had his feet washed and had not brought him food or drink. And now he was threatening him with death.

'If I tell you the truth, do you promise you will bring my message to the kings of the Achaeans?'

'I promise to take you with me; you can tell them yourself.

I have no reason to believe you and I do not know who you are. They'll believe you if they want to. If someone recognizes you. Now speak, for my patience is at an end.'

Anchialus spoke: 'Andromache told me, of her own free accord. Do not hurt her; she did not wish to harm you.'

'Andromache . . .' repeated the young king.

'Oh *wanax*,' Anchialus spoke again, unable to hold back his feelings, 'if the blood of Achilles truly flows in your veins, be generous with her, give her her freedom, respect her pain. She has been spared no suffering.'

Pyrrhus returned to his stool and started to pet his dog, as if he had heard nothing. He held his head low, as if he were listening to a dim, distant song; his men were singing to themselves as they struggled to stay awake on guard.

When he raised his head, his dark gaze was streaked with folly: 'My mother was a silly, fearful girl who didn't even want to give birth to me, afraid as she was of the pain. I need a real mother. That's why I took away Andromache's son, that little bastard, understand? Because I wanted her all for myself. When I saw her I knew she was the mother I wanted . . . and you think that I would leave her after all I've done to have her? You must be mad, foreigner, if you think I would give her up.'

Anchialus looked at him, bewildered: he had journeyed so far, overcoming such danger, to meet up with a foolish boy whom the gods had deprived of the light of reason. And yet the blood of Thetis and Peleus ran in that boy's veins, the blood of Achilles! The race of the Achaeans, in keeping with some obscure destiny, had been corrupted and poisoned, and perhaps all of his troubles had been for naught. He thought of returning whence he had come, of seeking a crossing towards the land of Hesperia where he would find his king, the one man who would never disappoint or betray him; not even the mysterious lights that pulsed in the sky could touch him.

But Pyrrhus came to his senses; his voice changed suddenly and his look, now, was inexplicably firm and direct. 'You will come with me,' he said, 'son of Iasus. We will go as far as the

Isthmus and lay siege to Mycenae from the north. From the south and west will come Pisistratus son of Nestor, Orestes son of Agamemnon, and Menelaus as well, and perhaps even Ulysses, that bastard son of a bitch. If he has come back. Menelaus has promised me his daughter Hermione as my bride; she is the loveliest girl in the world, the very picture of her mother Helen, they say. Then we will turn against Argos and then Crete. They will all fall.'

'But *wanax*!' protested Anchialus. 'You are all running a mortal risk. A threat is gathering over the land of the Achaeans, from the north. They will come, sooner or later, and will find you weakened by these fratricidal wars. They will annihilate you; you will suffer the same fate as the Trojans did with us. All of you must unite and face this danger together! Promise me that you will warn the other kings, and then allow me to return to the Land of the Dying Sun, where my lord awaits me.'

Pyrrhus smiled, revealing a row of fierce white teeth: 'The Achaean kings have been away from their own lands for too long and many things have changed. We must engage in more combat so that things may return the way they were. When this war is over, we will certainly be united, that I can promise you. And no enemy who comes from outside will defeat us because I will govern this land ... There is no metal in the world that can threaten the sword of Achilles!' he shouted out, unsheathing the sword and striking hard at the shield hanging from the tent's central pole. The great bronze sword clanged out loudly and Anchialus saw, as if in a dream, the faded images of Ilium: Patroclus wounded, holding out that shield as Hector's blows rained down inexorably, one after another. He saw all the agony of that night, Ajax Telamon returning to camp with the corpse of Patroclus on his shoulders, the savage howl of pain of Achilles, son of Peleus, reverberating like thunder over the silent plain.

The heart of the fierce boy standing before him harboured none of those feelings: neither devotion to friends nor desire for honour; there was no compassion for the vanquished, no respect for elders and women, no tenderness towards children. Anchialus realized in that moment that the son of Achilles wanted to reign alone over the land of the Achaeans, and that nothing would stop him.

The Pelian breastplate that covered him seemed the scaly skin of a dragon or a serpent. But Anchialus knew that his mission was not yet finished and that he must follow him. Much time would pass before he would be able to return west in search of Diomedes.

He said: 'I will come with you, *wanax*, if you so wish, and I will serve you as I served my king, lord Diomedes, shepherd of heroes.' His voice trembled as he said those words, for he was thinking of his comrades, who wandered through a distant, unknown land. He was thinking of the solitary, weedy mound on the mountains of Buthrotum. And he was thinking of the woman who had found him at his most desperate; she who had taken him home with her and sheltered him from harsh cold and solitude.

The king made sure he was given some hides and a blanket and Anchialus stretched out on the ground at the edge of camp. He was exhausted but could not find sleep because of the emotions that troubled his soul. In his restless tossing, he saw the son of Achilles leave his tent and ascend a hill that overlooked the camp. The young king contemplated his army, with his dog curled up at his feet. But these were not the Myrmidons of his father sleeping under the tents; these were savage Epirotes whom he had convinced to follow him with the promise of pillage and rape. Anchialus finally drifted off, won over by weariness, into a heavy, dreamless sleep.

*

The guard leaned over the bastions, extending his torch to illuminate the clearing before the bolted city gate, and he distinctly saw a chariot with the insignia of the Spartan Atreides. Next to the driver stood a woman wrapped in dusty dark robes. The woman let them fall to her feet, baring a proud head of blonde hair with coppery reflections, circled by a golden diadem.

'The queen of Sparta asks to see her sister, Queen Clytemnestra,' shouted out the charioteer. The sentry scurried down the battlement steps to speak to his commander. Another man was sent running to the palace while the commander himself opened the gate and strode towards the chariot with a torch in his hand. When the light illuminated the woman standing alongside the charioteer, the commander was struck dumb: before him was the awesome beauty that had unleashed the bloodiest war that had ever been fought, the destruction of the greatest city in the world. In all of his life, never before had reality so amply exceeded his expectations.

Helen descended from the chariot and walked towards the gate. Although she wore humble travelling attire, the queen's body was the epitome of divine perfection. The folds of the gown, rippled by the evening breeze that whistled round the enormous door jambs, fluttered over her flat stomach and clung to her marmoreal breasts, slipping between her long, agile legs. Her walk was supple and bold at once, like a lioness's, her feet seemed to barely touch the ground and her golden hair rippled around her shoulders like ripe wheat ruffled by the wind in the summer fields.

The commander of the guards understood why the greatest army of all time had been assembled to bring her back to her homeland; why a nation had preferred to suffer annihilation rather than turn her over. Just to catch a glimpse of her as she walked down the road, or when she appeared on the temple steps or in the palace halls. He knew that any man would agree to have his throat slit from side to side, for the mere chance of holding her naked in his arms a single time.

A ceremonial chariot drew up just then, sent by the royal house; Helen entered and sat on its seat.

Queen Clytemnestra did not receive her in the great audience chamber, but had her accompanied to one of the private rooms that faced the plains. The little room was well lit by two candelabra, each of which burned with six lamps, but the last glimmer of dusk still entered a little from the windows, prolonging the spring day against the advance of night. Hesperus, the evening star, twinkled alone in the infinite sky, hovering over the shadowy chasm.

The walls of the room were completely frescoed by scenes of a procession of women offering gifts to the *Potinja*. They all wore the ancient gown that bared their breasts and swirled in big flowery flounces down to their bare ankles.

Helen was moved to see those figures; that was the gown she had worn the day the Achaean chiefs had come from far and wide to ask for her hand in marriage, and her breasts, high and white as the snows of Mount Olympus, had blinded their minds and unsettled their hearts. Only a solemn pact prevented them from murdering each other in duels to the death, to win her.

On an ebony table stood a precious Cretan vase decorated with fish, medusas and cuttlefish, filled with sharply scented yellow mountain flowers. There was a chest in the corner and two stools in the middle of the room, nothing else.

A maidservant came in and set two small tables before the stools. Bowing, she invited Helen to follow her to the bathing chamber where the black stone tub was already filled with warm, fragrant water. Helen let the maids wash, dry and dress her and then returned to the little room where dinner had already been served. On her feet before her was Queen Clytemnestra, thin and exceedingly anxious, wearing a white gown that seemed one with the pallor of her face.

She reached out her arms: 'Finally, I can truly see you, after all those meetings in the dark, those words whispered in fear, in suspicion . . .'

Helen embraced her, holding her close. 'Sister,' she said, 'my sister, how much time has passed . . .'

'When I was told you were coming here in person I couldn't believe it . . . you've made me suffer so! Why haven't you told me what I yearn to know?' She stepped back from her sister's embrace and gave her a strange look, full of amazement and fear. 'You haven't changed at all! That horrible war has not touched the perfection of your face; there's not a sign on your skin. But you had seemed different to me at the sanctuary of Nemea, you were different ... What is this? What about Menelaus? You had me told that his end was at hand ... is this why you are free to come and see me alone?'

Helen stood silently before her while her eyes brimmed with tears.

'What is this?' asked Clytemnestra, bewildered. 'What is happening?'

'This is the first time I have seen you,' said Helen, 'after all these years. I have never seen you before, nor did I send anyone to tell you that the end of Menelaus was at hand. The king ... is well.' Clytemnestra staggered backward, seeking support from the wall. Her eyes darted around, confused and frightened, as if she were searching for a way out. Helen continued, her voice firm, just slightly cracking with emotion as her tears flowed freely down her cheeks.

'I never went to Troy. In all of these years I remained hidden at Delos, among the priestesses of the sanctuary. A plan of marvellous intelligence, devised by Ulysses and helped along by an incredible stroke of luck ... No one was to know except for Menelaus.' Now her voice was trembling: 'I was never able to tell you anything, sister. They never allowed me the time, nor the opportunity, to do so. And now destiny is about to be fulfilled. They will have no pity.'

12

As these things were happening in the land of the Achaeans, King Diomedes advanced with his warriors through the heart of the land of Hesperia. The Blue Mountains were an uninterrupted succession of wooded summits and narrow valleys crossed by impetuous torrents that ran between smooth boulders and banks of sand and bright gravel.

They met with vast tracts of oaks and beeches, with huge maple trees and another kind of tree with an enormous, furrowed trunk and fruits as prickly as a porcupine's back. Inside was a sort of single, flat walnut. The infrequent inhabitants gathered them in the autumn and boiled them in bronze pots or roasted them among the ashes of the hearth, and depended on them for sustenance all winter. They lived in round huts built of stakes and clay-plastered grates, covered by conical roofs held up by tall centrally placed poles. The single room was their assembly chamber, banquet hall and bedroom for the entire family, usually very numerous.

Lamus, son of Onchestus, told them that he had tasted those fruits as a child when a relative of his who traded with the Thracians on the mountains had brought him a sack of them as a gift. Telephus, the Hittite, knew them as well; they grew abundantly in his mountain land where the great Halys river had its source. Certain primitive tribes lived on nothing else. The *Chnan* had never seen them but he said that the world, all things considered, was much the same everywhere. It was the men who inhabited it who made it different.

As they moved on, the men tried to procure women for

themselves, either buying them or taking them by force. Some of them had even taken young girls, who could serve them until they were old enough to share their beds with them.

In this way, although many warriors had been lost during the journey, in combat or ambushes, the group making its way through the mountains was no smaller than when they had commenced their upstream voyage on the Eridanus.

They did not march continuously, because the king did not seem to have a precise destination in mind, nor did the passing time seem to affect him. Whenever they chanced upon a place that offered food and shelter, the Achaeans would stop, even at considerable length. They raised tents using the hides of the animals they had seized in town or had trapped in the forest; their time was spent hunting and fishing. They slept on mats of dried leaves that made a great deal of noise whenever they moved, but their slumber was more tranquil. They had left the swamps and the dying lands along the banks of the Eridanus behind them, and the implacable revenge of Nemro was but a memory. Many of them had women and perhaps, soon, some of them might sire children. But there was not a single man among them who imagined that this might be his life. It was not for this that they had followed the son of Tydeus.

The king certainly allowed them to live that life so that they might be fortified in body and spirit, so that they might gain new strength. But one day they would reach a rich and prosperous land, inhabited, perhaps, by a strong, numerous people, and they would have to conquer it by spear, or perish.

Two mules always marched at the centre of the column with the heavy wooden chest that the king had brought from Ilium. This ensured that one day Diomedes would found his kingdom and would make it invincible.

There was no further fighting for a very long time, because the Achaeans were nearly invisible as they moved through the forest; some of the women had become fond of their men and led the army down safer paths. Whenever they had to cross one of the mountain passes, however, they had to take it by force, because the inhabitants of those places had been warned by Nemro's allies.

The Achaeans were journeying up a torrent and had neared the source, at the foot of a great pyramid-shaped mountain, but they found the pass occupied by a numerous group of warriors. The women called them *Ambron*; they were strong and belligerent, and inhabited a wild, beautiful land made of steep mountains and deep dark sea. They made their living by cutting down trees with heavy bronze axes to clear pastures for their flocks and land for their crops.

Those who lived on the coast braved the waves to toss their nets; they lived on the fish they caught and drank the water of the torrents that from the mountains descended steeply into the sea.

Telephus, the Hittite, came forward and asked the king to listen to him, because the Achaeans were not equipped with the proper armour nor were they accustomed to combat in the mountains, while he had fought hundreds of times against the bloodthirsty *Kardaka* of Mount Toros and of the *Urartu* Mountains.

'The column must be divided into several parts, and each group must ascend in stealth and silence,' he advised the king.

'The king of Argos does not hide. I will take on those savages face to face, and my comrades will do the same.'

'If you do, you'll be torn to shreds. They are numerous, and they know the territory. They are in a favourable position and, above all, they care nothing for glory or honour. All that matters to them is driving you out while losing as few men as possible.'

'How do you know? You've never been here before,' observed the king.

'They are poor and poor people are the same the world over. Heed my words, *wanax*, for I have fought in Egypt, Amurru and Babel, I have fought on the Toros and the *Urartu* mountains, and I fought against you at *Vilusya*. Only rich peoples have chiefs who want to fight on the open field face to face in order to gain glory and prestige. Poor peoples want only to survive. And this is why they are more fearsome: they have nothing to lose. Draw up your men in four files, sound the horns and launch a frontal attack: if you're lucky, one in five will get to the top. They'll crush you under an avalanche of boulders, they'll target you with arrows and javelins and at the end, when they have decimated you, when they are still fresh and you are weary and wounded, then they will face off in hand to hand combat. There is no code of honour here; they make up the rules.'

'The Hittite is right, king. Listen to him,' said the *Chnan*. 'He has fought many times in the mountains. Heed him, for he has already saved you once.'

Their words sent the king into a rage; although living so closely with his men had diminished his manifestations of rank, the *Chnan*'s advice stung like a whiplash. He could not tolerate a couple of slaves reminding him that he owed them his life. He dismissed them with a sharp gesture that did not permit further insistence.

'Stay back here with the women if that's the way you feel,' he said. 'I don't need you.'

He called Myrsilus and indicated the enemy assembled at the crest. 'This is the only place we can cross,' he said. 'We must take that pass. Draw up the men in four files and make sure the formation is as tight as possible: those savages will see a wall of shields bearing down upon them. They can't have weapons capable of piercing our bronze. Have the bugles ready. I will lead you myself.'

The wood thinned out a little past the foot of the slope, leaving sufficient space to form the array, although the mountain meadow beyond was still dotted with trees here and there.

Myrsilus drew up his men, and when the formation was complete the king took his place on the right side and had the battle notes sounded.

The bugles blared and the noise echoed through the valleys and the rocky mountain walls. The king shouted: 'ARGOS!'

The men echoed: 'ARGOS!'

And the army moved forward at a measured step in closed

formation towards the pass. Myrsilus noticed a certain wavering of the enemy lines at the crest and said to Diomedes: 'We have frightened them; they will flee before we reach the top.'

In fact, many of them seemed to scatter and disappear. The *Chnan* thought that they were fleeing as well, and said to Telephus: 'This time you were mistaken, Hittite, look at them sneaking off!' But the words were not out of his mouth when the crest became crowded with men once again. The Achaeans were close enough to see that many of them were armed with axes. These rushed towards certain points of the pass where dense bushes hid the terrain. They gave violent blows with their axes. A sharp rattling could be heard at first, and then a noise like thunder, and hundreds of stones were liberated all at once from some casing that held them, and plunged downhill.

Telephus, who had not even answered so as not to miss an instant of what was happening under his eyes, shouted out: 'Behind the trees! *Wanax!* Behind the trees! Or on the ground, under the shields!' And as he shouted, he ran forward.

Diomedes realized that the men who had followed him all this way were about to be destroyed by his foolishness and he cried out in unison: 'Behind the trees, men, seek cover behind the trees! Drop to the ground, under your shields!'

The front dispersed, the men dashing for the nearest tree or reversing at a run to find one. Those who were too far flattened on to the ground, covering themselves with their shields. Those who were not fast enough were mown down and mangled. Others were wounded despite the cover provided by the trees; still others were hit on the rebound by the enormous boulders and were smashed under their shields, like when a tortoise is crushed in his shell by the wheel of a cart and his blood and guts squirt out on to the dusty road.

When the avalanche had passed, the king gave orders to retreat towards the wood and to carry along the wounded. The men obeyed, but the enemy targeted them with a hail of slingshot stones and of arrows. More men were struck, and they hobbled to find shelter as they could, bruised and losing blood. As Diomedes withdrew, he saw Telephus, the Hittite slave, lying on the ground and bleeding from the mouth. He had rushed forward to help the king and his warriors, but one of the boulders loosed by the *Ambron* had hit him full in the chest. Heedless of the arrows and other projectiles raining around him, Diomedes bent over him and gathered him into his arms, but the man groaned in pain.

'I'm done for . . .' he said, 'fucked to save a handful of desperate *Ahhijawa* . . . stupid . . . stupid . . .' His breath was a rattle.

The king raised his head: 'Forgive me, friend. I am the stupid one. Stupid and blind.'

'Commander . . .' said the Hittite. 'I am the commander of a squadron of Hittite chariots. Call me commander . . .'

'Yes, commander,' said the king. Myrsilus had arrived at his side and was protecting him from the enemy's shots.

'Do what I tell you to do, *Ahhijawa*, or they'll tear you to pieces, and even that god that you're carrying with you won't be enough to save you.' Every word raised his chest and delivered stabbing pain. 'I'm dying, *Ahhijawa*, and you must do as I say. I don't want to die for nothing.'

'You are the commander,' said Diomedes. And he paid no mind to Myrsilus, who was saying: 'Let's go, *wanax*! If we don't go, we'll die ourselves!'

The Hittite pushed up on his elbows: 'Call back all your men and pretend to flee, to rout. Make a lot of noise, as if you were marching back down to the valley . . .'

'I will,' said the king. Myrsilus's shield popped under the slingshots as if hail were rattling down on it.

'Wait until night, and divide up into small groups, then make your way up . . . go up towards the pass from every direction towards two . . . towards two or three rallying points . . . in silence. Observe how the enemy is laid out, and then . . . and then . . .'

'I understand,' said the king. 'I understand. Do not tire yourself, say no more.' With the hem of his tunic he dried the sweat that dripped down the dying man's forehead.

'If we had been able to draw up all our chariot squadrons at *Vilusya* ... we would have chased you back into the sea ... *Ahhijawa* ...' he said, wheezing.

'Yes,' said Diomedes, 'perhaps you are right, my friend.'

The Hittite stared at him and a strange smile formed on his face: 'Your world no longer exists ... *Ahhijawa* ... do you understand? You must change, or you will perish ... and I will have died for nothing ... I ... I ...' and he gave himself up to death.

'Let's go, *wanax*!' Myrsilus shouted again. 'They'll be upon us.'

'No!' shouted the king. 'I will not let the enemies take his body and strip him!'

'Didn't you understand what he said as he was dying?' Myrsilus shouted back. 'Our world is done with! Gone! We have to save ourselves, king, that's all that is left to us!' Diomedes saw his eyes filled with despair, for the first time ever. 'He would tell you to abandon him, if he could, because there's nothing left to save but your own life, for your men's sake. We must go, *wanax*! Now!'

Diomedes stood and ran for the forest and Myrsilus followed, raising his shield so that the king of Argos would not be struck down, would not breathe his last in a desolate field of stones at the hand of nameless savages.

The king ordered all his men to hide and then to feign leaving; they shook the bushes along the trail leading down to the valley, to convince the enemy that they were retreating.

When night fell, the king divided the remaining men into three groups: one under his command, another commanded by Myrsilus and a third under the command of Evenus. They took off their heavy armour and kept only their swords, daggers and bows, with quivers full of arrows. They crept up separately amidst the trees in the forest until the point where it began to thin out. From there they crawled their way up, covering small stretches of ground at a time. They ran when they could, hiding behind a tree or a boulder, always careful not to be spotted, not to make the slightest noise.

Myrsilus was the first to arrive at the top, followed by Diomedes and then Evenus. When Myrsilus peered over the crest, he saw that they had left ten or so guards at the pass, while the others slept under a big rocky shelter. He motioned to his men and they crawled up behind the guards who were dozing, leaning up against the stone wall. At his signal, each of his men leapt out of the darkness brandishing his dagger; none of the guards survived, not one had the time to let out a groan. Diomedes led his men to the top of the rocky shelter, Evenus shut out the front and Myrsilus posted his men to the sides, to cut off any escape route. At Diomedes's signal, they all nocked their arrows and let fly into the heap of sleeping men.

The yells of the wounded awoke the others but the second and the third volleys of arrows were already rending the night and sowing the ground with the dead and wounded. Their cries spread panic and confusion, but the attackers were all under cover and well positioned to take aim. They were helped by a little moonlight that drifted through the clouds. The arrows raining down in every direction, even from above, disoriented the *Ambron*, who could not understand how to locate their aggressors. The survivors soon took to their heels, running headlong towards the valley and seeking shelter in the forest, but the Achaeans relentlessly pursued them all through the night.

At the first glimmer of dawn, the Achaeans gathered the bodies of their comrades and gave them burial. Diomedes buried Telephus, the Hittite slave, who had once been the commander of a chariot squadron in the plains of Asia; he had found death in a remote place, far from the homeland to which he had so longed to return.

The *Chnan* sat off at a distance on a big boulder, chewing on a blade of grass and watching the sky as it filled with light. When the men had finished burying the dead, the *Chnan* approached the grave where Telephus had been buried. He picked up a fistful of dirt and let it run through his fingers. 'You stubborn Hittite,' he said. 'Was this any place to die? You had to leave me, just now when I was beginning to have a little hope . . .'

He picked a deep blue mountain flower and laid it on the mound, then reached under his tunic and drew out a bronze clasp with coral and amber beads, and buried it next to him. 'It's all I can leave for you; you know how much I need these things . . . Sleep, now, *Telepinu*; sleep, commander. The air is good here, the sun, and the wind; it's a better place than many others, in the end. I must continue on my road until I find the sea again, and a ship. It was destiny; a mountaineer and a sailor could never stay friends. If I ever reach you where you are now, I'll be soaking wet and stinking of algae, I can feel it . . . stinking of rotten fish and salt water . . .'

Myrsilus gave the signal; it was time to go. The *Chnan* turned back one last time. 'You never asked me my name,' he said. 'If we should meet up again one day in the dark world, you wouldn't even know what to call me . . . there will be lots of *Chnans* down there, I guess . . . Anyway, friend, my name is Malech . . . Malech. Remember that.'

*

They resumed their journey, walking at mid-slope on the mountain crest, directed south. One of the women said: 'It takes thirty days to cover this road; it crosses the Blue Mountain range and leads to the land of the Mountains of Fire.'

'What does that mean?' one of the men asked Myrsilus, who was marching alongside her and listening attentively.

'I've heard,' said the woman, 'that there are rivers of fire that pour out of those mountains and devour everything below. Storms of flames are hurled towards the sky, and the sea boils all around like a cauldron bubbling on the fire. Sometimes the earth trembles from its deepest depths and splits open, loosing pestiferous fumes that make the birds fall dead out of the sky.'

Myrsilus caught up with the king, who was marching at the head of his people in silence.

'*Wanax*,' he said. 'There's a woman walking at the middle of the column who's talking about the land of the Mountains of Fire that is found at the end of this trail. At thirty days' march from here. I think she is speaking of the land of the Cyclops! I have heard it described by men who sailed very far from our land. No one has ever dared approach it; from the sea at night, you can see the Cyclops' blazing eyes, flaming, you can hear their wild cries. They devour those who the waves cast up on their deserted beaches. I know that you do not fear them, you fear neither gods nor men, nor monsters of the earth or sea, and you know that I am ready to follow you anywhere, even to the Mountains of Fire, even to the land of the Cyclops, but listen to me, I beg of you. I think that the time has come for us to stop, as soon as we find a place where we can live. We have women, and we'll take others. We can build a city, with walls, we can establish alliances with nearby peoples. We lost more comrades in taking that pass, brave men, skilled with spear and sword. How many more will we lose if we continue on this way? You have your bride . . . stop, and generate a child so that this land can nourish him and accept him as its own . . . or we will stay foreigners . . .'

The king did not turn and continued on his way.

They marched along the crest of the mountains all day, until dusk, leaving behind their lost companions, leaving behind Telephus, the slave who died as a warrior, as the commander he had always been.

The king advanced with his head low, the first of the entire column, and for the first time he looked small to his men against the immensity of the mountains and the sky. He looked lost, in that labyrinthine, wooded land where every valley might conceal new threats. As far as the eye could see, there were no places that could sustain a city, no fields where crops could be grown, no plains that led to the sea, to a port from which ships could depart, making contact with other peoples, striking up trade. All they saw, few and far between, were villages of huts inhabited by shepherds who withdrew fearfully into the forests upon their approach.

Some of the men began to envy those companions who had remained in Argos. Perhaps nothing had happened to them; they had certainly rejoined their families and were sitting at table now with their wives and children, eating fragrant bread and drinking strong red wine. And when they awoke in the morning their eyes beheld the walls and the towers of Argos, of all cities the most beautiful and gracious.

It even seemed to them that their king had been abandoned by the gods. Where was Athena, who was wont to appear to him in human form, or so they said, and speak with him? Where was the goddess who had been at his side in his war-car on the plains of Ilium, guiding his horses like a charioteer?

The king advanced alone, head low, as if he had lost his way, as if he no longer had a goal. Some said that perhaps by walking among the severed heads, he had unknowingly surrendered his inner strength, his indomitable courage.

They camped in a little valley, wedged between the forests, near a clear-watered lake. There was an island in the middle of the lake, connected to the shore by a thin, partially submerged isthmus. The island was bare, save for a single, gigantic tree. Diomedes reached the shore of the lake and sat on a stone; he seemed to be contemplating the huge tree that extended its boughs to cover the island.

The bride from the Mountains of Ice joined him. She had a name now, Ros, and she had learned the language of the Achaeans.

She stepped up lightly behind him. He heard her but did not turn. He said: 'I stole you away from your husband because I thought I could found a kingdom in this land for myself and my comrades. I thought I could build a city and make it invincible. I thought, when I saw you, that only you could erase from my mind and my flesh the memory of the wife who betrayed me, Aigialeia . . . But now my strength is abandoning me, the road has become endless. I abducted you from your promised husband . . . for nothing.'

'Nemro,' she said. 'I saw him but once, and I held his hand only at the moment when I was to become his bride. I cried when you killed him, but perhaps . . . perhaps I would have cried over you if he had killed you. I cried for his youth cut short before its time, for the day that darkens before it reaches noon. I could do nothing anything else; a woman cannot choose to whom she will bind her life. But you are my destiny now, you sleep beside me every night.'

Diomedes turned and looked at her in the moonlight. She was young and perfect even in the shabby clothing that covered her. If she had been able to dress in royal finery, she could have sat on the throne of a powerful kingdom in the land of the Achaeans.

'I want to be the man you wait for with longing in your bed. After making love, I want to feel your arms holding me, your body warming me. The cold seizes me when I leave your womb and you turn away to sleep. I'm cold, Ros . . .'

'But the season is warm and the nights are mild.'

'It is the cold that grips men who fear death.'

'You are not afraid of death. I have seen you fight, time and time again, as if your life was worth nothing to you. There is a pain inside of you that you cannot overcome, a wound that will not heal. Was your queen so very beautiful? So lovely her breasts and so ardent her womb? I turn away from you because it is she you are thinking of, it is she you dream of at night. It is beside her that you would like to awaken. Forget Argos, and forget her if you want to conquer this land and begin a new life. Forget what has been, or you will lose everything: your comrades, this land, and me, if you care about me. Your nights will become colder and colder, until one day you will be terrified even to fall asleep, to close your eyes.'

The king reached out his hands and the girl felt him tremble. 'Help me,' he said, and his eyes blazed, in the shadows, with fever and pain.

*

They marched on for many days, leaving the territory of the *Ambron* behind them. They could sometimes hear the wail of their horns in the distance, as if they were still observing them from on high, without daring to face them again.

'So you have a name,' said Myrsilus to the *Chnan* one evening as the men were setting up camp. 'I heard you talking to yourself up on that pass we took.'

'I wasn't talking to myself. I was talking to my Hittite friend who died to save the king.'

'Malech. Why didn't you ever say so?'

'Why should I have? It wouldn't have changed anything. I won't be living the rest of my life with you. When I'm gone, you'll just keep calling me "the *Chnan*" no matter what my name was, and you'd be right. My name doesn't hide anything import-ant. I'm not like *Telepinu*, whom you called Telephus; he was a commander of a squadron of war chariots in the land of the Hittites before he was made a slave. In my land, everyone is like me; we go to sea, transporting goods to be exchanged with other goods. In Keftiu, in Egypt, in Tarsish, everywhere. Our kings trade as well, with other kings, and they haggle over the price when they buy and swindle when they sell. The Achaeans of the islands call us the *Ponikjo* because the sails on our ships are red. That's everything. We never go to war unless we absolutely can't avoid it, and we hold on to our poor little land pinched between the mountains and the sea.'

'A place to return to . . . we've lost that. But our king will give us a new homeland. These steep mountains will end, and we'll find before us a fair, flourishing plain, rich with pastures and surrounded by hills, with one side open towards the sea. There we will build a city and gird it with walls.'

'You're looking for Argos. The place you've described is Argos.'

'Have you seen it?' asked Myrsilus, and his eyes sparkled like a little boy's.

'Yes. I've seen almost all your cities. But you must forget it. You'll never find anything here that resembles it.'

Myrsilus scowled. 'I'm going to draw up the guard,' he said, and he moved off towards a hill that overlooked the valley. On the other side of camp, Diomedes was taking his horses to pasture; they followed him docilely and ate grass from his hands.

Myrsilus walked along the slope, to see what lay beyond the wooded hillock that limited his field of vision to the east; when the territory opened into view on that side, he dropped to the ground immediately, hiding behind a stone.

A long line of warriors was crossing the valley, followed by carts and pack animals. He pounded his fist on his thigh; they were headed towards a valley which the Achaeans would also have to cross, heading south. It was not a route that the two groups could share. He remained at length to observe them, and tried to count them. There were many of them. Too many.

'*Shekelesh*,' said a voice behind him. The *Chnan* had followed him.

'You recognize them?' asked Myrsilus.

'Yes. But I can't understand what they're doing here. This is not their land. They live in Libya, although many of them have migrated to a large island with three promontories and attempted to drive away the native inhabitants, the *Sikanie*.'

'You know the world and many of its peoples . . .' said Myrsilus, without taking his eyes off the marching column. 'I've never left Argos, except to go to war. And once I was there, I never left the camp.'

As they were still speaking, he noticed that the column was slowing its pace and had stopped. They were bustling about the carts and preparing to set up camp for the night. Small groups positioned themselves on the hills surrounding the valley to head off any perils, protecting that main part of their forces, who were pitching their tents in the wider part of the valley near the banks of a torrent.

'They are on the same road as we are,' said Myrsilus. 'We must tell the king and ask him what must be done.'

'It seems strange to me that they have come so far inland,' replied the *Chnan*. 'Perhaps they've settled on the coast, some place with too few resources for them to live on. They may have sent this group towards the interior to seize livestock or women, or both. Look, see there at the end,' he continued, pointing, 'there are flocks of sheep, and what look like cattle as well.'

'I think you may be right,' said Myrsilus. 'Perhaps tomorrow they'll turn back, and never give us any trouble.'

'But they might go on. And in that case, we'll have to decide whether to attack them or let them go by. Or change our own itinerary.'

Myrsilus pondered his words for a while, then said: 'If we capture one or two of them, we can make them talk and learn their intentions. I don't want the king to send men out in an attack, we've lost far too many as it is.'

'You are becoming wiser,' said the *Chnan*. 'Perhaps there's hope we'll be saved.'

'Wait for me here,' said Myrsilus. 'I'll be back soon. Do not let yourself be seen and don't move.' He crept off, low to the ground, and reached his comrades. He chose three of them, Eupites, Evenus and Crissus, and told each of them to pick out one of the *Shekelesh* and follow him in secret, carrying only a bow and dagger.

They advanced separately, shifting from one cover to another with rapid, silent moves. Myrsilus thought of how that strange land had changed them; how long it had been since they had drawn up in the open field, shield to shield and helmet to helmet, awaiting an encounter with the enemy who faced them drawn up in the same formation!

The *Chnan* pointed to a spot at mid-slope, in front of them: 'See them? There are three of them, and they're stretching out under that jutting rock. Do you want one or all three?'

'One is enough, I think.'

'Fine. As soon as it is dark, send a man back to camp to get some fire.'

Myrsilus gave an order for the *Chnan*'s plan to be carried out, and remained at his side to observe the three *Shekelesh* who were sitting in their shelter and speaking among themselves. Every so often one of them would stand up and walk around, checking the area. As soon as darkness fell, they stopped moving altogether and their shapes could barely be made out against the whitish rock.

The *Chnan* explained to Myrsilus what he planned to do; he

took the embers that one of the men had brought in a clay jar and started up a fire. Just a few moments passed before the *Shekelesh* noticed the bivouac. They got to their feet and consulted amongst themselves, then one of them started creeping cautiously towards the fire. Myrsilus never took his eyes off him and strained his ears to hear the little noises brought about by his movements. When he was rather close to the fire, Myrsilus put several men at his back to prevent any possibility of escape. When the intruder was about to turn back, they jumped at him and immobilized him with a dagger to his throat. He did not move nor breathe, aware that any resistance on his part would result in the blade slitting his neck open.

They dragged him off to a solitary place, not within view of his companions or the Achaean camp.

'Do you understand my language?' asked the *Chnan* in Canaanite. The prisoner nodded his head.

'Good,' continued the *Chnan*. 'I know that you understand us, even if you sometimes pretend not to. You will have realized that these friends of mine will cut your throat if you try to make yourself heard by the others. But if you tell us what we want to know, we'll keep you with us for a while and then we'll set you free. We don't want your sorry bones.' The prisoner let out a sigh of relief.

'Well then, where do you come from? Libya, or the island of the three promontories?'

'From Libya. We fought under King Mauroy against the king of Egypt but we were defeated and the wind pushed us to the northern gulf.'

The *Chnan* gestured to the man holding the dagger to ease up so that the prisoner could speak a little more freely.

'Where are you headed now?'

The *Shekelesh* seemed to hesitate a moment, but as soon as he saw the *Chnan* gesturing to the man with the knife, he hurried his reply: 'We have built a city on the coast, near a place called "the Elbow" but our chief wants to know if the island of the three promontories can be reached from the interior.'

'The island of the three promontories? But it is very far from here, very far south!'

'Perhaps not so far . . .' said the *Shekelesh*, twisting his neck a little.

'And why do you want to reach the island of the three promontories?'

'Because our people are there. Here we don't know if we can manage to survive. But we had no choice. We had crossed the sea when we ran into a storm; almost all of our ships were destroyed on the shoals and the rocks. We lost all our tools, our provisions. We could not rebuild the ships, or even repair them.'

'The *Borrha*,' said the *Chnan*, as if speaking to himself; it almost seemed as though the thought gave him a strange satisfaction.

'What were you doing in the northern gulf in the first place?' he insisted.

'I told you; the wind pushed us there after the great battle, and we were sailing up the eastern coast looking for food.'

'Did you find any?'

The *Shekelesh* shook his head: 'Nothing. Only empty villages inhabited by shepherds who ran off to the mountains with their sheep as soon as they saw us. The only ship we met before the storm was nearly empty as well; only water, dried fish and a little wheat.'

'I understand, my friend,' said the *Chnan* with a confidential tone, aiming to put his guest at ease. The man looked relieved, and cracked a half smile. '*Peleset*, I imagine. We met some of them ourselves around those parts.'

'No. *Ahhijawa*,' he said, still smiling. Myrsilus quivered at the word but the *Chnan* grabbed his arm to warn him not to speak or make a move.

'Ah,' said the *Chnan*, 'those bastards. We ran into some of them too and they tried to attack us. They must have been famished. I hope you gave them a good lesson. Were there many of them?'

'You'd better believe that we gave them a good thrashing! No, it was just one ship alone; they tried to slip off to the south, but we caught up with them. Not a single one of them survived, if I remember correctly. But they put us to a lot of trouble, for nothing. They put up quite a fight. Good at using their fists, too. Warriors, that's what they were, and tough ones at that, no merchants, that's for sure.'

The *Chnan* turned towards Myrsilus and said something under his breath.

'So, what do you know about the land that lies before us?' asked the *Chnan* then, indicating the mountain chain that extended south as far as the eye could see.

'Little or nothing. I think that further on there must be some *Teresh*, up ahead of us. We've run into them here and there in the villages. The inhabitants of these valleys captured some of them while they were out hunting or putting the horses to pasture, and they've kept them as slaves.'

'*Teresh!*' murmured the *Chnan*, astonished. '*Teresh* in the Land of Evening.'

The *Shekelesh* seemed relieved and looked at his questioner as though waiting for permission to return to his camp. 'Why don't you let me go?' he said. 'There's nothing more to tell.'

'No,' said the *Chnan*. 'I think not.' He looked at Myrsilus. The eyes of the Achaean warrior were full of ire and his hand gripped the hilt of his sword. The *Chnan* turned away as Myrsilus's sword cut the prisoner's head clean off.

'I had promised him that we would spare him,' said the *Chnan*, getting to his feet.

'I didn't promise anything,' said Myrsilus. 'He killed our companions . . . he killed Anchialus! The king's message will never reach our land. The invaders will arrive without forewarning . . . it will be a massacre. Our cities . . . our land . . .'

'You can't be sure,' said the *Chnan*. 'You can't be certain. It might be an incredible trick of chance. Perhaps there were other Achaeans in the northern gulf . . . perhaps. You don't think that there may be other madmen of your race wandering those inhospitable seas? There are *Teresh* here as well, can you believe it? *Teresh* in the Land of Evening.'

They walked slowly towards camp, still keeping an eye on the valley behind them.

When they were close, Myrsilus stopped. 'They say that the Trojans even asked the *Teresh* for help when they were forming the great coalition of *Assuwa.*'

Evenus, who was right behind them, said: 'But they refused. They feared that we would devastate their cities on the coast. That's what I heard.'

The *Chnan* stopped as well and turned back in the direction of the valley, motioning for everyone to stay quiet. Not a sound was coming from the valley. 'It's true,' he said after a while. 'And yet they were forced to join a much bigger coalition, under King Mauroy of Libya, against Egypt. Hunger was their real enemy, a dearth of crops, one bad harvest after another. But the coalition lost, and the *Teresh* nation was destroyed. The group ahead of us are probably as desperate as we are . . . as the *Shekelesh* are. They say that after the defeat, when the king of the *Teresh* returned to his homeland in Asia, he found it ravaged by famine. He decided then that one of his two sons would leave with half of the surviving population. They drew lots, and his second-born, whose name was Tyrrhens and whom the king loved dearly, was chosen to go. That is what people were saying the last time I sailed from the port of Tyre with a favourable wind . . .'

'Everyone is fleeing,' said Myrsilus. 'But from what? From what?' He watched the pale clouds crossing the sky.

'From death,' said the *Chnan*. 'What else?'

13

WHEN NIGHT HAD FALLEN, a chariot with the insignia of the Mycenaean Atreides stopped in front of the atrium of the king's house and the grooms came forward at once to take the reins of the two Argive stallions. The horses pawed the ground, still excited over their long race through the dark, and the charioteer, noble Pylades, calmed them by stroking their muzzles. In the meantime, Orestes got out of the chariot and entered the vast dark courtyard surrounded by a great colonnade dimly illuminated by lamplight. His slight figure seemed swallowed up by the big empty space that echoed with his rapid steps.

At the entrance to the palace, Hippasus, the master of the house, awaited him, accompanied by one of his sons. The old man had been the *lawagetas* when Atreus reigned over Mycenae, and Menelaus had restored him to a place of dignity in his palace. Next to him was the king's nurse, Marpessa. She was a woman of great age, but she had always run the household. She still had authority over the handmaids and the servants and she managed them with a steady hand.

'Your uncle the king and the queen await you for dinner,' said Hippasus and ordered that the youth's spear and sword be put in the armoury. 'They are impatient to see you and embrace you. But please follow the nurse first; she will take you to the bath chamber and give you fresh clothing.'

Marpessa kissed his forehead and eyes: 'You are as beautiful as the sun, my boy,' she said, 'but you stink of sweat and you're covered with dust. The water is perfectly hot; the maids have kept the fire going under the cauldron all day since we did not know when you would arrive. Come, the princess herself will help you wash and prepare for dinner.' She was already striding down the dark corridor with a quicker step than one would expect for a woman her age, and the young prince followed her. 'How long has it been since you saw your cousin?' she asked. 'Oh, I imagine she was still wetting her bed the last time you saw her. Much time has passed. You'll see, she's as lovely as the morning star, with skin as white as the moon, her mother's deep black eyes and the flaming hair of her father the king.'

The youth entered the bath chamber and the handmaids approached immediately to undress him. As soon as he was immersed in the tub, Princess Hermione appeared. She was so beautiful she took his breath away and left him without words.

'Welcome to our home,' said the girl. 'We have been waiting anxiously for you. I hope you are well and that your journey was a good one.'

'I am well, Hermione,' he said, 'and happy to see you. I had been told that you were as beautiful as your mother, but now that I've seen you, I'd say you were beyond compare.'

The girl lowered her head with a little smile, then approached him; taking a sponge, she dipped it in the hot water and squeezed it over his head, his back and his shoulders, as he closed his eyes and stretched out his legs in the stone tub, savouring the pleasure of the water's warm caress.

Hermione passed the sponge to one of the handmaids, who continued to wash the prince, and she sat down to supervise the guest's bath, as befitted her rank.

'You know,' she said, 'just a short time ago Telemachus, the son of Ulysses, bathed in that tub. It was a day of celebration; I was about to depart with my dowry, to become Pyrrhus's bride at Phthia in Thessaly. Telemachus had arrived from Pylus together with Pisistratus and we offered him hospitality here at the palace; he was seeking news of Ulysses. But my father did not have much to tell him. He did offer to help throw out the suitors who invade his father's house, but Telemachus refused. He said that he was sure that his father would return and annihilate them all. He is a nice boy, Telemachus, gentle and good. Pisistratus has become his good friend, and I hope that one day he will find a bride worthy of him.'

'If you were about to go to Phthia that day, how is it that you are still here?' asked Orestes with a certain anxiety.

'Because Pyrrhus is no longer there. His grandfather Peleus refused to keep him in his house, and he left for Buthrotum in Epirus. It would have been too long and dangerous a journey for me. I will go later, if we win the war; he will come here to fetch me.'

Orestes couldn't take his eyes off her as she was speaking. When he had finished, he stood up, and the handmaids covered him with a big linen cloth that Marpessa had taken from a chest. They dried him and dressed him with a fresh tunic, handsomely embroidered in bright colours at the hem. Helen's brother Castor had worn it one day, before the gods had called him to their abode. Orestes turned towards the nurse and said: 'Grandmother, prince Pylades will have unharnessed the horses by now and he will be entering the palace. Go receive him as well, please, and have a bath prepared for him.'

The old woman nodded and walked away down the corridor. Orestes drew close to Hermione as the handmaids were dressing him and pouring perfume on his hair. He touched her cheek with a light caress. 'If you were not already promised,' he said, 'I'd ask for you myself.'

The girl started slightly. 'Do you mean that?' she asked.

The prince answered with a look worth more than many words. He remained silent, contemplating her, and then said: 'Have you ever seen him?'

'No,' said the girl. 'But if we want to win this war, his strength is indispensable. That's what my father the king says.'

'We'll win in any case,' said Orestes. 'We have justice on our side.'

'If Pyrrhus fights with us, the conflict will be shorter. The king believes that we can also thus prevent others from convincing him to join them against us. The scale will be tipped in favour of whoever he takes sides with. Those who have seen him fight say he is an invincible fury. Like his father,' she said, her voice growing softer, 'but . . . fiercer, more cruel.'

Orestes took her hand and clasped it between his own. 'I would treasure you like a precious gem,' he said, 'like ripe grapes in the vineyard . . .'

Hermione's gaze trembled, her dark, shiny eyes became moist. 'If the war is shorter, there will be fewer losses, less blood spilt, understand? Too much has already been shed.'

Orestes tried to say something else, but his voice died in his throat. Hermione pulled back her hand, gently, and went towards the door that led to her apartments. Before disappearing, she turned back towards him and bade him farewell with a look. In the uncertain light of the lamps, the prince thought he saw a tear glittering on her ivory cheek.

'He won't have you,' he said.

*

The king himself, Menelaus the Atreid, came to receive him at the door of the great hall. He was flanked by two warriors from the army of Ilium, for they were the only ones he trusted.

The king strode towards him and greeted him with a warm embrace, then preceded him into the banquet room. Marpessa reappeared and gave orders to bring tables and food, and the prince began to eat eagerly, because he hadn't stopped during the day and the bath had made him hungry.

'Prince Pylades is with me,' he said. 'He will lead the Phocian army at our side.'

'Excellent,' said the king. 'He will be a welcome guest in Hippasus's house tonight; they will see to the plan of battle. King Nestor of Pylus will be sending the warriors who fought at Ilium under the command of Pisistratus, the strongest of his sons. Another allied army is descending from Epirus; it is led by the son of Achilles, Pyrrhus, who has sworn to help us. You will lead the chariot charge with me, if they dare to challenge us on an open field.' Orestes listened, but his eyes seemed to drift away at times.

When they had finished dinner, the king had the tables cleared but had them leave the wine.

'Your aunt, the queen,' said Menelaus, 'regrets that she was not with me to receive you at the door, but she will be joining us soon.'

Orestes seemed disconcerted; a troubled look crossed his eyes, an ill-concealed embarrassment.

'I understand,' said the king, 'I know what you are thinking . . .'

'My sister Iphigeneia . . . and my father died because of her,' said the prince, a sudden chill in his voice.

'It's not the way you think,' said the king. 'And it is time that you know the truth. That's why I had you come.'

The queen entered at that moment and greeted him: 'Welcome to this house, son.' But Orestes barely managed to bow his head. Her presence obviously created deep discomfort in the boy.

'The tunic of my beloved brother fits you well,' observed the queen. Her gaze was veiled with sadness and regret.

'Helen was not the cause,' said Menelaus. 'She was, instead, one of the combatants. Perhaps the most formidable of us all.'

The youth gave the queen an astonished look. She seemed not to notice, lowered herself into a chair and put her feet up on an elegant ivory-adorned stool.

The prince shook his head, bewildered. The king rose, poured wine into the young man's cup and waited until he had drunk it, then said: 'Get up and come with me.'

Orestes followed him without understanding what was happening. Before starting down the corridor, he turned back a moment to see the queen sitting there, as lovely as a goddess; she smiled at him. They soon reached a sort of gallery, closed off by screened shutters.

'Come,' said the king. 'Look.'

Orestes neared the screen from which a reddish glow filtered. The room he saw was illuminated; there was a girl there, playing a lyre and singing, while others around her spun wool of beautiful colours. At the centre, sitting at a large loom, was a woman whose head was covered with a light blue veil. He could only see her hands, her long, delicate fingers flying swiftly over the weft, passing the reel back and forth. Woven into the top part of the cloth was a peaceful scene, a shepherd guiding his sheep to a blue-watered spring. Green meadows surrounded them. The lower part showed a scene of war: a ship leaving port with warriors seated at the thwarts, manning the oars; they were departing to wreak destruction across the sea. Weeping women waved at them from the beach, their heads covered by black veils as if they were following a funeral litter.

The lyre suddenly stopped, the woman's sweet voice fell still and the lights dimmed. The woman sitting at the loom rose to her feet and turned around: it was Helen of Sparta, the bride of Menelaus the Atreid.

'Helen never went to Ilium,' said the king behind him. 'She never left the land of the Achaeans. The whole time we were at war she was hidden away at Delos, protected by an impenetrable secret.'

'I . . . I cannot believe what I see,' said the prince, and his eyes were full of stupor. 'How can this be? Is it a prodigy of the gods? A trick . . . an illusion for the eyes?'

'She is as you see her,' said the king. And he returned on his steps. Orestes, still as stone, couldn't take his eyes off the queen, her soft, proud step as she crossed the shadowy room, as the oil that the handmaids had poured into the lamps was consumed. A moment later, the divine Helen disappeared into a dark corridor. Her maidservants followed her as the lamps went out, one by one. The last one remained lit for a while, illuminating the marvellous weaving. The quivering light licked at the lamenting women and in the silence that enveloped the great house, the young prince thought he heard weeping.

*

They returned to the banquet hall and the prince approached the woman who was still sitting there. She held a golden cup that the handmaids had brought her in her hands; it was full of wine.

'This is the woman who followed Paris to Ilium,' said Menelaus behind him. Orestes drew nearer until he was very close.
Her gaze was unperturbed, her lips curling in a slight smile, her
forehead very smooth and perfectly white. She touched his face
with a caress and said: 'Welcome to our home, son.'

'But . . . but this is the same person,' stammered the prince.

'No,' said the king. 'Look, the mole she has on her right
shoulder has been tattooed. A priest from Asia came all this way
to do it. No one here in the land of the Achaeans knows this art.'
He brushed it with his fingers. 'See? It is not a mole, it is perfectly
flat. Otherwise she is the very portrait of your aunt.'

'But that can't be . . . the gods cannot have created the most
beautiful woman in the world twice.'

'I saw her by chance among a group of slaves that a *Ponikjo*
ship had unloaded at the market on the seashore. She was dirty
and ragged, her hands were black and her nails broken. She was
full of bruises and wounds and yet I was awed by her beauty and,
above all, by how much she resembled the queen. I couldn't
understand why she was in such a sorry state. Even the stupidest
of merchants realizes that a slave in those conditions isn't worth
half her real price.

'I thought that if I cured her, washed her and fed her, the
resemblance would be perfect. I bought her without haggling over
the price those greedy pirates wanted. I thought that somehow
this marvellous resemblance could prove useful to me . . . and I
knew that . . .'

Orestes listened as if he were beside himself, still not able to
accept what his eyes were telling him. He turned again and again
towards the woman seated so close to him; she had caressed
him, she had called Castor her 'beloved brother', she had said
'our home' as only a queen can say, she sat and spoke like only
a queen can sit and speak. And then he turned towards the king
who was continuing his story, but in his eyes a light of ire and
suspicion was growing.

'I knew that . . . in any case, she had to belong to me. I could not bear the thought that another man might, sooner or later, discover her beauty and take his pleasure with her as I take my pleasure with my legitimate bride.'

The woman got up just then, took a pitcher from the table and poured wine into two golden cups, which she handed to the prince and King Menelaus. She then said to Orestes: 'It is time for me to retire to my rooms and leave you alone, but first I will have your bed made up myself. May the gods grant you a good night.'

She took her leave of the king with a slight nod of her head and a smile, and went off.

The house was enveloped in night and silence. The only sounds to be heard were the steps of the warriors on sentry duty in the great outer portico, their voices as they exchanged orders and the barking of the guard dogs. The king's gaze was far away, his brow clouded over. Perhaps in that moment it was the call of the sentinels on the ramparts built to defend the ships from the fury of Hector and Aeneas that rang in his ears; perhaps he heard the groans of the wounded and the shrieks of the dying.

The prince stared into his absent eyes: 'You set off the war to recapture a slave ... the kings of the Achaeans suffered injury, pain and death over a slave ... kingdoms overturned, thrones bloodied ... all of this ... for nothing more than a slave!' He pounded his fist on the table, jolting the cups. 'I want nothing from you. I do not want your help and I will not remain in this house another instant.' He sprang to his feet but the king barred his way, towering over him, and the sudden movement of his head stirred up his long red hair like a vortex of flames.

'That was not the reason, I told you!' Menelaus's voice blared out suddenly in the silence like a war horn. 'She was not the reason the war was fought,' he said again, his voice lower after the prince had blanched and dropped his head. 'She was a combatant ... more fearsome than the cunning of Ulysses, than the ire of Achilles, than the might of Great Ajax!'

'But you told me ...' began Orestes.

'Yes, I told you that I could not bear the thought that another man might take his pleasure with the living image of my bride. And that's all. That's all I was thinking of when I had her brought to a secret place where she was washed, nursed to health and cared for. Every day I had her served the same food and the same drink as the queen. In the same identical quantities, at the same times. When I saw her again, months later, I was dazzled: she was the perfect image of my bride. I even thought . . .'

'That she was her twin sister?' asked the prince.

'Yes, I thought so. Castor and Pollux, Helen's brothers, were twins. If the gods had created a prodigy once, could they not do it again?'

'Yes,' said Orestes. 'Why not twice?'

Menelaus approached him, put a hand on his shoulder and squeezed tightly: 'You are tired, son . . .' he said, 'and you are so young . . . perhaps you would like to sleep. I sleep little and poorly, prey to nightmares.'

'I do not wish to sleep,' said the prince and he placed his hand over the king's. 'I have come to learn everything, before doing what must be done. You must not hide anything from me, if I am to be the one who leads the charge of the chariots over the plains of Mycenae, if I must raise my sword over the body . . .' He did not have the strength to say another word.

Menelaus poured more wine into the cups then, and continued. 'The queen's nurse was still alive then and I met with her one winter's night in the little house near the river where she lived alone and unwell, cared for by a handmaid whom Helen had ordered to stay with her as long as she lived and never leave her wanting for anything. The queen loved her nurse dearly, and often went to visit her, bringing her the sweets and fruits that she was so fond of. No one could have noticed me, for I was dressed as a farmer, and rode a mule loaded with bundles of sticks.

'When I entered, the servant recognized me as soon as I bared my head; she kissed my hand, and Helen's nurse recognized me then as well. She was ailing, and breathing with difficulty, but her eyes lit up when she saw me. I sat beside her bed and said: "Mother, I have bought a slave from some *Ponikjo* merchants. She was dirty and ragged, and her body was full of bruises, as happens with those slaves who won't accept their condition and rebel against their masters or try to escape. I handed her over to people I trust, so she would be treated well and cared for. Now, mother, that slave is the perfect image of Helen. So perfect she looks like the same person."

'The old woman's expression changed suddenly; her lips trembled and her hand gripped mine, squeezing it with surprising strength. She said: "Where was the *Ponikjo* ship coming from, son? Where had it been?" Her breath came in short gasps, whistling as it left her bosom.

'I answered, "I do not know, mother. The *Ponikjo* journey among all peoples, and cross the sea wherever they please."

'The nurse fell back upon the bed but her breathing was becoming more strained, and came in painful gasps. Her eyes were lost in time, as if searching for long-buried images. She made an effort and clasped my arm again: "Where did the *Ponikjo* ship go then? Has it ever returned to our port?"

'"I don't know where it went and we've never seen those merchants since. Tell me, I beg of you, what are you thinking? Why is your breath so short? What causes you such distress?"

'She did not answer. She would not answer, no matter how much I implored her. Perhaps she thought an uncertain truth would do me more harm than not knowing. She closed her eyes and seemed to be sleeping, and I did not want to tire her further with my insistent questions. She never awoke again, and several days later, we placed her on a litter and buried her with rites worthy of a family member.'

'So you still don't know who that woman is,' said the prince. There was an ambiguous expression in his eyes, as though he understood what had passed through King Menelaus's mind as he buried the queen's nurse with honours that long ago winter's day.

'Who was truly responsible for the war?' he asked then.

'We were,' said the king with a firm voice. He sat opposite his nephew and held his head in his hands. 'The Atreides were the repositories of a terrible secret that dated back to the time when Euristheus reigned in Mycenae. We knew that the day would come when we would be invaded by the descendants of Hercules who had been driven away many years before by King Euristheus, and we knew that these invaders would destroy the land of the Achaeans. We were responsible for averting this impending threat, for preventing the destruction of our cities, the devastation of our fields, the massacre and enslavement of children and women.'

The prince shook his head: 'And to ensure that this would not happen, you unleashed a war that lasted years, instead of saving your strength, instead of readying the armies and the fleets? I don't understand . . . I just can't understand.'

The king drew a long breath, as the outer courtyard rang with the footsteps of the guards who had arrived to relieve their comrades on the first shift. Then he said: 'What we needed, to ensure that this would not happen, was the talisman of the Trojans. The talisman would make us invincible; only with the talisman in our possession would we be able to gather the strength necessary to withstand the onslaught, but we needed to have it before our time was up. No army can challenge fate. The question was, how to win it from the hands of the Trojans? Well, one day your father told me that he was planning to go to Ithaca to consult Ulysses. The little king of the western islands was already famous then for his cunning, and both Agamemnon and I had good relations with him. His wife Penelope, as you know, is the cousin of your mother and your aunt Helen.

'Ulysses was against the war, and he opposed our plan for a great expedition against Troy. He did not believe in the honesty of our intentions; he imagined it was a desire for power and conquest that animated us. That was the only way we could explain the answer he gave us. "If it is only that statue of stone that you want," he said, "much less than a war is needed." Nothing is more powerful in this world than a woman's appeal over a man, he claimed. His plan was simple: invite one of the Trojan princes to Sparta and then convince Helen to seduce him and flee with him. Once inside the city she would be able to give us all the information we needed.'

'I would have killed anyone else who had even hinted at such a proposal, on the spot, like a dog, but I realized the true significance of his words. He meant to say: "If you Atreides want to drag the entire Achaean people into total war, if you want to ask thousands of warriors to suffer and die, thousands of wives and mothers to wail over their fallen husbands and sons for the rest of their days, then you have to prove that you are ready for anything, ready to be the first to sacrifice what you hold dearest."

'Now this would have been right, if it were true, as he thought, that the real reason for our seeking war was our desire for power. Ulysses lived alone, you see, and hardly ever participated in the large assemblies of the continental kings. His little island was enough for him, he oversaw the work in his fields like a farmer, he sheared his own sheep and butchered his own swine. He was happy with what little he had.

'And yet I hated him for what he had said, and I swore that I would kill him as soon as I had the opportunity.'

'I can't believe that my father would have dared to repeat such a request, even if Ulysses had suggested it to him,' said Orestes, shaking his head. 'My father was a man of honour.'

'He was. In fact, when he returned he was gloomy and taciturn; he would not speak with me. He simply would not be persuaded to relate Ulysses's proposal. And when he had finally told me, after my long insisting, he added immediately: "It's a provocation. He merely wants to say that we can't count on him, that it's not his war. We'll do without his help."

'It was then that I conceived of the idea of how I could trick the master of deception, the most astute of men. And so I said: "We won't need to. I will do as he says." As your father looked at me, stunned, as if I had gone raving mad, I continued: "Ulysses is right. We are asking the Achaeans to leave their wives and children, to face danger, to suffer wounds, to risk death. We must be the first to show that we are willing to pay the highest price. Tell him I will do as he suggests, on one condition: if war should break out, despite his plan, he must take part in it with his ships and his warriors and he must help us to win it."

'Your father looked at me as if he couldn't believe his ears, but he could not oppose my words. He had no reason to doubt my good faith.

'That same evening, I went to the secret chamber and met with the woman who drank with us tonight in this room. She was completely devoted to me; she obeyed me blindly, no matter what I asked her. She must have suffered enormously before I found her, so great was her gratitude. When I had explained to her what she must do, she said that it would be a great joy for her to satisfy my request. There was just one thing she was sorry about, she said, that she would not see me again for a long time, or perhaps ever again.'

Orestes listened, rapt. His long blond hair lay as still as stalks of wheat before a storm. He was hearing things he never could have imagined, was forced to confront ideas that revolted him. King Menelaus let out a deep sigh, rose to his feet and went to the window. The city slept before his eyes, and the earth slept.

'When Paris fled back to Troy, taking her with him, we sent messengers throughout the land of the Achaeans, summoning all the kings to a war council. The abduction of a queen has always been an act of war, implicating the coalition of all our forces to avenge the offence.'

'And Ulysses did not know this?!' asked Orestes.

'Certainly, but he was convinced that it would be resolved through negotiation. After all, our relations with the Trojans had always been rather good. War assemblies have often been held with the sole aim of inducing the adversary to negotiate. But Ulysses realized that he had been tricked, and then I feared that all was lost. He had come to Sparta secretly to instruct Helen about her mission to Troy. I had arranged everything to ensure that he wouldn't notice a thing. They met in my presence, at night, by lamplight, in one of the rooms of this palace. Yet, all at once he turned to me and said: "Who is this woman?"'

'That's impossible!' said Orestes. 'He hadn't seen Helen for years, the light was dim, the resemblance perfect. How could he have guessed?'

The king smiled. 'Her scent,' he said. 'Ulysses is a sailor, and like all sailors his sense of smell is very keen. That's how they know they are nearing land, by the smell. They know precisely what land lies before them by the odour that wafts over the waves. One day, long before then, he had kissed Helen's hand and he had breathed in her fragrance. The woman he had before him was different. 'I must know everything,' he demanded. 'Everything which regards this woman. And everything which regards Helen. You must hide nothing from me if you want our plan to succeed.'

'I realized that he was not indignant over my deception; on the contrary, that amazing resemblance excited him. It was an irresistible challenge for his mind.'

'I convinced the kings to entrust him with the task of going to Troy to ask for the return of Helen, and I went with him. He was very sure of himself. He said: "Paris has had what he wanted for many months. King Priam will not want to drag the city into war over the passing fancies of his son. He will oblige Paris to turn Helen over to us, and we will bring her home, along with the talisman of the Trojans."'

'So why didn't Priam return the woman?' asked Orestes. 'Anyone would have done so, anyone in their right mind. Priam was a wise man and a great king, esteemed by all.'

'I don't know. No one knows. Not even Ulysses expected a refusal. He grew visibly pale when they gave us their answer, and looked at me in dismay. I believe that Antenor was the cause. He rose up with such passion to demand that Helen be immediately returned, that Priam reacted badly. Antenor spoke in the name of the Dardans, obedient to Anchises and his son Aeneas. To the king's ears, his demand had the ring of an imposition, coming from a minor branch of his dynasty, and he could not tolerate it in front of us and in front of the assembly of elders. If Antenor had held his tongue, Helen – or rather, the woman they thought was Helen – would have been returned to us. The war would have been avoided.'

Orestes held his head in his hands and drew a long breath:

'There's another reason, is there not? A hidden reason, that torments you.'

The king did not answer. He was tense and weary, his eyes were as red as one who had not slept the entire night. His gaze was absent again, his mind distracted. Tumultuous images passed behind his brow, like storm clouds dragged by the wind.

'You feel, within yourself, that you did not really pay the true price, the highest and most precious tribute, the only one that would have allowed you to ask an entire nation to combat and die. You feel that your trickery turned the benevolence of the gods against you. Everything went badly from that moment on. Everything went out of control. From the hands of man to the hands of fate. Am I right?'

The king's forehead creased deeply, but not a word came from his mouth. The crackling of flames could be heard from the courtyard, and the soft murmuring of men sitting around the fire.

'The responsibility was ours,' he said then, 'and we acted as we had to act. No one had foreseen the war. Not even the Trojans.'

'But if Priam had returned the woman, would you have obtained what you wanted? Had she succeeded in learning the secret of the talisman of Troy?'

'No. Not until many years later, after Paris had been killed, after she had become the legitimate wife of Deiphobus his brother and was thus recognized as part of the royal family. In the end, we did succeed in winning the talisman of the Trojans, but at what a price! The laments of my fallen comrades do not let me sleep at night. Their cries rising from Hades lick at the feet of my bed: Achilles, slain by Paris before the Scaean Gates, Patroclus, murdered by Hector ... Antilochus, son of Nestor; today he would reign over sandy Pylus. Ajax the Locrian crushed between the rocks ... my brother, butchered like a bull in the manger. Ajax Telamon, who threw himself on his own sword; it pierced through his back, running red with his blood. Diomedes and

Idomeneus forced to flee, perhaps already dead in some far off, unknown land. And Ulysses . . . Ulysses has not come back.

'We had time to become friends under the walls of Troy but now, now that I need his counsel and his help so badly, he is not here. Perhaps he wanders still over the boundless seas.

'The other night I had a dream. I was on the seashore, and I could hear the voices of my comrades calling to me from the depths of the nether world. They called me by name; they asked for my help, tormented as they were by cold and by solitude. I tried to answer, tried to speak with them, but my voice did not leave my throat. I opened my mouth but no sound came out. Then I suddenly saw the ship of Ulysses emerging from the mist covering the expanse of the waves. I saw him land, and sacrifice a black victim to the infernal gods. And the souls of the dead rose up to him from the depths of the abyss. One of them, a venerable old man with a long beard, spoke to him but I could not hear him, I could not perceive the sound of his words. I could only see Ulysses's face turn white in dismay.

'When the old man finished speaking I heard the voices of my comrades again. I saw them all, one by one, passing before the son of Laertes: Achilles, Ajax, Agamemnon, Eurilocus . . . but their voices no longer had the same deep, forceful timbre as when they sent the ranks to battle on the fields of Ilium. Shrill sounds came from their mouths, like the screeching of bats in a cave; piercing cries that contrasted with their weak aspect, with the pale shining of their armour. Oh gods, I saw them all, I saw my companions and my brother in the cold squalor of Hades . . .'

Orestes watched him intently and saw terror, panic, emptiness, solitude painted on his pale, sweaty face. 'It was only a bad dream, uncle. You did as you thought best, and now justice is on our side again. We will win, and restore order to the land of the Achaeans. Do not despair: you have many years of serene life to look forward to, here with your people, alongside your bride and your daughter.'

'My daughter,' said the king, lowering his head with a sigh. 'I have promised her to Pyrrhus, in order to bind him to us and obtain his alliance.'

Orestes suddenly started, but immediately regained his composure. The wind was picking up, whistling softly through the courtyard and the portico, stirring the flames of the torches and lamps. The prince strained his ears as if the wind carried distant whispers. He said: 'Were you aware of the plotting of the queens?'

'I was.'

'What did you know?'

'Everything. I can tell you everything, if you are not tired, my son.'

'I am not tired.'

Menelaus began to speak again: 'It was a night like this one, long and silent, the west wind was blowing. Paris, the Trojan prince, was our guest and he had already fallen into our trap. Ulysses sat on that stool you see over there and he seemed to be staring at the shadows cast by the wavering flames of the lamps. He suddenly said: "Tomorrow I want to see the queen again and speak to her before I go. Then I will return to my island and wait until it is time to go to Troy."

'I answered him: "Then you will have to rise at the first light of dawn; the queen will be leaving the palace to visit her sister Clytemnestra. She will stay away for several days."

'Ulysses seemed to take no note of my words. His eyes were half closed and his head was leaning against the wall. Then he said: "Did you know that Queen Aigialeia of Argos will be visiting Clytemnestra as well?"

' "No," I answered. "I did not."

'Ulysses fell silent again and he seemed to be listening to the wind that whispered light through the courtyard.

' "Do you know that the queen of Crete has landed at Mases to attend a secret meeting? No, you don't know. But I do. I also know that Queen Clytemnestra has sent a man she trusts to Ithaca, taking advantage of my absence. What do you make of all this?" said Ulysses.

'I was astonished. "How do you know all this?" I asked him.

'He did not answer. He said: "Send the other woman to the meeting, and have her make sure it takes place in the open, after sunset. We cannot run any risks." I did as he had told me to do, and we came to learn of their pact. Ulysses and myself. No one else.'

The prince shook his head incredulously: 'Not even my father? Why? It could have saved his life . . .' The boy's gaze was murky, challenging again.

'It wasn't clear in the beginning. It seemed to be a pact of friendship among the queens, an agreement to meet every year to celebrate rites in honour of the *Potinja*. Only Ulysses continued to scent danger, and the day the fleet set sail from Aulis he was still tormented by suspicion.

'Many years later, the night we stopped at Tenedos on our return voyage, he boarded my ship. I was awake, out on the deck, watching the bloody light illuminating the sky to the east: Troy was still burning . . . He came close without making a sound and put his hands down on the ship's railing, next to my own. He said to me: "Do not trust anyone, when you arrive home. Put ashore secretly, at night. Allow only the men who fought with you at Ilium to come close to you. I've warned Diomedes as well, but I fear he confides too much in his strength. He has not yet learned that deceit is infinitely more powerful."

'He turned towards the curved stern which my companion slept under, exhausted by the emotions and the hardships of those last days and nights. He said: "Send her to meet with the other queens, if they invite her." '

'And why didn't you return?' insisted the prince. His eyes flashed with barely restrained ire.

The king lowered his head: 'I sailed for Delos because I could no longer stay away from Helen. I had forced her into long, bitter solitude. I couldn't wait any longer. I left the woman who was with me to the priestesses, so they could take her to a secret place in the Peloponnese. And I stayed with Helen.'

'As you bedded Helen, my father was dying! Downed like an animal, along with all of his comrades!'

The king's hands trembled, his eyes filled with tears. 'It is as you say,' he said. 'I heard his last breath, distinctly, I felt the knife that cut his throat slash my own flesh, I saw his funeral mask rising like a bloody moon, hovering over the tower of the chasm! Son, my grief for his death bites into me every day and every night, like a ferocious dog. Do not condemn me, for you know not what paths your life may still take! You do not know if your courage will fail you one day, suddenly, if passion will cloud your mind and your good sense. Our destiny is not in our hands, and if the gods grant us a moment of happiness they make us pay for it bitterly, sooner or later. Do not judge me, do not condemn a man who suffers.'

He stood before the young man as if he was awaiting a verdict. Orestes looked up at him: his red eyes held an expression of dazed heartache, his face was deeply creased, his chin trembled imperceptibly and his mouth twisted in agony. Orestes got to his feet as well, and stared into his eyes for a moment, then burst into tears and clasped his uncle close.

They remained thus for some time, both wounded by the same pain, tormented by the same obscure fears. In the end, the youth pulled away and stepped back: 'For that which they have done,' he said, and his voice was cold and ruthless, 'no mercy.'

14

THE MOUNTAINS SEEMED TO have no end in the land of Hesperia, just as one day, long ago now, it had seemed to Diomedes and his men that the plains were without end. The Achaeans managed to avoid the *Teresh* who controlled the region to the west by journeying along the crests of the mountains, but they ended up in the land of the *Ombro*, where they had to struggle to force their way through, although the *Chnan* at times tried to negotiate with them. Their small communities were very belligerent and mistrustful, and they were scattered everywhere, behind every corner. The Achaeans were often forced to seek shelter in the forests, so that too many men would not be lost. Whenever they neared a town in search of food, Diomedes's men were often attacked and forced to engage in unsparing combat.

The *Ombro* inhabited a splendid land, made of gentle hills and valleys full of flowers of every colour, edged with sparkling torrents. But it was a poor land, and very far from the sea; the *Pica* lived in the intervening territory, on the eastern side of the mountains. They were quite similar to the *Ombro*, cultivating the earth and raising animals in wooden pens. They burned their dead on woodpiles, then put their ashes into clay jars which they buried with a few humble belongings.

The *Pica* were dangerous because they knew the art of crafting metal, and they made spears, axes and knives and sometimes even laminated bronze vases which the *Chnan* considered with great interest, carrying off as many as he could when they managed to seize a town. Their women were beautiful, with long, smooth braided hair; they wore gowns woven at the loom in bright colours.

In the chiefs' huts they sometimes found abundant quantities of amber, which certainly came from far away, perhaps from the fabled Electrides islands celebrated by sailors in every one of the Achaean ports.

At the centre of each village, the *Pica* planted a pole topped with the image of a woodpecker, their sacred animal or perhaps their god. They took their name from him. Their land was very bare, suited mainly to grazing sheep and goats. Sometimes the sea could be seen in the distance, a sea as green as the meadows and edged with white foam. But the coast was completely uniform and there was not a port to be seen; no promontories from which one could gaze into the horizon, no coastal plains that could be cultivated. Myrsilus claimed that that was the same sea that they had crossed years earlier when they had left Argos to head north, and that if Anchialus had lived, he would be looking for them along that coast. He wondered what fate had befallen their homeland, since Anchialus had surely died in the hands of those bastard *Shekelesh* without ever delivering Diomedes's message of alarm.

One day, having pushed on in the direction of the eastern sea, Myrsilus returned with little objects of no value, but that he was never to part with; they were small vases and drinking cups that came from the land of the Achaeans. He showed them to the king, saying: 'See, *wanax*? Someone from our land has ventured this far. That must mean that nothing terrible has happened to them. If we succeed in founding a city one day, we can make contact with merchants who come from our land and have news of it whenever they come out this way.'

The king had taken those humble little objects into his hands and caressed them, so Myrsilus gave him one to keep for himself.

Diomedes still tried to breed confidence in his men, but he realized as time passed that they were living from hand to mouth. They always ate as though it were their last meal, slept with a woman as though it might be the last time they ever made love.

It was sad, and made him sick at heart, but there was nothing he could do to change it.

Ros, the bride from the Mountains of Ice, loved him after all the time they had spent together, but she had not given him a child and this instilled a dark foreboding in Diomedes's soul; if that woman had been summoned from lands far away to restore life to a dying people, then he must be the one who bore the seeds of destruction and annihilation within him. He realized that Aphrodite's revenge would persecute him to the very end, to any corner of the land or sea. He had wounded her on the fields of Ilium and she punished him by extinguishing life wherever he now tried to sow it.

At times, in the dead of night, he would awaken suddenly when a wolf or a jackal howled from a mountain top or wood, because he had become convinced that in that land the gods made themselves heard through the voices of the animals. Why else had they so often found signs of animal worship and votive offerings?

One evening he returned to his tent after a raid, covered with dust and sweat. He lay down his weapons and poured a jug of water over his head. Just then his bride appeared, and he saw deep sadness in her eyes, or compassion perhaps. Or pity.

He had not seen himself in a mirror for years, but it was enough to see those eyes and that gaze to understand everything.

'A goddess once mounted my chariot and fought at my side,' he said. 'Do you believe me?'

The girl came closer. 'If you believe it then I believe you,' she said.

'No, you don't believe me,' said Diomedes. 'For the man you see before you is not the same, and this land is not the same and not even the sky is the same. I feel the weight of the end. I passed between the severed heads: did you know that?'

'Yes. But that will not be the cause of your death.'

'My comrades follow me because I promised them a kingdom, a city with houses and families. And I've given them nothing but hardship, grief and death.'

'Your comrades love you. They are ready to follow you

anywhere. And after all, didn't they suffer with you when you fought under the walls of that city so far away?'

'Don't you understand? This is why my heart aches! Then we knew what our sacrifices were for, then we lived in a world where we knew the rules and the confines. Not any more. I don't know where to lead them. Years have passed since we reached the mouth of the Eridanus. We have crossed plains and mountains and forests, we have forded swamps and swirling rivers. We have fought with many peoples but we have conquered nothing. This land saps our strength from us day after day, robs me of my comrades, one after another. How many have I buried until now?' Tears brimmed in his eyes but his voice was firm and strong. 'I remember them all, each one of them. I remember their names, their families, their cities. But they no longer exist. No one will ever take an offering to their tombs, no one will pronounce their names on the anniversary of their deaths. I had hoped that one day, when I had built a city and a kingdom, I would be able to raise a lofty cairn to them, with many steles of stone, each one carved with a name. Every year I would have offered a sacrifice and celebrated funeral games. Even for the Chetaean slave who died as a warrior to save my life.

'Perhaps I shall never succeed. One day my strength will abandon me and I too shall fall. Perhaps I will be left unburied. Another man will have you, just as I took you from the man who was destined to have you.'

'That is not true,' said the bride. 'This land could welcome you, if you could only banish the ghosts of time past. One night, while you were sleeping and I was wakeful, I went to the campfire to warm myself. The small, dark man that you call the *Chnan* approached me, and he sat down in silence next to me. I asked him: "If you were certain that the king would listen to you, what would you ask him?"

'He understood my sadness and he had many times seen the despair on your face. This is what he said: "I would tell him, go towards the sea and find a place which is big enough, near a little promontory and a source of fresh water. Build a village by cutting down the wood of the forest. Learn to extract salt from the water and to preserve fish, establish good relations with the nearby inhabitants, exchange gifts and swear to hold to agreements. Take women in marriage and bear children. Live off what the earth and the sea can give you. Sow the fields, graze flocks of goats and sheep, so you will have food in abundance in the winter, when the cold wind blows over the sea and the mountains. You will have wood to warm you, soft fleece on your beds. One day, perhaps, you will plant olive trees and grape vines and you will have oil to fortify your bodies and wine to warm your spirits. No one will ever know you exist, but you will live in peace and die one day, enfeebled by age, watching the sun set on the sea with clear eyes."

'This is what the small dark man that you call the *Chnan* told me, and I think he is right. Why don't you listen to him? Perhaps you would find peace. You would see life flourish, instead of wandering aimlessly, pursued by death. Finally, I believe, you would become my husband, my man. I could bear you a child whom you would see growing strong as a colt, beautiful as a tree in bloom.'

The king looked at her without speaking, and for a moment, it seemed to the girl that she could see a serene light in his eyes, like a golden sunset, but only just for a moment. Myrsilus came running up, breathing hard. His weapons clanged against his shoulders and the crest swayed on his helmet, stirred by gusts of wind. She shuddered as if she had seen a starving wolf galloping towards her: Myrsilus was the only adviser Diomedes listened to.

'*Wanax!*' he was shouting. '*Wanax!*' He stopped before his king with a mad gleam in his eye, like delirium. The king had him enter his tent.

'*Wanax*,' he said again when he had calmed down. 'I was advancing westward with my men as you had advised me, to see if there was richer, more open land in that direction. We found villages populated by an unknown people and we attacked them to take their animals. The *Chnan* says that they are the *Lat*, and that they come from the north. They are tough, combative. They venerate a she-wolf as their god and are led by her.'

'Is this why you are so excited?' asked the king. 'We already know that there are many unfamiliar peoples roaming this land.'

'Yes, that's true,' said Myrsilus. 'But when we burst into the largest house, belonging to their chief, perhaps, we found a prisoner, a man, bound. We've brought him here with us. You have to see him. Now.'

Diomedes followed him, directing a fleeting glance towards his bride, as if to ask her forgiveness for not having listened to her, and he went down the slope until he found his armed comrades thronging around someone or something. Myrsilus led him to the centre of the circle and showed him a man sitting on the ground at the foot of a tree. He was unbound, and when he saw Diomedes he leapt to his feet as if he had seen a ghost. He stood still and silent, staring at the king. He was a man of about thirty-five, tall and slim, well built. His face and body showed signs of hardship.

'He's a Trojan,' said Myrsilus. 'His name is Eurimachus.'

'A Trojan,' said the king, drawing closer. 'A Trojan, here . . .' Then he turned to Myrsilus: 'Have you done him harm?'

'No, *wanax*.'

'Have you interrogated him?'

'Yes, but he hasn't said much.'

The king turned to the prisoner: 'Do you know who I am?' he asked.

'Your appearance tells me that the gods have justly punished you for what you did to us, but I recognize you nonetheless. You are Diomedes. You wander without a homeland or a family in foreign territory. Destiny has been no kinder with you than with the vanquished.'

Diomedes bit his lip. He was ashamed of his wretched semblance, of the dwindling ranks of his men. The last time that man had seen him he was flying over the plain of Ilium on his chariot in a cloud of dust, clad in shining bronze, followed by an army as numerous as the stalks of wheat in the fields. He felt stabbed by deep humiliation, and yet he understood that strange, giddy enthusiasm that had possessed Myrsilus: that man was a part of his lost world; he obeyed the same rules, spoke the same language.

'How did you get here?' he asked, and hope seemed to quiver in his words.

'From the sea. With Aeneas.'

Diomedes was struck dumb. He remembered the night that he had spent in the swamps near the banks of the Eridanus, the black mirror of water that swelled up under a mysterious force. There he had seen the Dardan prince, Aeneas! Covered with bronze, advancing towards him with a menacing air, brandishing his sword. This was the meaning of his vision! Only a final bout of single combat between the two races would satisfy the gods! Only thus would they be satisfied, and assign dominion over that land. The gods had led him here, through mud and dust, and they had led the son of Anchises to the same place. This was the reason, without a doubt! The gods were not content with the savage encounters that had bloodied the plains of the Hellespont for years; they demanded to watch the last duel, from up on the top of Mount Olympus, as they drank ambrosia from their golden cups. They could not be disappointed; if they were granted their pleasure, they would surely assign the prize. Perhaps Athena, who had once protected Diomedes's father Tydeus, would appear to him again, a diaphanous figure in the mists of sunset. She would take up the reins at his side, on his war chariot.

'Where is he?' he asked. His voice had lost all uncertainty; it was metallic and hard, peremptory.

'You will never know.'

'There's no place for both of us in this land. It must be either me, or him. You don't have to tell me where he is; I'll find him nevertheless, and I will challenge him to a duel. But if you do tell me, you can be certain I won't attack him from behind, when he least expects it. I will send a herald, and you can accompany him yourself. If you accept, you can return to him and remain with him, if he wins. But if I win, this land will be mine, mine the people who populate it far and wide.'

'Isn't the blood you spilled for years and years enough? All those innocents, mown down by death, all those tears . . .' said the Trojan. 'Isn't it enough that your homeland has become a nest of vipers, cursed by the gods? Do you know what has become of the great master of deception? He who designed the trick that defeated us, do you know what fate has reserved for him?' Eurimachus's eyes blazed, the veins on his neck stood out.

'Ulysses! What do you know? What do you know?' shouted out Diomedes.

'We met one of his comrades in the land of the Mountains of Fire, in the region of the giant cyclops. The poor wretch had been cast ashore and forgotten; for months he had been living like an animal, eating roots, worms and insects. He seemed crazed when he saw us, he threw himself weeping at Aeneas's knees, he embraced his knees, do you understand that? He told us what happened to the great deceiver: Ulysses has lost all his ships and wanders the sea aimlessly, persecuted by implacable destiny.' The Trojan's eyes glittered with cruel, fearless joy. Diomedes lowered his head and felt anguish invading his soul: Ulysses . . . had not returned. His faithful bride and the little prince still waited for him, gazing out over the distant waves day after day, in vain. Ulysses, the greatest sailor in the land of the Achaeans, had lost his way! Or perhaps he was so shattered by the loss of his ships and his comrades that he dare not return to his homeland to face the elders and the nobles.

'Do not rejoice too soon, Trojan,' he said, staring wildly into his eyes. 'Ulysses will return. Ulysses always finds the way. His mind fears not even the gods; he can win any challenge. But consider now what I have told you. If you accept to take me to Aeneas, you will witness a fair duel. If you refuse, I'll sell you as a slave, trade you for some food or animals.'

When Diomedes returned to his tent, his bride ran to him. 'What did Myrsilus show you? There was a man down there; who is he?' she asked, and her fear was plainly written in her eyes.

'The past,' said the king. 'My past has returned. I must kill if I want to conquer the future. Only then shall we found a city for the living and raise a mound to the dead. Only then.'

*

The Trojan prisoner leading them to Aeneas had lost his way. Autumn was ending, and the weather worsened abruptly. Snow fell heavily on the mountains and covered the trails and the passes. Diomedes tried nonetheless to advance in the direction of the western sea, but peril abounded on the steep windswept summits and in the forests crawling with packs of starving wolves.

One day, as the sun was setting, as the column of warriors advanced along a steep, narrow path in the deep snow, one of Diomedes's horses stumbled and fell. The steed tried to get back up by digging in his hooves, but the ground crumbled beneath them. He slipped further down, letting out shrill whinnies of pain. And his companion, erect on the rim of the precipice, answered, calling him desperately.

Diomedes plunged down the slope, nearly falling headlong himself, finally reaching him. The magnificent animal could no longer move: his spine was broken. He raised his head, snorting great clouds of steam from his nostrils, his huge eyes wide and full of terror.

Diomedes knelt before him: he couldn't believe that this had happened. This was one of the divine horses that he had taken from Aeneas in battle after having defeated and nearly killed him.

They understood him, they understood human words, they understood, in the night, the mysterious voices carried by the wind and perhaps, when all other creatures had given themselves up to sleep they spoke to each other in a language that no one could understand. Diomedes pummelled the snow and wept as the horse whinnied weakly, his head falling backwards. The king stroked him gently, at length, then tore off a strip of his cloak and tied it over the horse's eyes. From above, his comrades watched in silence, while the other horse called his companion frantically, rearing up and wildly kicking the air, whinnying sharply towards the grey, impassive sky.

Diomedes pulled out his dagger and struck the animal at the base of his head. A clean blow. The snow was stained by a scarlet stream and the horse surrendered his life.

The king trudged slowly towards the path. He reached his comrades and silently resumed the march. But the other horse would not follow them. The efforts of Myrsilus and the others to coax him on were futile: absolutely immobile, he stared at them with flaming eyes.

The king turned towards them: 'Let him alone,' he said. 'He has reached the end of his road.'

As they began to march again, the horse turned towards the bottom of the escarpment and began, tentatively, to test the terrain with his hoof. Then, slowly, he began to make his way down. Myrsilus turned around and said, *'Wanax!'* and the king stopped as well. He turned and watched with a swollen heart as the horse descended slowly in the snow up to his breast and finally reached his dead companion. He nudged him with his muzzle, neighing softly, trying to move him with his head, to make him stand up. In the end, he placed himself in front of the other, his head high, nostrils dilated, ears pointed, whipping the air with his tail, scraping the frozen earth with his hoof.

'It will be dark soon,' said Myrsilus, 'the wolves will come.'

'I know,' said the king. 'And so does he. But nothing will separate him from his lost companion. He'll wait to gallop with him again in the Asphodel fields.' Large tears lined his bristly cheeks. 'It's never cold there; there is no snow, or frost. It's never dark and night never comes. A divine light shines endlessly over meadows blooming with white lilies and scarlet poppies . . .' He pulled close the cloak that the icy wind snapped like a tired banner. 'It's never cold there, never cold . . .'

In that moment, the darkness was animated by yellow eyes, by rustling noises, by dull snarling, while a shrill whinny broke the silence, raising a challenge as clear as the sounding of a trumpet.

Myrsilus drew closer to Diomedes and fixed him with a firm gaze: 'You'll conquer others no worse than these,' he said. 'And you will harness them to your chariot. Let us go now, *wanax*, the night is upon us.'

*

At that moment, under another sky, Anchialus jerked awake abruptly and left his tent, searching the darkness in the direction of the mountains and then, opposite them, the beach glittering in the moonlight. He thought he had heard a strange sound, like distant galloping. He approached a guard on watch near the fire, one of the Epirotes marching with Pyrrhus.

'Did you hear that?' he said.

'What?'

'Someone . . . someone approaching on horseback.'

'You're dreaming,' said the guard. All he heard was the sound of the lapping waves, the sleepless motion of the sea. But Anchialus was certain of the sound in his ears and, unsheathing his sword, strode through the camp immersed in sleep. The plain stretched between the mountains and the sea, extending at the end into a narrow sandy strip between the high promontories.

The waves of the sea glistened in a silver wake that led, like a path, to the horizon. To the pale face of the moon. And the sound of the galloping was always closer, more powerful. He heard it, here, and there, striking the hard rocks which rang crackling under the pounding bronze hooves and then beating the compact earth with a dull roar. It came from the right, no, perhaps from the left. He couldn't say. Suddenly, out of nowhere, it was on him. He heard shrill whinnying, he felt panting, snorting breath steaming from quivering nostrils, he smelled the sharp odour of sweat and then it was behind him, towards the sea. He turned and he heard it pounding the sand and whipping the waves of the sea until the sound died off, amidst the billows, towards the pale light of the moon.

He saw nothing, but remained at length to watch the swells, white with foam like flowing manes tossed by the wind, to watch the shivering silver wake stretching infinitely to the shores of distant Asia and the deserted fields of Ida.

He retraced his steps and sat down on a stone covered with fragrant moss. Whose wild galloping had that been, bursting upon him from the west and fading off over the sea towards Asia? What message were the gods sending him? He closed his eyes and tried to crush an ominous premonition.

The next day Pyrrhus gave orders to turn south along the coast. And thus the son of Achilles left behind the vast plains of Thessaly and Phthia, his birthright, which he had been allowed to see for so brief a time. He was reminded of the suspicion with which old Peleus had questioned him upon his return, and how he had enjoined him to leave his land, his ships and his Myrmidon warriors, whom he was not worthy of. The old man had driven him off, banished him to the sea, forced him to take up his journey again.

But the day would come when he would return, and it was close now. The old man would die, and he would become the most powerful sovereign in the land of the Achaeans.

They marched all that day and all the next, following the coast of Boeotia, the cursed land of Oedipus, of Eteocles and of Polynices, and they reached the borders of Phocis and Locris. There they united with the Locrians, the warriors of Ajax Oileus who had survived the waves of the sea. Many of them could no longer enjoy the peace they had longed for during years of war. The clang of weapons and the sound of bugles had them rushing to join. Pyrrhus's savage vitality and untiring fervour reminded them of his father, and they would follow him, enthralled, even to the gates of the underworld.

A few days later, they were camped on the Isthmus. No one remembered to offer sacrifice to the sea and to Poseidon, so Anchialus did so, alone. He sacrificed a lamb, thinking of his comrades who perhaps still wandered the seas, and of those who perhaps had not yet found the road of return.

The army soon found itself on the road that ran between the dominion of Argos and of Mycenae. They could see sentinels in the distance, posted on the mountain tops. Smoke signals rose at night, as their passage threw the entire land into confusion and dread. The ferocity of Achilles's son was legendary; the survivors of the long war in Asia had told many a tale during the long winter nights, to their wives and children gathered around the hearth. They knew that war and slaughter were his reason for living, that he feared neither gods nor men, that the odour of blood filled him with an accursed, inexhaustible energy, sated only by the destruction of his very last enemy. Anchialus asked himself whether Menelaus, having unleashed such an annihilator, would ever succeed in containing him or inspiring him to peace. Anchialus felt such loathing towards him that he had even considered doing away with the monster in his sleep after the war was over, but the possibility of succeeding was remote. He was always guarded by Automedon, his father's charioteer, and by the bronze-covered giant Periphantes, armed with two double-edged axes.

They finally reached the plain of Argolis one evening as the sun was setting. On one side, to the left, they could see the lights of Mycenae and the citadel, still reddened by the last light of dusk. Beyond Mycenae, still hidden from sight, was Argos, and Anchialus imagined the city immersed in the peace that precedes the evening.

They pitched camp, but suddenly, in the dead of night, the sentinels roused the king who was sleeping in his tent next to his dog. Pyrrhus threw a cloak over his naked body and peered out at the mountains that closed off the Argive plain to the west. On the summit blazed a gigantic fire, spreading its glow over a vast area. Menelaus's army had reached the mountain top and was ready to descend into the plain. The pincers were about to close.

'Light a fire,' said Pyrrhus, and he went back to sleep under his tent.

15

THE WAR COUNCIL WAS held shortly before dawn in a farmer's house near Nemea; Hippasus's sons had secretly made all the arrangements several days earlier. King Menelaus entered first, followed by his nephew Orestes and by Prince Pylades who commanded the Phocian warriors. Shortly thereafter Pisistratus arrived, accompanied by his charioteer; he was covered with bronze and an enormous double-edged axe hung from his belt. He lay it on the table, took off his helmet and kissed Menelaus on both cheeks.

'My father the king sends his greetings,' he said, 'and has told me to tell you that, starting today, one bull from his herds will be immolated to Zeus every day so he may grant victory to our armies. Naturally, he did not fail to say that were he not so old, he would be leading the army himself, and that men today are not made of the same wood they used to be, and we should have seen him that time that the Arcadians invaded his territory to raid his cattle . . .'

Menelaus smiled: 'I know that story. I think I heard it told one hundred times when we were fighting in Asia. But trust me, there's much truth in what your father says. They say that when he was young, he was a formidable combatant. I'm sorry he did not come: Nestor's counsel would have been precious.'

The owner of the house brought a basket of fragrant bread, just baked. Menelaus broke it and distributed it to everyone. Pisistratus gulped down a few pieces, then said: 'It took quite some effort, from my brothers and me, to convince him to stay home. He wanted to come at any cost. But he is very old now, and weakened by the strain of war. Bringing him with us would have been too risky.'

The noise of a chariot and the pawing of horses came from outside, then the sound of footsteps.

'It's Pyrrhus,' said the king, rising to welcome the guest.

The son of Achilles, decked in his father's armour, stood for a moment at the open door, filling the space completely with his bulk. His adolescent's face contrasted strangely with his wide shoulders, his powerful muscles, his disquieting gaze. There was something unnatural about him, as though he had not been born of woman. As though the god Hephaestus had fashioned a soulless exterminator in his forge.

Menelaus greeted him and broke some bread for him as well. 'We are all here now,' he said then. 'The council may begin.' A pale reflection entering the window at that moment announced the birth of a new day.

Pyrrhus spoke immediately, before the king had invited him to do so. 'Why do we need a battle plan? We will wait for them to come out and annihilate the lot. If they don't come out, we'll scale the walls and burn down the city.' Orestes looked at him and was gripped by a feeling of deep aversion, almost repugnance, for that creature capable only of blind violence, but he said nothing.

'It's not so simple,' said Menelaus. 'We know that there's an Argive contingent marching towards us, and we cannot rule out Cretan ships landing at some hidden spot. As far as the city is concerned, I don't want to destroy it. Hippasus has told me that many of the inhabitants have remained faithful to the memory of my brother. I believe we should detach a contingent to cover us from behind in case the Argive army should turn up unexpectedly as we are attacking Aegisthus's forces. I was thinking that Prince Orestes could command it.'

Pyrrhus laughed derisively. 'You're right,' he said, 'that way he can't get into any trouble. I can handle the Mycenaeans alone. I have to earn your daughter's bed somehow, don't I?'

Orestes blazed with indignation and jumped to his feet, drawing his sword. 'I fear no danger!' he said. 'And I don't fear you, even if you are the bastard son of a demigod!'

Pyrrhus also rose to his feet. 'Then come outside,' he said, 'and we can solve the matter immediately. We don't need you anyway.'

Orestes was heading towards the door, but Menelaus barred their way. 'That's enough!' he thundered. 'Woe betide an army divided before its first battle! No matter how strong the heroes who lead it are, it is destined to be destroyed, and its leaders with it.' The two princes stopped cold. 'The Achaeans have suffered tremendous grief for the ire of your father, don't you know that?' he said to Pyrrhus. 'Do you know how many generous young men were mown down in the fields of Ilium because of that murderous quarrel? How much remorse, how many tears were shed? When your father saw the mangled body of Patroclus, his corpse immobile in the stiffness of death, he would have given anything to have repressed his wrath while he was still in time, to have never abandoned the army to the fury of Hector. Now eat the bread that I have had baked in this house, so that the bond of hospitality, sacred in the eyes of the gods, may unite you!'

Pisistratus handed some bread to both. 'The king is right,' he said. 'This challenge is ill-considered. There will be glory for everyone on the battlefield today. You, Pyrrhus, will be sufficiently rewarded by marrying the daughter of Helen, whom every Achaean prince would want as his bride. There will be no slaughter of the vanquished nor plunder, for this is a war between brothers, between people of the same blood. Thebes was cursed and then destroyed for having permitted the sacrilegious duel between Eteocles and Polynices, sons of the same mother and of the same father. If this were to happen here, the gods would curse us and there would be no more peace for our land.'

The two youths took the bread they had been given but barely touched it to their lips, and repressed their anger. It was clear to all that the challenge had only been deferred. The king allowed silence to fall over that gesture for several long moments, then began to speak again in a firm, commanding voice.

'So, Pyrrhus will draw his phalanx up at the centre, in front of the city gates, while Orestes will remain at the rear with a squadron of chariots to prevent an attack from behind. I will draw up to the right, along with Pylades's Phocians, and Pisistratus will position his men to the left. I believe that Aegisthus will come out to fight. Over these past years, the city has extended outside of the walls. Many of the elders have requested that these houses and properties not be abandoned to destruction. Hippasus's sons will signal with the horns when I give the order to attack. Now return to your men, and may the gods assist us.'

Pyrrhus left first; he got into his chariot and raced off towards the north in the direction of the hills. Pisistratus followed soon after, but before stepping aboard his chariot next to the driver, he said: 'Take care, Orestes. He provoked you deliberately, certain that you would react. That's a very bad sign. But don't think about it now. Today we must win.' He rode off as a veiled sun rose over the mountains. Menelaus, behind them, heard those words with anguish, and his heart was sickened by dark foreboding. He feared that sooner or later Orestes would accept the challenge of the invincible son of Achilles and that he would succumb.

Prince Pylades approached Orestes and said: 'Pisistratus is on your side. This is important. Whatever Pyrrhus has in mind, he knows that everyone will be against him. Stay away from him, do not let yourself be provoked. Do not play his game.' And then, when they were in the middle of the courtyard, ready to take their separate ways, Pylades continued in a low voice: 'It's evident that the king is greatly afflicted by this; he thinks he made a grave mistake considering Pyrrhus indispensable for the success of this endeavour and asking for his alliance. Say something to hearten him: he must not have doubts and regrets passing through his thoughts today, as he does battle. He must have only revenge on his mind. Farewell, my friend. This evening it will all be done.'

Orestes turned then towards Menelaus and he smiled: 'Do not worry yourself, uncle. He's just a boastful boy, and we're all excited at the eve of the battle. He has already been in combat, while for me this will be the first time on an open field. He merely wanted to lord it over me. That's all.'

The king shook his head. 'I am worried,' he said, 'I am afraid that this war will generate more bereavement, more sorrow without end. Blood will have blood.'

'You are right there, uncle: the blood of my father and his comrades must be avenged. Remember that you are Menelaus the Atreid, shepherd of armies. No one can stand up to you in the land of the Achaeans.' He jumped on to his chariot and flew off towards the south in a cloud of dust. Menelaus remained alone in the middle of the courtyard watching the sun rise slowly in the milky sky. The sheep bleated behind him as their keeper led them out of the fold. The king looked at him, and for a moment wished he were like him, a man of no import who thinks only of finding food for his dinner.

*

Pyrrhus assembled his Epirotes, lined them up in a column and began to descend towards the plain. Automedon held the reins of his war chariot. Anchialus approached him. 'You will allow me to speak with King Menelaus? You promised me, remember?'

Pyrrhus regarded him with an ambiguous smile, then gestured to his guards. 'Keep him here at camp until the battle is finished and you see me return. I don't trust him; he might be spying for our enemies. No one has ever seen him before, no one knows where he comes from.'

Anchialus struggled as two of the guards led him away to tie him with a rope to a pole at the centre of the camp. He shouted: 'Man of no honour and no word! You are not the son of Achilles, you are a bastard!'

Pyrrhus turned and shouted back: 'Do not fear! When I return this evening I shall send you personally to say what you like to my father; you can tell him yourself that I didn't keep my word!' His laughter was lost in the pounding of his horses' hooves and in the roar of the bronze wheels of his chariot.

In the meanwhile, a host of warriors had exited the gate of

Mycenae, descended along the valley of the tombs and taken position on the slope that overlooked the plain. Menelaus saw them and signalled to Pisistratus and Pylades to draw up to the right and to the left while waiting for Pyrrhus to come and occupy the centre. As they had established, Orestes deployed his chariot squadron further south to intercept any Argive foray at their backs. Pisistratus, who was the closest to the walls of Mycenae, noticed that the ranks of the enemy were swelling; he whipped his horses and joined Menelaus. 'There are a great many of them,' he said. 'Many more than I expected. What is Pyrrhus waiting for to take his place? I hope they do not attack now. They could put us in serious difficulty.'

'No, I don't think they will. And if they are as numerous as you say, that means we have all of Aegisthus's forces lined up before us; all the better for us, we can keep a close watch on them. For the time being, we will only shorten the distance between the two arrays.' Pisistratus obeyed, but Menelaus was mistaken about the strength of the force. Aegisthus was hidden to the north with a strong contingent of Argives and a selected group of Mycenaean chariots. His informers had been reporting on the advance of the Epirote army for some time, and he had been waiting for them since the night before in a well-sheltered valley. When Pyrrhus's column passed in front of them, he had the attack signal raised in silence. The chariot squadron was arrayed in a wedge formation, and at his next signal they stormed full force at Pyrrhus's column, still in marching order. The Argive infantry charged forward at a run.

By the time Pyrrhus realized what was happening, the head chariots were already upon them. They mowed through his marching column like a scythe cuts down stalks of ripe wheat, leaving the ground behind them red with blood and scattered with mangled limbs. The cries of the wounded tore through the heavy morning air, resounding over the nearby mountains, and the echo cast them down to the plain. But the armies of Menelaus and Pisistratus were too far away to hear them and Orestes, even more distant, had the neighing of his stallions in his ears, and the din of the chariots as they patrolled vast stretches of the territory all around.

The Locrians of Pyrrhus's rear guard withdrew to the hills, and the concerted shouts of their commanders lined them up rapidly in combat order. In the immense confusion, the warriors who had fought at Ilium with Ajax Oileus exhorted their comrades to throw all the stones they could find on to the ground before them to hinder the charge of the enemy chariots, and their commanders had the archers advance on all sides. But the terrified Epirotes fled in every direction, falling in droves under the spears of the seasoned chariot-borne marksmen of Aegisthus. The Mycenaean had meanwhile identified Pyrrhus's chariot and was loosing his squadron, widened into a pincer formation, upon it.

The sun, veiled since early that morning, was now hidden by a front of black clouds driven by a strong northern wind that made the dust swirl under the racing horses' hooves and under the wheels of the chariots launched at full speed across the plain.

Pyrrhus saw the tips of the pincer closing in on him from the right and from the left, and he felt that all was lost. He turned his eyes towards the hills and saw the barricaded Locrian contingent shooting swarms of arrows at the assailants, decimating the warriors on the enemy war chariots.

'There!' shouted Pyrrhus at his charioteer. 'You must get us there before they close us off. Save me, Automedon, and I will make you king of Tiryns!'

But Automedon had already seen the only route of escape and was urging on his left horse, pulling at the reins with all the strength of the arms that had once prevailed over the gallop of Balius and Xanthus. His pursuers, intuiting the manoeuvre, whipped on their teams to cut off his path. Automedon shouted: 'I will take you to safety, son of Achilles, but look out! The chariot there on our left will succeed in cutting us off unless you slay the driver.'

But Pyrrhus was not listening, and seemed to be out of his mind; 'Faster, faster! Force over!' he shouted.

Automedon could not complete the curve any more sharply

without causing the chariot to overturn. He pulled a javelin one-handed from the quiver at his side and thrust it at Pyrrhus, shouting: 'Strike the charioteer, now!' Contact with the weapon seemed to rouse Pyrrhus; he grasped the massive ashwood pike in his fist and turned towards the closest chariot, where the enemy was already taking aim with his bow. He weighed the javelin and hurled it with all his might. The point of bronze tore through the charioteer's cuirass at his waist, pierced through his belly and came out the other side. Without its driver, the chariot careened and overturned, dragging down the two chariots close behind it in a tangled mass of men and horses. Automedon urged his team onward, loosening the reins at their necks; they flew towards the line of the hills, to safety. Aegisthus and the others pulled up short, finding themselves on too wide a curve, and regrouped with the rest of the squadron confronting the Locrians.

Pyrrhus meanwhile had penetrated behind the lines where many of his Epirotes had gathered, and he jumped to the ground, instantly regaining his composure. He reformed the lines into a close, compact array, shield against shield. He ordered the front line soldiers to kneel; each warrior planted the shaft of his weapon into the ground so that only the spearpoints emerged. That would do to hold back the chariots, while he had the rest of the army retreat to more uneven ground. There the enemy would be forced to attack them on foot; they would gain time and perhaps he would be able to open a passage through to Aegisthus . . .

*

Menelaus was exceedingly worried. He could not imagine what could have happened to Pyrrhus, and the massive Mycenaean line-up was becoming more and more menacing. He ordered Pylades to join up with Orestes and head north with the chariot squadron to see what had happened. It was risky to leave the battlefield exposed in the direction of Argos, but an attempt had to be made. The sky was getting darker and flashes of lightning shot from peak to peak, while violent gusts of wind bent the tops of the poplars down in the valley and the crests of the warriors' helmets. The horses quivered impatiently at their yokes, pawing the dirt with their hooves, as they felt the storm gathering in the sky and on the ground.

When Orestes had received Menelaus's order, he left a small garrison to hold the position and he flew off, with Pylades and all of his squadron, towards the line of hills standing out to the north. It wasn't long before he realized what must have happened, and he was about to stop his horses and turn back, abandoning Pyrrhus to his destiny, but Prince Pylades convinced him to advance. 'There are Locrian troops with Pyrrhus,' he shouted. 'This is the best way to settle your score; the son of Achilles will be in your debt his whole life!'

Orestes launched his chariots forward in attack; he deployed them in three lines across the entire plain, so that they would strike the enemy in waves. Aegisthus realized too late what was happening; he tried desperately to turn his front in the opposite direction, giving up on the ground battle with Pyrrhus's men. He ordered his men to go back to their chariots and to retreat towards the sides, before Orestes's chariots reached them, but the manoeuvre failed before it could begin. His warriors had just jumped into their chariots when they were hit by the first wave and decimated. Then came the second wave, and the third. Aegisthus's chariot was overturned, and his driver was dragged away and trampled to death by the crazed horses, on the stones of a dry river bed. Aegisthus got to his feet and turned in confusion to seek a way to escape, but Pylades spotted him and shouted to Orestes, whose chariot was rushing past at a short distance: 'On your left! Look to your left!' Orestes enjoined his driver to hold the horses, and he spotted Aegisthus. He leapt from his chariot and ran straight at him.

'You will pay for the blood of Agamemnon!' he shouted in a rage. 'You will appear before him this very day in Hades, with your nose and ears cut off!'

'Then come and get me, you cur!' shouted back Aegisthus, standing up to him. 'I fucked your mother and butchered your father! Yes, that's right, he was bleeding like a pig!'

Those words pierced through Orestes like a white-hot blade as he charged forward, and devastated his soul. A veil of blood dropped over the eyes of the prince. His fury vanished all at once and was replaced by an icy calm. Near his enemy now, he halted his charge and weighed his spear. Aegisthus's sneering confidence disappeared all at once; he looked around wildly and spotted an abandoned shield. He dropped lightning quick to gather it, but Orestes was left-handed and threatened him now on his undefended side. Orestes heaved the ashen pike and it sank through his shoulder blades, between his neck and his back, where his breastplate gave no protection. It nailed his enemy to the ground in that position, on his knees; Orestes watched as a great stream of blood poured from the mouth of the retching, choking man. But before he died, he wrenched the spear from his body and knocked him over on to his back. He drew his sword and cut off his nose, his lips, his ears and his genitals, so thus he would appear to the shade of his father the Atreid in the house of Hades.

Aegisthus's soul fled sighing into the cold wind that battered the countryside, and Orestes found himself face to face with Pyrrhus. He was spattered with blood from head to foot and he had bits of flesh and human brains on his shield and greaves. Orestes felt a cold chill at the sight of him. He was panting, and stank unbearably.

'The Argive infantry is wiped out,' he said. 'I imagine I should thank you for getting the war chariots out of my way.' And then, observing the desecrated corpse of Aegisthus: 'By the gods, I didn't think you were capable of it. I have to admit you've got it in you.'

Orestes was uneasy at this praise, and answered: 'Pisistratus and King Menelaus may be in difficulty. We must return to Mycenae.' He leapt on to his chariot, followed by Pylades and his squadron, and set off swiftly towards the city.

Pyrrhus turned back to his men and said: 'Start marching and catch up with me as soon as you can. If you get there when the battle is over, there will be nothing left for you.' Then he mounted the chariot that Automedon had just brought to his side, and hurled off after Orestes's squadron.

'Tonight you will be king,' he said to Automedon, 'as I have promised you.'

'I didn't do it for you,' replied the charioteer. 'I did it because you are the son of your father.' He whipped on the horses.

*

Meanwhile, the commanders of the Mycenaean army had given orders to attack, sure that Aegisthus had by then got the better of Pyrrhus, and taking advantage of the fact that the chariot squadron commanded by Orestes had taken off to the north. The forces were balanced; they might even win.

Menelaus then joined forces with Pisistratus's Pylians; he drew up at the centre, leaving the right wing to the son of Nestor. The enemy army were favoured by the slope and the direction of the wind; they had gained ground and were managing to push back their adversaries, even though Menelaus, at the centre, was fighting like a lion. The king felt that he was battling under the eyes of his brother; he could hear his cries roaring from the penetralia of the palace. He shouted to those he had before him: 'Stop fighting! Accept the truce or you will be exterminated! Abandon the usurper!'

But few could hear him in the din of the battle, and those who heard him could not understand him. They continued fighting desperately because they had been told that the victors would exterminate them all and sell their families into slavery.

Pisistratus brandished his enormous two-edged axe on the right wing, toppling his enemies one after another, his men so close behind him that the entire formation was slowly rotating to the left. Thus, when the chariot squadron led by Orestes came into sight, Queen Clytemnestra's army had their backs almost completely turned to him. Orestes did not slow his onward charge and mowed into the enemy, drawing all of his men behind him. Pylades returned to the head of his Phocians and led them into the attack. Pyrrhus, who had been following at a short distance, threw himself into the fray as well, as the sky was rent by blinding lightning and shaken by loud peals of thunder. Rain pelted down on the raging conflict, soon turning into hail, and the two armies were immersed in a magma of mud and blood, in a chaos of screaming and neighing, that completely obscured the minds of the warriors, plunging them into a blind frenzy, a delirium of destructive folly. Certainly, had the gods dissolved the thick mist that clouds the vision of mortals, Menelaus the Atreid, Pyrrhus, Orestes, Pylades and Pisistratus would have seen the bloody ghosts of Phobos and Deimos passing among the storm clouds, announcing the arrival of the god of war.

The Locrians and Epirotes had arrived and had drawn up in columns behind Pyrrhus's war-car. The son of Achilles had pushed his way through the entire formation and was battling on the front line; since the terrain there was too rough for chariots, he had descended and was fighting on foot with such fury that the enemy line wavered and split, leaving an opening at the centre through which hundreds of warriors poured. The Mycenaean army was breaking ranks and retreating haphazardly towards the gate to seek haven within the city walls. Pisistratus cut them off and, finding themselves completely surrounded, they threw down their arms and pleaded for mercy. Menelaus saw this and stopped, ordering the heralds to have the fighting cease. The blasts of the horns sounded amid the claps of thunder and Pisistratus was the first to hear them and call off his warriors. Orestes heard them and he halted his chariots. Pylades heard them and he withdrew his Phocians on the left wing, but Pyrrhus continued the massacre, and he incited his Epirotes to attack the undefended quarter close to the walls.

*

Anchialus was alone at the centre of the camp, for the Epirotes who had been guarding him had taken to their heels when the storm broke, seeking refuge in a mountain cave. He waited until the rain had soaked the earth, then he propped his feet against the pole and pushed it back and forth until he had uprooted it. He freed himself of his bonds and ran back to his tent to recover his weapons. He approached one of the terrified horses who was trying to kick himself free of the reins that kept him tied to a tree at the edge of camp. He loosed the steed and jumped on to its back, riding off before his guards had realized a thing. He galloped over the plain lit by flashes of lightning and pelted by the wind and rain. When he reached Mycenae, his head was bleeding and his body ached from all the hailstones that had struck him, but he distinctly saw Menelaus's army immobile under the downpour. At that very moment a young blond warrior passed on his battle chariot; he was heading towards Pyrrhus, who was continuing to advance towards the city. The youth cut in front of him and came to a halt, shouting: 'Stop, and call off your men! The king has ordered that the fighting cease. The survivors have surrendered. Enough blood!'

'I greatly regret it,' replied Pyrrhus, 'but I promised my men rich spoils, and that is why they followed me here. You stop them, if you're capable of it.'

'I will stop you, if you don't order them to withdraw immediately,' shouted Orestes. 'Follow the king's orders!'

'I am the king,' shouted Pyrrhus. 'I am the strongest. Get out of here before I topple you into the mud. Do not defy fortune!'

Orestes took up his spear. 'This is my city, for I am the legitimate heir of Agamemnon, and you are on my territory. Withdraw and call back your men. I am saying this for the last time.'

'If you want me to go, you will have to kill me,' said Pyrrhus. 'There is no other way.'

Orestes jumped from the chariot, gripping his spear in his right hand. King Menelaus saw him and shouted: 'No! Do not leave the chariot; he will kill you!' But it was too late: the two warriors faced off, spears tight in fist, each seeking an opening in the defences of the other.

Pisistratus approached Menelaus. 'You must stop him,' he said, 'or Pyrrhus will hack him to pieces. Look, he is a whole head taller. No one can resist against such might.' But Pyrrhus had already thrown his spear, grazing his adversary on his right side. Blood spurted from the wound, staining the earth red. Orestes gritted his teeth. He knew that his spear was his last chance to end the encounter. If he missed, we would have to accept a swordfight and it would be all over for him. And that was why he had always held his spear in his right hand. He attempted a few feints to throw his adversary off balance, but Pyrrhus was as solid as a mountain, and the last drops of enemy blood slid down his armour like raindrops off a smooth cliff. But then he noticed that Pyrrhus was seeking a secure hold for his right foot, unsteady on a slippery stone. Lightning swift, he dropped his shield, passed the spear to his left hand and cast it. Pyrrhus reacted in the bat of an eye and raised his shield high to the right. The spear hit the rim of the great bronze and bounced off to his side. The Pelian shield thundered under the impact.

Pyrrhus burst into loud laughter as Orestes, deadly pale, bent to pick up his shield. 'I knew you were left-handed! I saw you kill Aegisthus, remember? And now you're dead, you stupid boy.' He drew his sword and flew at him.

'Stop!' shouted Menelaus. 'The bond of kinship joins you! Do not commit such a horrendous crime.' But the son of Achilles was unstoppable, and struck with immense power. Orestes tried to surprise him with a lunge, but Pyrrhus responded with an awesome blow which shattered his sword.

Orestes felt death biting at his heart. Soaked in a cold sweat, he retreated, trying to raise his shield, but he knew that his end was near. He turned disheartened to the ranks of his men as if to seek help and in that moment a man slipped between the lines and shouted: 'You'll win with this! Catch it!' And he threw him a sword. Orestes bounded backwards and caught the weapon, turning again to face his adversary. A flash lit up the sky and the great sword glittered with blue light in his hand, like a lightning bolt. It was not made of bronze, but of some metal he had never seen. Pyrrhus saw, and a shock of fear crossed his eyes. He had never seen anything like it either.

'Strike!' shouted Anchialus, who a moment before had pushed his way through the ranks. 'Strike! It is hyperborean metal, nothing can defeat it!'

Orestes looked again at the sword. He drew up all his force behind his shield and began to advance. His eyes shone with the same reflections as the blade, his hand like a claw gripped the horn hilt tight. Pyrrhus reacted against the nameless fear that had wormed its way into him. 'It's another one of your tricks!' he shouted. 'You won't fool me again!' He lunged forward and rained down a rapid succession of hammering blows from above, aiming directly for his head. Orestes raised the sword to fend off the blows but, before the impetus of the assault was spent, Pyrrhus's weapon was sheared off at the hilt. Pyrrhus's astonishment lasted an instant and cost him his life. Orestes thrust the long blade deep into the side of his adversary, who dropped the stump and collapsed to his knees.

His gaze was already veiled with death and the heat of life was rapidly abandoning his limbs. He raised his head with great difficulty to meet the eyes of the victor who stood tall before him. 'You are the king of Mycenae now,' he said. 'The king of the Achaean kings . . . and Hermione is yours as well. Have mercy, if you believe in the gods . . .' His adolescent's face, dripping with rain, was as white as wax.

'What do you want from the king of Mycenae?' asked Orestes, and his soul filled with vague dismay.

'Have my body taken to old Peleus, in Phthia, among the Myrmidons. Ask him to accept me . . . I beg of you.' He brought his hand to the wide wound and held it out to Orestes, full of blood. 'This blood . . . he will have pity perhaps on this blood.'

He reclined his head on his chest and breathed his last breath. The evening wind gathered up his soul and carried it away down the valley of the tombs to the sea, to the promontory of Taenarum where the entrance to the world of the dead lies, and to the dark houses of Hades.

*

Menelaus and Pisistratus ran to embrace him, but Orestes trained his gaze towards the city and towards the tower of the chasm, where a figure cloaked in black stood out against the leaden sky.

'Before nightfall,' he said, 'fate must be fulfilled.'

Menelaus bowed his head. 'Son,' he said, 'your father has been avenged. You have slain Aegisthus. No one can blame you if you spare your mother.'

'No,' said Orestes. 'Agamemnon's shade will have no peace until the guilty have paid. And she is the most guilty of all.'

He walked towards the city while the last claps of thunder died out over the sea. The bastions were deserted and the Gate of Lions was wide open. He advanced along the great ramp, passed before the tombs of the Perseid kings topped by rain-washed steles, and reached the courtyard of the palace where he had played as a child, where he had watched his father mount his battle chariot and leave for war.

There were neither servants nor handmaids in the courtyard or under the porticoes, nor guards posted in the atrium. The door yawned into the darkness. Orestes drew his sword and entered, and the silence immediately swallowed up the sound of his steps which faded away into the deserted house.

The clouds slowly parted at the horizon, towards the sea, revealing for a few moments the golden eye of the setting sun. Flocks of crows and of doves descended on to the walls and towers of the city to find shelter for the night. But just then a scream of pain from the depths of the palace rent the silence and made the birds take fright and scatter off with a swift beating of wings. They sailed round the bastions as the echo of that scream drifted off over the valley. But before it had faded completely, another cry, even louder, more crazed and desperate, rose towards the dark sky; it pursued the first and joined with it like some mournful choir, and then the two voices plunged together into the chasm, dying on the bottom like a hollow lament.

The doves settled then, one by one, on the walls and rooftops of the city, looking for their nests. Only the crows remained aloft, flying in wide circles over the palace, filling the sky with their shrieks.

16

ANCHIALUS WASN'T BROUGHT INTO the presence of King Menelaus until two days after the great battle of Mycenae. That same
night, the king had sent word that Anchialus should remain his
guest in the tent he had had prepared for him until he was
summoned. And then the king had gone in the dead of night to
the palace of Mycenae: Orestes had not returned.

There was no trace of the prince in the palace; when Menelaus
entered all he found was Clytemnestra's body. She was wearing
the gown of the ancient queens that bared her breasts: a deep
wound lay between them. Her blood had flowed so copiously
that it stained the steps before the throne. It was said that the
queen had dressed in that way to welcome her son, certain that
he would not dare to sink his blade into the breasts that had
nursed him as a baby.

Menelaus's men toiled until late that night to put out the fire
that the Epirotes had set in the quarter of Mycenae that rose
outside the walls. Everything had been destroyed, and the houses
had been reduced to ashes by the flames.

The king waited at length for Orestes, in vain. He finally
asked Prince Pylades to send his Phocians to search for him.
They looked high and low, guided by the light of the fire that
had devastated the undefended quarter of the city. They carried
torches into the corridors and underground rooms of the palace,
searched the city's houses one by one and inspected the valley of
the tombs as well.

That was where they found Electra, sitting in silence on the
stone that covered the grave of her father. They brought her to

Menelaus, who held her long in his arms as she cried all her tears. When she finally found the strength to speak, she told him that her brother had left; she said that the execution of their mother had ravaged his mind and his heart. Pursued by her restless shade, he had gone to a distant sanctuary to seek purification for the blood he had shed. Only when he was healed would he return.

Prince Pylades slept in the palace, on the floor outside of Electra's room on a bearskin, to assist her if she needed help that dreadful night. Menelaus departed immediately, for that city called up only bitter memories for him. He ordered that the body of his brother Agamemnon be exhumed and buried in the grandiose tomb excavated in the valley, after dressing his body in his armour and his golden mask, as befitted a great king. He ordered that a tomb be reserved for queen Clytemnestra as well. He knew that no matter how evil men seem to be, they are still subject to the inescapable will of Fate, and he knew that death unites all men, and makes them all the same. Thus he also ordered that the body of Pyrrhus be bathed and embalmed and transported by ship to Phthia and the land of the Myrmidons, so he could receive funeral rites from Peleus.

The next day Menelaus marched towards Argos, where he arranged for the city to be blockaded on the west and the north, while Pisistratus set sail with his fleet; that evening, he landed his warriors at the bay of Temenium, closing the city off to the south. It was there that Anchialus was summoned to the king's presence.

As soon as he saw Menelaus, he threw himself at his feet and kissed his hand: 'Do you recognize me, *wanax*?'

'I do,' said the king, considering the pale bristly-bearded man before him. 'You are the man who threw the sword to Prince Orestes that saved his life. I am in your debt. Ask and I shall give you everything I can.'

'No, *wanax*, before then, in the fields of Ilium, don't you remember? In Diomedes's tent. I am Anchialus, son of Iasus. It was there that we met.'

The king stood and held out his hand, helping Anchialus to his feet. He felt like weeping, and his voice trembled. 'That cursed war,' he said. 'What grief! And yet now that I see you I am cheered to recall those times, the comfort and warmth of friendship. Tell me, of what was that awesome sword crafted? How did you get it?'

'Oh *wanax*, this is the reason I've come here. When King Diomedes realized that the queen had taken power in the city and was plotting to kill him, he decided to take to the seas and seek a new kingdom for himself, instead of unleashing a new war. Many of us followed him and we sailed the western sea at the height of winter towards the Land of Evening. But one day, as we were attacking a village to carry off food and women, we saw an immense horde descending from the mountains. There were thousands and thousands of them, and they brought their women and children and their old people with them. An entire people, in migration. We barely managed to survive their attack, and many of our comrades were lost. King Diomedes confronted their chieftain in single combat and risked his life; the man was armed with a sword similar to the one I gave Prince Orestes, and like him all the other warriors of his race. Their weapons are made of a formidable metal, as tough as bronze but as hard as stone; nothing can withstand it.

'The king managed to win the duel by hurling his spear from a distance, but he realized that no army could resist these invaders drawn up on an open field. They have thousands of horses, as well, but they are not harnessed to chariots, like ours are. Those men ride their animals bare-backed, forming a single creature with the power of a horse and the craft and cunning of a man. Like centaurs they fly over fields and mountains, swift as the wind. They can run in circles and jump over obstacles. This I know, because they later took me prisoner, and I spent nearly three years with them.

'We managed to escape with great difficulty, fleeing away over the sea, but Diomedes summoned me and ordered me to turn back, although I was loath to do so. He said: "You must return, you must warn Nestor and Agamemnon, and Menelaus, if he has returned, and Sthenelus at Argos, if he has survived. Tell them what you have seen, tell them to prepare their defences, to raise a wall on the Isthmus, to launch the black ships . . ." '

Menelaus was dumbfounded by Anchialus's words. He could still hear the voice of the Old Man of the Sea sounding within him; he could see the great cavern and the visions of his comrades: Ulysses prisoner on an enchanted island, Diomedes, in the swamps of a remote land.

'I obeyed with a heavy heart,' continued Anchialus, 'and I turned my prow south, but no more than several days had passed when I fell prey to *Shekelesh* pirates. We fought with all our might, but we were completely overwhelmed. I was the only one of us to survive, but I still have in my ears the screams of pain of my comrades as they were tortured to death. I swam ashore and began to march to the land of the Achaeans, although I had no idea of how far it was. I was twice made prisoner, and I ended up once again in the hands of those invaders, who kept me as a slave until I managed to escape again. After long wanderings and much suffering, I reached Buthrotum and the house of Pyrrhus. The son of Achilles had already departed for the war, but I met Andromache who told me how I could reach him. I crossed the mountains with his army and have at long last arrived here.'

The king fell still in meditation, then asked: 'How far are they?'

'It is difficult to say, *wanax*. They don't seem to have a destination in mind. They sometimes stop in a single place for years, but they do not know how to build cities and so they must keep moving in search of new pastures for their herds. When they do move, they head south and so, sooner or later, they will reach this land. I could not say when, maybe in a year's time, or two, or ten, but you can be certain that they will arrive. Oh *wanax*, heed the words of King Diomedes, who is bound to you through deep friendship. Build a wall on the Isthmus, ready the defences, launch the black ships to sea! This is what I had to tell you; now my mission is finished. If you are still willing to offer me a reward . . .'

'Anything I can,' said the king. 'Ask me for anything.'

'Give me a ship, so I can return to my king. I don't desire anything else.'

'You will have it tomorrow if you want. But I would ask you to wait until Argos has fallen! Wait to take to the sea, so that when you see your lord, King Diomedes, you can tell him that Argos is his. That he must return. We will make a pact of eternal friendship and alliance that no one will be able to sunder, and we will grow old together watching our children's children grow. If he will not return, tell him that he shall remain forever in my heart, like all the friends and comrades who suffered with me in the bloody fields of Asia.'

'I will do as you advise,' said Anchialus. 'If you like, I will fight alongside your warriors, as I once did.'

'That will not be necessary,' said Menelaus. 'Argos will fall without a fight. The army that was sent out with Aegisthus's forces has been destroyed. The survivors have come over to our side. The city cannot resist.'

'Aigialeia . . . what will become of her?'

'The war council will decide. But the queen of Argos is a proud woman. Perhaps she will take things into her own hands. But go now and take your rest. We all need to rest.' The king took his leave, kissing Anchialus on both cheeks.

Anchialus started to leave, but before crossing the threshold he turned back: 'There's something I have not told you.'

'What is it?'

'That people . . . speaks a language like our own. Different. And yet very similar. I have always wondered why.'

He went out into the night and the king remained alone in his tent with those words. 'A language similar to ours,' he kept repeating to himself. He lifted his hands to his face and closed his eyes. 'Oh gods,' he said, 'gods of the heavens. Destiny is fulfilled. The sons of Hercules are about to return. If you are just, allow me, please, to live until the moment in which I will know if the war in Asia was fought for the salvation of our people or if so much blood and so many tears were shed for nothing.'

A month later, Argos surrendered. Menelaus and Pisistratus entered the city, welcomed by the rejoicing inhabitants. Queen Aigialeia killed herself.

Anchialus was given his ship and he left one day at the end of winter, sailing north towards the mouth of the Eridanus. He remembered Diomedes's promise: when they had come to a suitable place, he would found a city on the coast and would place a signal on the beach so that Anchialus could find them. The king never broke his word.

*

Meanwhile, in the land of Hesperia, Diomedes had crossed the snow-covered Blue Mountains and had descended a great river until he reached the confines of a plain which extended all the way to the western sea. It was inhabited by the *Lat* who had settled there not long ago, having crossed the Mountains of Ice, some said, or perhaps the eastern sea. Eurimachus the Trojan told them the *Teresh* lived north of that land, and that Aeneas had occupied a territory on the coast that he had won from the *Lat* in battle.

If nothing had changed during his absence, the Dardan prince could be found at no more than two days' journey along the shores of the great river. Diomedes decided to set up camp there. The climate was mild and the pastures were lush. One night he summoned Eurimachus and said: 'Tomorrow you will leave.' Then he called Lamus, son of Onchestus, and ordered him to accompany the Trojan as his herald. 'When you see Aeneas, you shall say: "Diomedes, son of Tydeus, who has already defeated you on the fields of Ilium, is here. He thinks that there is not room for both of you in this land, and that the quarrel that set our peoples one against the other for long years must be settled once and for all. Why else would the gods have made us wander at length over land and sea only to find each other here in this far land? He awaits you in a valley along the great river, and he challenges you to this duel. He who wins will certainly have the favour of the gods and the dominion over this land." '

'I will do so,' said Lamus.

They left the next day, and the *Chnan* departed with them. And thus the wait began. Myrsilus raided a village in the mountains and carried off some fine horses. He assembled the king's war chariot, greased the hubs and fixed the shaft on to the wagon. He shined every decoration until they gleamed like they once had. He chose the two proudest stallions and had them run every day from dawn to dusk along the shores of the river. He accustomed them to the harness and reins and trained them well in every manoeuvre. They were very different from Asian horses, and from Argive horses as well. They were tall and slender, not as fast, perhaps, but more powerful, with a fiery temper. Diomedes spent most of his time alone and took little interest in the training; the great effort that Myrsilus was making to provide him with a chariot worthy of a king, worthy of a hero, a chariot that would raise his fame to the skies, seemed not to matter at all to the king.

This was not true; Diomedes kept to himself in order to gather his strength and concentrate all the power of his spirit. He was preparing for the encounter by distilling every last drop of his life energy. Myrsilus feared that the king would take his own life if Aeneas were not to accept his challenge.

One evening towards dusk, Myrsilus saw Lamus and the *Chnan* riding towards camp on an ass. He raced to meet them.

'Did you see him? Has he accepted?'

The *Chnan* halted the ass and slipped to the ground. Lamus said: 'Yes, I saw him. He accepts. Take me to the king.'

Diomedes received him in his tent. He was pale, but his eyes shone with a feverish light. He did not move. He asked nothing. He waited for Lamus to speak.

'Aeneas accepts the challenge. He will come on the first day of the new moon. Alone, except for his charioteer. You too must use your chariot alone. You will fight as you did in Ilium. Three javelins from the chariot and then, if you survive, on the ground with a spear, a sword and an axe. No respite. A duel to the death. These are the conditions I accepted in your name.'

Diomedes's face lit up as though life once again flowed through his veins. 'Well done,' he said. 'I thank you. If I win, if I finally found my city . . .'

The *Chnan* interrupted. 'That's not all. The *Lat* fear him. At least a part of them, while others would be willing to accept him. When they learned of this challenge, they gave me a message for you. They ask you to join forces with all your warriors, to drive the Trojans into the sea. The *Teresh* are divided as well. Some of them are on the Trojans' side and are ready to form an alliance in the name of their common Asian origin, but others want Aeneas, and all his people, dead.'

The king looked at him in surprise: 'How did you discover all of these things?'

'I can understand the *Teresh* well enough, and they understand the *Lat*. That's all. What is your decision?'

'No,' said the king. 'I will not drag my men into a war against the Trojans. They have already fought against them once, and it was a cursed war. It brought nothing but grief and endless pain.'

The *Chnan* shook his head: 'I've yet to hear of a war that wasn't cursed, that did not bring grief and endless pain.'

'This is the war they have experienced; they have seen that the victors have suffered as much as, if not more than, the vanquished. With what spirit could they face another war against the same people? No. Tell the *Lat* that I will not make war at their side. Tell them, if you want, that we have already fought a long war that brought us every kind of misfortune. I will combat Aeneas alone. If I win, you will return to them and negotiate new conditions. From a stronger position. Perhaps this beautiful plain will soon be ours. Perhaps the day in which I will build my city is nearing.'

The *Chnan* smiled: 'This land has much changed you, since I have known you. It is harsh and primitive and forgives nothing. It has made you lose your world, a little at a time. You've lost pieces on the road, in the swamps, on the mountains, in the valleys and the forests, as your comrades fell, when your immortal horses were devoured by the wolves. Perhaps it would have soon stripped you of everything. No longer a king, or a hero. Only a man. Like me.'

'And that is a good thing?'

'I don't know. But it would certainly be the truth. Your truth. When someone has the truth in front of him, he knows what to do. If he likes it, he continues on his road. If he doesn't, he kills himself. But now this Aeneas has ruined everything. He has pushed you back, revived the old ghosts. Now you have fooled yourself into thinking that nothing has changed. You prepare for a duel as if you were under the walls of Ilium. Even if you win, nothing will change. This land is made of hundreds of peoples, speaking many different languages, coming from no one knows where . . .'

Diomedes fell silent, thinking of the *Chnan*'s words. They seemed right. They seemed true even though they were so terribly simple. But was it all really so simple? So simple to live, or to die?

'Yes,' he admitted. 'And yet a particular vital force burns in some of them more than in others, and the others are slowly attracted to them like lamplight attracts moths. Like a small seed becomes a great tree, perhaps one day a new nation will grow here.'

He rose to his feet and went to the entrance of the tent, contemplating the green expanse at his feet which extended like a precious carpet under the golden light of the setting sun. 'Look,' he said then, 'another day has passed in the land of Hesperia, but it has not passed in vain. Many seeds have fallen here, carried by the wind of fate. Some will grow roots, others will dry up and die. And tomorrow this land will be different than it is today. Something is born, something dies, but each thing must be true to itself. An oak seed cannot generate a rush, nor can an eagle give birth to a crow. I am Diomedes, son of Tydeus, destroyer of cities. Even if I were stripped of everything, I would still carry my world inside of me, whether right or wrong. I will combat so that my world may live. If I die, it will mean that my death was meant to happen. This is what the Land of Evening has taught me.' The *Chnan* lowered his head and did not speak.

*

The next day, Diomedes summoned Myrsilus and said: 'There are only four days to the new moon. Where are my arms?'

'But *wanax*,' said Myrsilus, astonished, 'I have been doing nothing but taming your horses and preparing your chariot and you have never said a word to me. Your weapons will be ready very soon, if this is what you want.'

The king lay his hands on Myrsilus's shoulders: 'This is what I want. They must sparkle on the day of the duel like the day they were crafted.'

'They will gleam, *wanax*. They will be ablaze like the noonday sun. You will look awesome and invincible, like that day a goddess took the reins of your chariot against the god of war before the Scaean Gates.'

Myrsilus took the king's armour from his tent, the embossed greaves and breastplate, the shield and the helmet, adorned by a horsehair crest. He ordered a slave to shine them, to remove the patina that darkened them. He himself took a long ashwood stick from the forest; he removed the branches and the bark, polished it with a pumice stone, and shod it with the heavy, solid bronze head. He weighed it in his hand until it was perfect, and then fitted on the bronze socket at exactly the right point. He then took the baldric which was remarkably crafted in gold, enamel and silver and he cleaned it with his own hands, making it gleam. It had once belonged to Tydeus, when he fought under the walls of Thebes. Last of all, he took the great sword of solid bronze; he sharpened it with a whetstone, tested the long edge and the sharp tip and greased it with pork fat melted over the fire, until he saw it shine. The king had used it only once, when he had fought Nemro; never since had he found a worthy adversary.

When his work was finished, Myrsilus put the arms back into the king's tent so he would see them and his courage would grow within his soul. His bride saw them as well, and her eyes filled with tears.

*

When the day of the new moon arrived, the king asked Myrsilus to be his charioteer. He awoke him when it was still dark and spoke to him: 'If I should die, bring my body back to my bride so she can bathe it and prepare it for the funeral rites. You yourself will dress my body with this armour and bury it in front of the

Achaeans. Raise a cairn and set a stele that I will be remembered by. Shout out my name ten times and then entrust it to the wind. And then depart; you will lead the comrades. No curse weighs upon you. Perhaps the gods will forget and you will succeed in beginning a new life in this land. Otherwise, if they so wish, take them back to Argos. The *Chnan* will know how to find you ships.'

'None of this will ever happen,' said Myrsilus. 'It is as you say: the gods want this duel to be fought to its end, and then we will be able to live a new life and build our city. You will fight and you will win. As you always have.'

He shook the reins and urged on the horses, who took off at a gallop. Myrsilus drove the team up on to a small ridge of land near the great river, a softly sloping hill from which the valley and plain of the *Lat* could be seen.

The rising sun had just begun to lighten the horizon behind the mountains, but the plain was still in shadow. A slight mist covered it, like a light veil. Birds chirped their welcome to the morning. A large heron passed through the sky in slow, solemn flight. The king watched him at length as he vanished in the distance over the sea. He said: 'Sometimes I dream that I am a bird, a great bird with white wings. I dream that I am flying over the foamy swells of the sea, my heart free of worry, of pain, of fear. It is a beautiful dream. When I awaken my heart is light.'

But Myrsilus's eyes were fixed on the plain. '*Wanax!*' he said, and the king turned that way as well. A chariot advanced through the mist, appearing and disappearing with the rippling of the ground. Then the light of the sun struck it in full and the point of a spear sparkled with dazzling fire, a white crest swayed in the morning breeze. Diomedes's hand tightened on the shaft of his spear. At that moment, the chariot stopped and the blast of a horn sounded over the vast plain, struck the peaks of the mountains and echoed over the snow-covered summits. The son of Anchises was launching his challenge.

'He has seen us,' said the king. 'Let us go.' And Myrsilus drove on the horses.

They were face to face, after so many years, dressed in

resplendent bronze, as they had been then. Diomedes shouted: 'It's you or me, son of Anchises! Only one of us will see the dawn tomorrow!'

Aeneas answered him: 'It's you or me, son of Tydeus!'

Myrsilus sent the team galloping over the plain. Aeneas's charioteer shouted out and set the war-car racing off against his adversary of old. Diomedes took a javelin from the quiver; he weighed it in his hand and when Aeneas's chariot was within range he hurled it with all his strength, aiming low, at the belt. The tip hit the parapet and shattered it into pieces. Aeneas flung his javelin as well; it struck the edge of the shield and rebounded to the right. For an instant, as the chariots flew past each other the hubs of the wheels were so close they nearly touched, the two warriors glared at each other and the ancient fury was rekindled. Aeneas saw in those eyes the sinister reflection of the flames that had burned his homeland, Diomedes saw the arrogant challenge of Hector and Deiphobus, the fire that had burned the rampart and the ships.

They reached the confines of the field and the charioteers took the reins and assumed their positions again. The warriors took a second javelin from their quivers.

'There's a strong cross wind, *wanax*, adjust your aim to the left.'

Diomedes nodded. 'Go,' he said.

Myrsilus whipped his stallions' backs with the reins. The steeds raised a long whinny into the air, distantly echoed by Aeneas's horses, then broke into a gallop. 'I'll take you right into him; you'll have him directly in front of you, but just for an instant,' shouted Myrsilus. 'Careful! Weigh it both left and right before you throw!' When he was at the calculated distance, he swerved violently with his right horse, widening and then narrowing on the left at the last moment while Diomedes crouched low, holding on to the rear handles and leaning in to the other side, to keep the wheels gripping the ground.

Aeneas's charioteer was disoriented by the move and Diomedes re-emerged from behind the parapet with his javelin tight in his fist. He found Aeneas right in front of him then, for just an instant, and he hurled the weapon at his neck, at the collar bone. The javelin missed its target by a hairbreadth because Aeneas's chariot gave a jolt, but the bronze still cut into his skin above the shoulder. And while his adversary rode off, Diomedes turned and shouted: 'First blood, son of Anchises!'

But Aeneas's charioteer took him by surprise: he did not halt the horses, but widened their path in a full curve without diminishing their speed. When Myrsilus had started his team running again after having stopped at the end of the field, they were already upon him, racing at full tilt. Just an instant before he let his javelin fly, Diomedes realized that Aeneas was aiming to strike his charioteer. He raised his shield to protect Myrsilus, but this threw him off balance and he missed his throw.

'Thank you, *wanax*,' said Myrsilus. 'But you've lost your third javelin. Now you must do battle on the ground with your spear and sword.'

'It would have been worse to lose my charioteer and end up in the dust,' said Diomedes with a smile. 'You were magnificent. Sthenelus could not have done any better.'

Myrsilus set the horses off at a trot and turned back, then stopped at a short distance from their adversary. Diomedes and Aeneas descended from the war-cars, and the charioteers handed them their spears. The sun was already high over the mountains and was turning south, sparkling on the waters of the great river.

The two heroes faced each other warily, protected by their shields, spears in hand. The speed of the horses could no longer be added to the force of their arms. Now ability counted as much as strength. Diomedes chose not to throw his spear from a distance, but engaged Aeneas in hand-to-hand combat, crossing his ashen shaft with his enemy's. Wood and bronze crackled in the close assault, bronze points seeking out a gap in the other's defences, a space between the joints of the breastplate, a brief opening between the edge of the shield and the visor of the helmet. The whole valley resounded at length with the din of the battle.

Myrsilus stood pale on the chariot while the horses tranquilly browsed on the grass. He abruptly started: with a sudden surge of energy, Aeneas had leapt backwards to dodge a blow, crouched down and hurled his spear from the ground, shearing off one of the shoulder plates on Diomedes's armour. Blood reddened the chest of the son of Tydeus, who managed still to cast his own spear. The point of bronze struck the side of Aeneas's helmet with such force that the Dardan hero wavered and nearly fell. Diomedes raised his sword to finish him off but Aeneas reacted, lifting his shield against the furious raining of blows. He moved backwards and, one step after another, he regained his composure, stood tall again and drew his own sword.

They stopped for an instant, panting heavily, then attacked each other with renewed violence.

Myrsilus was astonished: he could not understand what mysterious energy upheld Aeneas's arm against Diomedes's fury. He watched the sun as it continued to rise in the sky. Perhaps Aeneas was truly born of a goddess, as he had heard, and he prayed to Athena to hastily infuse new vigour in the arm of Diomedes.

The ferocious battle went on. It went on and on, until their swords were blunted and deformed by the blows. They were useless now. The charioteers approached them and offered the double-edged axes. The two combatants were disfigured by the tremendous struggle. Blood dripped from innumerable wounds; sweat blinded them and they burned with thirst and fever. As he handed him the axe, Myrsilus looked the king full in the face: 'There's still enough fire in your eyes to burn a city. Strike him down, *wanax*, no one can stand up to you. You've already beaten him once, and forced him to flee.'

And the charioteer of Aeneas also spoke to his lord as he handed him the sharpened axe: 'His energies are waning. He's desperate. You have a son, a people with women and children. Strike him down, son of Anchises. You will be the one to see the dawn tomorrow.'

And the battle resumed with the axes: long, exhausting, cruel. Their shields were shattered, mangled by their blows, the straps holding their helmets and breastplates were ripped to shreds. At the end, the heroes faced each other, offering their undefended bodies to the axes. Skin and bone against bronze.

But a god, perhaps, took pity on them. As they attacked each other for the final time, even the handles of the axes split, and the two warriors remained on their feet, gasping, soaked in bloody sweat.

Diomedes spoke first: 'Son of Anchises, the gods have granted victory to neither one of us. See? Our weapons are broken and useless; we have nothing but our teeth with which to wound each other. It would not be worthy of us to attack each other like dogs. I . . . I believe that the gods have sent us a sign; is it not a miracle that we are both still alive? Look, the sun is already descending towards the sea. We have fought this entire day. Perhaps this is what the gods want: that there be peace between us.' Aeneas regarded him in silence. Only the rhythmic rising and falling of his chest accompanied his panting breath.

Diomedes spoke again: 'Listen. Achilles is dead. Hector is dead. You and I are the strongest warriors in the world. But neither of us is stronger than the other. Let us forget our ancient animosity. Let us unite our peoples in this land and form a new, invincible nation. Listen, son of Anchises. I am willing to share with you the greatest of my treasures, the most precious talisman of your lost homeland.' Aeneas listened with a look of deep apprehension. 'On the night in which we conquered the city, I managed to slip into the sanctuary and abduct the Palladium, the sacred image of Athena which had made Ilium the greatest and most prosperous city in the world. I knew where it was kept; Ulysses and I had stolen into the citadel some time earlier and we were the only ones to know where it was. I've been carrying it with me all these years. I was waiting for the day in which I would found a new city. I would have placed it in a beautiful temple and there I would have built a new kingdom. And now I offer it to you, so we can build this kingdom and this nation together. Enough blood and enough tears. Enough.' He bowed his head and awaited Aeneas's response in silence.

The Dardan hero stared at him without saying a word. There

was no longer hate in his eyes, but rather melancholy and pity. He said: 'Son of Tydeus, I fought for years to defend my homeland and I fought you now in the hopes of destroying the last shadows of my past before beginning a new life here, in the land of Hesperia. The gods wanted our last encounter to end this way, and now let us separate, so that each of us may take his own road. Too much hate and too much blood have divided us. Our wounds are still bleeding.

'What you believe to be the talisman of the Trojans is nothing. It is nothing but a false image, one of the seven replicas that King Laomedon had made to mask the true idol. All of you searched for it that night, blinded by the dream of endless power: you, Ajax Oileus, Agamemnon. Ulysses himself. Cassandra fooled you all. She alone knew which one was the true idol, and that night she revealed the secret to me. I returned unseen amid the flames which were still devouring the city and recovered it, and I took it with me, to Mount Ida. It was the smallest and poorest image of them all; just two cubits tall, I could easily carry it in my arms.

'Only Ulysses realized the trick. He had always suspected something. That night at Tenedos, while you were all sleeping, overwhelmed by weariness, he searched your ship and Ajax's ship and found the false images. That is why he turned back; he wanted to warn Agamemnon, but when he landed on that deserted beach, the Atreid king had already departed.

'I saw Ulysses rummaging through the ruins of the citadel that night as I slipped away. I spoke to him; I appeared to him as a ghost amid the pillars of Priam's palace, reduced to ash. I did not kill him; I knew that the worst torture for him would be having been deceived. This is why he still wanders the seas without purpose and without hope.

'The sacred image now protects my camp and for this reason I know that this small refuge will become a city and that this city will generate one hundred cities, all beautiful and prosperous, and will unite all the peoples of Hesperia, from the Mountains of Ice to the Mountains of Fire, along the crests of the Blue Mountains, for ever. Farewell, son of Tydeus. May the gods have mercy on you.'

17

DIOMEDES FELT LIKE DYING. He fell on to his knees and wept, as Aeneas mounted his chariot and disappeared over the plains of the *Lat*.

Myrsilus brought him back to the camp by force and there he lay for three days and three nights, devoured by fever, touching neither food nor drink. Myrsilus had all his weapons taken away, for he feared the king would take his own life.

On the fourth day he spoke to him: 'Oh king, I and my companions know the truth now and yet, although we are sick at heart, we have not given ourselves up to despair. All these years we have followed you and we have fought with you so that your dream and ours might become reality. The gods have willed differently, and we mortals can do nothing against Fate. But we love you, and we want to live with you or to die with you.

'I saw you fight with spear, sword and axe against the son of Anchises, and I heard your words. There is no man on the face of the earth who can match you. We have come to a decision, and we want you to know this: if you live, we will live; if you die, we will die.' He stretched out his arm: 'This is the sword I have borne with honour. Take it. If you use it against yourself, I will take my life with the same blade, and our comrades will do the same and we will sleep here together, under this sky, lulled by the voice of this great river. If you eat and drink with us, we will be happy and we will follow you until we find a place to live in peace in this land and together we will await the end that the gods have reserved for us.'

Upon hearing those words, the king wearily got up from his

pallet and showed his pale face, his blood-matted hair, his unkempt beard, his eyes red behind dark rings, and he burst into bitter tears. His back was shaken by sobs and big drops coursed down his hollow cheeks. Myrsilus stood before him unmoving until he saw him begin to calm, to wipe his eyes with the edge of his tunic. He nodded then to the bride, to long-haired Ros, who crouched in silence in a dark corner of the tent, and she took a jug of spring water and gave it to him so he could drink. She touched his face, then got up and had some water heated. When it was ready, she removed his clothes and bathed him, she poured scented oil over his head and then she lay down beside him, under a warm sheep's fleece. She embraced him, caressing his tortured body with light fingers, passing on the warmth of her body until sleep descended on his eyes.

*

They departed at the beginning of spring and headed eastward until the Blue Mountains stood between them and the people of Aeneas, and after wandering at length they found the sea that they had long ago crossed in search of the mouth of the Eridanus.

A people called the Messapians lived on that land, ruled over by a king called Daunus. The *Chnan* negotiated a treaty with him, and obtained a small territory on the shores of a lake to found a small city. They called it Helpie, which in the Achaean language means 'hope'.

*

It was a long time before the threat announced by Anchialus came to pass in the land of the Achaeans. King Menelaus had had a wall raised on the Isthmus and he built new bulwarks in Mycenae and other cities; cisterns were dug and stores assembled. But what truly gave the king hope for the survival of his people was his certainty that he possessed the talisman of the Trojans. He had placed it in a temple on the citadel of Argos, for that was the highest site on the whole plain; from there, one could see Tyrinth and Temenium and, at night, the fires of Mycenae. In Argos, to keep the memory of Diomedes alive.

One day, Orestes returned to Sparta and Menelaus granted him the hand of his daughter Hermione, who had long awaited him, so that they might reign over Mycenae together and generate many descendants to carry on the line of the Atreides.

Ulysses returned as well, as Prince Telemachus had hoped: one day he showed up at the palace in disguise, dressed as a beggar, and for days he observed all that went on without revealing his identity to anyone, not even his bride. When he suddenly made himself known, he appeared as he truly was to the eyes of all; he grasped his bow and shot down the suitors who were banqueting in the great hall as Prince Telemachus and his servants barred the doors and prevented them from fleeing. He slaughtered them all, one after another, he hanged the maidservants who had betrayed him and then he finally revealed himself to his wife.

And yet his homecoming was bitter: he returned on a foreign vessel, having lost his ships and his comrades, and he had to shed much blood to reassert his authority. The massacre never ceased to weigh upon him. He left his throne to his son and departed once again in a final quest for peace. They say he was seeking a distant, solitary land in which he could immolate a sacrifice that would free him from the persecution of the gods and allow him to live the last days of his life in serenity on his rocky island. No one knows whether he succeeded, and no one knows what end he met. The twilight of the last heroes has faded into confused, uncertain accounts for which there have been no witnesses.

I've often asked myself who the serene woman was who welcomed Telemachus to Sparta when he went to ask King Menelaus for news of his father; she showered him with gifts and gave him a beautiful peplum for his bride to wear on the day when he would chose a maiden for himself among the daughters of the Achaeans. I've wondered whether this happy, gracious queen who was always seen thereafter in Sparta was the same woman who had screamed with horror over the corpse of her sister Clytemnestra, rent by the blade of her son. On the day of her sister's funeral Helen was said to have gouged her face and wept inconsolably, cursing the atrocious destiny of the Atreides. I know nothing else.

I know that, for a very long time, threat seemed to disperse without harm over the land of the Achaeans, like when clouds gather and thunder booms in the sky but then the wind scatters the storm without a drop of rain or hail. But the will of the gods is always difficult for men to discover.

One day a ship reached Pylus with terrible news: a horde of invaders was descending from the north, burning and destroying everything in their wake. Nothing seemed capable of stopping them. Pisistratus, who now reigned in the palace after the death of old Nestor, immediately issued the alarm, sending messengers to Sparta and Argos; he summoned the scribes and instructed them to contact all the garrisons on the coast and relay orders to send their warriors into the field and their ships to sea. But as the scribes were still engraving the fresh clay with their styles, the palace was already ringing with cries, the rooms filling with smoke and flames. Pisistratus ran into the armoury and took down his enormous double-bladed axe . . .

*

The echo of that devastation spread everywhere; it crossed the sea and lapped at the coast of Hesperia, where for years Diomedes had been leading an obscure life in the poor village he had built. His bride was long dead, along with the child she had tried to bear him.

One evening, at the end of the summer, a boat laden with refugees came ashore near Helpie. They were Achaeans who had fled their invaded homeland with their wives and children. Nothing was left to them; their houses had been destroyed, their cities burned to the ground. As soon as he heard of them, Diomedes hastened to greet them, bringing them dry clothing and food.

When they had eaten their fill, when they had finished telling their stories, the hero asked them: 'Do you know who they are? Do they rule over the entire land of the Achaeans?'

'They are called *Dor*,' replied the eldest among them, 'and they are invincible. They form a single, dreadful animal with their horses by mounting them bare-backed. They have weapons stronger than the best bronze; not a shield can withstand them, nor a cuirass or helmet. Our warriors never had a chance against them, and yet they never gave up the fight. Only Mycenae has resisted, and Argos; their walls still protect them, but their destiny is in the hands of the gods, if they still think of us.'

Diomedes turned to Myrsilus, who sat next to him, bouncing on his knee the small son he had generated with a native woman. He had a strange light in his eyes, a light that Myrsilus had thought gone for ever. The king said: 'Argos is holding out. Did you hear that? Argos resists!'

Myrsilus regarded him with bewilderment: their days of weapons and blood were so far away, now. Every evening he sat with his son on the shores of the sea to watch the waves changing colour. Sometimes Malech, the *Chnan*, who had never taken to the seas after all, came to sit with them as well. Myrsilus told his boy the story of their king, who had once lain siege to a great city in a far-off land; he told him of the gods who had fought at their side and of the endeavours of the heroes: Ulysses master of deceit, Great Ajax, big-voiced Menelaus and Diomedes son of Tydeus, victor of Thebes of the Seven Gates. But the stories he told were like fables of a remote time, as enchanting as they were no longer true.

But suddenly, looking into Diomedes's eyes, he realized that time had never killed the spirit of the Argive hero; the fire was still burning after so many years under the ashes.

'I'm leaving,' he said. 'Perhaps a ship can still land at Temenium. Perhaps the fortress of Tiryns still defends the road from the sea.'

Myrsilus felt his heart plummet. He looked at his son and then said: 'What you are thinking is pure folly. Those cities will have fallen by now. Thank the gods that they have reserved this place for us, where we can live in peace. Look at those wretches: they are miserable, they have nothing.'

Diomedes smiled: 'Do not fear. You men will stay here and live in peace. You have your children, and your wives. It is right for you to stay. But I have nothing, only my memories. I lost my bride and the child who was about to be born, but Argos is still alive at the bottom of my heart. She is the beloved homeland I have never forgotten. Listen to me: an oak cannot generate a rush, nor can an eagle give birth to a crow. Now I know what I must do. I will die with my sword in my fist, but I will see the sun shine on the towers of Argos, one last time.'

It was impossible to dissuade him, and for the first time after years and years his comrades saw him as he once was. He seemed reborn to a new life, not a man rushing towards death.

He asked King Daunus for a ship but the man burst out laughing and said: 'With what will you pay me? A handful of sea salt, and the wool of your sheep?' The king was coarse and greedy.

But Diomedes did not react. 'With this,' he said calmly.

He lifted the blanket that covered the pack on his mule's back. Sparkling gold wounded the eyes of the native king, who was struck speechless. A suit of armour of dazzling beauty, all gold, gleaming in the sun. The armour once worn by Glaucus, the Lycian hero. He had given it to Diomedes on the field of battle as a hospitable gift, exchanging it with his own copper armour.

'Will you give me a ship and oarsmen?' he asked again. Daunus drew closer, his hand hovering over that wonder as if he were afraid that he would burn himself by touching it.

'Yes . . . yes . . .' he whispered, still not believing his eyes.

'Good,' said Diomedes. And he covered the armour and led off his mule. 'I want it to be ready as soon as possible,' he said as he left the courtyard. 'The sooner it is ready, the sooner you will have what I've shown you.'

He walked off to return to his city. Daunus started, as if awaking suddenly from a dream: 'Who are you anyway?' he shouted, as the other walked away. But Diomedes did not answer, nor did he turn.

'Who are you really?' repeated Daunus, more softly now, as if speaking to himself. He watched as the man walked towards the sea with long strides, his wide arms alongside his body, as if the suit of armour still weighed on his shoulders.

'But then it's true,' said Daunus again. 'You truly are Diomedes, the king of Argos.'

*

As soon as the ship was ready and the crew enlisted, Diomedes went to the sea to board, bringing with him only his clothing and his weapons. He wanted to leave immediately, although the weather was not good and a cold wind blew over the sea, agitating the waves. But when he arrived he saw the ship empty and his comrades drawn up on the beach. With them were Malech, the *Chnan*, and Lamus, son of Onchestus. They had never had the heart to abandon him.

'Where is my crew?' he asked in surprise.

Myrsilus stepped forward: 'We're here. Remember, *wanax*? If you live, we shall live. If you die, we will die with you. You were right: an eagle cannot become a crow. Let us set sail.'

'No,' said Diomedes. 'No. I will go alone. Return to your city. I command you to do so, if I am still your king.'

Myrsilus smiled: 'If we obey, will this be the last order you give us in this land?'

'The last,' nodded Diomedes. And his voice was veiled with sadness.

'Very well,' said Myrsilus. 'All aboard then,' he shouted to his comrades. 'Argos is our city!'

The comrades shouted: 'ARGOS!'

Diomedes watched as they took their places at the thwarts and cast off the moorings and his eyes brimmed over. As the ship began moving, he leapt up to grab the rail and vaulted aboard. He stood beside Myrsilus at the helm.

The men hoisted the sail and the ship gained speed, bound towards the open sea. Diomedes's plan was to head east towards a small group of rocky islands and then to turn south and sail steadily in that direction.

The wind was picking up, but no one thought of turning back. The *Chnan* glanced nervously up at the darkening sky. A shout suddenly echoed from the bow: 'Ship starboard!'

Diomedes ran to the ship's side and scanned the sea; a vessel was approaching them from the north. The insignia of the Spartan Atreides stood out on the faded sail.

'Strike the sails!' shouted Diomedes. 'It's a Spartan ship!' The crew furled the sails and the oarsmen manoeuvred to maintain their position.

When the ship was within eyeshot, an incredulous expression came over the king's face, as if a ghost had suddenly appeared before him.

'Anchialus!' he shouted out. From the ship a voice even louder than his own answered: '*Wanax!*'

In a few moments, the two vessels were side by side. Anchialus jumped on board and embraced the king with tears in his eyes. 'I've been searching so long,' he gasped between sobs, 'so long!' All of the comrades gathered round and embraced him. Only the *Chnan* remained at the helm and gravely watched the white seafoam that frothed leeward, pounding the ever-nearing islands.

'Where are you headed?' asked Anchialus when he had calmed a little.

The king raised flaming eyes. 'To Argos,' he said.

Anchialus looked at him in dismay. 'To Argos?' he said with a broken voice. 'Oh, unhappy wretches! Don't you know? I met refugees on the sea just yesterday, fleeing the city. Argos no longer exists.'

A stony silence fell over the ship, broken only by the sharp whistle of the wind.

'To the oars!' shouted the *Chnan*. 'Men, to the oars! Reefs ahead!'

Myrsilus turned towards the little rocky islands, beaten now by huge billows rimmed with white foam, and then towards the cloud-dark sky. He shouted, as if out of his mind: 'You gods have betrayed us! You will have no more suffering from us! You will have no more tears! To the oars, men! To the oars!'

The comrades exchanged glances and understood; they looked at the sky and at the boiling surf and they threw themselves at the oars, rowing with savage energy as Myrsilus gripped the helm forcefully, guiding them straight into the rocks. Diomedes understood as well and stood tall at the side of his pilot, firm against the fury of the storm.

Myrsilus yelled out at the top of his lungs to overcome the roar of thunder. He cried: 'ARGOS!' And his comrades echoed him, shouting with everything they had in them and making the surface of the sea boil with their oars.

The stern dipped down, pushed by the aft wind and by the force of one hundred arms and the ship rammed straight into the reefs. The keel crashed into the rocks and shattered; the ship rolled like a wounded whale, its stern shooting up and its bow going under. A gigantic wave smashed into the hull, already nearly dismembered by the terrible impact, and dragged it down into the abyss.

The storm raged on for many hours with huge billows, and the sky became blacker than night. It ceased only towards evening, when a cold ray of sun pierced through the grey clouds. A flock of seabirds rose up then from those desolate rocks. Among them was a great white-winged albatross which lifted above all the rest, higher and higher, letting out shrill shrieks of grief. He sailed through a rift in the clouds and was swallowed up by the darkness.

*

The foreigner finished his story thus, one evening at the end of winter. He left the day after, and we were never to hear of him again.

I've often asked myself who he was, really. Of all those who lived through those events, who could have had complete knowledge of all the facts? I have never been able to find an answer. Or perhaps I have never wanted to find one. Whoever he was, he had the right to oblivion, for destiny had forced him to live despite himself.

The last thing I remember about him were his eyes, when he turned to look at me before disappearing behind a curve in the road. They were no longer the eyes of a man. They were as empty and black as the circle of the new moon. There was nothing left inside of them, for he had given everything over to us: memories, pain, regrets, everything. Now he could finally look at the world as if he were no longer a part of it, as if he had long crossed the last horizon.

GLOSSARY

Ahhijawa – the Hittite word for the Achaeans.

Ambron – word (Ambrones) used by Pliny to indicate the Ligurians.

Assuwa – Hittite word, probably meaning Asia.

Borrha' – northeast wind; origin of *Borea* in Latin and *Bora* in Italian (and English). Etymology uncertain.

Chnan – what the Phoenicians called themselves, meaning Canaanite. The term continued to be used in Northern Africa until the third century AD.

Derden – One of the Sea Peoples listed in ancient Egyptian documents. (Dardani; the race of Aeneas).

Dor – word used here to indicate the Dorians.

Elam – Near Eastern region corresponding to the area of the Zagros Mountains in western Iraq.

Enet – the Enetians, a people of northern Anatolia, named in the catalogue of ships in Book II of the Iliad as allies of the Trojans. As early as the fifth century BC, they were identified with the Venetics who settled in eastern Italy. Their Trojan leader, Antenor, was said to be the founder of Padova.

Kardakas – a people appearing in Assyrian documents of the seventh century BC, corresponding perhaps to the Karduchians of eastern Anatolia. Probably the modern Kurds.

Kmun – word used here to indicate the Camunians, a people of the eastern Italian Alps famous for their stone carvings.

Kussara – Hittite city in central Anatolia, located not far from the capital, Hatti.

Lat – word used here to indicate the proto-Latins.

Lawagetas – a Mycenaean word (la-wa-ge-tas) indicating the head of the army.

Lukka – one of the Sea Peoples, perhaps corresponding to the Lycians.

Nbyt – sanctuary of the crocodile god Sobek on the upper Nile, today's Kom Ombo.

Ombro – word used here to indicate the proto-Umbrians.

Pakana – Mycenaean word (pa-ka-na) for sword, giving origin to Homeric Greek *phasganon*.

Peleset – the Sea Peoples, corresponding perhaps to the biblical Philistines.

Pica – word used here for the Picenians, a people of eastern central Italy.

Ponikjo – a Mycenaean word (po-ni-ki-jo) probably used to indicate the Phoenicians.

Potinja – (po-ti-ni-ja) a divinity known as 'potnia theròn' (literally, the lady of the animals or the lady of living creatures) in historical times; the great Mediterraneasn mother goddess.

Sherden – a people commonly listed in ancient Egyptian documents; one of the Sea Peoples. May correspond to Sardinians.

Shekelesh – one of the Sea Peoples, perhaps indicating the Siculians or Sicels, ancient inhabitants of Sicily.

Sikanie – word used here to indicate the Sicanians, among the most ancient inhabitants of Sicily.

Sobek – the crocodile god of the ancient Egyptians.

Telepinu – a first name in Hittite; may correspond to the Greek Telephos.

Teresh – one of the Sea Peoples. May correspond to the Greek *Tyrsenoi*: that is, the Tyrrhenians or proto-Etruscans.

Urartu – ancient name of Armenia, present in Assyrian-Babylonian documents and in the Bible.

Vilusya – Hittite site recognized by many scholars as Ilium, or Troy.

Wanax – Mycenaean term (wa-nax) for 'lord,' origin of Greek *hanax*.

Wanaxa – (wa-nax-a) the female form of *wanax* origin of Greek *hanassa*.

AUTHOR'S NOTE

This story is liberally inspired by the lost poems of the Trojan cycle, especially those which narrate the returns of the heroes of the War of Troy. The most famous of these returns is certainly Homer's *Odyssey*, which enjoyed such fortune from the very start that it outshone the poems of the 'lesser' journeys, which were subsequently lost. The tales they told, mentioned in Book XI of the *Odyssey*, must nonetheless have been fascinating, and would provide a wealth of material for the great tragic poets of the 5th century: Aeschylus's Orestean trilogy (*Agamemnon*, the *Libation Bearers* and the *Eumenides*), Sophocles's *Ajax* and Euripides' the *Trojan Women*, not to speak of Virgil's *Aeneid*.

My aim in this novel was, in a way, to fill in that huge gap between the events that immediately follow the Trojan War and the situation depicted in the *Odyssey*. The myths of this period describe the total destabilization of Mycenaean Greece, with most of the kings dying during their homeward voyages, assassinated upon their return or driven from their lands. This situation, however, seems to be at least partially reversed in Books III and IV of the *Odyssey*, when Telemachus, the son of Ulysses, visits Pylos. The normalization seems to be the work of Menelaus, king of Sparta, who enjoys a privileged relationship with Nestor, has bound Achilles's son Pyrrhus to him through marriage with his daughter, and has plans to send Ulysses to settle in the Peloponnese. Furthermore, Menelaus's return from Egypt seems closely connected with Orestes's killing of Aegisthus (*Odyssey*, III, 306).

The killing of queen Clytemnestra and the usurper Aegisthus at Mycenae is usually seen in myth as Orestes personally exacting revenge for his father's death, but we cannot exclude actual dynastic internecine wars; there is archeological evidence of possible traces of partial destruction outside the walls of Mycenae that may have preceded the fall of this civilization, traditionally attributed to the Dorian invasion which coincides with the era in which the palaces were destroyed.

Modern historical reflections, supported by archeological research, no longer uncritically accept the so-called Dorian invasion. In his introduction to the latest edition of *The World of Odysseus*, M. Finley actually calls into question historical authenticity of the War of Troy tout court, claiming that it could only have occurred, if at all, in the Iron Age and not the Bronze Age.

This novel certainly does not mean to propose solutions to historical problems which are still open, but rather to explore the fascination and power of myth and the traces it has left everywhere, in our territory and in our past. The myths which have inspired this novel have their roots in the still little known period of transition between the end of the Bronze Age and the start of the Iron Age, when the entire Mediterranean world was shaken by a series of catastrophes: the Hittite empire of Anatolia collapsed, Egypt was invaded by the so-called 'Peoples of the Sea', and the Terramara civilization in Italy was extinguished in less than half a century, leaving nothing in its wake. The Mycenaean world – the world of Homer's heroes – disintegrated as well, perhaps as the result of an invasion, as discussed above, or perhaps due to as yet unidentified causes, such as severe climate change, for example, which may have forced sizeable populations out of their original settlements.

Some researchers have interpreted the myth of Phaethon's chariot scorching the earth before being downed by Zeus's thunderbolt as the metaphor, or historical memory, of a catastrophic natural event. The novel hints at this event in the mysterious object which plunges into the swamps of the Po valley, in accordance with the myth that locates Phaeton's fall at the mouth of the Eridanus river. His grieving sisters were transformed into poplar trees on the banks, and their tears into drops of amber, the same Baltic amber that archeologists have found in such abundance in the late Mycenaean settlement of

Fratta Polesine, located near the extinct northern arm of the Po, which the ancients called Eridanus.

Among the lost and wandering heroes of the Homeric saga, I've chosen to follow Diomedes, retracing an itinerary celebrated in the traditions of the Greek colonies of Italy; there is evidence of a cult of Diomedes along the entire Adriatic shore, from the Illyrian coast to the Venetian lagoons, from the mouth of the Po to the wide river valley, from Ancona to Puglia and the Tremiti islands, where a certain kind of seagull with a woeful cry is still called 'Diomedean'. I've attempted to weave his wanderings into the rich background of epic tradition.

This epic tradition includes the tale of the two Helens, and the myth of the Palladium, the idol which was said to make the city which possessed it invincible. Many Greek and Italian cities, through the age of written history, claimed to hold the true idol in their sanctuaries, Rome included. Other myths include the fall of Phaeton's chariot at the mouth of Eridanus, as already mentioned, the Oracle of the Old Man of the Sea at the mouth of the Nile, the legend of Aeneas's landing on the plains of Latium (later elaborated by Virgil) and the tradition which has Padua founded by the Enetians, led by the Trojan Antenor. The diffusion of these myths in Italy have helped current scholars to trace the earliest colonial penetration of the Greeks into Adriatic, Ionian and Tyrrhenian waters, without excluding the intriguing possibility that this penetration may have taken place on much more ancient routes, dating back to Mycenaean times and thus, once again, to the epic Homeric cycle of the 'returns'.

Modern philological and archeological knowledge allows us to integrate these traditions so as to create the most likely sequence of events. The battle beneath the walls of Mycenae, for example, incorporates what we currently know about that type of conflict, knowledge which Homer would no longer have been aware of in his time. For example, in the Iliad, the chariot is used as a means of transport, to carry the combatants to the battle site, while in reality it would have been used in Mycenaean times as a war machine; simply, at the time the poem was set down, this memory had been lost.

The reader will have noticed an intentional Homeric 'patina' which seeks to evoke the atmosphere of epic poetry, set against the background of the Mycenaean culture in Greece and of the late bronze age in Italy, which remain our chronological reference points. This picture includes the presence, in Italy, of the peoples who would populate it in the following centuries: Etruscans, Latins, Ligurians, Apulians, Picenians and Venetics. Although current historical knowledge cannot demonstrate their presence in this obscure period of archaic migration, I've suggested it to accentuate the theme in the novel of the newly forming Italic and European peoples, hinted at, for example, in the myth of the Pelasgians ('sea wanderers'). For the sake of compacting the narrative, the events described here take place in a much shorter period of time than is conventionally accepted both in the epic tradition and in the archeological indicators of historical events; I've done this to render them more dramatic and to allow myself to weave a possible itinerary which blends myth and imagination.

The author's dream is just this: that fortuitous intuition, or simply love for a lost world, can succeed in retracing the steps of the heroes celebrated in the epic tradition, and transform them into flesh and blood, animated, however, by energies and ideals whose memory has been long lost to us.